TOM DEITZ

Other Avon Books by
Tom Deitz

FIRESHAPER'S DOOM
THE GRYPHON KING
WINDMASTER'S BANE

Coming Soon

SUNSHAKER'S WAR

DARKTHUNDER'S WAY

TOM DEITZ

AVON BOOKS ◆ NEW YORK

DARKTHUNDER'S WAY is an original publication of Avon Books. This work has never before appeared in book form. This work is a novel. Any similarity to actual persons or events is purely coincidental.

AVON BOOKS
A division of
The Hearst Corporation
105 Madison Avenue
New York, New York 10016

First Avon Books Printing: December 1989

AVON TRADEMARK REG. U.S. PAT. OFF. AND IN OTHER COUNTRIES, MARCA REGISTRADA, HECHO EN U.S.A.

Printed in the U.S.A.

RA   10 9 8 7 6 5 4 3 2 1

To Klon
for more than he can imagine

Acknowledgments

Mary Ellen Brooks
Monnie D. Dean
Beulah N. Deitz
Adele Leone
Chris Miller
Jon Monk
John R. Newell
Vickie R. Sharp
Barbara Strickland
Brad Strickland

and a special thanks to
Frances Wellman and Karl Edward Wagner

PART I

THINGS FALL APART

Chapter I: Raven's Call

(Enotah County, Georgia—
Friday, August 16—afternoon)

Mad David Sullivan had been reading so much Welsh poetry the last few days he had almost begun to think in triads.

His three best friends, for instance, Alec McLean, "Runnerman" Darrell Buchanan, and Gary "G-Man" Hudson.

Or, a couple of hours earlier that August afternoon, the three hottest places on earth: the Sahara Desert, Death Valley, and the Fiddlers' Convention at the Enotah Mountain Fair.

And for the moment, and rather esoterically, the three aspects of music that were simultaneously impacting on his psyche.

There was the literal music in the air to start with: the plunking and sawing that blared from beneath the huge green tent that dominated that portion of Enotah County High's athletic field not given over to parking. But instead of the bluegrass and country that had been the fair's sole issue for as long as David could remember, this year the

3

sponsoring local Lions' Club had magnanimously decided to set aside one day for folk music in its less insular manifestations. So it was that "Down Yonder," "Wildwood Flower," and "Orange Blossom Special" had given way to the Irish jigs and reels of Doctor Paddy, the Middle Eastern mandolin melodies of Nelson Morgan, and the soft, plaintive dulcimer of Bethany Van Over. Only a few moments before a North Carolina singer billed only as "John" had marched himself and his wide black hat and his silver-strung guitar offstage. David had particularly enjoyed his set. The guy apparently knew hundreds of ballads so ancient and obscure no one else recalled them at all; but more to the point, there had been a special magic about him, as if he *believed* the strange things he sang of. Never had David heard "Tam-Lin" performed with such conviction.

It was a song about the Faeries, he knew: whimsy to most folks—or romance, if they understood it at all. But for him it held darker implications. For Mad David Sullivan, like the fabled, willful Janet of the song, had also rescued a loved one, if not from the Queen of the Fairies' apocryphal Tithe to Hell, at least from the clutches of the quasi-mythical beings the Irish called the Sidhe. Over a year had passed since he had met them, and things had never been quite the same after.

But music (to continue that particular triad) was not only a thing of the ear that day; it was a thing of life itself: of a late summer afternoon in a north Georgia county so remote it was nearly in North Carolina; of a sun that was hot like the blacksmith's forge in the Early Settlers display; and earth that was dry as Byron Herbert Reece's elegized bones—but with the first cool wind of an early autumn taking the edge off both and a pile of clouds in the west that hinted softly of thunder. David had only to look around him to see that world; to gaze beyond the glaring windshields and shimmering paint of countless outland vehicles and the sunglasses and hats of their even more countless passengers to where mountains rose in an ever-receding tumble of age-softened humps, each in a paler shade of blue, all accented here and there by the clear blaze of warm, sunlit water. Music of the earth, for certain. And of the skies.

But of all the musics haunting Mad David Sullivan, the one that sang most joyfully in his soul was that constant, silent symphony he heard whenever he looked at the red-haired girl walking beside him through the trampled grass, her slender body clad in white shorts, green Alarm T-shirt, and with a certain silver ring on her finger. Liz Hughes was her name, a friend since childhood. And now, so recently he still couldn't quite believe it himself, his . . . His what? Girlfriend? Nah, that sounded far too frivolous. His lady? Too pompous, too remote. Maybe just *his*—except that also sold her short, because in spite of being only seventeen, Liz Hughes was for sure and for real her own woman. She also loved him, and he loved her, and both those things looked like going on forever.

(The three women he loved most: all Liz Hughes.)

But if that was so, why had she just said what she had?

They had left the tent only moments before and were threading their way around the hulking Winnebagos that packed this part of the field. A snack had been their avowed intention, but something about the music, something about the songs of betrayed or unrequited love—"Little Matty Groves," for instance—had made David raise *that* topic one more time.

A clearing of throat, a pause, a cough, and the words had tumbled out for at least the tenth time in half as many days: "Look, Liz, are you *sure* you won't change your mind 'bout going back to Lakeview?" Lakeview Academy was the private high school Liz had attended the previous year in Gainesville, Georgia: fifty miles to the south, beyond the mountains.

And the inevitable response: a heavy sigh, a casting of green eyes to the left as shoulders and neck muscles tensed and prettily pointy features grimaced irritably. And this time a dead stop. He halted too, and stared at her, blue eyes wide and waiting. Then came the words he had dreaded, though her tone carried less anger than frustration: "Do we *have* to go through this again? Can't you ever take me at my word? It's not like I'm doing it to hurt you; it's something I have to do because it's best for me."

"But *Liz*," David protested feebly. "School's not *that* bad up here. 'Sides, we've only got one more year. Surely you can stick it out that long."

"Yeah, one more year; then it's off to U.G.A. for both of us. Surely *you* can stick it out *that* long!"

David raised a quizzical black eyebrow into the unruly blond mop that a month before had been quite a high-tech haircut, and chuckled evilly. Liz promptly blushed to her ears.

"Only a year," she repeated, to get unflustered.

"But I can't *wait* that long!" he exploded. "I mean, crap, girl; things have just started goin' good for us. We've been fiddling around so long, not knowin' and wonderin' and makin' fools of ourselves, and then suddenly it just happens. I *love* you; can't you see that? I can't stand the notion of not havin' you around!"

"I'll be home on weekends, David, most of 'em, anyway, now that I've got a car. And believe me, I won't be spending 'em sitting in my mama's parlor! Besides, you've still got Alec and your MacTyrie Gang buddies. I don't have any close friends in Gainesville—not like here, anyway."

David stuffed his hands in his scruffy cutoffs and looked away. "Yeah, but Alec's a... Well, it's just not the same! I mean he's my best friend, and all; always has been, always will be. But he's—well, there're some things you just can't *do* with him! I—"

He stopped in mid-sentence and blushed, wishing he hadn't put it quite that way for fear Liz would think him thrall to the same gonadal zombiehood as all the other local boys—not that it wasn't necessarily true, sometimes, or that she necessarily disapproved. In fact, *that* had been one of the things they'd discovered that summer—shoot, that *month*. They'd not *done* it yet—not quite. But oh Godallmighty, what an almost! For the millionth time, he recalled that magical first occasion; him fresh from six weeks at the Governor's Honors Program in Valdosta (he was wearing the black Commarts jersey even now, the same one he'd had on that night), and Liz home from a trip to San Francisco. They'd met at B.A. Cove out from his house, had finally opened up to each other, and things had simply followed the logical progression . . . to a point. They'd chickened out somewhere around the waistline and compromised by going skinny-dipping.

Things had taken a more sinister turn, then, as David found himself taken prisoner by a vengeful Faery woman and drawn once more into affairs of that other World which lay unseen around his own. But he didn't want to think about that now—he'd had enough arcane adventures to last him a lifetime. For the moment, he just wanted to be a normal kid: a nice north Georgia boy with a good mind, a strong, healthy body, and a mighty fine-looking girlfriend who was smart as a whip in the bargain. *Startin' to sound like Uncle Dale, kid,* he told himself, and realized they were walking again.

Liz broke in on his reverie. "You were glad enough of Alec's company until this summer."

David's face clouded. "That's not fair! We grew up together—course you and I did too, but it wasn't the same. And anyway, I haven't seen him much lately, in case you haven't noticed."

"Would you like to?"

A shrug. "He's been part of me forever, always the same, always solid, reliable Alec. But things with you and me have changed, gotten better—which I guess doesn't mean I still don't want to keep the other good things in my life." He shook his head as if to clear it. "Gaaa—I can't even talk straight. I mean a man can have a girlfriend and still hang out with his buddies—can't he?"

Liz regarded him seriously. "I hope so, 'cause I truly wouldn't want anything to happen to that friendship. Besides, I'd like to know somebody's keeping an eye on you while I'm gone."

David ventured a smile. "Back to that, huh?"

A countersmile. "You can't convince me."

David's only response was to twine his strong, tanned

fingers around Liz's fine-boned freckled ones. This was it; he'd wagered as much as he dared; it was time to play his ace in the hole. He brought her up short by a section of split-rail fence that marked the northern limit of the fairground. Beyond was only forest. It was cooler there, and shady. "Okay," he sighed, "I won't say another word about it. But please at least *try* to see my side, and maybe... maybe I'll try a little harder to see yours, too. Maybe we can talk it over one more time at Uncle Dale's party."

"I'm looking forward to that."

David glanced up hopefully. "You mean you'll—"

Liz poked him in the tummy. "Not to bringing it up again, foolish boy; to the party!"

"That's goooood," David whined nasally in his best Peter Lorre imitation. "'Cause I've got a surprise for you after."

Liz released his hand and hugged him, which shocked him considerably since it wasn't at all the response he'd expected—especially not when it turned into a lingering kiss right there in front of God and somebody's Chevy.

Rustle-rustle-rustle: a sound in the thick leaves above their heads.

David ignored it. He was letting his hands curve around a denim-clad fanny, and Liz seemed to have similar inclinations.

The noise again, louder: probably a squirrel.

"Message!" a harsh voice croaked loudly right in his ear.

David jumped about three feet and lost hold of his sweetie. "Jesus! Talk about crappy timing!"

"Message," the voice repeated implacably.

David squinted into the branches beside his head and saw a large white raven perched there. "Go ahead and spill it, then," he growled, eyeing it distrustfully.

"Summoned!" cried the bird. "Summoned you are, to the Track as quick as can happen. Nuada Silverhand wants you."

"Damn," David grunted. "I don't suppose he bothered to say what for."

"Play," the bird replied dumbly—evidently not one of Silverhand's first-rate messengers, to judge by its awkward English.

David frowned uncertainly. "That doesn't make a bit of sense!"

"Message!" squawked the bird, and flew away. In a moment it was lost in the blue glare of heaven.

"I guess you gotta go," Liz groaned.

David grimaced sourly and pounded the splintery wood beneath him. "I guess so. But why *now?* Why can't the bloody Sidhe just leave me alone?"

"Would you really want that?"

"I'd like to at least give it a try! It's not even been two weeks since I saved their collective heinies."

"Yeah, and it's only been a year since you'd have died to get a chance to talk to them."

"I *did* almost die, if you remember."

Liz propped her chin atop his shoulder. "You might as well go. They'll keep at you until you do."

He nuzzled her hair. "Yeah, I reckon. At least it's a friend this time, anyway—if you can call Nuada a friend."

"I think you can."

"But Jesus God, girl, why does it have to be *today?*"

"That," Liz whispered, "is something you'll have find out from them."

"If I ever see that raven again, I'm gonna have something to say about its timing, though."

"You may have to race me for that." Liz giggled, and pinched his bottom.

Hands stuffed in each other's back pockets, they made their way past the school building, which housed most of the craft and commercial exhibits, and entered the hot, dusty chaos of the midway. Sensory overload engulfed them: the sticky smell of cotton candy and the prickly odor of stale sawdust; the din of conversation and the shouts of barkers and the heavy rumble of machinery that was descant to the screams of the riders on Tilt-A-Whirl and Trabant and Octopus—all encompassed by the glint of gaudily painted metal and the frantic shimmer of bright summer clothing on ten-thousand hot, sweaty tourists. David found himself searching in vain for the fortune-teller's tent that had been present the previous summer. A lady there had told him something valuable—and had given him something far more precious in the form of a certain rare volume called *The Secret Common-Wealth*. He had meant to return it this year, but the woman had not been back. No one seemed to know when she had left the carnival.

He was still musing about her whereabouts when a tug of Liz's hand brought them beneath the overhang of the tent that marked the fair's entrance, where they joined the exit queue—far fewer folks going out than coming in. David stood on tiptoes to survey the masses jostling in the other way.

The sea of faces spun and shifted, and eventually cast up a figure he knew: blandly handsome beneath dark, spiky hair; tall, slender body neatly dressed in a black R.E.M. T-shirt, winter camouflage fatigues belted with a length of chrome chain, and black sneakers. A ghost of moustache stained the upper lip; a silver cross on a chain hung from the left earlobe.

"Alec!" David cried over the din of the mob. The boy glanced around, gray eyes questing until they found David and stabilized. His face lit in a grin David realized he had seen all too rarely lately. But then the gaze slid toward Liz, and the joy dimmed minutely, shadowed by lowered brows.

"Come up for a burger," Alec called. "I'm on duty for the next three hours."

David shook his head in a reluctant abdication. "Can't! Got a blessed *appointment*." He gave the word a peculiar intonation.

Alec's grin faded completely.

"I've gotta *go!*" David reiterated quickly.

A final vague, sorrowful nod from Alec, and Liz was pulling him onward. David slipped her grasp and dashed sideways, scanning the crowd, but his friend was already gone, swept away beyond the metal fence that separated *out* from *in*. Once David thought he saw his dark head bobbing along near the Ferris wheel, but could not be certain. Suddenly he wanted to talk to Alec, to reassure his best buddy all was well. But he couldn't.

Not when he had a summons he dared not ignore.

A stab of brakes, a jerk of steering wheel hard right, and David swung the Mustang of Death (as Alec called his lately battered pride and joy) into the loose gravel of the Sullivan Cove road. The Lovin' Spoonful's "Summer in the City" thundering from the radio was a frantic counterpoint to the stones that spat and crunched beneath his tires as he momentarily lost it. *Better slow it down, kid; you know what can happen when you get crazy.*

He did for a fact; a quick glance to where the right front fender *wasn't* was proof enough of that. Little more than a week had passed since he'd stuffed the Mustang into the bank up on Franks Gap, though so much had happened in between it felt far longer. There'd been extenuating circumstances, of course, and magical ones at that, but the damage was real enough. This had been door week: three days from sunup to sundown in his father's sorghum fields to pay for the used (and hideously incongruous blue) door that replaced the pristine red one he'd shredded on rocks. Half a week before that for the tire; most of September still to come for the new fender, grill, and bumper. It would be a long time before Mad David Sullivan and the Mustang of Death roamed the night again.

The rightward glance made him notice something else too: an empty bucket seat. He was startled at that, surprised to realize how rarely that position was unoccupied anymore. But where before it had been Alec occasionally riding shotgun (*cowering* was more like it, considering David's driving), now it was Liz practically every day. As for the nights, she drove then, in Morgan, her little black Ford EXP, the tiny two-seater with the nice long cargo deck that was good for a lot more than hauling.

A couple of bounces further, hard left this time, and he was scrabbling up the steep, rutted slope of the narrow logging road that did duty as the family driveway before continuing on its way up the imposing mountain on the lumpy roots of which squatted Sullivan Manor (his name for the family homestead), whitewashed and agglutinated within its arc of barns and stables. Beyond it was the long straightaway he had just turned off of, one end leading back to Enotah and eventually to Liz and Alec, the other onward to Atlanta. There were *other* roads nearby, too, but them it was best not to mention—not that he could have, even had he wished. The Ban of Lugh forbade it: that magical prohibition laid on him and his partners-in-secrets by the King of the American Faeries himself, which literally froze their tongues against any mention of Faerie except to one another.

The Faeries! *Damn* them!

He parked the car in the dusty side yard, glanced at his watch, and frowned: It wouldn't do to keep Silverhand waiting. And he still had to come up with some kind of ruse to fool his pa, though he already had a good idea what that would be.

A tinny slam of door, and he sprinted across the yard, leaping three unaware chickens before pounding up the rickety back steps. His mother was in the kitchen—baking, which was unusual, and (more predictably) with three half-read romance novels stashed around the counters and a fourth on the kitchen table. His father was nowhere to be seen, nor was his brother, the cursedly savvy and obnoxiously pestiferous Little Billy.

(*Three most troublesome relatives: his ready-to-start-first-grade-and-therefore-full-of-himself brother; his religiously-unimaginative-and-ineffectually-overbearing pa, and his dithering-herself-into-apoplexy-so-as-to-avoid-thinking-about-what-was-really-bothering-her ma.*)

"Have a good time?" his mother called as he passed. She did not turn down the Alabama tape on her Walkman, nor did she look up from the dough she was rolling. Her shoulders alternately tensed and slackened beneath a red Clifton Precision Softball jersey on which was emblazoned JOANNE.

"Uh, yeah, sure." He paused, grinning in silent amusement. A thick strand of blond hair had escaped from her ponytail and was threatening to invade the incipient baking. "But, hey, I gotta go!"

Eyes blue as his and bluer than her faded jeans, snapped around, flashing sudden fire above a mouth gone thin and hard.

"It's one of *those* situations, Ma," he called as he broke that uncomfortable contact and trotted down the hall toward his room.

"David, I don't like—"

Her words were cut off by the closing of the door. *No time to talk,* he told himself; no time for the same old story: how she didn't like anything she didn't understand, nor believe things she had actually seen, hard to accept though they might be.

"Caught ya!" a child's voice crowed behind him.

Already half undressed, David spun around and leapt across the room to sweep the small, blond boy who had been hiding in the closet corner high into the air, invert him, then cross to his bed (one of a set of twins that bracketed opposite walls) and gently (but not *too* gently, no sense spoiling the brat) plop him down atop it, tickling him all the while.

"You're goin' off to see the Shiny People, ain't ya, Davy?" Little Billy gasped as soon as he stopped giggling. His blue eyes glittered, but whether with glee or dread, David could not determine.

"'Fraid so, kid," David replied, turning to his chest of drawers. Still wondering exactly what the raven had meant by *play,* he stripped, tugged on a jockstrap, and replaced his cutoffs and T-shirt with a pair of burgundy Enotah County High gym shorts and a matching de-sleeved sweatshirt from the neckhole of which a winsome-looking appliquéd possum hung by its tail, clutching a football to its furry chest. He had just finished tying his running shoes when his brother piped up again.

"Can I go?"

"Do you *want* to? You've always been scared of 'em."

"Yeah," Little Billy replied solemnly, "but the Thunder-cats say you're supposed to face what you're 'fraid of. So I thought if I went with you, I could . . . you know . . . ?"

"Yeah, I know, punk," David said, reaching over to ruffle the little boy's fair hair before banding his own, scarcely darker locks into a stubby ponytail and knotting a red bandanna around the lot. "But no, you can't go, not this time. I don't know what I'm gettin' into exactly, so I don't want you mixed up in it."

"But someday?"

"Maybe," as he darted into the hall, with his brother a small shadow behind him.

He reentered the kitchen just as his mother was setting a tray of hot oatmeal cookies on the table. The smell (cinnamon and walnuts) took his breath—there was nothing in the world he liked more than hot cookies. Automatically, he reached out to snag a handful—seconds ahead of his brother—only to receive a sharp smack on the wrist from a spatula.

"Not even one!" JoAnne admonished. "These're for the party. I swear, I don't know if I'm gonna be able to make it, I got so much to do."

David paused by the door. "Well, Uncle Dale doesn't turn seventy every day!"

"And Aunt Katie's leavin'," Little Billy added, skirting around behind his mother to claim the batter bowl. David wished he had time to contest it.

"And about time, too," JoAnne snorted.

"Ma!"

She stuck a floury hand on her hip and fixed David with a put-upon scowl. "It ain't that I don't like her, she's done a lot for us, for Dale, and all; but—"

"Yeah," David interrupted, wishing he could wind this down, but knowing that if he humored her he might be able to beg at least a couple of the sacred goodies. "She sure has."

"But it's just scandalous, them living together like that."

David couldn't help sniggering when he thought of the old Irish lady who had moved in with his great-uncle after last week's adventures. She had at least ten years on the guy, but that didn't necessarily mean anything—as his mother was oh-so-quick to point out. But still, he felt compelled to come to the defense of his favorite relative. "We didn't have room, he did."

"We've got the *attic!* We could have put you up there and her in your room."

"We offered."

"And she refused. Said Dale needed a woman around to keep him straight. Hmmmph! Straight my hind end!"

"Stiff, anyway." David chuckled, and winked at her.

She looked sharply at him, then turned back to her baking. Little Billy stole three cookies and snuck one to David, who hid it behind his back as he edged toward the door. "I ain't told you the worst part," JoAnne added over her shoulder.

"What?"

"Uncle Dick's coming tomorrow." She snapped her fingers contemptuously. "Just like that! Whole passel of 'em. No notice a'tall."

"Oh Lord," David groaned. "Not the Terror Twins. I really will have to hide out upstairs."

"An' that yucky girl," Little Billy opined through a mouthful of contraband.

"God, you're right! The Dread Cousin Amy!" *(Three most obnoxious younger cousins . . .)*

"Yeah. Yucky, yucky, yucky."

"What's yucky?" his father's voice rumbled through the screen behind him. David hopped out of the way as Big Billy Sullivan shouldered in, briefly filling the whole doorway with his ruddy, red-haired, Levied form. He snagged a dishrag from a nearby hanger, mopped his face and bare chest, and tossed the sodden mass atop the washing machine, then sauntered to the refrigerator to grab a Bud and help himself to a handful of cookies, oblivious to his wife's sharp protests. Eventually his eyes fell on David. "So where're *you* off to?"

"Goin' runnin', Pa; gotta get in shape for school. Gonna try to make the track team again." It was a lie, and he hated it; but there was no way he could tell the truth, not with the blessed Ban in effect. Besides, he *was* going running—sort of.

"You're too short," Big Billy grumbled, wiping his forehead with a meaty hand. "I done told you that."

"I'm faster than Gary, who's on the team. Besides, it's all I'm good for. Softball's dull as dishwater; so's football. I'm *really* too short for basketball, and we don't have swimming or wrestling—or gymnastics, which is what I'm built for."

"Seems to me you got enough to waste your time on already, anyway. 'Sides, I'm gonna need you every minute come harvest time."

"He's got a girl, Bill," JoAnne cautioned.

"His fine young butt's still mine long as the sun's shining, though; and it's shinin' mighty late these days."

David was bouncing from foot to foot with impatience. "Uh, look, folks, I *really* gotta go. But, hey, Pa, thanks for lettin' me off today. The music was really excellent."

"No big deal," Big Billy mumbled awkwardly. "I got by. But come next week when that little gal gets gone, whooee, we gonna see how much you can sweat."

"When you gonna be back?" his mother wondered. She stared at him, and he found it hard to meet her gaze. She knew what he was really about, he was certain of it— knew a lot, as a matter of fact, had seen things no woman of her background should have. They had spoken of it once or twice, but not in the last couple of days. It was as if she was denying, as if her newfound knowledge was too much for her mind—or her faith—to accept. David understood. It had taken a lot for *him* to acknowledge the fact that his everyday reality was not the only one.

And his pa . . . Big Billy did not know either, yet even he was sharp enough to know something was wrong; that reality was ever so slightly out of kilter around Sullivan Cove. He would have had to be a fool to miss the troubled glances, veiled references, and sudden silences that passed between his sons and his wife. And Big Billy Sullivan was no fool.

"Back around supper's all I can say," David called, and was out the door.

As soon as David was an eighth-mile up the logging road, he stopped running. Big Billy would have seen him head up the mountain and assumed he was following one of his several cross-country courses. But he was safe now, so he slowed to a steady walk up the rutted path, letting the last tin and shingle rooftops of the farm fall away behind as he settled himself into the woods. Trees closed around him: dark pines or bright-leafed maples. Laurel and rhododendron crept in from either side—the road had got so rough this year the forest service had not bothered clearing the ditch beside it. Another year or two of similar neglect and it really would be a trail—which would suit him just dandy.

Another half mile he climbed, into wilder territory, nerves keying up in anticipation—or dread. Did he really want to do what he was about? Should he have agreed to such an ill-timed summons? As if to answer his unvoiced fear, the trees slipped in closer, became oak and ash advising *no, no, no,* even as the laurel thrust out slick leaves to restrain him.

He paused and looked back. This was probably far enough; it was time to begin his *real* journey. What would it be this time? he wondered, as he began to focus his senses, feeling the brush of wind against bare legs, arms, and belly, the heat of sunlight on his hair beneath its ruddy confinement, smelling damp soil and distant pines, and the ticklish scents of a thousand pollens; hearing the wind sigh and hiss past leaves. But most of all he centered on his vision, ever alert, searching . . . searching . . .

He became aware of a noise from the dense foliage to his right: the soft, precise crunch of dry moss trod by hooves. A peculiar tingle that was not quite pain eased into his eyes, and then he caught a head-high flash of white among the branches. An instant later his guide pushed its mighty chest and shoulders through the laurel.

A stag, it was, and totally white from its delicate hooves

to its extravagant antlers. Only its eyes held color: the green of still forest water. A toss of the beast's head surely meant he was to follow, so he thrust aside the thick shrubbery and entered the wild.

Not yet a mile from home, he might already have been in another World, to judge from the tall, straight trunks that rose about him, the hush of wind on sun-dappled branches. But he had no time for aesthetic appreciation, for the stag was trotting away, its ivory hooves eerily silent upon the leaves, leaving him no choice but to jog noisily along behind.

It did not take long at all to reach it: a thin screen of blackberry briars along a strip of ground that glittered more than it should where the sun slashed across it from the crown of a lightning-shattered oak; a faint depression where nothing grew beneath the dusting of leaves but thick, dark moss. Looking at it made David's eyes itch and burn. The stag paused at its margin and lowered its head until its antlers barely skimmed the earth.

David gasped at the sudden burst of pain that briefly filled his eyes as light flared into being there: a golden strip wide as his outstretched arms and extending out of sight along the ridge to either side. Straight Tracks they were called, and straight they were, as arrows. They were the roads of the Sidhe.

The stag stepped onto the Track and once more inclined its head to have him follow. Taking a deep breath, David closed his still-smarting eyes and stepped onto it, then walked five full paces along its length before opening them again.

He exhaled quickly. Good, he had done it right, he was no longer in his World—not quite; a subtle difference in the light told him as much. A shudder raced through him. Did he really want to finish what he had started?

Of course! In his heart of hearts there was no doubt. But did fear and wonder have to keep such close company as they had done in recent days? He hoped not. Still, not everyone in Georgia had the Second Sight, which was what had allowed him to see the Track in the first place; in fact, as far as he knew he was the only one, though Alec and Liz seemed to be growing increasingly sensitive lately as well —due, no doubt, to ever more frequent exposure. But did there have to be a such a high price for something he had not asked for? Something that was a lot more trouble than it was worth; that had stolen precious moments from his lady?

Yet Silverhand had called him, and that had happened but once since that amazing Sunday morning nearly two weeks gone when two enemies had died and a would-be friend had rejoined the living. That, he supposed, was enough. The last time, David had shown his immortal mentor a cheap hologram pendant he had bought in a Valdosta flea market. The Faery lord had been so intrigued David had given it to him. And now this summons. What did it imply?

The stag tossed its head impatiently. David sighed and trotted after, trying not to pay too close attention as the landscape around him slowly altered. Briars were everywhere, of course, totem plants of the Sidhe—yellow ones, this time, spiraling in and out among the gold-trunked trees like the interlaced borders of an illuminated manuscript. But then boulders began to dot the spaces between the trunks and gradually replaced them, so that David eventually discovered he was jogging down a file of rough-hewn, house-high monoliths that emptied at last into a rock-girt clearing. The Track faded abruptly, and he found himself in the center of an empty circle of those same rustic pillars, above the heavy capstones of which loomed the topmost branches of a fog-shrouded forest. The breeze, when it found him, was cool. The stag was nowhere in sight.

"Took you long enough, foolish Mortal!" a clear male voice hissed in strangely lilted English in his ear—just as David found his arms prisoned from behind and felt something hard and cold and very sharp press against his jugular.

Chapter II: Threats

(Tir-Nan-Og—high summer—
late afternoon)

Lugh Samildinach, High King of the Daoine Sidhe in
Tir-Nan-Og, let the thin golden chain slide once more
through his slender fingers and flipped the crystal disk on
the end so that it spun and put forth its own, paler shimmer—a gold that was no match for the heavy cast panels
on the limestone walls, the sun-in-splendor inlaid in the
wooden table before him, or, beyond it, the circlet on his
closest friend's hair. In the tall, arched window behind him
a gilt-silver wind chime tinkled in a rising breeze, sending
ghosts of its own reflected yellow flitting across the airy
chamber. That wind was warm and held a thin, nervous
tingle; the westering sun was a hot topaz a hand's breadth
above the mountains.

His friend—Nuada Airgetlam: his warlord and the nearest of the four at the table—stretched a gleaming hand
toward him in a whisper of well-wrought joints. Of silver
that appendage was, for he had lost his fleshly arm to a
blade of cursed Iron in the Battle of Mag Tuired. But it

moved no differently—and with no less speed or finesse —than the real one beneath his white tunic.

Lugh snatched the spinning bauble away, barely in time, grinning slyly beneath a moustache black as his shoulder-long hair and little shorter. "Oh no, Silverhand, this trinket is mine, for did you not give it to me?"

Nuada frowned slightly, then lifted a slanted eyebrow, dark eyes flashing with cheerful wickedness. "I *lent* it to you to examine. The boy gave it to me because I liked it—a small thing to him, and not costly; a curiosity of his people, really—but a gift nevertheless, and also his first one."

"A fine thing, this," Lugh chided, "that a man begrudge his king the gifts of Mortals!"

Nuada snorted amiably and cast his glance round the chamber. "Mortals made all this, or most; certainly the finer portions."

"Aye," muttered the red-clad woman whose face was hard as the beak of the crow that reached up from her shoulder to peck at the circlet of stylized skulls binding her inky tresses. "Mortality does have its virtues. Fear of death is a mighty incentive, and the desire to be remembered after perhaps even greater."

The grizzled-looking man to Lugh's left scratched his thin chest through his robe of moonlight gray. "Either that, or the promise of immortality, which you cannot deliver though your Mortal wrights desire it—not, at least, as they would have it."

"Right you are, Oisin—as usual." Lugh chuckled, casting his eye toward the speaker: the one alone among them who showed any signs of age. And well he should, for Oisin had himself been born a Mortal. His own willfulness had been his downfall; blindness and eternal decrepitude the legacy. But he was wise in the ways of more Worlds than Faerie, and there were things he knew and magics he could work that were beyond the ken of any present. Lately he had become Lugh's Seer.

"Humph," growled the woman. "Surely you did not call us here to talk of trinkets!"

"Patience, Morrigu," Lugh whispered easily, "all in good time." With a finger he stopped the bauble's spin and studied that which hung before him. It was a simple disk of some transparent material that did not exist in Faerie. A hoop of thin half-gold bound it, and inside was a stag's head. Not a flat picture, but the actual, round head; for as Lugh turned the disk, the head moved about within. He turned it over and saw the head again, still from the front, once more moving.

"A *hologram*, men called them," Nuada said. "Magic of light and mirrors."

Lugh smiled and stuffed the object inside his red silk robe. "If you permit, I will study this a while longer, but have no doubt I will return it. It is not seemly to claim gifts made to others. Only ill-luck attends."

"Keep it as long as you like." Nuada smiled back. "I have made another and contrived a more useful variant which you should see in action very shortly."

"Enough of this," the woman snapped, starting to rise. "I have other business."

Lugh leaned back in his chair and fixed her with a stare so fierce she slumped down in her seat again. "You *business,* Morrigu, is this kingdom and the preservation thereof, to which a remarkable number of things are related, including, perhaps, that toy. But you are right. I have called you here not to examine Silverhand's curios, but to speak of grimmer matters."

As one they watched him, waiting. Save for them—and Angharad, Lugh's pet golden enfield—the room was empty. Only a solitary guardswoman stood beyond the brazen doors to ward them and wait their pleasure. A risk that was, but Lugh had taken precautions; the spells woven into her golden helm would mask whatever words might pierce walls and doors and trickle outward—nor could she remove it, not while she waited there.

"I suppose," the Morrigu said finally, with ill-concealed annoyance, "that this meeting has something to do with the message from Finvarra you received this morning."

Lugh inclined his head, stole a morsel from the plate of

sauced kraken upon the table and passed it to Angharad. He watched absently as she took it: eagle talons bringing it to a fox's head to nibble. As casually as he might have scratched her ears, he reached into his robe and laid a roll of ivory parchment on the table. "The High King of Erenn is displeased at some late occurrences here," he said. "You may read it if you like, but I imagine you already know what it means."

Indeed they did, though it was a complicated matter: Finvarran of Erenn's half-brother Ailill had fathered a son on the Fireshaper Morwyn verch Morgan ap Gwyddion, a woman of the fearsome Powersmiths who lived beyond Arawn's realm of Annwyn. The child had subsequently been fostered in Erenn, whence he had been sent with his father when Finvarra named Ailill ambassador to Tir-Nan-Og. Ailill had no love for mortals, though, and had soon begun stirring up trouble with the Lands of Men that were very close there. Eventually this had led to him to accidentally slay the boy, who had also become enmeshed in mortal affairs. For this crime, along with his treasonous acts, Lugh had imprisoned Ailill in the shape of a horse, and there matters stood until two things had happened.

One was that Ailill's twin sister, Fionna, had deemed Lugh's judgment too harsh and an insult to Finvarra's crown, and had taken it upon herself to set things aright by sneaking into Tir-Nan-Og and releasing Ailill, intending to spirit him back to Erenn. And the other thing was that Fionna had not considered the feelings of a mother bereft of her child.

For Morwyn had vowed vengeance on her son's slayer, as was her right under the ancient Laws of Dana. Thus, she too had come to Tir-Nan-Og seeking Ailill, but for quite a different reason. *A life for a life,* the Laws proclaimed, and so she would have had it be: Ailill's life for that of her son. She had succeeded too well, though, for not only had she slain Ailill, but in so doing had likewise caused the death of Fionna, thereby upsetting the balance of the Law. Affairs had become even more complicated when her son had turned up alive, further skewing the balance. And so it stood: two dead unlawfully, one alive who by Finvarra's thinking should not be, and another alive who had caused it all by a too-hot desire for vengeance.

"It seems a well-reasoned case," Nuada said, "if you look at it from Finvarra's side—except of course that he blames Morwyn for the death of his sister when it was in fact her own doing. Morwyn merely provided the instrument."

The Morrigu frowned thoughtfully. "Save for that, though, it is as Nuada says. Why then does he threaten war?"

Lugh slapped his hand on the table. "Because he says it was through my connivance that all this happened! He claims I allowed Morwyn to steal the Horn of Annwyn, which then brought about his sister's death. But let me read you his words." He picked up the scroll and began: " *'It was by a certain dreadful thing you had in your keeping that my sister found her doom—a thing Morwyn stole yet could not have stolen without your consent. That is ever your way, brother prince of Tir-Nan-Og, to plot and scheme, but nowise leave any mark of your passing. Mortals it was this time, aiding my kindred's killer, one a far-son of our own shadow-land!'* "

"And so he threatens war if you will not surrender the Lady Morwyn to him for judgment?" Oisin asked.

"Those are his words," Lugh replied, passing the enfield another morsel. "Finvarra would like for me to heed them as easily as this beast heeds my hand. I imagine you know my answer."

Nuada smiled grimly. "You have no intention of acceding to his demands—nor could you and still have right to your crown. 'A death for a death,' Finvarra tells us. But what of the equally ancient law of hospitality? Morwyn has done *us* no harm, at least not directly, though her actions certainly have potential to cause trouble, and not only with Erenn. Arawn too is displeased because of how you have used the Horn."

"He is *displeased*," the Morrigu corrected sharply, "because the Powersmiths have at last confirmed what they have suspected for centuries: that he does not have it, though it was their gift to him; and may I add it was the poorest kept secret in Faerie, thanks to Ailill. Still, Arawn has lost face—which I have no doubt he would like to regain. I am surprised we do not find him already at our borders with a force of Powersmiths driving him on."

"But Morwyn is herself part Powersmith," Oisin noted. "Her mother was of that land."

"Yes," Lugh said. "And her father is brother to Arawn's queen, and together that complicates the problem, because I truly have no sovereignty over her, beyond hospitality which I offered and sanctuary which she has claimed by right of trade: sanctuary for a service."

"And a mighty service that was indeed," Nuada said, "for had not Ailill's minions been fomenting dissension in this land for ages, with their talk of war with mankind, and their constant stirring up of trouble here? And did not Morwyn herself expose yet another threat in Fionna? Should you then surrender one of Arawn's people—worse than that, one who is half a Powersmith—to a foreign monarch? I think not. It is you who are ruler, here, not Finvarra."

Oisin took a sip of wine. "Aye, Lord. If anyone has a right to demand you give up Morwyn it is the Powersmiths —or Arawn of Annwyn, she being also his kin."

"And if you defy Finvarra?" The Morrigu's question hung in the air like one of her crows at hover.

"He will attack. He will have no other choice. His ships have already passed onto the Sea Road—a wise thing, considering the Roads' condition."

"Such would be a grievous thing," Nuada said. "I know Finvarra is your friend."

Lugh sighed wearily. "Do friends let spies creep into their brothers' kingdoms and stir up trouble? Not by my thinking—nor do kings, at least not those who have any right to their crowns. A strong king would either have known Ailill for what he was before he sent him here as Ambassador—which Finvarra did not, I would stake my throne on it. Or else he would himself have encouraged sedition, and we *know* Ailill acted of his own volition."

"Finvarra must therefore be a weak king," Nuada said. "By your logic."

"Which he is not," Oisin inserted.

"Deluded, then," the Morrigu spat. "—or mad; it runs in the family. You have only to look at Ailill and Fionna."

"They had different mothers," Oisin pointed out. "Finvarra's mother—"

"He is also arrogant," Lugh interrupted. "Had Finvarra couched his demands in less forceful words, I might have accepted them. At least I would have considered. But they *were* demands, and stated so, and demands I will not countenance—not from anyone. Certainly not from one who cannot even master his own subjects!"

"They are still here, too," the Morrigu noted. "We have not yet discovered everyone Ailill corrupted."

"War he wanted," Lugh said bitterly. "War with mankind."

Nuada looked down at the table. "And now we face war with our brothers in Faerie—war with Erenn if we do not accept Finvarra's demands, and war with Arawn and probably the Powersmiths if we do."

"Alas, that is true," Lugh replied, rising. "Whatever choice we take, I see all roads leading to slaughter."

"Only the crows will be happy," the Morrigu said flatly.

"Not even you, Great Queen?"

"No single person is worth a kingdom's honor. Not when we still have the Mortal problem to consider."

"What is your counsel, then?"

"That you get Morwyn back to her own country as soon as possible, and preferably on her own vessel. Failing that, that you make ready to take war to Finvarra. War on someone else's soil—or seas—is always preferable to war on one's own."

"You think we will not win?"

"I have never lost a war," she said. "But all things have an ending."

"So be it, then," Lugh sighed. "You have heard my

thinking. I go now to send my reply. One word will I tell Finvarra: *never.*"

Nuada rose to follow. "And what of a certain young human, who has the vessel Morrigu mentioned—that might prove very useful, if things reach the end we foresee."

Lugh turned in place. "What of him?"

"Oisin and I were just on our way to meet with him, to begin what once we spoke of."

Lugh's eyes narrowed thoughtfully, but he nodded. "It would serve us well, if it comes to that eventuality. In any event, he will have to be contacted, though perhaps we should wait until we see our way clearer. For myself, I go to speak with the Lady Morwyn." And with that, he stalked from the chamber.

His counselors followed him until they, too, went their own ways: the Morrigu to inspect Lugh's forces, Oisin and Nuada by the shortest route to a certain place that was neither in the Lands of Men nor in Faerie, but closer to the latter.

The young guardswoman also went with them, but turned down another way as soon as it became convenient. A moment later she ducked through an archway and removed her golden helmet, then reached for her ear and popped out the golden spiral she had set there. Ailill had given it to her before he was murdered. Poor Ailill—poor, loving Master. She remembered the feel of his body against hers and allowed herself a single tear—and then a triumphant smile. Lugh might have warded her helmet so that she could not know of what they had spoken, but Ailill had foreseen such things. The spiral in her hands made every word very clear, and now they were locked away in her memory. A second spiral she left, so that no one could read her thoughts and thus betray her.

And what thoughts!

A Mortal boy, was it? She certainly knew who that was. And a particular vessel? She had a notion about that as well. Already a plan was forming.

Chapter III: He-Goes-About

(a Place Between—no time)

"Fionchadd, you fiend, let me go!" David gritted, as he twisted beneath the painful wrestling hold that had somehow pinned both hands hard up between his shoulder blades before he had known what was happening. Had there been anything but edged metal (*not* steel, he knew) at his throat, his assailant would now be sitting on his butt somewhere in front of him, courtesy of a soldier-uncle's training. The grip was poor, really; easy to escape—if only there hadn't been the dagger.

Abruptly the pressure vanished, the weapon swept away. David spun around to face a boy apparently his own age—except that Fionchadd mac Ailill of the Daoine Sidhe was centuries older.

Eye to eye they met each other: both slim and muscular and a little shorter than was normal for their races; both still gaining depth in chests and width in shoulders, fullness in arms and legs. Even their blond hair was similar, save that the Faery's was curly, slightly more golden, and somewhat longer than David's bandannaed mass. Their eyes were different, though: David's blue and level; Fionchadd's green and aslant. And the Faery's face was thin, his cheekbones high above a pointed chin—a prettily handsome face, but somehow disconcerting. By contrast, David's features showed a typical adolescent synthesis of a man's clean angles and a boy's softer curves. At the moment, the Faery was dressed nearly as lightly as his human counterpart: in a sleeveless, hip-length tunic of green-and-white checked wool, and baggy gray breeches drawn snug around his waist and ankles. He wore no shoes, but his narrow feet looked hard and competent.

"A *fiend*, am I?" Fionchadd laughed, his voice low but clear—his real voice, not the half-heard talk the Sidhe used among themselves, that rang more in the mind than the ear. He clamped his arms around David and gave him a swift, brotherly hug that took him completely by surprise.

"Some folks would say you are," David acknowledged solemnly when he had caught his breath.

A flash of wicked grin. "Would you?"

David scratched his nose. "I'm not sure. I haven't got that far in my bull sessions with Silverhand yet. 'Course, *some* say you were angels who wouldn't take sides when Satan rebelled."

To which a deeper voice—bronze rather than brass—appended, "And some say we're the souls of the mortal dead!"

David started at that, and whirled around to see two more figures enter the stone arena.

One was an old man, white-haired; his thin body bent and stiff and clad in a plain robe the color of a full moon's corona; and with sightless eyes that shone dark silver. He carried a long wooden staff clinched in dark, gnarled fingers, each of which bore at least one ring of gold or silver.

"Oisin!" David cried, and the man inclined his head. He looked, David thought, either preoccupied or worried, to judge from his furrowed brow.

The man who stood beside him was much taller, fair-haired, and wearing a short white tunic above matching hose and thigh boots. His right arm appeared to be cased in articulated metal armor of fabulous workmanship, though in fact it was part of his body. He it was who had spoken.

"I *know* that's not true, Nuada," David said quickly. "About the souls of the dead, I mean."

"*Do* you?" the Faery lord gave him back. A lifted eyebrow showed humor the rest of his face denied—apparently something was bothering him too. "Have I told you as much?"

"No, but you have souls; you can have kids and be injured. Even die, if you do it right."

"Which proves nothing except how limited are your kind's notions of life and death. But that is not the matter of this meeting."

David bit his lip and frowned. There was no use putting it off any longer. "Okay, so what do you want with me?"

In reply, Nuada reached to his golden belt, unhooked two plain, cross-hilted swords, and held one out in either hand. Fionchadd claimed one immediately; and at his nod David reluctantly took the other.

"I sense misgivings," the Faery said, as David backed away. "Yet you yourself once agreed that it would be worth your while to learn something of weapons work."

"I wasn't expecting it quite so soon, though," David replied, relieved to discover that Silverhand's mysterious summons held no more ominous portent. "I kinda thought we were talking in abstracts."

"Ah, but it is never wise to expect anything of the Sidhe," Oisin said, chuckling. "They pride themselves on being unpredictable."

"Yeah, tell me about it, man."

"But you should consider yourself honored," Fionchadd teased. "You are to have the best master in all of Tir-Nan-Og; for who better to instruct in weapons-work than the Warlord of the High King himself?"

"And to observe than Oisin," Nuada added.

"But he's blind!" David protested before he could stop himself.

"So much the better," Nuada said calmly, "for eyes can

be deceived. But Oisin can tell how blows fly, where they land, and with how much effort; all from the pitch of parting air and the sound and rate of your breathing."

"Uh, speaking of blows," David interrupted, surveying his scantily-clad body, "shouldn't we be wearing, like, *armor*, or something? I've got some back in the boat Morwyn gave me."

Nuada shook his head, though his eyes glittered briefly. "Armor is only as good as the body it protects. For a master, there is no need. Besides, there is a special quality to these weapons."

David raised a dubious eyebrow.

"When they bite flesh they do no damage."

"Well that's just *great*," he muttered, with heavy sarcasm.

"That does not mean there will be no pain," Nuada went on obliviously. "For pain is a necessary thing for a man to learn. But the blows will do no lasting harm."

David glared at him askance. "How *much* pain?"

"Enough that you will avoid it, enough that you will remember."

"But Finno'll chop me to ribbons!"

"Of course he will. Yet he too has things to learn."

"And we'd best be at it," Fionchadd said, laughing, grabbing David by the arm. "Otherwise this cowardly human will surely talk away his lesson."

"There is always time in Faerie," Oisin noted, "though sometimes less than others."

"I don't know about this," David grumbled, as Fionchadd led him to the center of the stone circle. He felt rather like a sacrifice about to be made at some Druidic rite, and found himself wondering who had built this enclosure.

"You are not required to be good," Nuada told him, when they had taken their places. "And truly you will never be as accomplished as the least of the Sidhe; but you might find a basic competency very useful."

"Yeah, sure," as he faced Fionchadd.

"The first thing you have to learn is how to stand," Nuada told him. "And since you will not be using shields, you must stand to present as little target as possible. Observe how Fionchadd does it."

David did, or attempted to. The Faery boy faced him side-on, left leg leading, the sword in his right hand and poised horizontally above his shoulders so that blows might be delivered with the full force of the body behind them. That much, at least, David thought he could manage, so he copied the pose.

Nuada frowned and strode forward, made minute adjustments on David's posture, then frowned once more. "You're wearing your body wrong," he said at last. "Relax. It knows what to do, even if you do not."

David made another attempt, but something was still slightly off.

"Let me show him," Fionchadd suggested.

"Huh?" David snorted. "What do you know that Silverhand doesn't?"

"Nothing," the Faery boy replied patiently. "But there is a thing you and I can do that you and he cannot."

"Yeah, sure."

"Do you not remember, foolish mortal? Once before, when I had no form, you and I shared bodies. Allow me to do that again, and I will show you."

David hesitated, though he knew what Fionchadd had said was true. The Faery had only lately returned to the realm of the living; before that his soul had been trapped in a well-lizard in Tir-Nan-Og. But then David had tasted of that well, and for a while both their consciousnesses had occupied his body. It had been interesting—and had saved David's life. But did he want to do it again? Suddenly the idea appalled him. Still, he was here to learn. And it wasn't like they hadn't done it before.

"Oh, go ahead," he sighed.

Fionchadd's hand brushed his, their gazes met. And suddenly the world slid out of focus, and it was as if he had been thrust out of his body. But then his own brain overrode, and he tensed automatically.

No! a thought rang out. *Relax!*

I . . .

Let go and trust me.

David did—reluctantly. And felt his body slip into a new, more comfortable stance. The changes were subtle: an inch here, a half inch there, a slight twist somewhere else. But the whole felt exactly right, felt, in truth, as if raw energy coiled right between his shoulders, ready to strike out at any threat.

Abruptly that second presence vanished, and he found his vision clearing.

Nuada eyed him critically. "It is close enough for now; his body will remember."

"Where shall we begin?" Fionchadd asked.

"I think sword blocks will be sufficient for today," Nuada replied, facing David. "There are three basic ones: head, body, and legs. Each starts with the weapon in the same configuration: vertical before you. To stop a blow to the head, you swing the blade up and twist the wrist, bringing it horizontal. For a body blow, a simple left or right suffices. For legs, swing the blade down to meet your opponent—show him, Fionchadd."

The Faery nodded and readied his weapon. His eyes glittered disarmingly above the white flash of his flawless grin.

"Now, David, strike him, quickly! Aim for the head!"

David swung the sword, feeling arm and shoulders and back—even hips—swing smoothly around in one fluid motion he would not have guessed he possessed. The blade flashed straight for the Faery's ear.

But did not connect.

Because Fionchadd's sword was there before him, whistling up and over to intercept him. Metal clanged on metal. The hilt thrummed painfully in David's hand, and before he knew it, he had flung up his other one as if to fend off further attack.

"No!" Nuada shouted. "Tuck your free hand in your waistband, otherwise you will try to use it for a shield."

David followed his instructions, then resumed position.

They practiced the other forms, then, with David throwing blows more or less at random and Fionchadd showing him how to counter. The first few rounds were deliberately slow and gave him little trouble, but gradually the pace increased until eventually the Faery's arm was a silver-tipped blur. Not one of David's blows connected, though; and in no time at all his arm began to ache.

"Now it's your turn." Fionchadd chuckled wickedly. "Your turn to defend, I mean. I will call out the blows and you parry."

"Crap!" David groaned. He was already worn out simply from swinging the sword's unfamiliar mass. His fingers hurt, too; and likewise his wrists and shoulders. It was like slinging hay, he thought. Only more elegant—and far more demanding.

"Head!" Fionchadd cried abruptly.

David blinked. Almost too late he swept his blade up.

"Body!"

—Sword lowered, swinging to the left to block the blow that hissed in from that direction.

"Body!"—but from the other side; blade flipping sideways to meet it.

"Leg!"

He met it—barely.

"Body!"

Yeah, okay; he managed that one too.

"Head!"

"Body!"

"Leg!"

"Head!"

"Leg!"

Too fast—or he was too slow, the weapon a burden in his hand. Metal slammed into his unprotected thigh, and a fine, clear pain slid through his flesh. Before he could stop himself he glanced down—and saw Fionchadd's blade embedded almost an inch deep in his leg.

The world went momentarily colorless.

Fionchadd jerked the sword away, and David gasped. There was no blood, no wound—and no pain any longer.

"The hardest thing for our kind to learn," Oisin said

from his place between two stones, "is how to deal with pain."

Fifteen minutes later it was over, because by then David was so numb with fatigue he could not have raised a weapon if his life depended on it. "Sorry, guys, I've had it," he panted, as he flopped down on a slab of mossy stone beneath a trilithon.

"Already?" Fionchadd sighed. "Surely you can go a *little* longer."

David could only stare at the Faery in helpless frustration. *How dare he look so calm!* Oh true, Fionchadd's usually pale face was flushed a little, and there was the merest sheen of sweat along his long, smooth limbs, but nothing else gave any indication of exertion. The little sleaze was not even panting—damn him!

A shadow fell across David's face. "Not a bad beginning for a mortal," Nuada said. "Perhaps in another few decades you might even prove quite accomplished."

"Decades!" David moaned. "I'm not gonna be able to *move* for at least a century. And anyway, who am I gonna fight? My kind don't go in for that sorta thing anymore; and you folks don't need to bother with it to get at us. Two words and snap-your-fingers and we're goners. Even me —now that the ring Oisin gave me's lost its ability to protect me."

Nuada glanced at his companion. "A sorry thing that, though ruined in a righteous cause."

"Yet a man must be the source of his own strength. Reliance on anything beyond oneself can only lead to disappointment."

David scowled thoughtfully. "I'm not sure I agree with that. No man is an island, and all."

"No," Oisin replied. "But a man should be able to *function* as an island if he must. I have not said that isolation is desirable, only that the ability to deal with it is. A man should be the source of his own strength, but likewise should he let it flow out from him and merge with others, and drink from their strength as well."

"Okay, okay," David protested wearily. "My poor old brain's too addled for this kind of heavy thinkin'."

"And in any event, we must depart," Nuada said. "Lugh has a grievous problem on which we must be ready to advise him. Fionchadd, are you coming?"

"In a moment."

"Ah." Oisin laughed softly. "I heard him called a *fiend* before, but I think a truer word for him is *friend*."

David simply closed his eyes and did not reply. He was tired . . . so tired. He did not see Nuada and Oisin leave.

Almost he slept.

But suddenly water was splashing into his face—only it wasn't water, because when he licked it from his lips it was sweet, and when he opened his eyes it was a thin stream of red that Fionchadd was squirting from a white leather bag straight toward him.

David blinked, then allowed the Faery to fill his mouth. His aim, of course, was perfect. "Damn, that was good." He giggled, after Fionchadd had turned the arc toward himself in a flicker of movement that did not waste a drop. "What is it, anyway?"

Fionchadd's eyes sparkled with humor. "Why Faery wine, of course!"

"Not the kind that dooms you to an eternity there, I hope." David yawned, letting his lids close again. "If it is, just go ahead and take me. I'm too tired to care."

"Would that be so bad?" The Faery's voice was suddenly serious.

"You've *heard* my answer to that. I've had one chance already, and turned it down."

"You'll die, you know, eventually."

A shrug. "It's what we're designed for."

"I'll miss you."

"Me too," David grunted.

A long pause, then: "I'm sorry."

"For what?"

"For the pain I cost you when first we met: most particularly for wounding your kinsman. I . . . I did not know you then, nor any Mortals. My year as a lizard gave me a great deal of time to reflect."

David opened his eyes but did not turn his head to look at him, nor immediately reply. *Jesus,* he'd almost forgotten that: how Fionchadd had once shot Uncle Dale with an arrow that had caused him to have a stroke, thereby starting the whole chain of events that had brought him to his present pass. And here he was hanging out with the guy like they were best friends or something. He wondered for a moment if Fionchadd had somehow cast a glamour on him to make him forget, but rejected the notion. They'd both grown up a lot in the year since that had happened. And wasn't forgiveness part of growing up? Fionchadd had been acting in a perfectly acceptable way for his kind and culture at the time; for most Sidhe considered mortals as little more than animals. But the Faery had changed now, he could tell; and wasn't that change partly David's own doing? Besides, it was partly through David's actions that Fionchadd's father had died, and the Faery had evidently forgiven him for that as well. Could he afford to do any less? Fionchadd had also been acting out of family loyalty, not spite, which was a thing David certainly understood. Lord, what a complicated mess!

"I will understand if you do not wish my further company," Fionchadd said finally.

David sat up and looked at him. "Oh gee, Finno, I— *Shit!* I mean, so much has changed since then. I guess if I wanted to I could get really pissed, but . . . well, it's like you were a different person then. It was a bad thing from my point of view, but your reasons were honorable—to you."

"I am forgiven then?"

"If I am. Now—I reckon I'd best be movin'. Think I'll grab a swim down at Lookout Rock and get on home—if I can make it that far without fallin' over."

"May I join you?"

David flopped an arm across the Faery's shoulders. "If

you'll show me the way out of this confounded bogus Stonehenge."

David had never seen a sight as welcome as the pool on Lookout Rock when Fionchadd finally got him there. The journey hadn't been difficult, really: a jog down the Track, then off by a certain silver-leafed tree, and suddenly they were in the middle of the logging road a mile or so above the turnoff. From there it would normally have been a quick, painless trek to the rocky outcrop whose precipitous overlook gave the place its name.

But he was not normally this tired.

He stood at the water's edge now, the forest a semicircle behind him, the sheer cliffs diving straight down a hundred feet away to his right to reveal a vista of purpling mountains, and just up ahead, a steep, black slab down which a waterfall slid into a pool perhaps fifteen yards across and four feet deep at the deepest. He stepped closer. A tickle of spray touched his face, and he could smell the odors of wet leaves, pines, and sun-baked rocks.

Lordy Jesus, he was bushed. Idly he wondered how he would explain that fact to his father. Usually when he got back from a run he was mildly winded and a bit flushed. Sweaty. But now he had almost no energy at all except what was trickling into him from the wine Fionchadd had given him, and all that was doing was making him giddy.

"This place has Power," the Faery noted from beside him.

David giggled wearily. "I always said that, back before . . . . I knew."

"It has Power anyway. Things have Power because you give them Power. And anything that is beautiful has Power."

In reply, David threw down the sodden sweatshirt he'd been carrying and commenced prying at his sneakers— then hesitated. He swam here often, skinny-dipping with Alec or his other MacTyrie Gang buddies; he wasn't particularly shy or modest, nor had any reason to be. But suddenly the idea of undressing in front of Fionchadd gave him pause.

His companion, however, had no such inhibitions. Before David knew it, he was out of his tunic, his breeches, the small bit of fabric underneath.

Though he had seen the Faery naked before, David could not resist a surreptitious glimpse at him. Exposed, the differences between the races were clearer: in proportion, in thickness of bone, in smoothness of contours. The Faery's body was also blemish-free: no moles, no freckles, no scars nor random hair.

Fionchadd caught him peeking and returned the stare more frankly as David finished stripping. David blushed furiously and dove into the water.

A second splash was the Faery.

They swam a lap or two, then David flopped over and floated, moving only enough to keep his head above water, while Fionchadd paddled lazily beside him. David closed his eyes, gave himself over to the magic of the place: the glitter of sunlight, the call of birds, the susurration of falling water that was surely the earth's first music . . .

And then music of another kind; *real* music, and fast approaching; harmonica it sounded like. Abruptly he recognized the tune: Beethoven's "Ode to Joy," of all things. "Oh, crap, Finno," he whispered, "you better hide. Somebody's coming!"

The merest tremor shook Fionchadd's body. "It is too late for that; eyes have touched me already—but I will do what I can."

"I'd appreciate it." David scrambled toward the bank.

He was not fast enough. A bare instant later a figure emerged from the deep shadows of the forest and passed into the lesser gloom at its edge. David's breath caught. At first he thought it another of the Sidhe, for something about the way the stranger moved, something about the way he carried himself reminded David of that immortal race. But then the visitor stepped full into the light and David knew he had been mistaken.

It was a boy roughly his own age, though somewhat taller and good bit more muscular. He was dressed in worn blue jeans, purposeful-looking hiking boots, and a red T-shirt emblazoned with a white falcon at dive. An immense blue backpack towered above his head, and thick black hair hung from under a beaded headband to sprawl across his brawny shoulder, setting off the reddish cast of his skin. He looked, in short, a very great deal like an Indian.

The boy started toward the pool then paused, squinted into the long afternoon shadows. His eyes brushed David, who had retreated to the deeper water in the middle, and he started. "Sorry, guys," he shouted quickly in a Southern accent David could not place more specifically. "Didn't know anybody was up here!"

David risked a furtive glance at Fionchadd who was hanging back even further, then looked back at the intruder, startled to see the boy's eyes also dart toward the Faery and linger there—he'd expected Fionchadd to shapeshift or make himself invisible, or something, but evidently his efforts had gone awry. "No problem," he called back, as he slipped as close to the edge as modesty permitted; fortunately the pool was fairly deep at that corner, so he could stand waist deep and still make himself heard above the sound of rushing water. "I was just coolin' off a little."

The stranger crossed the remaining distance and squatted on the edge. A leather thong hung around his neck, and there was a small bulge between his pecs: probably some kind of pouch—which made sense, if David's suspicions were accurate.

"Just saw the damnedest thing," the boy allowed.

David's heart flip-flopped, as a thousand disturbing possibilities unfolded. "Oh yeah, like what?"

"White deer. I was just comin' over the gap and saw one runnin' through the woods ahead of me. Tried to follow, but it was too fast. Damnedest thing I ever saw."

David exchanged glances with Fionchadd. "I bet."

"Yeah, well, it's gone now."

"Right."

The boy nodded toward the pool. "This stuff fit to drink?"

David folded his arms. "Be my guest."

The visitor slipped off the backpack and scooped a hand into the pool, then cocked a thick black brow. "You didn't pee in it or anything, did you?" His eyes were brown and penetrating—and, for the moment, full of humor.

David sniggered and was surprised to find himself echoed by Fionchadd. "Not this time."

"What about your buddy?"

David glanced toward his Faery companion. "Huh? Oh, yeah. Don't reckon: he's civilized—housebroken anyway!"

The boy helped himself to a half-dozen efficient scoops, then sat back on his haunches and sighed contentedly. "Nothing like the real thing, straight from the bosom of the earth, thanks be to it. Name's Calvin, by the way, Calvin McIntosh. And yes, in case you're curious, I'm an Indian."

"All right!" David exclaimed, "I thought you might be—uh, what with the headband and the hair and all. Our folks don't get hair that black."

"It's usually best to settle that kinda thing right off," Calvin noted. "Saves a lot of misunderstandin'."

"Huh?"

"Some folks aren't exactly thrilled by Native Americans. I'd rather know how the land lays to start with."

"Well *I* think it's just excellent to meet one," David said. "So you don't have to worry about me. Oh, and I'm David Sullivan, I reckon."

"You *reckon?*"

Real smart, David told himself as he tried very hard not to display his embarrassment. "Sometimes I'm not real sure."

"Well, David Sullivan I-Reckon, *I* reckon I'm glad to meet you." Calvin stretched a surprisingly graceful hand across the water. David took it. The grip was firm but relaxed.

"And your friend . . . ?" the boy added, turning his gaze back to Fionchadd.

"Call me Finn," the Faery said, gliding forward. "Would you like to join us?"

Calvin squinted again, then blinked, as if he were having trouble with his eyes. "Uh, thanks, but I've had enough cold baths the last few weeks to last me a good, long lifetime, even if goin' to water *is* part of my heritage." He paused for a thoughtful moment. "But if either of you fellows know where I could get a *hot* one, I'd be mighty grateful. And maybe point me to a laundry? That'd be real good. I've been livin' in these britches so long they can walk by themselves and whistle 'Dixie.'"

"You can come down to my house," David volunteered before he had truly thought it through, and could have kicked himself. It was not that he distrusted or disliked the boy. Indeed, given that they'd known each other rather less than five minutes, it was remarkable how comfortable he felt with him already—like an old friend newly returned. But what would his mother say when he came trotting in the back door with a for-real redskin in tow? Especially now, when she had about a ton of cooking to do, not to mention all the other preparations for the party and the impending company. It was too late to call back the invitation, though, now that he'd made it.

"That'd be great." Calvin grinned, looking vastly relieved. "Not too far I hope. I'm bushed."

"Tell me about it, man," David said with a chuckle. "But no, it's just down at the foot of the mountain. My folks've got a farm there."

Calvin's eyes shifted once more toward Fionchadd. "Both of you?"

"I live further away," the Faery offered before David could reply. "And while I speak of that, I had best be going." He slipped out of the pool and calmly commenced drying himself with his nubby tunic. A moment later he tugged on his baggy trousers and pranced off. David was glad they looked more or less like modern sweatpants. "I will see you again," the Faery called over his shoulder. "Both of you, perhaps." He entered the forest, then, and was gone.

When David turned back toward Calvin, he was still staring after Fionchadd. He hoped the Indian hadn't noticed anything too odd about their late companion. 'Course for that matter, he rather wished he hadn't noticed him at all, and wondered once more how he had.

As if sensing that appraisal, Calvin jerked back around and once more lifted a quizzical eyebrow. "Well, *he* was certainly a strange bird. Never saw anybody quite like him."

"Yeah, well, old Finno's pretty special; that's for certain."

"He part Japanese, or something?"

"Or something."

"Didn't think he could be full. Hair's wrong—'course I *have* seen a couple of blond Orientals."

"Yeah," David said noncommittally.

Calvin continued to press the subject. "Not from around here is he? Couldn't place his accent."

"Nope," David replied, admitting nothing.

The Indian's eyes narrowed minutely.

"But you are—a native, I mean."

"Yep—and proud of it." David was grateful for any chance to turn the conversation away from the Faery. The last thing he needed was to start a friendship by lying, though something about Calvin's face told him he'd have to be extra careful. The Indian was *awfully* sharp.

Calvin commenced unlacing his boots. "Maybe I *will* take you up on your offer, at least partly. You don't mind if I just cool my bunions a little, do you?" He grinned again, displaying a mouthful of very white teeth. David grinned back and slipped back into deeper water as the Indian rolled up his jeans and lowered his feet into the pool. A gasp followed, then a moan of blissful contentment. "Oh, *mama mia* that feels good!"

"*Mama mia?*" David echoed. "Where're you *from,* anyway?"

Calvin's expression turned serious.

"I was afraid you'd ask that; and if I were true to the better part of myself, I'd say I was from here: the woods.

But unfortunately, I'm from Atlanta—mostly. My dad's a construction foreman down there. He's half of the People, but doesn't like to claim it. Mom was full, though. She died when I was born."

"Sorry."

An absent shrug. "Can't miss what you never had. 'Sides, they were separated by then, anyway. Fortunately Mom's dad stepped in and made sure I got to spend some time with her folks up at the reservation."

"You mean Cherokee?" David asked, thinking of the big settlement a couple of hours away to the northwest. He'd been there once or twice, but he hadn't been impressed. As far as he could tell the place was simply miles of handicrafts from Taiwan and Hong Kong—that, and bored-looking Native Americans wearing more feathers and beads and fringes and leather and paint than the Cherokee (at least) ever would have. Even the traditional drama, *Unto these Hills*, which depicted the Trail of Tears, had failed to move him—though he had to admit that an intermittent threat of thunder hadn't helped any. "That your tribe?" he finished.

"That's what *you* folks call it."

David scowled. "And what *should* we call it?"

"Well, the right name for the place is Qualla; the proper name for the tribe's *Ani-Yunwiya*."

"*Ani*—" David began. "What was the rest of it?"

"*Ani-Yunwiya*. Means *the people*, or *the principal people*. Cherokee is somebody else's name for us. Means *people-who-live-in-caves*, more or less."

"*Ani-Yunwiya*," David repeated. "Is that it?"

"Close enough. Most folks don't even bother."

"Names can be important," David said. "Hey, isn't there something about you folks having secret ones? That's what my uncle told me one time. Supposed to be as much a part of you as your hair, and all, right?"

The Indian's expression became very serious. "Right. I only tell mine to certain special people; people I can trust with my life—because that's what it is."

"Yeah."

"Edahi," Calvin said suddenly.

David looked up. "What?"

"Edahi: my true name."

"Jesus!" David cried. "I sure wasn't expecting *that!* I mean, we barely know each other!"

"Surprised me too," Calvin whispered gravely. "But something told me to do it, and I can usually trust my instincts."

"And what did they tell you just now?"

"That you're a guy who's used to keeping secrets."

"Well, thanks . . . Edahi." He paused. "I . . . I don't suppose you'd be willing to tell me what it means, would you?"

"He-goes-about."

"I see," David replied, though he didn't.

"My grandfather gave it to me. He was one of the last of the old-time medicine men. Read my fortune when I was born and saw that I'd always be wandering around lookin' for something. My middle name's a pun on it."

"Yeah?"

"Fargo."

"Oh." David chuckled. "I get it! But, hey, thanks again, man, for trusting me."

An awkward silence fell on their conversation for a moment, but eventually David spoke again. "So, you spend much time up there on the reservation—at Qualla, I mean?"

Calvin nodded. "Spent summers with my grandfather until he died last year."

"Sorry to hear that," David said. "So what brings you here, then?"

The grin returned. "Legs' taxi."

"All right, *Fargoer,* get serious!"

"The Appalachian Trail."

Which explains the bodacious backpack, David thought, flipping an indignant handful of water at his new friend.

Calvin easily dodged the tiny tsunami. "Well, then, *seriously,* David-I-Reckon; I . . . I guess I'm searchin' for my roots, or something. I grew up in the white—in *your* world and thought I'd adjusted, but a couple of years ago I found out it just wasn't enough. 'Course the reservation doesn't work either, in the long run—all that drinkin' and show biz and stuff'll drown your spirit in a second. So anyway, when my grandfather died, it really bummed me out, so I thought I'd hike the old Trail and try to get a handle on myself that way. Find out which world was mine."

"How long you been at it?"

"'Bout a year."

"A *year?*"

"Started at the north end, worked south."

"But what about—"

"School?"

"Yeah, right."

"Dropped out."

"But you're not stupid!" The words were out before David could stop himself.

Calvin grimaced. "Yeah, I'm plenty bright; made good grades, and all—but it's *your* people's history I was learning, *your* literature, *your* science—which is fine, if that's the world you wanta live in. But my grandfather showed me there's more, and I've gotta follow it, learn my *own* history, and lit, and science."

"And music?"

"Yeah!" Calvin laughed, but then turned serious again. "Uh, look, man, were you bein' straight about that bath?"

"Absolutely. And laundry, and all. Supper, too, if you want it—'course you'll have to watch my ma. She's okay, but we're planning a big birthday do for my favorite uncle —he'll be seventy tomorrow—so she's kinda wired right now. Got a six-year-old brother who's a real pill, too. He'll just *love* you. Probably think you're a Thundercat."

"And your dad? I don't want to, like, make you uncomfortable, and all; but—well, a lot of folks up here don't exactly appreciate my kind."

David could only shrug. "Well, to be perfectly honest, I've never heard him comment on the subject. Probably won't say anything anyway, 'cept about the farm. Just sulks and grumbles a lot. We're not much alike."

"You don't act much like *any* of the folks around here."

"I'm not, I guess."

"Ever read Tolkien?"

"Of *course*," David replied archly, wondering what had brought that up. "Hasn't everybody?"

"And *Dune*, and . . ."

"All I can get my hands on. Ever read *Gods and Fighting Men?*"

"Never even *heard* of it. What's it about?"

"Never mind," David told him, suddenly wishing he hadn't mentioned that particular book, since he was trying to shy away from Faerie these days, not drag other people in—which any protracted discussion might well do, especially if the wrong kind of questions set him flirting with the Ban. "We've got enough in common without gettin' into that."

Calvin did not reply, but he stared at David so intently that David felt compelled to duck under water.

"Guess I'd best be gettin' on home, too," he gasped when he had resurfaced. "My stomach's startin' to sing opera."

"Sounds good—the food, I mean, not your tummy."

"I hope not." David laughed, as he headed for shore.

Calvin slid his feet out of the pool. "Uh, look, Dave, is there anything I can do around your place to pay for supper and all? I'm pretty handy with farm chores."

David barred his teeth evilly. "Oh, I'm sure Pa could find *something* to keep you busy. How are you at mucking out stables?"

"Fine," Calvin said, turning his head discreetly as David climbed out of the pool and commenced toweling himself off with his sweatshirt—to little effect, though it had been lying in the westering sun. "Sure they won't mind?"

"No," David told him; then: "Shoot, why don't you spend the night? That is, if you want to."

"It'd beat the ground I've been sleepin' on for the last week, that's for sure."

"What about before?"

Calvin grinned from ear to ear. "There was this girl up

near Silva had a cabin, see; that, and curiosity—and raging hormones . . ."

"Aha!" David chuckled, tugging on his gym shorts. "I
gotcha." He slipped on his shoes, wadded the sopping shirt
into a bundle, and started toward the trail that led out to the
logging road. Calvin shouldered his pack and followed,
and for a moment they walked single file through the
woods. That was a little disturbing, too, for David could
almost feel the Indian's eyes boring into his skull. Once or
twice, too, during the hike down the mountain, he caught
Calvin slipping him strange sideways glances—though
their conversation was the usual sort of banter typical of
kindred spirits.

But still, he thought, as he trudged into the kitchen almost an hour later, there was something a little disconcerting about Calvin Fargo McIntosh.

Chapter IV: Speaking of Ships

(Tir-Nan-Og—high summer—sunset)

Lugh stared at the red-haired woman lounging on the red silk cushions beside him and tried not to be swayed by her beauty, which held all the fascination—and danger—of a flame. He had found her by the long, shallow pool in the Court of the Summer Stars, and there they remained, drinking pomegranate wine from ruby goblets of the lady's own making—she had insisted.

White marble was warm beneath them; breezes cool across their faces where the first breaths of evening drifted past the square pillars of the surrounding colonnade and brought with it the scent of cedars from the next courtyard down, where a lone guardswoman waited. Silver inlays set in the pavement showed the constellations, and diamonds large as olives marked the particular stars and sent rainbows sparkling over the pinkening stone as they caught the last rays of the sun. The woman's eyes, too, sparked brightly, but there was little softness there, for she and Lugh had been speaking of war.

"Truly, Lady Morwyn," said the King of Tir-Nan-Og, "I

have no choice, if I would preserve my realm. Do not forget that I warned you of this already, and still I have given you shelter—sanctuary—call it what you will. All has been as you asked and Dana's Laws demand. But my land must come first. I may not turn you out, but it is certainly my right to ask you to leave of your own volition."

The corners of the woman's lips lifted slightly in an ironic half-smile as she took a sip from her goblet. "Indeed, Lord, I have no desire to foster contention between you and your brother princes. Yet it is as I have said: I have little choice *but* to stay, if what you have told me is true."

"True it is: the ravens have seen what comes. Finvarra's ships have already passed onto the Sea Road, no matter that the Tracks are weak this season. He intends, I am certain, to lay siege to Tir-Nan-Og unless I relinquish you."

An eyebrow lifted delicately. "And will you withstand this siege?"

Lugh's face was grim. "For a while. I will seal the borders, if need be. Once, already, I have done so."

Morwyn dipped her fingers in the pool and watched the drops trickle through them, a gleam of diamonds in the waning light. "Long has it been since Faerie went to war."

"And now—forgive me, Lady—over so small a thing as the lives of a pair of half-mad twins."

"—who happened to be littermates to the King of Erenn!"

Lugh shook his head. "That, I expect is but an excuse. Finvarra, I doubt it not, grows weary, as do I. The years weigh heavy when they have no end. Sometimes any change from boredom is sufficient."

"What of the Lands of Men? Would it not profit both of you more to turn your attention there? *They* are a threat; the matter of myself a mere legal bother."

Lugh sighed heavily. "In that you echo your one-time lord's thinking but never mine. We could not win such a war and remain unchanged. I doubt we could win it at all."

"Yet you have just spoken of change as a thing desired."

"But there is change and change."

"And none of this addresses your problem."

"True, and I can find no simple solution. I have cast the Runes and read the Tracks, and all I have found is thunder. Even Oisin is baffled."

Morwyn set down her goblet and folded her arms decisively. "We must therefore trust to our own devices! Well then, there are two things I have to tell you: One is that I would not bring war upon one who has given me succor and greatly honored my son—thus, if I can find a means to accomplish it, I *will* leave. But the other thing is more fell, which is that to which I alluded before: the reason we may already be too late."

Lugh's eyes narrowed abruptly. "I think it is time you told me."

The Fireshaper took a deep breath. "There is a secret known to my people that I have learned by certain means that we employ, of which I should not speak lest it mark me a traitor . . ."

"I would not have you do *that*," Lugh told her, "whatever may be your reason."

"That is for *me* to decide, a matter between myself and my conscience. But the news I bear is this: For a very long time, Finvarra has been building a navy in secret. Human wrights he has employed, as well as the dwarf folk."

"All this I have heard," Lugh said. "Finvarra's fondness for ships is widely known."

"Ah yes, but what is *not* so widely known is that he has had other aid as well: the aid of my mother's people."

Lugh's mouth became a thin, hard line. *"Powersmiths!"* he whispered. Then, louder, "What *kind* of aid?"

"With keel and prows, with sails and oars—and with Power—such Power, Lord, as will render the seas open at any season!"

Shocked silence was Lugh's only response.

"What this means, of course," Morwyn continued, "is that you may not have as much time to prepare as you had expected. *That* is why it may already be too late for me to leave your country."

"I have ships as well," Lugh said heavily.

"Ships swifter than the Winds Between the Worlds?"

"Far swifter, and also of Powersmith crafting. Who do you suppose built the airy navy that found you on the mountain in the Lands of Men?"

"But Finvarra's ships are newer—and far, far faster!"

Lugh gnawed his moustache thoughtfully. "This is all ill to speak of, Lady: yet there is one thing you may have forgotten, and it is a surprise to me that you have not yourself recalled it."

Once more an eyebrow lifted. "And that is?"

"There is still one ship that should be faster than any of Finvarra's."

"What ship is that?"

"The one you gave a certain Mortal. I have heard Fionchadd speak of it often, how it uses all the subtlety of your people's art—and all their latest delvings into Power. Surely that boat would easily outdistance any fleet of Finvarra's."

"It might, Lord, but it is no longer mine to offer."

Lugh's eyes glittered dangerously. "No, it was a gift given *freely,* I presume. Or was there, perhaps some *other* motivation? A desire to protect it, maybe? To hide its secrets from my druids?"

Morwyn smiled cryptically but did not reply.

"I am right then!" Lugh cried triumphantly. "I knew it, and curse you for screening your thoughts so that I might not see the truth."

"Yet if I had that ship . . ."

"And I swore to keep my druids from it . . ."

"—I might slip away this very evening, and none the wiser."

"You might even evade Finvarra . . ."

"One problem yet remains, though."

"Besides retrieving the ship, I assume?"

"Aye. The vessel was made for speed only, not for confrontation. It is vulnerable to attack. Therefore I must leave as soon as possible, to minimize chance of engagement."

"Will you see to it, then?"

Morwyn nodded, and stood. "I go to make myself ready. And by the way, have you seen my son?"

"Fionchadd?" Lugh asked, as he retrieved his goblet and joined her. "I believe he is somewhere with Nuada."

Morwyn frowned. "And I have a notion where that might be."

Chapter V: Odd Man Out

(Enotah County, Georgia—
Friday, August 16—early evening)

Though he should have been flipping burgers, Alec McLean had been spending rather more time that hot August afternoon staring at his fingers. There was nothing remarkable about them, really; they were merely the hard, knobby digits due a moderately active seventeen-year-old boy—unless he rearranged them. He did it again: thumb and pinkie folded, the remaining three extended scouts-honor-wise. *Three,* he thought—until he shifted his index finger sideways. *Two-and-one, now—except that all of a sudden it's one-and-two,* whereupon the indexer rejoined the others, and the ring guy was on his own.

Back and forth; in and out: *three, two, one; one, two, three . . .*

"For heaven's sake, Alec, pay attention!" his father called behind him. "That's the third batch you've ruined today! I didn't get you this job to burn up the profit!" He sounded more put-upon than exasperated.

"Huh? Oh—sorry, Dad!" Alec spun around and tried to salvage the six patties charring on the grill beside him.

Maybe the black wouldn't show if he squirted on enough mustard and catsup.

Dr. McLean, a solid three inches shorter and a flabby forty pounds more portly than his only child, rolled his pale eyes toward his purple-and-gold Lions Club hat and pried the greasy flipper from his son's nonciphering hand. "Just forget it, boy; these are goners anyway. You might as well go home, much good you're doing here."

Alec frowned. "Sorry, I . . . I guess I'm just not with it today."

"I guess you're not. But do try to be tomorrow."

"Tomorrow's David's uncle's party!"

"Not in the *morning*, it isn't! Or at night."

"Da-aad!"

"I signed you up for thirty hours in here, and thirty you're gonna do! Now scat! I can get by till Gary comes on board—assuming he's on time."

It was Alec's turn to roll his eyes. "What would you do without the MacTyrie gang as slave labor?" he wondered aloud, as he untangled himself from his stained white apron and sidestepped his father on his way to the concession stand's flimsy wooden door.

Dr. McLean applied himself to methodically dismembering an onion. "Darrell's picking you up, right?"

"Yeah," Alec replied offhandedly. "I still say it'd be easier if you let me drive."

Dr. McLean's round face furrowed in resignation. "That'll be enough of that. That part comes in, you can drive your car. Mine stays home where it's safe. No way I'd let my new Swedish baby in this traffic."

"Which reduces you to bumming rides with my buddies."

"Which *means*, my son, that I've an excellent feel for both irony and convenience."

"Gaaaa! Not English again!" Alec shrieked as he leapt down the steps. "You really are trying to get rid of me!"

"Tell your mom I'll—"

"Yeah, I know: You'll catch a ride with G-Man later this evening."

"You got it."
"Carry on."
"You got it."

You son-of-a-bitchin' child! Alec was railing at himself
as he shuffled through the late-afternoon crowd on his way
out of the fairgrounds. Once more he recalled the image
that had soured the whole half-day and made him burn
more than that last half-dozen burgers in the process. It
hadn't been much, really, certainly nothing to justify such
an overblown reaction—just a thing he had seen a thousand times before: David's head bobbing away in a crowd.
Except that this time that head had bent close to a copper-
red one only a little shorter, and that made all the difference, because it reminded him yet again (as if he needed
reminding) of exactly how much David's friendship priorities had shifted. He hated it, too; and hated himself for that
hating. *Two-and-one; one-and-two; son-of-a-bitchin'
child, for sure!*

He just shouldn't *feel* that way, dammit! David was his
friend, practically his brother. So why should it bother him
that his best friend was apparently happier than he'd ever
been?

It wasn't like he wasn't partly to blame, either. Hadn't
he been pushing David toward Liz all summer? He'd sure
given him a lot of grief about her while they were down in
Valdosta, and more upon their return. But that had all been
rather abstract; more McLeanian vicarious living. It was
real now; and he was having trouble adapting to True-
Love-Meets-Mad-Davy-Sullivan.

Love! Ha! That was a giggle!

One definition of it, he had heard, was supposed to be
when someone else's happiness was more important than
your own. Which meant that if he loved David, which he
did, platonically; and if David was happy by virtue of
being in love; then he should himself be happier still. Only
somehow it didn't work out that way. Nor did it tell him
what to do about Alec. Poor, odd-finger-out Alec McLean.

Abruptly he stumbled, bounced off an unyielding surface, then a considerably softer, though more vocal one.

"Hey, watch where yer goin', boy!"

Alec froze, looked up, and realized he'd not been paying the slightest attention to where his feet were taking him. He'd simply been plodding along with his hands in his pockets, scruffing his B.K.'s through the ubiquitous midway sawdust, and feeling sorry for himself.

"Sorry," he mumbled to his victim—a fat, sweaty man in Bermuda shorts and a hat: Floridian, without a doubt.

The man scowled, grunted an obscenity, and turned away.

Alec did too, biting back a flash of anger that his logical part knew all too well was a function of his preoccupation. But so quickly did he spin around that before he could stop himself, he slammed into someone else and tumbled backward to the ground. Blushing furiously, he picked himself up, still seeing stars—and came face-to-face with the prettiest girl he had ever seen.

She was as tall as he was and black-haired, with skin like ivory and a touch of strangeness to her bone structure, the cant of her eyes and brows: Mexican, maybe, or Indian, or even Oriental. Except that her eyes were dark blue, wide and frank, yet shy in their appraisal. He found himself staring straight into them, only half aware of her smile as she met his gaze and gave it back. For a moment the stars returned, and he looked away, but not before he had glimpsed her clothing: white linen blouse and a long fringed skirt of obviously foreign manufacture. The body beneath was slim yet well developed; maybe she was some sort of athlete or one of the carny women out for a lark. "S-sorry," he managed, and could not resist another glance at her face.

"No damage done," the girl replied. She had an accent, though he couldn't place it except that he knew he'd heard it before. "I should have been more careful," she continued.

"But I really *am* sorry," Alec stammered. "I don't usually make a habit of running into b—" He stopped himself a bare syllable short of saying *beautiful women*, and colored again. What was wrong with him? It wasn't like he'd never seen a pretty girl before. Except, he realized he hadn't—not like this one, anyway. And she was so . . . so *approachable*, he supposed; not like the spiteful, self-centered airheads at school, who he was convinced carried a gene for bitchiness along with the ones for blond hair, perfect skin, and great bods. Liz was the only truly pretty girl he knew who wasn't stuck-up about it—and she was taken.

The girl blinked, as if waiting for him to complete his sentence. "I don't usually run into people," he finished lamely. "I'm usually more together than that."

"Apology accepted!"

"Uh . . . anything I can do to make amends?" Alec blurted before he was truly aware of what he was saying. "Buy you a Coke, or something?"

Again that smile: red lips above perfect teeth; and God, didn't she have nice eyes? "I'm not hungry now. But maybe—sometime."

"Sometime?"

She nodded. "I have an errand that will not wait."

"An . . . an errand? Need any help? I know my way around the fair pretty well."

"Alas, no. I must find out certain things—though I think I have already found one of the things I sought."

Alec's heart flip-flopped. Could she possibly mean . . . *Surely not!* On the other hand, maybe she did. He wasn't bad looking, he supposed. And she was foreign, she might be grateful for any kind voice in a storm. Now he thought of it, too, she did look a wee bit troubled; he could see it in the gentle furrowing of her brow. (Lordy *Jesus*, what wonderful eyes!)

Already she was backing away, on the verge of being swept into the mob. "I— Wait," he called. "I don't even know your name! I—" He froze, amazed at his own forwardness. Usually he was shy around girls—certainly shyer than Davy had recently become. Except that somehow all that had left him. Suddenly he felt newborn, as an unfamiliar confidence welled up in him, making him almost giddily reckless.

The girl ducked past the skinny, hard-looking woman who had threatened to come between them. "Call me Eva!" She pronounced the first letter somewhere between *E* and *A*. "And you are . . . ?"

"Alec. Alec McLean. I live over in MacTyrie."

The girl's face brightened. "MacTyrie! Ah—truly I may see you, then. I am visiting this area, you see, and—"

"Where're you from?"

Another laugh, like silver. "Many places, my sudden friend, many places!"

"But—"

The crowd eddied in once more. "Truly, I must leave," Eva cried, as it took her. "But perhaps we will meet again. In fact, I think I would like to."

Alec's grin stretched so wide it made his cheeks hurt. *"Wait!"* he called, as the girl turned to go. He started after, but found his way blocked as the sweaty throng swirled in to make way for the hot-dog cart a clown was pushing past. Then someone jostled him from behind and someone else from the side, and when he found his balance again, Eva had vanished.

How strange, he told himself. *How very strange*. Now that had certainly been interesting. Jesus, she'd been pretty, and nice, as far as he could tell. Maybe not *too* nice, though: because she sure hadn't been the least bit shy. She had actually appeared to like him, too. Was it possible . . . ? Nah, no such luck, not for skinny Alec McLean. Not with all the hot-blooded muscular young jocks on the prowl. But still—she'd said she might see him again. Suddenly he was looking forward to that encounter with a fervor that bordered on irrational.

Eva, Eva, Eva: The name was still dancing through Alec's brain when he climbed into Apocalypse Now, Runnerman Buchanan's tan VW van ten minutes later. He could still lower his lids and see her, see that secretive flash in her eyes, the devilish curve of her smile. He had tried to find her, of course; had searched the fairgrounds until he had no choice but to abandon his quest or miss his ride, and that was a for-real bummer.

And now, perhaps ninety seconds into the journey home, he found himself presented with another.

They had just trundled noisily through the morass of traffic in the fairgrounds parking lot and eased onto the MacTyrie road. Their first bits of shouted conversation (Darrell had a Guns N' Roses tape on full) had been casual enough: a round of cheerful kidding about Dr. McLean's refusal to allow the new Volvo 760 in such heavy traffic. And then Alec had fallen silent, too distracted to pay much attention to his dizzy buddy's random chatter—which was hard to hear anyway over the thundering stereo and the rude-sounding blatts of the Vee-dub's near-nonexistent muffler.

Until, he suddenly realized, the voluble Mr. Buchanan had just raised *that* subject again.

"Okay, McLean, fess up. It's time you leveled with me, man."

"Huh? What'd you say?"

Darrell glared at him sullenly from under brass-blond hair caught back in the impressive ponytail the members of the Enotah County High track team affected. His narrow face looked sharp and weasel-like. "Don't give me that shit, man; you know what I said: What went on at the Traders' camp that time? What was all that B.S. with the fire and all, and you and G-Man and Mad Dave and his sweetie bein' gone all night?"

Alec grimaced in irritation. He didn't need this right now. Shoot, even if he had wanted to spill the facts, there was no way he could have, at least not to Darrell. The whole mess had been an affair of Faerie, and the Ban of Lugh was therefore in effect. The upshot was that Alec *couldn't* tell his friend what he wanted to know. The best he had been able to manage when the topic had arisen in the almost-two-weeks since the incident was to say that he had sworn an oath to the Traders not to tell and feared their wrath if he did. David's tongue was under similar interdict, as was G-Man's—which meant that, except for Aikin Daniels who had been out of town the whole time and still was, the illustrious Mr. Buchanan was the sole member of the MacTyrie Gang who was still ignorant. Unfortunately, it looked like staying that way. Certainly there was nothing *Alec* could do to change the situation.

Darrell, however, was not so easily dissuaded. "Come on, Mach-one, spill it; I mean it's not like I wasn't involved or anything. It was *me* had to spend three hours tellin' the cops I didn't know shit about you guys disappearin', and then *blammo* back you are on Sunday mornin' like nothin' happened. That ain't cookin' with gas, man."

Alec took a deep breath and turned his gaze to the vistas of motels and marinas flashing by on his right, all blocking the gray-purple humps of the mountains. "I told you, I can't! I mean look, I would if I could, but I can't, okay? I took an oath."

"Bullshit."

Alec's fists clenched automatically. "I *can't*," he repeated. "You're just gonna have to make do with that."

Darrell's glare almost pinned him to the window. "Bullshit, I say. I've had enough of your and Sullivan's secrets: boys-in-white, shiny people in the woods, that ring that burned G-Man that time. . . . I mean, *Jesus*, you've even got him doing it! You guys took an oath as a member of the MacTyrie Gang, too; remember? Straight talk, honest answers to honest questions, no secrets. *No* goddamn secrets, man!"

Alec's only response was to lower his head and close his eyes in despair.

"Oh . . . *shit!*" Darrell spat in exasperation. "Damn it, McLean, I'm sick of this!"

Alec slumped down even further, wishing this trip would end sooner than the fifteen or so minutes it would take.

Darrell's face suddenly lit with a fiendish glow. "By God, I bet I know *one* way to get the truth out of you!"

He bent forward over the steering wheel—and jammed the accelerator to the floor.

The van farted and jerked and spat out a cloud of oily black smoke, then slowly began to gather speed, though with far more noise than enthusiasm.

"Look, Darrell," Alec began reasonably—or tried to, though he could feel the shuddering of worn-out suspension as the van hustled along at speeds it was no longer easily capable of, especially given the tourist-season traffic. "If you want to talk about being straight, and all, you oughta realize there're some things a guy just can't tell anybody—like confession and all. I mean, I'm in a moral dilemma, man. I don't like it any better than you do!"

Tank-topped shoulders shrugged in calculated nonconcern. "So level with me, then."

"Darrell, I—oh, *crap!*"

Darrell slammed on the brakes to avoid a dawdling Nissan Sentra that changed lanes right in front of them, then turned hard right into the little-used back road that had once been the main route to MacTyrie. The van began to gather speed again. He reached over and cranked up the stereo, let "Welcome to the Jungle" thunder through the cavernous space behind them. *"Tell me!"* he screamed.

"I can't!" Alec shouted back, wondering helplessly if his companion had finally gone off the deep end.

Darrell began to weave across the road, inscribing ever-widening arcs. Once, Alec was certain, the right-side wheels lifted off the ground. He knew they were going to flip—but Darrell lifted off a fraction, and the van thumped back to the pavement. But now there was a hill ahead, and beyond it a series of long, tight curves. And perhaps no place in the whole county filled him with such terror, because if you were a good driver and had a fast enough car, you could get completely airborne coming over the top, and still live to tell about it. Unfortunately, though, Darrell was *not* a good driver; and even Alec, who was not much of a car nut at all, knew that there were considerable differences between the dynamic qualities of classic Mustangs like David's or late-model Lasers like Gary's, and decrepit Vee-dub vans like this one. If they went off, they'd not even have to bother about a coffin.

And Darrell was obviously going to do it.

The VW gathered speed; the volume of the stereo increased; Axl Rose's voice broke into a staccato chatter.

"Tell meeeeeee!" Darrell shrieked gleefully, by now so far gone with his game that Alec doubted he much cared about the information.

All Alec could do was close his eyes and pray.

Faster and faster, and then the engine note changed and an awful, sick feeling slid into Alec's stomach, followed immediately by a falling sensation and—the longest moment of his life later—a sickening crunch as the van landed hard, fully compressed its inadequate shocks, and slewed across the road, miraculously still under control and upright.

Darrell swerved onto the shoulder. His face, when Alec looked at him, was white. "Dammit, McLean!" he raged. "You *know* what you just did? You almost got us *killed!*"

"*I* almost got us killed? *You're* the asshole who came over Oh-shit Hill at ninety in a friggin' Volkswagen van!"

"And you're the asshole that made me so mad I did! Shit, man, I've had it with you! I'm sick of all this secret stuff. You can take your goddamn secret and walk! Just get the hell out of my car!"

Alec stared at him incredulously. "You're not serious."

"The hell I'm not! Get out! Get out right now!"

Alec sighed and opened the door. It wasn't that far to MacTyrie, and who needed jerks like Darrell anyway? Guys that wouldn't take you at your word, and then went off the deep end and tried to kill you, and then blamed it all on you when they got the shit scared out of them.

Before he was truly aware of it, he was standing on pot-holed pavement, with a stand of pines leering down at him from the bank at his back as he watched the tan breadloaf putting angrily away amid a symphony of clanks and a billow of smoke that had not been there before.

"Bullfuckingshit!" Alec spat, and started walking.

Fortunately, it was not a long hike on to MacTyrie, and as it turned out, he did not have to walk most of the distance, for less than a mile down the road an older neighbor insisted on picking him up in her Lincoln Town Car. The gray-haired woman tried to engage him in conversation, but he was still too pissed to bother with more than mumbled thanks when she let him out at the end of his street.

Even with such unasked-for aid, though, it was nearly suppertime before Alec finally found himself turning up the sidewalk between the banks of ivy that fortified his folks' Cape Cod. He was not, however, in any mood for food.

Nor did he know what he *was* in a mood for, what with the emotional (and almost literal) roller coaster he'd just gotten off of. First meeting that girl—the marvelous Eva whose very name filled him with an excitement he had never known; who made him wonder if perhaps even he, skinny Alec McLean, might at last be about to join the ranks of the amorously experienced. And then having the whole thing ruined by a real-and-true fight with his number-three best buddy. The whole thing made his head hurt.

What he wanted to do was talk to somebody. He pushed through the front door, ducked into the den, and picked up the phone, too impatient to bother with his own upstairs—then paused, wondering whom he should try. Not David this time; *he* was part of the problem. And besides, maybe it was time Alec started putting his emotional eggs in some other basket, just in case the old familiar one became *too* full. His friend *had* been mighty distant lately—well, not exactly distant, more like love-struck. Not that Alec blamed him, exactly or had any right to: Liz *was* awfully nice-looking and obviously a perfect match for him, and if what David was going through now was anything like what Alec had gotten a taste of that afternoon, he thought he understood a little better. Still, David wasn't as available as he once had been, and that was a fact; and though Alec's rational part understood the reasons, it was still not very pleasant to deal with when he needed him but did not dare call.

Gary was at the fair, and Aikin was out of town, which,

of his close friends, left only Liz—but he certainly wasn't going to call *her*, even assuming she was home; even though he knew she'd probably lend a sympathetic ear. He simply wasn't ready for that yet, not to deal with the person who had sundered him from his brother. *No, you fool, don't think like that; that's selfish*. Yet he did think like that, couldn't help it. Logic and emotion were at war in him—had been all summer—and right now emotion was winning. Which, for better or worse, left him back where he'd started: with good old Mad Davy Sullivan.

Reluctantly Alec dialed the number, heard the phone ring twice before it was picked up.

"'Lo?" a heavy voice grunted.

Damn. It was Big Billy.

"Uh . . . uh, yeah," he stammered. "Uh, this is Alec. Is . . . is David there?"

"Nope," Big Billy rumbled. "Gone runnin' or somethin'."

"Know when he'll be back?"

"When he *gets* back, I reckon."

"When'd he leave?"

"While ago."

"Okay . . . uh, well . . . thanks."

Alec thumped the receiver into the cradle. *"Crap,"* he groaned and slumped down on the bottom stairstep. What to do, what to do? The one thing he was certain of was that he had to get out of there.

Abruptly he stood, pushed through the front door.

"Where're you going?" his mother called from the kitchen.

"Out," he said, and slammed the screen over her surprised protests that his dad would be home in a minute and they'd have supper. A moment later, he was hurtling the new 760 over the back route to David's, driving faster than he'd ever dared.

Chapter VI: Secrets

By the time Alec eased the co-opted Volvo between David's battered Mustang and Big Billy's pickup truck, he was his old self again—almost. He had sublimated most of his anger, mastered most of his hurt; had finally stopped along the roadside to wipe the embarrassing tears from his eyes and cheeks, and to comb his hair: in short, to present the image of calm rationality that was his normal persona. When he sprinted up the back steps, he had even managed to coax a casual smile to his face.

The smile persisted as he knocked on the screen door and waited, though he could see David's mom fumbling around at the stove. An idle sideways glance showed him laundry flapping on the line: jeans and T-shirts and a sleeping bag he didn't recall.

He had just started to puzzle over that when JoAnne Sullivan opened the door.

"Hey, Alec," she said without enthusiasm. "Come on in."

Alec nodded, used to her occasional coolness, and

slumped into a kitchen that was empty except for the two of them, which only added to his apprehension. He wondered where everybody was. Big Billy, he supposed, was off fooling around with the cows or some such; it was that time of day. And David probably was too, if he was back. The daily milking was officially one of his chores, though one he loathed and frequently evaded. Even Little Billy was absent, though he could hear the closing theme from *"The Real Ghostbusters"* thumping along in the adjoining den. Uncle Dale, he imagined, was home sparking.

"David around?" Alec ventured, wrinkling his nose appreciatively at the scent of pork chops frying.

"Somewhere," JoAnne replied absently, handing him a cookie he had not requested.

"Mind if I check his room?" Without waiting for permission, he stood, but just as he did a door opened in the darkened hallway opposite his chair. An instant later David emerged and sauntered toward him, head obscured by the mass of towel he was applying to his hair with considerable vigor with one hand while he shook out a plain white T-shirt with the other.

Alec was already stepping forward when the figure came into the light: jet-black hair, bare reddish skin above jeans that were far too tight, some kind of small leather bag flopping against the chest . . .

"You're not David!" he blurted before he could stop himself.

"No, I'm Calvin," the stranger replied, extending a still-damp hand. "Calvin McIntosh."

Alec was dumbfounded. Who in the hell was *this?* Not one of the family, that was for sure, because this fellow was obviously a Native American, and he was certain that David had no such kin. No way he'd not have bragged about it.

"Calvin's stayin' here tonight," JoAnne volunteered, as Alec took the proffered hand without really feeling it. "David found him up on the mountain and invited him home for supper 'n washin'."

"Yeah." Calvin grinned. "He loaned me these britches

while mine're drying. Little snug through the fanny, though."

Alec glanced down. Sure enough, those were David's jeans, his brand-new 501s. *That* was a sign of more than casual favor. "Looks like it," he mumbled.

"You must be Alec," Calvin said, still grinning ingratiatingly.

Alec started at that. He hadn't introduced himself, and that was rude—not that he much cared just then. "Uh, yeah," he stammered.

"Thought you must be, since you're pretty obviously not the famous Liz. David's told me a lot about you."

"Yeah, I bet. Where is the big D, anyway?"

"Milkin', I reckon," JoAnne offered over the sudden crackle of flour being added to grease to make gravy.

Calvin stuffed the towel in the washing machine and slipped into the T-shirt, which was also too sung. "I was just goin' out there, wanta join me? You don't need anything, do you, Mama Sullivan?"

Alec stiffened. Who did this guy think he was, wearing David's clothes like they belonged to him, acting like he lived there, assuming an easy familiarity with David's mother that Alec never achieved in the years of his and David's friendship. And now asking *him* if he wanted to join them like he was some kind of tagalong? No thanks. No bloody thanks!

"Uh, I don't think so," he muttered, slumping against the wall. "I just thought I'd drop by—but if you folks're busy..."

"Nope," Calvin assured him. "Not me anyway, though I 'spect Dave's dad's got a big day planned for me tomorrow. But hey, isn't your last name McLean, or something?"

"Yeah."

"Hey, so maybe we're related."

"But you're..."

"An Indian?" Calvin supplied with practiced smoothness. "Sure, but we've got last names too, and lots of 'em around here married Scots."

"Oh yeah, like old William McIntosh, and all. Wasn't

he the one who sold his people down the river?"

"And got killed for it. Yeah, but he's no kin."

"Oh . . ."

"He was a Creek, for one thing; I'm Cherokee."

"So? You could still be related . . ."

"Creeks and Cherokee were enemies," Calvin replied flatly.

Alec didn't know what to say. He'd come here looking for comfort and an end to confusion, and had found more trouble instead—and had just made an utter fool of himself in the bargain.

"I could tell you the whole story, if you want," Calvin volunteered. Evidently Alec's *faux pas* hadn't bothered him—or else he was playing games too.

"Can't right now," Alec grunted. "I kinda need to talk to David."

As if in reply, footsteps sounded on the back porch, and David shouldered awkwardly into the room, a pail of fresh milk swinging from either hand. He staggered over to the kitchen counter and set them beside his mother, then turned, rubbing his fingers to return the circulation. "Hey, Alec, my man, what's hap'nin'? I see you've met our resident redskin!"

Alec's gaze darted toward Calvin. He frowned minutely. "Yeah, we've met."

David's eyes narrowed. "Sorry I wasn't here earlier. I was . . . occupied." He put a particular stress on the final word and lifted an eyebrow slightly.

Sidhe? Alec mouthed where no one could see him.

David nodded. "Tell you later," then paused and studied Alec's face for a moment. "'Scuse us a minute," he sighed to Calvin, then grabbed his friend by the arm and pushed through the screen door again. Once on the porch he bent close and whispered in Alec's ear, "I was *summoned*, Alec, to meet with Nuada. That's why I was in such a hurry when I saw you at the fair. Fionchadd and Oisin were there. Claimed they wanted to teach me sword fighting— which they did, or tried. But I think something else is up. They looked *real* worried. Like I said, I'll tell you more when I can. This isn't exactly the best of times, as I'm sure you've noticed."

Alec wrinkled his nose sourly. That was all he needed: one more bit of exotica competing for David's attention. Maybe if he dyed his skin blue or took up skydiving or something . . .

David clapped a comradely arm across his shoulders. "So have a seat; stay for supper. Calvin is."

"No thanks," Alec said abruptly. "I—I really did need to talk to you, but I guess you're right about this not being a good time. Maybe I'd just better leave."

David eyed him levelly. "You okay?"

"I'm fine, David—fine as I *can* be. Everything's just hunky-dory."

"The hell it is! You wanta tell me what's goin' on?"

"Oh, just that goddamn Darrell . . . that . . . that. Oh, just *everything!*" He pushed past David and paused at the edge of the porch, barely missing the yellow tomcat that had come out looking for the ear-scratching Alec usually gave it, and found itself almost flattened instead.

"Alec!"

"Oh, just *forget* it! I'm not fit to be around right now, anyway."

David caught him by the arm.

"What in God's name's *up* with you, McLean? You on the rag, or something?"

"That's *it!*" Alec shouted, and bolted down the steps. For once he was able to outrun his friend and was already in the Volvo and accelerating away before David could catch up with him. The buzzing of the seatbelt reminder was an irritant he contemptuously ignored.

"Sorry 'bout that," David said to Calvin, when he had slumped back into the kitchen. "He's not usually like that, but—well, I guess things haven't been goin' too good for him lately." He sprawled into a chair and sat staring at the cup of coffee Calvin had poured himself.

"It's 'cause David's got a *girlfriend,*" Little Billy proclaimed loudly, appearing from nowhere to scoot past and steal another cookie. "He's jealous. Jealous Alec! Jealous Alec!" he continued, as he fled the room with his booty. The TV skipped across three channels before settling on what sounded like "Win, Lose, or Draw."

"Smart kid," Calvin observed, stirring in a second sugar.

"No joke!" David nodded, grateful his mother had stepped out for the moment, or she might be adding her own none-too-kind opinions. "Unfortunately, I'm beginning to think it's true." He started to get up to strain the milk, but Calvin held him back with a firm grip on his forearm. "It's not 'cause of me, is it? I don't want to cause trouble between you and your buddies."

David removed the hand gently. "No problem. He gets like that sometimes. Me and him've been best friends forever, and—well, maybe Little Billy's right. I've got a lady now, and I guess my priorities *have* kinda changed. It's not that I don't still like him, or anything—shoot, I love him like a brother. But I guess maybe it's time he started making his own way and didn't rely so much on me."

Calvin finished his coffee and stood. "Maybe I'd better move on."

"Bullhockey, man," David cried, pushing him back down. "Sit still! You ain't goin' nowhere. Your clothes're still wet—and besides, if you don't do tomorrow's chores I'll have to."

"I don't know. . ."

David folded his arms and regarded him frankly. "Okay, tell you what: You stay through Uncle Dale's party, then you can get on your way. That's only one day. He's somebody you need to meet anyway; knows a whole lot about the Indians up here and all."

Calvin stuck out his hand. "Treaty time, man."

"Huh?"

"Time for compromise. I'll stay. But not here, I'll camp up on the mountain."

"You will not!"

"I will too. Besides, I heard your mom say she'd need all the beds she had for the weekend."

"Okay, then; but at least stay up on Lookout. Me and Alec've got a lean-to built up there."

"Yeah, I saw that. You got a blanket I can borrow? My bag's not dry yet."

"Do you one better, I'll lend you mine."

"I'd 'preciate it."

David levered himself up and led the way to his room. Calvin had not been there before, having gone immediately to claim the promised hot shower after quick introductions and a snack in the kitchen. David bent over and began sorting through the detritus in his closet, while the Indian wandered about the small room, examining David's odds and ends curiously. He paused by the bookshelf and scanned the titles. "Shoot, you weren't foolin', were you? *Dune* and *Stranger in a Strange Land* and—Jesus, you've even got the old Ace edition of Tolkien!"

"Got a 1938 *Hobbit* too, with the different text in the riddle game," David said proudly. "Library was throwing it out, so I grabbed it. That's where I got that other book I mentioned: *Gods and Fighting Men,* Irish mythology, and all. I—" He paused in mid-sentence. He'd done it again: brought up that book he did not want to bring up. Or did he? Faerie was still a wonder and a glory, a thing he loved. And the wonder of the myths it had bred was a thing to be shared with friends. But he feared and distrusted it too; and hated what it was doing to him.

Calvin was eyeing him curiously, "Got any Scots—or Indian?"

"Don't know of any Scots," David replied, relieved to change the subject. "And I'm afraid I've never been into Indian. Familiarity breeds contempt, and all that, I guess; though now you mention it, I think the MacTyrie library's got some stuff: Seems like there's even one called *Sacred Spells of the Cherokee*, or something like that. I looked at it once, but couldn't really get into it. I—"

Calvin was frowning thoughtfully. *"Sacred Formulas,* maybe?"

"That's it!"

"You're kiddin'! I've heard of that all my life but never seen it."

David twisted around to stare at him. "So what's the big deal?"

"You mean besides being my heritage and all? I'll tell you what the big deal is: My grandfather knew the guy who wrote it, Mooney, I think his name was. Grandfather used to swear by that book. Every time he'd run into something he couldn't quite remember he'd say he wished he had it."

"Look, then; stick around through Monday and I'll run over to the library and get it for you."

"All right! Grandfather tried to teach me all he could, but . . . well, he was real old when I finally came along, and nobody wanted to hear that stuff 'cept me, and by then he'd forgotten most of it."

"Didn't you say he was a medicine man?"

"Yeah," Calvin said, and fell silent.

David wondered if the note of interest in his voice had given too much away, then shrugged and decided it didn't matter. He had finally excavated his sleeping bag from the dig in the closet and was beginning to re-roll it. "It's a little smelly, I'm afraid," he apologized, mostly to reawaken the conversation. "Never got around to washin' it after the last time."

Calvin slipped a battered brown book from the shelf. "What's this?"

David looked up, scowling, wishing he'd thought to hide a few things. "Uh, well, you could call that Scots fantasy, I guess. It's a book about the fairies. A gypsy woman gave it to me at the fair I was telling you about. Meant to give it back this year, but couldn't find her."

Calvin snagged the thick blue book next to it and read the title aloud: *"The Fairy-Faith in Celtic Countries.* You must *really* be into this fairy stuff."

David froze, suddenly aware of an intensifying of Calvin's stare. "Somewhat," he hedged. "Hey, you wanta give me a hand?"

Calvin joined him, and together they got the bag rolled.

They had just started out when the Indian paused yet again. "Ho! What have we here?"

David's heart sank. Calvin had found it—the one thing he really *should* have hidden—and would have by the time the company arrived tomorrow. It sat on the small book-case behind the door and was normally obscured when it was open. But apparently Calvin had the proverbial eagle eyes and spied out every cranny. Reluctantly David closed the door and allowed his companion a clearer view.

Calvin held his breath and bent down to stare at the object that had drawn his attention. A perfect model Viking ship, it looked like: no longer than his hand and complete to the most minute detail, with rigging of gossamer fine-ness and an almost-invisible glitter of jewels on the bosses of each tiny, perfect shield. A miniature dragon's head marked its prow, a curve of reptilian tail the stern. The sail of red silk was furled. Beside it lay an intricate finger ring: a silver dragon twining with a golden one, their heads side by side but facing opposite directions, the angles of their jaws locked in an eternal embrace that hinted at both love and contention.

"Oh wow!" Calvin exclaimed. "Did you *make* this?"

"Uh, no," David managed. "It was a, uh, gift. One of my friends brought it back from the old country."

Calvin whistled through his teeth. "Must have cost a fortune."

"She could afford it. I kind of did her a favor."

Calvin screwed up his eyes. "*Damn,* this thing looks real! You can even see the pegs in the planks. I've never seen detail like this, 'specially not in wood."

"Careful," David warned. "Don't even breathe on it; the rigging's really fragile."

"Yeah," Calvin agreed, wide-eyed. "I can see that. Jeeze, it's like—like something the fairies would make."

"Or the Nunnehi?"

"Wha?"

"The Cherokee fairies. Them I *do* know about. Uncle Dale can tell you more, though."

"Supper," David's mother called from the kitchen.

"I'd like to have another look at that model, sometime," Calvin said, as David hustled him out the door. "Something about it bothers me. It's kinda like that weird feeling I got from that swimmin' buddy of yours. What ever happened to him, anyway?"

"You didn't say anything about a weird feeling," David replied quickly, choosing to ignore the more difficult part of the question.

"Hummph," Calvin snorted. "Indian talk too much, should keep own counsel."

"*Calvin!*" David groaned, and aimed a kick at his new friend's Levied backside, grateful the conversation had shifted, yet wondering if, in fact, it had.

Alec's stomach growled again, and he cursed it, adding a muttered "*damn*" to the unkind epithets he had already affixed to Darrell Buchanan, Volkswagen vans, Liz Hughes—and Mad Davy Sullivan and his new redskin sidekick, not to mention to his own wimpy self for being such an asswipe. Somehow he'd managed to miss supper first at home, then at the Sullivans. The fast-food joints in Enotah were jammed with tourists, even if he had felt like waiting—which he didn't; and he just wasn't ready to go home and face the music over the Volvo yet.

He had to get his act together, though, *had* to. Otherwise he wouldn't be able to deal with the scene when his dad caught up with him. He had not been a notably rebellious adolescent and wasn't at all certain how his parents might regard the sudden onslaught of irresponsibility and temperament. But he was not real keen on finding out, either.

So he did the only thing he could: he sought out his own Place of Power.

He passed the turnoff for his street and took back ways through town (if a town with perhaps twenty blocks total could be said to *have* back ways) and eventually found himself turning into the old athletic field where the Irish Horse Traders had camped two weeks before. Their presence there had disturbed him by its proximity to *his* place, though he had not let on, because even David did not know of *this* place.

He hesitated for a minute, still at war with himself: knowing he should go home and face the music, but determined not to. Finally he squared his shoulders, shut off the car, and climbed out, noting as he sprinted across the open field, the scorch marks and mounds of ash and rusting metal where arcane fire had claimed the Trader's wagons. But further on, around the west side where the honeysuckle grew thick along an outthrust knee of the small mountain that bordered the field on that side. . . .

It was still there, behind the concrete retaining wall that backed the rotting bleachers: a nearly-overgrown trail that angled sharply back into the woods, then followed the curve of the mountain in a quick-rising arc that dead-ended halfway up a forested slope. Only a quarter mile or so that trail ran, but it was enough. To his right Alec glimpsed a glitter of lake agleam through the dark trunks of pines. Anytime now. . . Ah, yes, there it was, to the left, hidden by a mat of ferns unless you knew to look for it: the first of a long series of masonry steps that zigzagged up the mountain to his goal.

A moment later he was there: the concrete-and-brick ruins of a burned-out dwelling that had once overlooked the town, and, more recently, the field; but had eventually been forgotten when progress moved another way. A whole story's worth of walls remained, though: and before them a broad stone terrace, half covered with vines. Trees grew thick around, hiding the ruins from below, so that Alec could see without being seen, which was precisely his intention. He could lie here and ponder and think, and that was exactly what he planned to do.

He crossed the terrace and ducked through the gaping front door. The concrete floor inside had resisted the flames that had taken the roof and ceiling, and directly opposite the entrance was a fireplace with a wide hearth. He flopped down there, set his back against the crumbling bricks, and watched the evening arrive.

Eventually he dozed, to awaken into almost full dark.

Mist was rising, drifting in from the nearby lake, giving the field below an aura of mystery that was at odds with its prosaic utility. *Crap,* he groaned, as he sat up and check his watch. He really should go home. But suddenly he heard soft footsteps and, to his horror saw a figure coming up the steps through the woods. *That* was all he needed, to have his personal place violated.

"Alec," a soft voice whispered. "Alec, is that you?"

His heart flip-flopped. "Eva! Over here!" And then he was leaping across the terrace and running through the mist to take her hand before he even knew he had done it. An instant later he was drawing her up by the fireplace. She was dressed the same as before, he noticed: white linen blouse and long, fringed skirt.

"What are *you* doing here?" he asked. "How in the world did you find me?"

"I . . . I was not doing anything, really; I was only wandering about your town, and then this fog appeared, and I became lost, and I thought I heard someone breathing . . ."

"You must have awfully good ears, then."

"I do. I followed them—and saw it was you."

"You can see that good in the dark?"

"I also have very good eyes."

"So do I, but I can't . . ."

"The starlight revealed you."

A shudder ran though him. Lord, what a voice. He could hardly stand it: the mystery of the accent, the undercurrent of sensuality that hid in that simple phrase. This was no ordinary girl, not by a long shot.

Eva curled up on the hearth beside him and rested her head on his shoulder. Alec tensed, unable to believe this was happening, that this wonderful girl was here, that she was sitting close to him . . . *so* close to him. He took a deep breath and put his arm around her.

She snuggled closer. "Do you come here often?" she asked.

"Sometimes."

"When you want to be alone?"

"How'd you guess?"

"Because there are too many people in this town for you to be alone unless you choose."

"Yeah, I reckon. But look, I really don't want to talk about my problems."

She pulled away and looked up at him. "Do you not?"

Alec met her gaze and swallowed. "Okay, maybe I do." *God, what eyes: beautiful even in the dark.*

"You must tell me, then. You do not know me; we may never see each other again, since I am only visiting here. You may talk freely to me."

"You're here for the fair?"

"You could say that. I have some business to attend to for a friend, something he wants me to find."

"Where're you staying?"

Eva laughed softly. "A woman must have some secrets. But come, you were about to tell me your sorrow."

"I was?" *Those eyes again, how can I resist them?*

"Were you not?"

"I . . . I guess I was."

So Alec told her the whole sorry mess, about David and Liz and Darrell. Almost he told her everything, even about the Sidhe, since that was part of it too. Certainly he would have liked to, if not for the Ban of Lugh.

"This friend of yours sounds like a fascinating person," Eva murmured, when he had finished.

"Yeah, well, evidently a lot of people think so, all of a sudden."

"Tell me, is he interested in sailing?"

"Not particularly. Why?"

Eva laughed. "Just a thought. I have them sometimes. Call it a premonition."

Alec stared up at her, startled. The moon was new, and the stars were in their full glory, shedding a surprising amount of light across the fog-shrouded field and illuminating Eva's face. She was looking at him, frankly, openly, with maybe a touch of—of what? in her expression. Was it possible . . . ?

"Eva, I . . ." he began.

She stopped him with a finger against his lips. "You talk too much, my Alec."

"I—maybe I do."

"There is a cure, you know."

"Which is?"

A kiss gave him the answer.

It was full dark when Alec awoke. Stars still glittered in a black sky, and the fog in the field below his mountain aerie was even thicker, so that he seemed marooned in a sea of white. The fog was warm, too, and that was strange.

He was alone, lying on the terrace where he and Eva had—had *what*? He hardly remembered, hardly dared hope things had gone as they had—if they had. And that was also odd. He recalled the taste of her lips, though, and the warmth of her body against his, the feel of her hands in places . . . places hands had never been before, and never mind where he had put his hands, and then another, even more intimate thing.

But when had she left him? They had talked, he knew, and then had followed—what followed. Finally, still half-breathless, he had laid his head in her lap and droned on about who-knew-what. It had been so relaxing, so comforting. He must have dozed off. And she had left him.

"Eva?" he whispered, and sat up. "Eva? Are you still here?"

His right hand brushed something that rattled. He reached down, found a single sheet of thick bluish paper on which was written, visible in the bright starlight: "Thank you for your company, my Alec. You were sleeping so prettily I could not disturb you, but I had to be elsewhere. Meet me here in two days, same time."

Two days, Alec thought. *Two days!* He wondered if he could stand the waiting.

It was eleven o'clock by the digital clock in the Volvo's dash when Alec finally eased it into the narrow driveway between the beds of ivy and surveyed the old home place. Usually his folks had turned in by now, but this time there were lights burning in the living room, and that was a bad sign—especially to someone with a guilty conscience. It was not the hour *per se* that was the problem, but the manner of his departure—and the vehicle. With considerable trepidation, he turned the knob, only to feel it twist further than he had intended as the door was pulled out of his grip and he found himself facing his father.

Doctor Gerald McLean was shorter than his son and built more like a fig than a fighter. Certainly he was bespectacled and balding. But none of these lessened the anger that burned in his eyes, the twitch of scarce-restrained rage that haunted the corners of his mouth.

"I see you've finally remembered where home is," he said. "I think we need to have a discussion."

Chapter VII: Sails

(Tir-Nan-Og—high summer—morning)

Morwyn looked up from her packing, suddenly wary. A noise had disturbed her. She dropped a scarlet velvet cloak onto the red carpeted floor and cocked her head. Footsteps approaching; probably Lugh. Good, she would be ready to depart as soon as she dealt with one remaining item, which was the whole vast chamber around her. The Room Made of Fire, it was, that portable place she carried with her which could fold in on itself and yet include all she could ever conceivably need. At the moment it occupied a space within Lugh's twelve-towered palace that had heretofore been an empty chamber: white marbled outside, frozen flame within. Soon, though, she would say the Word and work the spell and—

A knock on the section of wall that masked her door and Lugh entered without waiting permission. That galled her a little. For an instant, she thought to rebuke him, crown or no. But then she saw the black mood that hung across his forehead like thunderclouds across a mountain.

"I am almost ready," she ventured. "Have you procured the vessel?"

"Not yet," Lugh spat, "but it no longer matters. You are not going."

"Why, Lord?"

In reply Lugh simply reached inside his robe, drew out a plain disk of crystal bordered with gold, and flung it tinkling to the table. A Word, and the disk stood on end. Another Word, and it began to expand, until a moment later it was an arm span across. A final Sound, and images began to take form, and Morwyn saw, as the High King did, the one thing they both had most dreaded.

In the foreground was a strand: a strip of beach almost as white as the morning stars that still twinkled in the pearly, predawn sky; with a low, pillared pavilion stretching to the limits of sight on either side. The midground was a mass of foam: restless breakers cavorting and snapping at each other, then rising higher into dire waves whipped by no wind.

But the background—the whole top half of the image —was ships: ships as far as one could see from horizon to horizon. Low slung and narrow they were; black-hulled, and with sails the red of war. Dragons carved from night-colored wood rode the prows of those vessels, and also gryphons and wyverns and other beasts of battle, even as fleshly crows and ravens scoured the skies above them, filling the air with strident, taunting cries. Oars rested in the water but did not move; and Morwyn knew that no one manned those oars, now or ever.

Yet men there were, thousands of them—or warriors of the Sidhe of Erenn, to call them right. They stood those decks in their endless files, dour and grim; with armor of black and cloaks the same red as the sails.

One of that number broke rank, strode to the prow of the largest ship, the one in the center. No sooner had he taken his place there, than the vessel began to glide forward among the breakers until the knife edge of its keel was almost in the sand—almost, but not quite touching dry land. That man drew himself to his full height, then, and flung back his cloak to stand revealed in armor that glittered like the newly-risen sun. His hair was black and his voice was fell. A quick flash of hand toward his waist and he had drawn his sword, which shone blackly in the ruddy light.

"Hear my words, Lugh Samildinach, Ard Rhi of the Daoine Sidhe in Tir-Nan-Og," that man cried, his voice harsh in the heavy air. "I am Finvarra, Ard Rhi of the Daoine Sidhe in Erenn. A message I have sent you, my princely brother, demanding that you surrender the Fireshaper Morwyn verch Morgan ap Gwyddion to me for judgment. And a reply I have received from you this hour: one I must reject, for it denies me what is mine by right. You have left me no choice now, if I am to be an honorable prince, which surely you know I am. My answer you see before you, but yet I would forestall this thing if I can. One final time, therefore, I ask you: Deliver Morwyn to me within seven cycles of the sun, or you will find me upon your borders with all my host coming after. The seas belong to us all, brother prince, and I do not yet offer you confrontation. But it is a little thing to land now. Do not force me. I will await your word."

He lowered his sword, then; and the shouts of his men were drowned by the rumble of drums.

Morwyn looked at Lugh, and her face was grim. "And your answer is . . .?"

"The one I have already given."

Chapter VIII: Company

(Sullivan Cove, Georgia—
Saturday, August 17—morning)

"Yeah, but look, Liz," David was whispering into the telephone, "are you *sure* you can't get here any earlier?" He shifted his weight and scratched his bare midriff absently, then glanced down and noted that a sneaker was untied. A monstrous yawn was token of the hour: 6:30 A.M.

"I'm sure," a sleepy-sounding Liz replied. "I told you: today's the only time Dad's got to help me move. I've still got some packing to do, and it's gonna take all afternoon to lug my stuff down to Gainesville. I'm lucky I can come back at all."

"See? See?" David chided. "That's what you get for moving away from me: just a bunch of hassle."

"What I get, David Sullivan, is a better education!"

"Maybe too good."

"What's that supposed to mean?" David could practically see Liz's eyes narrow and her fist smack on her hip in indignation.

"What do you think?" He chuckled.

"I'm not gonna be going out with other boys, if that's what's bothering you!"

"It wasn't."

"*Wasn't* it?"

Another yawn. "Uh, well maybe . . . But look, try to get back as soon as you can—I'll . . . well, it just won't be the same without you. Even Uncle Dale said that. He's looking forward to seeing you too."

"That's guilt-tripping, David."

"Just the facts, ma'am. Shoot, I wouldn't be surprised if you two weren't—"

"*What?*"

Another chuckle. "Oh, never mind. But look, I really do need to talk to you—about Brother Alec for one thing, and . . ."

"You already told me that."

"Oh, right. Anyway, gotta go."

"Love you."

"Yeah, me too."

David hung up the receiver and yawned again. God, he was tired. Yesterday's exertions had apparently taken more out of him than he thought, as had been evidenced the night before when he'd dozed off in the middle of a conversation with Calvin. He'd awakened in the empty den sometime past eleven and stumbled off to bed, only to be roused again far too soon after by the relentless chiming of the alarm summoning him to what he knew would be a morning of last-minute cleaning.

But at least the kitchen was done—which was a miracle considering the cooking that had been going on for days. Still, one's favorite great-uncle didn't turn seventy but once, as Uncle Dick and crew were driving up from Tampa to attest. Nobody knew when they were arriving, though: which was one reason he'd had to resort to such an early hour for his call. Once Big Billy's youngest surviving brother arrived with his pushy wife and his hellion kids, there'd be no privacy at all. Worse yet, their very presence made for a degree of domestic chaos he could barely stomach, and he was grateful for Calvin's offer of help with the chores, because it really would take a lot of the load off him. They were going running, too—as soon as soon as the Indian got there; but in the meantime, there was still one piece of unfinished business.

He dialed another number.

"Hello?" a groggy voice answered.

"Uh, hi, Alec: how's it goin?"

"Fine, except, of course that it's six thirty-five in the morning and I'm grounded. Beyond that I'm as good as I can be, considering . . ."

"Grounded?"

"Tell you later. Walls have ears, y'know."

David frowned. It was hard to tell from Alec's tone whether he was merely sleepy or being sarcastic. He sounded a little reticent and David wondered if his best friend might not be in some kind of trouble. Come to think of it, he'd been driving the new Volvo yesterday. That almost certainly explained it.

"Uh, yeah, well, sorry 'bout the time, man," he hedged. "But look, I just wanted to apologize for last night, but—well, Calvin just kinda showed up. Hadn't been there even an hour before you came over. But I mean if you'd had something you really wanted to talk about . . .?"

"No problem."

"You sure? You were in pretty bad shape when you left."

"I'm *okay*, David."

"I tried to call you a couple of times."

"I was out."

"M. Gang honor?"

A pause, then: "Word of honor."

"Sorry, man; I shouldn't have said that."

"It's fine."

"Look, are you still coming to the party? I really want you there."

"Well, as I said, I'm kinda on my dad's shitlist right now, and I've gotta work morning and night at the bloody concession stand. But I think I can make the afternoon."

"Good job! Maybe we can slip off and talk some of this out before—"

"Before what?"

"Before Liz gets there. She's gotta move a bunch of stuff down to Gainesville today and won't be in till late afternoon, so we've got till then."

"You sure?"

"What's that supposed to mean?"

"What about—oh, never mind."

"Calvin? Well, he's gonna be there, but he's not my shadow or anything; he's a free and independent person. I mean I like him, and all; but you've got nothing to worry about—if you were worrying."

"Yeah, well—"

"You were, weren't you?"

"I can't *help* it," Alec blurted.

"We'll talk, then. But look, I see Ma coming this way with a broom in her hand, so I better run or I'll get put to work. So we'll see you later?"

"You got it."

"Catch you then, bro. Gotta—"

"Boogie?" came another voice, as footsteps pounded on the porch and Calvin bounced into the room.

"You got it!" David repeated, grinning as he surveyed Calvin's attire: green jogging shorts, Nike running shoes, the freshly washed falcon T-shirt and a much smaller pack. "We'd better be at it, too," he added, dragging Calvin back outside.

"Not till you finish the chores," Big Billy drawled cheerfully from the yard beside them.

"So who is this uncle of yours we're going to see?" Calvin asked an hour later. He and David had finally finished the morning routine: milking and feeding the livestock, which Calvin had virtually taken over. David had contented himself with emptying every trash can in sight. They'd all been full, too, what with his mother's incessant baking. She was in a state bordering on panic.

"He's really my great-uncle," David said, as he helped

Calvin through the barbed-wire fence that separated his family's upper pasture from Uncle Dale's—there was no sense going the long way round if there was a straighter and more picturesque route, especially since they had reluctantly decided to delay their jogging. "He's my grandpa Sullivan's next-oldest brother."

"Is he still alive?"

"Of course!"

"Your *grandfather,* dummy."

David shook his head. "'Fraid not. He died before I was born: *his* pa outlived him by ten years."

"What happened?"

"Car wreck. He was in his late forties, which is probably fortunate, considering. He was a pretty wild character, apparently—loved the women, but married very late. Almost got himself disinherited. If he had, Lord knows where we'd be living."

"How so?"

David sighed as they picked their way across the pasture. "Because he was a younger son— Oh fiddle, Calvin, this is complicated." He paused, pointing westward toward a glimmer of water almost masked by a fringe of trees. "See that lake? The old home place is under there. My five-times-great grandpa, Patrick Brian Sullivan, settled there in 1817—soon as we secured it from—oh no!"

"From the *Indians?*" Calvin supplied, nonplussed. "Probably the Cession of July 8, since this is east of the Chattahoochee, but don't worry about it; you can't help your history any more than I can mine."

"Yeah, well, it's still a bum rap, I guess. But anyway, he came over from Ireland as a boy right after the Revolution and fought in the War of 1812 and got a land grant for his trouble, built a cabin out there where the lake is. His son, Thomas Kevin, was the first one born here. First one buried here, too, since old Pat B. just wandered off one day and didn't come back."

Calvin cocked an eyebrow. "Any idea what happened?"

David shook his head again, though he had a notion or two—considering what he now knew about the surrounding territory. "But to get back to the younger-son business," he continued, "the property kept getting passed down through the male line: first son to first son. It wasn't like they tried to exclude the women, or anything; they just all kept getting married and moving away. Anyway there got to be a tradition: the oldest son got the home place, and any younger ones got farms further out, and when *they* had kids they had to subdivide again, or leave—which most of 'em did, 'cause the lots were too little for farmin' by then.

"Anyway, when the R.E.A. built the lake in the forties, it drowned the old place, so the rightful heir—Uncle Dale's older brother—got displaced and had to move, and got mad and joined the army and got killed in the Second World War. His two sisters had married and gone by then, and that left two farms and a bunch of cash—since the girls wanted no part of the government's blood money, as they called it. Pa's still living on part of it. So anyway, Uncle Dale got one of the two remaining farms that were still above the water, and my grandpa, his younger brother, got the other: the furthest-one out. When he died, Pa got half his place and Uncle Dick the other, only he sold his to Pa and left."

"What about your grandmother?"

"She remarried and left too. Seems she was secretly in love with Grandpa's brother, but when he got killed, she got real down on the army and all, and when Dad joined up and Uncle Dale took up for him, they had a falling out, and haven't spoken since. We haven't heard from her in years."

"Your mom's folks from around here?"

Another shake of head. "Dad met her while he was up at Fort Bragg. She's a North Carolina gal, just like yours was."

"So you don't have a lot of close kin around, then?"

"It's like I said: the boys stayed if they could, and the girls left. Oh, I've got third and fourth cousins out the wazoo, 'specially over in Union County, but they don't count. Leastwise I don't count 'em."

They had crested the ridge now. Below them spread the rolling hillsides of Uncle Dale's farm, good mostly for raising cattle, though he had a little corn patch on one side, a tiny vegetable garden on the other, and a scraggly strip of sorghum in the creek bottom. Straight ahead was a line of outbuildings: weathered gray corncrib, barn, woodshed, and smokehouse; and beyond them, the compact lump of Uncle Dale's house—scarcely more than a cabin, really. It had only gained indoor plumbing in the fifties. Its tin roofs reflected the early-morning sun.

And to the left, at the summit of the hill on which they stood, almost at the shadow line of trees, was a small area enclosed by rusty wrought-iron fencing. A single scrawny cedar guarded the center. David had already started toward the cabin, but twisted around abruptly and redirected his steps that way. "Might as well show you the family plot."

Calvin nodded silently and followed. A moment later they passed through the rusty gate. Tombstones rose all around them: some marble or granite, the oldest scarcely more than iron-colored boulders. Baskets of faded flowers, both real and plastic, were scattered about. David indicated a pair of markers to the left: BRIAN ARMAGH SULLIVAN, one read; a smaller slab beside it bore the name KATHERINE WILSON SULLIVAN. "My Civil-War ancestors."

Calvin inspected Brian's dates. "1843–1860! He was awfully young when he died."

"Yeah, I guess I'm lucky to be here, considering that he got married the day before he joined up. They must have done it right the first time, 'cause they never had another chance. Yankee bullet blew him away."

"But didn't most folks up here side with the Union?"

"Yeah, but we were all crazy Celts, and the Union was mostly Brits, 'least that's what old Granny Kate here told Uncle Dale."

"*Told* him?"

"He was eight when she died."

"And who's this real new one over here?"

A shadow crossed David's face. "That's Pa's youngest brother," he said after a moment, his throat constricting. Even after four years the memory was too painful. "We called him David-the-elder, 'cause he had the same name as me: David Kevin Sullivan, only he was a second and I'm a third. The named me after him 'cause he took such a shine to me when I was born. Uncle Dale raised him, really. Grandma was pregnant with him when Grandpa got killed and never wanted much to do with him. He never knew his own pa."

Calvin was studying David's face intently. "But he knew you didn't he?"

David nodded mutely. "He was the older brother I never had. There's a streak of dreamer that shows up in the family every now and then—more of the Celt, I guess. Uncle Dale's got it, I've got it in spades, but Pa missed it and so did Uncle Dick. I'm not sure about Little Billy yet."

"But your uncle . . ."

"I never thought of him as an uncle, 'cause he was only eight years older'n me; I just called him David. But to answer your question: yeah, he had the dreamer streak—'course he had everything: brains, looks, athletics —even art. I wish I was half the man he was."

"What happened?"

"Joined the army 'stead of going to college, 'cause he wanted to see the world. Got to see Lebanon and the inside of a coffin in about six weeks of each other."

"You loved him, didn't you?"

David nodded sadly. "Every good thing I am I owe to him—what I don't owe to Uncle Dale."

"Speaking of which, we'd better get over there, or I'm never gonna get to meet him."

David turned his head to wipe away the single tear he hoped Calvin hadn't noticed.

"Glad to meet you, boy," Dale Sullivan said five minutes later. "I reckon Davy can't keep from making interestin' acquaintances." He released the hand he had been shaking and ushered them into the coziness of his living room, where he plopped his bony, khaki-clad body into the rocker beside the rough stone fireplace. The dull splashes and sharp clicks of dishes being washed came from the adjoining kitchen. Someone was also humming.

"Yeah, well he's pretty interesting himself," Calvin said cryptically, as he took a seat on the sofa, which faced the hearth where David had ensconced himself. "He's been tellin' me about the family."

"Oh-oh." Dale chuckled, his blue eyes agleam beneath his wire-rimmed spectacles. He scratched his goateed chin absently. "Pretty borin' stuff, ain't it?"

"Not at all, sir," Calvin said quickly. "Kept my interest, anyway. 'Sides, most kids our age don't know their history at all."

Dale eyed him keenly. "But you do."

Calvin nodded. "No thanks to my dad. He wanted to ignore the family heritage and live like a normal Atlanta 'burbie, but my mom's father stepped in and said I was to spend summers with him. He turned me onto the old ways, taught me the genealogy and all."

"How far back?"

"Far as he knew it. The calendars don't convert very well."

"What was that you said about him being a medicine man?" David asked pointedly. "He teach you anything?"

Calvin grimaced in resignation. "Well, sorta. Basic herb lore, mostly. He wanted me to settle down a little before we got into the hard stuff—the chants and spells and all—and then he got too old to do much. 'Bout all I learned of *that* was the discipline and a little of the ritual: goin' to water, respect for the earth, and that kinda thing. How to look at the world through Indian eyes. I've met my totem, but that's about it."

"All right!" David cried. "What was it?"

Calvin fidgeted uncomfortably. "I shouldn't even have mentioned it. It's supposed to be a secret."

"Like your name?"

Calvin glared at him. "You tell me about that model, I'll tell you about the totem."

Dale cleared his throat warningly. "You boys up for a little coffee?"

"Yeah," David said, glancing at Calvin, who shook his

head. "No thanks. I've already had three cups this morning."

"Then one more won't hurt, will it? 'Sides, this is *special* coffee."

"How special?"

"Trust me." Dale shuffled off to the kitchen and returned shortly with two steaming mugs in hand. David stuck his under his nose and inhaled deeply, motioned for Calvin to do the same. An unmistakable underscent hid within the rich aroma.

Calvin wrinkled his nose in turn but did not taste it. "Moonshine?"

"Let's just say there's a secret ingredient the law might be more than casually interested in."

Dale laughed loudly. "The only interest the law's ever shown in that stuff's in how much I can let 'em have."

"And I've been meanin' to talk to ye about that too," came a woman's voice from the kitchen door.

David looked up and grinned as Katie McNally tottered into the room. Instantly he was on his feet to give the old Trader lady a quick hug and help her to a seat beside the window. She was at least ten years older than his uncle, stooped, gray-haired, and frail, with a bad left eye which she squinted. But there was strength in her too, and feistiness. David knew: he had seen both, and more besides.

Calvin raised an inquiring eyebrow.

"Oh yeah, Calvin: this is Katie. She's Uncle Dale's—"

"Houseguest!" the old man finished quickly, grinning above his white goatee.

Katie said nothing, but her eyes twinkled merrily as she tugged her fringed paisley shawl closer. "Katie's been staying here the last couple of weeks, while her folks are traveling," David volunteered. "I guess you could say she's a friend of the family."

"Like I told you, this family attracts strange friends," Dale said, gazing at her fondly. "Sure am gonna miss her when she leaves." His gaze shifted to David. "I 'magine you know the feelin'."

"I am *not* strange!" Katie laughed, her voice still alive with the lilt of her native Ireland.

"Oh, so the woods are full of Tinkers?"

"Tinkers?" Calvin wondered aloud. "You mean—"

"Irish Horse Traders," David told him quickly. "Katie's family were up here and had—an unfortunate accident. She got sick and we agreed to take care of her while the rest of their folk got their act together."

"Besides, she's a hell of a cook!"

"*Mr.* Sullivan!"

"Things have sure been a lot better around here, too."

"Couldn't hardly o' been worse! You lads have no idea how messy an old man livin' by hisself can be!"

"And you have no idea how cantankerous an old woman used to livin' by *her*self can be! She ain't had nobody to boss for years. Been like a kid in a candy store!"

"How's yer mama holdin' out?" Katie wondered. "I wish she'd o' let me help her."

David shrugged. "Done with the baking, put the turkey on last night and the ham on this morning. Too bad we couldn't roast a pig like we wanted to."

"You know your ma and her notions," Dale said, chuckling.

"Yeah," David nodded, slapping his hands on the stone. "And I've got an idea we'd better be gettin' back there. I just wanted to bring Calvin over to meet you so he wouldn't get lost in the mob later."

"Glad you did. You boys come back anytime."

"Right."

David finished his coffee (Calvin hadn't touched his, he noticed), stood, and headed for the door. "See you at lunch?"

Dale shook his head. "Me and Miss Katie are just gonna have us a nice quiet one here. There'll be enough of a to-do this afternoon to keep us all busy. And to tell the truth, boy; I'm not so keen on making a big fuss, but your mama wanted one, and I didn't have the heart to argue."

"Yeah, I know," David said, rolling his eyes. "Come on, Fargo, let's travel."

"Well, he was certainly an interesting old coot," Calvin observed, as they started up the Sullivan Cove road a moment later. "But you didn't tell me he was *livin'* with somebody. I thought Aunt Katie was really your aunt!"

David laughed loudly. "Yeah, well, I wanted to surprise you."

"You sure did that!"

"Neat, ain't it? An old guy at his age, and her even older. Ma's completely scandalized, of course."

"Of course."

They jogged on in silence for the next quarter-mile.

"Just one thing puzzles me," Calvin panted, as they turned up the Sullivans' driveway.

"Which is?"

"From what I've heard, Traders are pretty clannish. How'd y'all get hooked up with 'em?"

"That's a long story."

"I got time."

"Not *that* much."

"Just as well," Calvin replied. "Now when are you gonna tell me about that model?"

"When you gonna tell me about that totem?"

Calvin stopped in place and regarded him seriously. "You *really* wanta know?"

David nodded. "I'm trustworthy."

"Yeah, I suspect you are, but you'll have to prove it. I already told you one secret; don't you think you owe me one of yours?"

"I don't know about that," David said.

"No," Calvin replied smugly. "But I do."

The rest of the morning passed quickly as David and Calvin found themselves pressed into duty as housemaids in anticipation of the company who would soon be arriving. David thought once of calling Darrell to see if he could get another slant on the Alec situation, but just as he picked up the receiver his mother handed him the vacuum cleaner and a stack of clean sheets and dispatched him to make up the unused attic bedroom.

He had barely finished straightening the heirloom doll-pattern quilt his great grandmother had made when he heard a knock on the front door.

"Can you get that, David?" his mother hollered. "I've got my hands full."

He exchanged mournful glances with Calvin and headed for the stairwell, wondering where Little Billy was, since he usually co-opted the role of doorman on such occasions.

More knocks, again, louder.

David pounded down the stairs and turned left into the living room. "Liz!" he exclaimed, when he saw the slender shape silhouetted beyond the screen. "What the heck are *you* doing here?"

"I'm on my way to Gainesville, stooge. But I thought I'd run some stuff by to help out with—if I can get somebody to come out to the truck and give me a hand."

"You're coming *back,* though, aren't you?" David asked in panic, joining her on the porch. "I mean you said you would, and all."

"In about four hours," she replied easily, as she led him down the steps and across the yard to where her dad's silver Ford pickup waited. David assumed Papa Hughes was in there somewhere, but it was hard to tell from the near-black tinting that covered the windows. Liz trotted to the back and popped open the camper's tailgate. The inside was crammed with suitcases and boxes, but carefully wedged into the corners were a series of covered trays. She snaked one out and handed it to David.

"My God, girl," he groaned, as the load grew rapidly higher, "what *is* all this stuff?"

"Oh, just some things I whipped up to help out with the party." Liz smiled, casting a coy glance sideways as she filled her own arms and started back toward the house. "Brownies and fudge and . . ."

"Brownies! Oh no! Not brownies, not *your* brownies!"

"And what's *wrong* with my brownies?"

"Nothing!— 'Cept that I don't want to have to share 'em!"

"You'll get fat and ugly if you eat 'em all!"

"He's already halfway there, then." Calvin laughed, stepping from the shadows of the porch.

Liz did a double take, while David shot daggers over her shoulder.

"Uh—yeah," Liz began uncertainly.

David cleared his throat. "Oh . . . this is Calvin. I kind of found him yesterday. He'll be here through the weekend. Calvin McIntosh: Liz Hughes; Liz: Calvin."

"Family?" Liz ventured.

"Not hardly. I guess he's a—"

"Native American," Calvin volunteered. "Raincheck on handshake or whatever, seein' as how your hands are full. Unless you'd like a kiss?"

Liz looked flustered and made her way down the narrow hallway between the brothers' bedrooms and into the kitchen.

"Nice lookin' lady," Calvin observed, following David back into the yard for a second load. "She the one you told me about?"

"Sho' is," David replied a little irritably.

"Looks like she's got you well trained."

"I just let her *think* that. I wear the pants."

Calvin's face broke into a mischievous grin. "I wouldn't wear 'em very long, then, if I was you; least not around her, not if she'd take 'em off me. Jesus H. Christ, she's a fox!"

"An apt description, what with the red hair and all."

Calvin bent close behind David and whispered in his ear. "So, you guys makin' it?"

"For *Chrissakes*, Calvin, her pa's up there in the cab!"

"Well *are* you?"

David stared at him indignantly. "Look, man; I like you

a lot, but you don't know me well enough to ask me those kind of questions."

"But I told you about the girl up at Silva, the one with the cabin and the—"

"—raging hormones. Yeah, I know. But I didn't *ask* you, if you notice, and besides—"

"You know," Calvin mused, "that red hair sure would make a nice scalp . . ."

"So would that black mess of yours," David shot back fiendishly, as he piled Calvin's arms full of more trays. "And *I* know where you're sleeping."

"Indian know woods like back of hand," Calvin replied with a laugh. "Indian not sleep where expected."

"Ah, but I know more about those woods than you ever will."

"I don't doubt it," Calvin said seriously, "not for a moment. And I've not forgotten you owe me an explanation."

The sputter of flying gravel interrupted them, and David looked up to see a battered blue Chevy Caprice wagon start up the driveway. A red-haired man was at the wheel, a blond woman beside him, and three shapes moving too fast to tell in the back. David sighed; that would be Uncle Dick, Aunt Evelyn, and their eleven-year-old sons, Jason and Jackson, the Terror Twins—and their even more obnoxious eight-year-old sister, the Dread Cousin Amy.

"It's gonna be a loooong day," David confided, as he and Calvin trudged back inside. "A very long day for sure."

"I think," Calvin said very carefully, "I'll have lunch up on the mountain."

David reined him back by the collar. "The hell you will, *keemo-sabe!*" he cried fiendishly. "You'll stay here, or I'll *kill* you!"

"Humph! White man break treaty."

"Show me the paper, kiddo!"

"Speak with forked tongue, then."

David hissed loudly and followed him inside—just as

Liz was leaving the kitchen. He risked a quick kiss as she scooted past.

"Love you," he whispered.

"Love you too."

"Yuck!" squealed the Dread Cousin Amy from the door.

Chapter IX: Revelation

(Tir-Nan-Og—high summer—
midday)

"War?" Fionchadd cried, green eyes suddenly aglitter. "How soon?" He laid down the bow with which he had been practicing and paused to stroke the silver-scaled head of Dylan, his pet wyvern—far taller than he now and no longer totally reliable. It would not be long, he knew, before he would have to relinquish the creature to the wild.

"Soon enough," Oisin replied heavily. He lowered himself onto one of the blocks of rough-cut stone that littered the half-finished courtyard, then turned his silver gaze toward the boy. Fionchadd flinched, in spite of what he knew of that stare.

"A shame, too," Oisin added. "We were just beginning to initiate young Master Sullivan into another mystery, and now I fear we may have to end the lessons."

Fionchadd's face fell. "I was enjoying it, too."

"I know," Oisin said wistfully. "And I think you were enjoying other things as well."

"Such as?"

"Why, the boy's company itself!"

The resulting shrug was tinged with arrogance. "And where is the wrong in that? I owe him a debt I can never repay! Were it not for him I would still be a voice on the wind—or worse, a nightmare for a small green lizard. Besides, I like him. He is intelligent, talented, quick—for a mortal. He is not even bad to look on. I find, in fact, that he is often better company than our own folk. Certainly he is less predictable, and that has a certain charm."

"*I* would not have predicted war," Oisin noted dryly.

The boy shook his head, suddenly serious. "Nor I."

"You do not seem so eager, now that you have had a moment to consider it."

"No . . . I suppose not." Fionchadd straightened and stared at the old man, arms folded. "It is not that I fear, though; indeed, I would relish a good fight. It is only that it is so . . . so pointless. We will fight, some of us will die, and we will all live again, and nothing will be changed. And all because of my mother."

"She is only the most immediate cause."

"It seems enough for Uncle Finvarra."

"Yet you love her."

"I have no choice."

"You chose not to love your father."

"Again, I had no choice; he gave me none. At least she has not manipulated me."

Oisin sighed and rose. "Enough of this. Tell me truly of David Sullivan: does he have the making of a warrior?"

Fionchadd's brow furrowed. "He moves well enough. He has more strength than is common for one his size. He wears his body nicely, now I have shown him how. And he appears to be able to use his body and mind as one thing. But there is fear, too, and that makes him hard to teach. Fear of death, fear of pain: these are different for men than for us. For us they pass."

"And for men they do not," Oisin finished, as he turned to leave. "Do not forget to whom you speak."

"Never, Lord. But another thing David Sullivan has, and that is Power, of a sort—and while I speak of Power, I met a strange thing that day of which I have not yet told you."

Oisin paused in mid-step. "A strange thing?"

Fionchadd nodded. "A boy of the human folk, yet not like our fair-haired friend. This one had skin like red copper, hair coarse and black. Brown eyes that saw. . ."

"That saw what?"

"Enough. He glimpsed me before I could hide myself; and after that I could not. His mind was hard to cloud."

"Another mortal with Power?"

"Possibly, but of a strange kind. Neither like ours nor the usual Mortal sort. I have never met its like."

Oisin bit his upper lip thoughtfully. "This boy you spoke of—could you show him to me in your mind?"

Fionchadd nodded, and Oisin laid a hand upon his brow. He left it there for perhaps five heartbeats, a strange light awake in his sightless eyes.

"It is as I thought," he said when he had dropped the hand. "And a fortunate thing that may be."

"How so?"

"Because, if that boy is what I suspect, we may have an answer to the trouble that floats at our borders. He has reminded me of something I had long forgotten—and in that may lie our salvation."

"And what might that be?" Fionchadd asked eagerly, as Oisin once more turned to go.

"I think," the old man said slowly, "that our King should be the first to know!"

"But Oisin!"

"No, boy, there is no time for wasting." And with that he strode away, leaving Fionchadd alone with his wyvern and his questions.

Chapter X: Partying and Parting

(Sullivan Cove, Georgia—
Saturday, August 17—afternoon)

"I'll give your folks credit for one thing, Sullivan," Gary Hudson slurred happily. "They sure know how to throw a party." He giggled and flopped his brawny shoulders against the rough boards of Uncle Dale's barn behind which he, Calvin, and the available members of the MacTyrie Gang (which was basically Alec, Darrell, and David—Aikin was still out of town) had been hanging out for the last thirty minutes. It was four o'clock in the afternoon, and dinner-to-die-for (to use Darrell's phrase) was still at least an hour away—though they were already so stuffed with finger-food and punch it hardly mattered. "Yep, Davy, m'man," Gary continued, "this is one helluva do." He wiped a lock of dark hair out of his face and took another sip from the Mason jar of 'shine he had surprised them with, then handed it to Darrell on his right, who took a longer swig and gave it in turn to Alec, who peered at it apprehensively for a moment, and took two.

That was a good sign, though, David decided from where he slumped against an abandoned tractor opposite.

Apparently they'd patched up whatever problem they'd had. Or at least the brief private conversation he'd snatched with Alec when he and Gary had arrived (they both had to work that evening and had ridden together) had indicated as much. At any rate, they were speaking more or less civilly, and that was enough. Now if he could only find out what was up with Alec's grounding . . . It had evidently taken a special parental dispensation to get him here.

Alec caught David watching him, took a third, more decisive swig, and passed the jar on to him with a tentative smile.

It was strange, David thought as he accepted the offering, how easy it was to take people for granted, though Alec didn't seem the worse for either of yesterday's downers, except for a certain reserve that was probably due as much to Calvin's presence as anything. And if he kept on hitting the sauce like he just had, he wasn't going to be showing even that pretty soon.

"You gonna drink or grow cotton?" Darrell prompted.

"Huh?" David started and smiled sheepishly. "Here's lookin' at you, boys." He raised the jar to his lips and let a trickle burn across his tongue, then swallowed more carelessly. It wasn't as good as Uncle Dale's stuff; not by a long shot. He wondered where G-man had got it; probably his dad had taken it in as part payment on some car repair or other. He was still gazing at it curiously when Gary cleared his throat loudly. David poked Calvin's elbow. "Firewater, Geronimo?"

Calvin shook his head. "Nyet, don't touch the stuff."

David started to say something, then remembered the morning's coffee.

"Oh come on," Darrell blurted. "Give it a try. One won't hurt you."

"No," Calvin gave him back. "But considerin' the trouble my people have with this crap already, I'd just as soon avoid temptation."

"It's real preemo hooch, though," Darrell persisted. "You won't get better."

In reply, Calvin reached for the canteen that hung at his

side—incongruous beside the mixture of David's and Big Billy's Sunday clothing he was wearing—and took a long draught of Budwine, the syrupy sweet cherry drink that was bottled in Athens, Georgia. "I'm not philosophically opposed, or anything, you understand. It's purely personal. 'Sides, if I stay out, you guys get more."

"He's got a point there," Darrell noted sagely.

"We could share a pipe, though," Calvin added. "I've got some rabbit tobacco."

Darrell's thin face puckered in disappointment. "Nothing stronger?"

"Watch it!" Gary chortled, pounding the side of the barn, "One of those bo-vines in there could be a narc."

"*All* of 'em, even," David amended knowledgeably, as Darrell's eyes grew wide with the guileless incredulity of the slightly gone.

"And speaking of watchin'," Gary continued, "what're *you* watchin' for, Sullivan?"

"Huh?" David asked, realizing he had been gazing toward the dusty red line of the Sullivan Cove road. "Oh, nothing."

"He's waitin' for his *woman*," Gary confided to Calvin. "She's really prime."

"No shit, man; I've met her," Calvin replied, nodding vigorously.

David saw Alec's jawline tighten.

"She *is* coming, isn't she?" Gary asked casually.

David nodded. "Oh yeah—gonna be late, though."

"Still planning on going to school in Gainesville?"

"'Fraid so. She's leavin' tomorrow."

David was awaiting Gary's reply when he chanced to glance toward the house. "Oh, Christ, boys; varmint alert." It was the eleven-year-old Terror Twins with a strutting Little Billy in the lead.

"Quick, hide the evidence!" Darrell cried, taking another desperate hit off the jar. Somehow they managed one more round, though David strangled on his, and it made his throat burn abominably. Already he could feel himself getting lightheaded.

"So *here* you are!" Little Billy squealed as he strode into the shadows behind the building. "Ma wants you *right now!* Gonna make some pictures." Beside him, the red-headed cousins sniggered behind their hands, looking wicked and surly and sly. One of them—Jackson, David thought it was—glimpsed the empty jar and narrowed his already slitted eyes even further. "I got some beer in my suitcase," he proclaimed. "Stole it from Mama's stash."

"Should we be impressed?" David sniffed, heaping a full measure of older-adolescent contempt onto his words.

"Daaaavy, come on! They want you!"

David shrugged helplessly and unhitched himself from the tractor. "Gotta run, guys. You comin'?"

"Not even breathing hard," Darrell snickered, poking Gary in the ribs and doubling over while Alec and Calvin exchanged eye-rolls of resignation.

David scowled back at them, then spared one final glance toward the still-empty road. He had just started to follow his brother when his eyes suddenly took on a familiar tingle. He frowned and scanned the line of trees that crowned the hill above the farm, then frowned harder when he saw—what?

"You guys run on," he told Little Billy. "You folks too," to his buddies. "I gotta check out something first." He locked gazes with Alec, slid it across to Gary, but avoided Darrell's out-of-focus stare.

"Davy!"

"Just a blessed minute, kid! Tell 'em I'll be right there."

"Daaaaaavy!" But already David was dashing up the hill. An instant later he was in the forest.

Fionchadd stood there, slipping out from behind a tree in the full glory of his Faery shape: gray velvet tunic and gray silk hose and a gray leather hat with a feather. He held a pair of small, tightly coiled scrolls, which he handed to David, who took them hesitantly.

"I do not understand what cause for joy there is in aging," the Faery said. "Our kind do it but slowly, and after we get our full growth—which takes long and long, as I can tell you—we do not further mark it, except for the strengthening of Power it brings." He paused for a moment, then continued. "Two things we *do* honor, though, are aid unasked for and friendship freely given, and we know what it is to lose a friend, especially a dear one. For that reason, the Ard Rhi has asked that these be given one to Katie McNally, whom he understands is returning to her people, and one to Dale Sullivan who remains behind. These he sends in acknowledgment of past efforts in behalf of his folk and his kingdom."

"Thanks," David said, glancing around nervously. "I know they'll appreciate them. And I hope you'll 'scuse me if I boogie, 'cause I really do have to get goin'."

David had already turned away when the Faery spoke again. "Wait," he called. "I too have a gift—an atonement; call it what you will."

David stared at him uncertainly, but before he could speak, Fionchadd had reached into a pouch at his waist and brought out a golden chalice, completely plain, except for a delicate etching of interlace around the base, stem, and rim.

"Maybe it will make up for the pain I caused him," the Faery said. "It is made from a nugget I found on his farm. I meant to leave it where he would discover it himself, but our discussion of yesterday put my conscience and myself at odds. I had my mother craft it in the night."

"I'm not sure he'll accept it, though," David said as he took it. "He's funny about such things, and he may consider it a bribe as much as a gift—either that, or too fancy a present, but I'll pass it on. And hey, thanks. If not from him, then from me."

Fionchadd's knuckles brushed the ground in a deep formal bow. "I hope to see you again shortly." And with that he turned and was gone, leaving David to call, "Carry on," to suddenly empty air.

"Yeah, carry on," he repeated, as he tucked the scrolls in his jacket and jogged off down the hill.

"Took you long enough," his mother grumbled when David finally stumbled breathlessly into the chaos of Uncle

Dale's living room, having taken a time-consuming detour by his car to stash the gifts beyond the reach of nosey-cousin eyes and fingers.

"Took you long enough," one of those very cousins, the Dreaded Amy, echoed in the self-righteously indignant tone David found so irritating in girls her age. He glared at her, wondering what was keeping Liz, who was a much better example of red-headed female. And then found himself trying to remember if Liz had been like Amy when she was eight. *Uh-uh, no way.*

"You stand over there, Davy," JoAnne said, flourishing a complex Minolta and pointing toward the fireplace. "I want one of you and Dale first."

David rolled his eyes, but allowed himself to be positioned, feeling the critical appraisals of at least a dozen relatives. The only consolation was knowing that his uncle probably felt as silly as he did—especially in the three-piece blue suit the old man hadn't worn in at least three years.

The next fifteen minutes were spent preserving every possible combination of Sullivan kith, kin, and associate for posterity—including an excruciating three shots with the Dreaded Amy who insisted on pinching him with her sharp little fingernails when no one was looking. He busied himself by inventorying the other folk in the room.

Besides the immediate family and Uncle Dick's crew, there were about twenty other cousins, mostly Uncle Dale's first and second, ranging in age from fifty to over eighty. In addition there were various neighbors from the community—if Sullivan Cove could be said to be one, though actually there was only one other house on the road. These folks had come in from nearby, or were tradespeople from businesses Uncle Dale frequented. Most of them had simply gotten wind of a party and had come uninvited—but with food, of which there was God's plenty. Over to one side two lonely-looking chaps were army buddies with whom the old man still corresponded. One of them—a jovial, bewhiskered chap from Virginia named Klondike John—was the subject of many an amus-

ing tale, including a particularly hilarious one involving a
Nashville transvestite. David wished there was time in
which to get to know him, but he had volunteered to take
Katie back to her home in South Carolina and would be
leaving shortly after dinner. Of her folks, the Traders, there
was not a soul. Not that she missed them, much, David
thought, considering the way she was gazing at Uncle
Dale.

And then it was time for the massive buffet supper that
sprawled all the way across Uncle Dale's front yard like
dinner on the grounds at the Sullivan Cove Church of God
across the hollow. The food, at least, was excellent, even if
the same could not be said for the company, since there
was still no Liz and David found himself obliged to sit next
to the Dreaded Amy.

Another hour elapsed before David was able to get
Uncle Dale down to the car to pass on the scrolls. Very
cautiously the old man unrolled the creamy parchment.

It was not large, but David, staring over his uncle's
shoulder, gasped at the magnificence of the intricate interlaced illumination that spun and twisted around the border
in a riot of color. Though obviously hand-done, the writing
(printing, actually) was clear, if perhaps a bit spidery, and
executed in the style he knew was called uncial. There was
a rust-colored smudge at the bottom, which bore an unmistakable fingerprint. "Read it," he said, "I think you're supposed to."

Dale put on his spectacles and began.

Lugh Samildinach, High King of the Daoine Sidhe in
Tir-Nan-Og herewith sendeth greetings to Dale Yearwood Sullivan on the occasion of his seventieth year
in his World. In recognition thereof, and in honor of
past services done Myself and My realm, I herewith
grant unto said Dale Sullivan one boon which, if it be
within My power and a just thing, I will render unto
him upon his stating his desire aloud and the burning
of this parchment. Know that I have sealed it with
My Blood, and My Blood is My Word and in it is

My Power. By my hand this 17 day of August, as Mortal Men number the Circles of the World.

Lugh Samildinach, Ard Rhi

"Well, that was mighty nice of mister Lugh," Dale mused. "But I reckon we'd better run and give Katie hers 'fore she leaves."

"Hang on a second," David said. "There's . . . there's one more." Without further explanation he produced the chalice.

"Who's this from?"

"A . . . a friend, I guess. It's from Fionchadd."

"Fionchadd? Ain't that the boy we resurrected? He think he owes me something for that?"

"No," David whispered. "He thinks he owes you for something a lot worse. He was the one who shot you."

The old man did not reply, and David was at a loss as to how to proceed, because for once he could not read his uncle's face.

"He didn't know you then, nor any of us," David blurted finally. "And he feels real bad now. I think this is a peace offering. He's already asked me for forgiveness. If you take this, he'll take it as a sign you forgive him too."

"Hmmmm. That's a pretty big order, Davy, to forgive somebody for tryin' to kill you."

"Yeah, I know. And I guess I owe you an apology too, for not telling you when we brought him back, but so much was going on, and all that stuff last year seems so far gone . . ."

"It does to me too," Dale said. "And I seen enough men caught between two kinds of duty durin' the war to kinda understand, so if you see Mr. Finnykid, you tell him I'll consider the case closed—if he'll share a drop of 'shine out of this here fancy goblet with me."

"I'll tell him," David said.

"Well, I reckon you and me better be gettin back up to the house, boy. You wouldn't mind hangin' on to these here goodies till the crowd's gone, would you? Might raise some mighty nosy questions. And hey, ain't that Miss Lizzy's car a-turnin in there?"

David's face lit automatically. He grinned. "You tend to your lady," he said chuckling, "let me tend to mine!"

Eventually evening rolled around and the first stars began to show themselves above the valley. The company gradually drifted away, including most of the older relatives, as well as the Terror Twins, who had been so scandalized at Uncle Dale's lack of cable they had hied themselves back to the relatively more luxurious quarters of David's house to drown themselves in the MTV Enotah County had finally acquired that month.

Finally only David, Liz, Alec, Gary, and Calvin of the young folks remained on Uncle Dale's front porch; sharing it with the birthday boy himself (back in khakis again), Katie, and a much mellower Klondike John.

"I remember," Dale said, gazing westward, "when all that land was farms."

"What about that mountain?" Calvin wondered, indicating a nearly perfect cone that erupted from the surface roughly a mile away. The setting sun struck red highlights from the sheer cliffs that crowned its summit. "Surely they didn't farm that."

"Old Bloody Bald?" Dale scratched his head. "It wasn't more than half a mile from the house, but we stayed away from there."

"How come?"

"Spirits, mostly," he said darkly, though he spared a glance at David and a more intense one at Calvin. "Your people had a burial ground near there, and to be honest, we just never thought of it. It was hard to get to, anyway: had a thick wall of briars all around it that resisted burnin' and everything. We just sorta give up on it."

"Haunted, like?"

The old man nodded, and David fidgeted restlessly, realizing for the first time that everyone present except Calvin and Klondike John were initiates to the true secret of Bloody Bald: that in another, taller manifestation which overlapped it in another World, it was heart and center of Lugh's kingdom. That though here the summit showed shining slabs of quartz that blazed with red at dusk and dawn, there it bore a castle that dwarfed anything in the Mortal World.

Klondike John belched happily and rose from his rocker. "Well, Miss Katie," he said, "I guess you and me better be travelin', if we're gonna get you home before bedtime."

"I reckon so," the Trader lady sighed wistfully, unpinning the purple orchid Uncle Dale had surprised her with that morning. "But God help me, now that time's here, I hate t' go."

"You don't have to," Dale said softly.

Katie shuffled over to him and patted his head, smoothing the wayward white hair. "Oh yes I do, Mr. Sullivan. But ye haven't seen the last o' me, don't ye doubt it. Why, I . . ." Suddenly her eyes misted with tears.

David touched Liz's shoulder and rose softly. "Uh, hey, look folks," he muttered to the others as they started toward the steps. "I think it might be best if the rest of us kinda vanished. I sorta need to spend some time with my lady, anyway"—he stared pointedly at his buddies—"so could you like . . .?" He did not finish the sentence, but raised his eyebrows expressively.

"Nod, nod, wink, wink," Alec snickered, nudging Gary with his elbow. "Come on, we better boogie, or Dad'll be frying us instead of burgers."

"Yeah, me too," Calvin grunted. He looked intently at David. "Think your mom'd mind if I dropped by for a snack? I've still got one toe that's not full."

"Probably wouldn't even know you were there."

"Catch you later, then."

David took Liz's hand, and escorted her to his car. She frowned at him as he opened the trunk and commenced rummaging through the mess inside. "I promised you a surprise, don't forget," he reminded her.

She pinched him on the fanny and grinned.

"*Jesus,* girl!"

"But we were talking about surprises!" Her eyes twinkled so mischievously in the fading light that it was all he could do to keep from laying a good long smooch on her right there.

"Well, I'm afraid this one is, shall we say, a little more complicated." He snagged his backpack and slammed the deck lid. A nod indicated the scrap of red-clay trail that split off from Uncle Dale's driveway and ran between his little vegetable garden and the sorghum patch and toward the forest. "I thought we'd sneak off to the lake for a little while."

Liz raised an eyebrow. "We got in trouble last time we did that."

"I don't think we will now, though."

"I hope not."

But as they entered the dark lane between the pines, a darker shape slipped in behind them.

"Okay, David," Liz said. "Don't you think it's about time you told me what this is all about?"

David squeezed the hand she had joined with his own and shot her a wink, then patted the backpack. "No way, lady; not until things are *just* right."

"I'm not sure things *can* be just right around here, David."

"Things can be right anywhere," he replied quickly, "long as I'm with you!"

Liz squeezed his hand again, and together they soldiered on at a quicker pace. Around them stretched the woods—a finger of the Enotah National Forest that splattered across Georgia's northmost tier of counties. Second-growth, this was: pines instead of the older ash and elm and oak and poplar. Tall and sparse-branched this low down, the trunks of those trees reminded David of the pillars of Chartres Cathedral he had once seen in an art history book. The scent of their resin was like incense.

It was dark, yet not fully so—especially not to David's eyes, which could see more than most men, whether by Faery light or his World's own. And there was enough starlight filtering down between the meshing pinwheels of branches to glitter across the ground for them to easily make their way.

"Jeeze, I'm gonna miss this," Liz said softly.

"You don't have to—"

"Don't spoil it, David. I'm gathering memories."

"Okay, then—and you're right: it is neat—and for once it's nice just to be in the woods with no hint of Faerie. I'm so used to having things suddenly *change* on me, I almost expect it."

"That why you don't go roaming around by yourself as much as you used to?"

"Well, there's at least one *other* reason."

"Such as?"

He stopped in place, took her in his arms, and gave her a long, slow kiss. "Such as this," he murmured, feeling his body flush, already tingling as Liz molded herself to him. But he forced himself to draw away, leaving her gazing at him in wonder.

"Just a little further, Liz, I promise."

Silence closed in on them, yet not silence, for there was a whisper of wind, a hiss of breathing, the soft padding of some animal behind them to the left. As one they found themselves trying to enhance the quiet, placing each foot upon the ground cover with utmost care.

And then David pushed through a man-high tangle of laurel and stepped out onto coarse sand. He heard Liz's breath catch in wonder.

Before them lay an isolated cove, scarcely more than a quarter mile across. Trees framed it on all but the northern side, which merged with the greater body of the lake, shimmering to the right like a slab of dark mirror. All around rose the soft humps of the mountains, close and comforting, and further off to the north the perilous cone of Bloody Bald. It was a symphony of shape and reflection and subtle shadow, highlighted here and there—upon leaves and treetops and the endlessly repeating crests of shoreline ripples—with silver.

"Oh, David, this is wonderful," Liz said. "How come you never showed me this before?"

David shrugged. "I hadn't been here in so long I'd almost forgotten about it. But something made me remember it the other day. You know, like how you can get set in familiar ways and ignore the new or exotic when it's right under your nose, and all?"

She regarded him skeptically. "I would have thought you'd had enough of that."

"That's not what I mean. You can have exotic without resorting to Faerie. There's more magic in our own World than we can ever know."

"I know one kind," Liz whispered, and kissed the nape of his neck.

"So do I." David chuckled, seizing a wandering hand and bringing it to his lips. "But that doesn't mean you shouldn't take advantage of the other when you can!"

"Oh?"

"Oh."

David slipped out of her grasp and deposited his backpack on the sliver of beach, then squatted beside it and pulled out a flat, square box. Holding his breath, he opened it reverently and removed something. The only sound was the slap of the wavelets on the shoreline.

Liz gasped. Starlight glittered off the tiny mast and rigging of the model boat, set rubies to sparkling off the minute shields along the sides. The eyes of the dragon prow glowed softly, as if lit by some inner flame.

From his pocket David drew out the dragon-headed ring and slipped it on his finger. Then, very gently, he placed the boat on the water, knelt beside it, and stroked the head of the silver wyrm. A tiny jet of fire flashed out and brushed the nearest bit of rigging.

"No, David!" Liz gasped.

"Just wait," he told her. "Wait and watch."

The rigging began to glow, then erupted into tiny blue flames that quickly spread to mast and spar and sail; to hull and prow and keel. But instead of leaving ash and destruction in their wake, they sucked substance from the very air and mixed it with that of the model so that it began to expand, until scarcely a minute later, a full-sized, full-rigged longship floated silently in a hidden arm of Langford Lake.

"Your barge, madame," David intoned in a formally British accent. "*Waverider* awaits you."

"*Waverider?*"

"The vessel's name, madame; the Lady Morwyn told me."

"But how do we get on?"

Drat, David thought, feeling his face color with embarrassment at a very important detail overlooked. He frowned down at his clothes: new black cords, clean black Reeboks, gray-and-black striped dress shirt over the California Renaissance Festival T-shirt Liz had sent him a few weeks before from San Francisco, the twin of which he knew she wore beneath her own white jeans and oversized green shirt. *Oh well,* he sighed, *can't be helped,* and commenced tugging off his shoes and socks. A moment later, pants rolled to the knees, shoes and top shirt resting on a stone above the waterline, he scooped a giggling Liz into his arms and waded out to help her over the low gunwale amidships. He followed immediately, scrambling over the side and leaving dripping puddles over the wooden deck. A quick series of Words to the dragon prow, and they were off.

"Excellent!" Liz cried, as the ship slipped silently across the water.

Barely a minute passed before it glided to a stop in the middle of the cove. All around lay forested mountains; above spread the infinite sky; below, its reflection that held its own inborn glitter. Together David and Liz walked to the prow, stood behind the tall curve of carved dragon.

"This is the first time I've used it," David admitted. "I don't dare try it in the daytime. But tonight just seemed like too good a chance to waste."

Liz's eyes sparkled as she took his hand. "And why tonight?"

This was it, then: his trump card. The one final thing he

could do to convince Liz not to abandon him. He took a deep breath. "Because I want tonight to be magic."

"*Any* time with you is magic," Liz whispered back. "But I'm still going to Gainesville."

"I was afraid of that."

"You know it's the right thing, though." Liz slid her arms around him and laid her head beside his.

"Is that head or heart?" he murmured into hair that smelled of strawberries.

"Head, this time. I'm sorry."

For a long time they simply stood there, with David's face buried in her hair, his lips occasionally wandering to nibble on her neck or ears. But finally he eased himself away, his body afire.

"What's wrong, Davy?' she asked softly.

"Nothing," he said, grinning. "Except that I happen to know there are some furs in the cabin, and I think there just might be some wine!"

"Are you trying to get me *drunk?*" Liz giggled, the corners of her mouth curving mischievously.

David started. Maybe he was. Certainly he was more than a little buzzed himself, from the steady stream of spiked-punch and moonshine he'd imbibed all afternoon. He shook his head. "You're enough to get me high." He laughed, and led the way amidships.

"This is a memory I'll always cherish," Liz said, when they had dragged a mound of fur onto the deck and David had found a skin of wine and two silver goblets in one of the cabin lockers.

"Me too."

"There's only one thing it needs to make it perfect."

"What's that?"

An eyebrow lifted ever so slightly, and then her fingers found the hem of his T-shirt.

A moment later they sank down together atop fur that was whiter than the starlight that shimmered across their naked bodies.

Chapter XI: Tracks and Tracking

Calvin was tired of waiting. It was not that he was uncomfortable, exactly; indeed, crouched as he was atop a low clay bank hidden between two clumps of laurel eight or so feet from where that preposterous ship had departed the cove, and with his back lodged firmly against a convenient boulder, he was quite at peace. It was just that it had taken all the patience he had—and all the woodscraft his grandfather had taught him—to follow David and Liz through the forest. Once, he was certain, they had heard him, though he walked barefoot—and shirtless, lest a twig snag some unwatched sleeve or collar and betray him.

And yet he waited. He had seen a Mystery, that much was obvious, but such things could not be. No one could do what this new friend had done: enlarge a toy ship with flame from a ring—never mind that proof of it lay before him in the form of a sensuously curved, furled-sailed silhouette floating on the dark water not a hundred yards away. Yes, it was a Mystery; though now he knew why David had been so secretive about the model. But Mysteries demanded answers, and for this one the only solution was watching and waiting.

An hour passed, and still he sat, unmoving.

David took another sip of Morwyn's wine and clicked the silver goblet against Liz's. The liquid was tart and sweet and sparkling, with a hint of mint. He could not tell its color in the uncertain light, but thought it might be green. Certainly it glowed very faintly.

Curled on the thick fur beside him, Liz smiled and stretched luxuriously. She ran a finger along his bare side from armpit to hip crest, then continued it along his thigh. He shivered, almost giggled because it tickled; and glanced down at her, slim and pale against furs that were paler yet. Every sense bombarded him with stimuli, from the texture of the fur to the smoothness of Liz's skin to the cool tickle of the wind across his own bare flesh. And there was the sparkling darkness: an endless panoply of black and blue and silver; and the smells of pine woods and cold mountain water and Liz's hair and the muskiness of their own sweat-sheened bodies. He wanted the moment to go on forever. It was ironic, he thought: he had tried to give Liz a memory, one to make her stay. And she had—without one word being spoken—given him a far more lasting one instead.

His plan had all been in vain, though, that much was clear; come the morrow, Liz would leave. But *her* endeavors had not been so futile, for he was bound to her now by a love that was deeper than love, by magic older than time. Man and woman; earth, sky, and water. He felt newborn: the first man—and more aware of himself as a man than he had ever been, now that he had shared the greatest mystery. Last summer he had undergone one change, born of magic, when his whole worldview had been turned upside-down by his encounter with the Sidhe. But now he was initiate to another, greater magic. Suddenly he felt at one with the whole vast scope of creation.

Liz moved beside him. He bent over and kissed her.

"What time is it?" she asked sleepily. "I really do have to get home."

"Do you?" He yawned and stretched. "I wish we could stay here forever."

"So do I," she murmured. "If it was always like this. But nothing can ever stay the same—even Faerie changes. Eventually the sun'll rise; eventually we'll see the knots in the boards and the thin places in the fur and the tangles in each other's hair."

"And the warts and moles, and—"

"David!"

"Liz!"

She ran a finger along his cheek. "And I guess eventually you'd have to shave, or else you'd look like a barbarian, and I couldn't stand that."

He glanced at her askance. *"What?"*

"You'd look yucky with a beard."

"And if we stayed here forever, we'd get all sunburned, and peel."

"And get gross and fat and old!"

"Not fat. What would we live on?"

"Love?"

"Fat for sure, then."

Their lips met again, then David sat up abruptly. "I guess you're right. We really ought to be gettin' back." He slipped into his skivvies, then grabbed his damp trousers.

He had just zipped his fly when he became aware of a subtle change in the air, as if every invisible dust mote were being charged with electricity. Abruptly his eyes began to burn and twitch, the sign of the Sight about to kick in—which meant that Faery magic was astir nearby.

Simultaneous with that realization, a fog began to rise, extending pale tendrils from the lake's suddenly-glassy surface to greet a strip of glitter that was coalescing off their port side into a tenuous tunnel of light, the closest part of which continued to thicken and brighten until a section of it ripped asunder and Fionchadd stepped through. A golden glow bathed him for an instant, then faded. He was clad in a short black tunic over dark blue hose, all beneath a long cloak the same shade as the nighted mountains. A gleam of metal at waist and fingers mirrored the cold sheen of the surrounding water. He looked breathless and unhappy.

David, still bare-chested, glanced around, automatically concerned for Liz's modesty, but she already had her shirt on and was tugging up her jeans beneath the long tail. As Fionchadd flopped wearily against the railing, her hand found his.

"David, my friend," the Faery panted, "I have an urgent message."

Calvin couldn't stand it any longer. Wasn't it enough that he was having to fight to stay awake while David and Liz were up to . . . he bet he knew what . . . out in the lake, while he sat there on the night-moist ground chewing on a stick of beef jerky and repeating one of the hunting chants, all the while rolling over in his mind the implications of what he had just witnessed?

But now there was *another* Mystery, a brazen glitter that lay a little above the water as if starlight had crystalized upon low-lying fog and turned to golden filigree there; and then a brighter glow right beside the ship that reduced his friends to shadows against it before it dimmed again.

His eyes were burning, too; as if they rejected what yet they told him. Yes, this was a Mystery he had no choice but to explore. Soundlessly he stripped off his remaining clothing—except for his medicine bag—and slid into the water. An instant later he was swimming silent as a shadow through the starlit lake toward what he hoped would be an answer.

"A *message?*" David practically shouted, while Fionchadd helped himself to a long squirt of wine.

"An Annwyn vintage," the Faery speculated absently, ignoring David's indignation. "From Arawn's southmost vineyards, unless I miss my guess. My mother must have laid a strong spell upon it for it to last so long in your World."

"You mean you can't tell?" David muttered sarcastically.

Fionchadd shrugged. "I was raised among my father's folk in Erenn and thus learned the arts of their tradition. They feared to have me reared among my mother's mother's folk, lest I grow mightier than they; and the Powersmiths, for their part, feared for their secrets to pass too far from their control." He paused to drink again.

"You said something about a *message?*" David gritted impatiently.

"Oh, aye," Fionchadd replied, wiping his mouth. "You are summoned, David Sullivan, and your lady as well, since she is here, to a meeting with High King Lugh."

"Lugh!" David gasped. "What could *he* want with me?"

Fionchadd shrugged again. "He has been much troubled of late, though there is no time now to recount the reasons. But come, I have wasted too much time. Already your escort approaches."

"*Now?* He wants us *now?*" He'd had other plans for the evening—like prolonging Liz's company as long as possible—and he was damned if he was going to have them ruined by any more Faery foolishness.

Fionchadd lifted an eyebrow ever so slightly. "I have no choice in the matter."

"Stranger and stranger," David mumbled, tugging on his T-shirt.

"Aye, passing strange, but let us be on our way."

"I have to go home," Liz reminded David softly.

Fionchadd glanced at her, and for the first time seemed truly to take in the ambience: fur and wine and the dishabille of clothing and hair. His face split in a grin. "Ah," he said with a chuckle, flopping his arm across David's shoulder, "I see what you have been about."

David grunted noncommittally, but could feel his face starting to burn.

Abruptly, Fionchadd released him and was kneeling at Liz's feet. "Have no fear, gentle lady. You know a little of the ways of time in Faerie, and I tell you now that you need not fear its passage. This aspect of the Tracks, at least, even I can master."

"How 'bout it girl," David sighed, moving to stand beside her. "You up for one last trip into the Otherworld?"

She nodded reluctantly.

"Then let's get this thing in port and travel."

He had not taken two steps before he felt Fionchadd's firm grip on his shoulders. "Actually," the Faery said, "we do not need to go to port. Let me show you."

David nodded sourly and turned, hands fisted on his hips. "Okay, get on with it!"

Fionchadd glared at him; eyes flashing sudden cold fire. "It is not *my* doing," he hissed. "Do not forget that. And do not forget that though there is debt and perhaps even friendship between us, our kind are not alike and our goals ofttimes at odds!"

David folded his arms stubbornly. "Suppose I choose not to go."

"Then you would be in peril! Now that Oisin's ring has lost the ability to shield you, your protection is by grace, not by right or Power."

Suddenly they were face-to-face and chest-to-chest, mortal and Faery gazes locked in challenge.

"*Okay,* you guys!" Liz shouted. "Grow up, both of you. I've had enough of this macho-man crap."

Fionchadd relaxed a fraction, and the spark of anger dimmed in his eyes.

"Oh, okay," David grumbled. "Do your stuff."

Fionchadd inclined his head stiffly, then moved his hands a certain way. The glitter in the air brightened immediately, and he stepped back onto the Track, motioning David and Liz to follow. David did—reluctantly, for he never truly trusted the surface that was *not* a surface to remain beneath his feet, those walls that were *not* walls to keep out the outer dark. And this time there was no ground beneath, only a yard or so of fog, then water. It was, he thought grimly, like trying to stand in a tunnel made of moonbeams.

Yet it held, gave back pressure in response to his weight. And at a word from Fionchadd, he stroked the golden dragon's head.

Cool air spurted from the tiny nostrils, quickly growing

into a far stronger breeze. It did not disturb the Track's drifting motes, but as it blew and twisted around the ship, the vessel shrank, until an instant later it was once more a toy floating on the water. A flick of Fionchadd's wrist raised it to their level. He snagged it from the air and handed it to David, then indicated a pair of white mares that stood beside his own black stallion a little way back down the Track. David nodded and climbed atop one, while Liz took the other.

Fionchadd also started to mount, then glanced over his shoulder. David followed his gaze—and saw other steeds fast approaching. Each bore a rider, and at the head rode Lugh Samildinach, High King of the American Sidhe.

"Christ!" David cried. "I didn't realize Lugh was coming *here!* Where's this meeting gonna be, anyway?"

"Well," Fionchadd replied, "we thought it would be best if we met at your uncle's house—since this matter likewise concerns him."

David started to reply, wondering if there was more to the earlier gifts than had first appeared, but by then the riders were upon them.

Lugh led that procession. Tall he was, and black-haired, and—rare among his kind—black moustached. He wore a dull red tunic with an ochre sun-disk worked upon it, and boots and gloves of burgundy suede leather.

Fionchadd was instantly on his knees. David started to dismount and do likewise, but thought better of it, and contented himself with a deep bow over the saddle's high pommel. Liz followed David's example.

Lugh reined in his horse and cocked an eyebrow at Fionchadd. "I see you have trained them well, cousin," he said, laughing. "But rise up, David Sullivan, for you are no subject of mine—though some among my folk already call you the Young Lord of the Mortal Lands."

"Good grief," David gasped before he could stop himself. "You're kiddin'!"

Lugh shook his head. "My jests are far more subtle, as a rule. Now come, the others are waiting."

The rest of the company crowded up, and David took

quick inventory. Nuada was there in white, and Oisin in gray. The black-haired woman in the red dress with the crow on her shoulder was the Morrigu, the evil-tempered Battle Mistress; she was supposed to be a triple goddess, though David had never dared ask her about it. Rash young Froech was there also, he who had once been Ailill's keeper, and with him quiet Regan the Healer in green. And there *she* was in a gown the color of forgefire: Morwyn verch Morgan ap Gwyddion. Fionchadd's mother; daughter of a Fireshaper sorceress by the brother of Annwyn's queen. A hasty exchange of greetings, and they were off, galloping along a stream of golden motes that faded from view behind them.

Calvin, however, knew a great deal more about seeing than most people. His grandfather had taught him a few things about the nature of perceived reality and looking out of the corner of one's eyes, and also that knowledge is sometimes more reliable than sight. So it was, then, that though the Track melted from the Mortal World, still its memory persisted, and the resonance of its Power. Thus it was, too, that though he had dived as deeply as he could when that Finn guy started making signs and passes, he had still resurfaced in time to heave himself through the remnants of that strange, shimmering surface before it healed entirely. But now he was lost: trapped in a kind of golden fog with only a strip of tenuous yellow light to guide him.

Chapter XII: Spies and Spying

No matter how many times he did it, David never really got used to traveling on Straight Tracks. It was an instinctive fear of heights, he supposed, or of falling—that terrible apprehension in his gut that no matter how solid the ground looked or felt, it might transform at any moment into a mere gauze of light, or dust upon the air, or even a hazy vapor across nothing at all. He was afraid of bridges, too; and this Track above the lake was very like a bridge when you thought about it, which he was trying very hard not to.

Liz rode beside him, but she had not spoken, and Fionchadd too was strangely silent—legacy, he imagined, of their almost-altercation. But he had been *right* to be upset, dammit: he was *tired* of being jerked around by the Sidhe —and everybody else, when it came to it. All he wanted to do was get his life in order: finish school, leave the farm, go to college, and see what happened. At least the negatives there (like bullies and chores) had a discernible end. But this Faerie stuff *didn't* look like ending anytime soon, and he was getting sick of it. The Sidhe wanted him, did they? Well, he'd grant them an audience this time, but he'd lay down the law, too, and tell them to let him be. They had the wrong man if they wanted him to be their ambassador. And as for dragging Uncle Dale and probably the rest of the clan into it—he'd have none of that!

The silence persisted, and for a while David was only aware of the half-seen landscape beyond the tenuous golden tunnel around him: none of the usual subtly altering woods this time, but a stranger way that passed through less tangible regions marked only by a weaving of shadows and rippling curtains of mist and fog.

He had just begun to wonder why Lugh had chosen this route, which was obviously longer than the path through the unfrequented woods of his own World, when the fog abruptly vanished, and he beheld, not a hundred yards away, the rusty tin roof and weathered posts of Uncle Dale's back porch. Straight ahead lay the split-rail fence that marked the limits of the old man's farmyard, and to the right was the loom of barn, its ancient SEE ROCK CITY ad still faintly visible on the shingles. At a word from Lugh they dismounted. Froech led the horses toward the stable.

"David, you had better go first," Lugh told him.

David nodded sourly, casting a distrustful glance backward toward the company. A quick check of his watch showed 11:30. He could not imagine how he was going to explain the situation.

"Well," said Uncle Dale five minutes later, "I don't reckon you folks come here to talk about the weather, did you?" He took a sip of coffee-and-'shine and surveyed the group arrayed around his living room. Nuada and Regan had been there before, but Fionchadd had not (the old man hadn't said a word when he'd entered, though he'd looked at him intently), nor had Lugh; and David, squatting on the hearth beside his uncle, could not help but be aware of the King of the Sidhe; how, in spite of his low-key (for him) dress, regality literally poured off him, so that he dominated the room like a flame.

Liz squeezed David's hand and settled herself against his other side.

Finally Lugh cleared his throat and spoke. "It is a long tale we have to tell, good folk, and yet there is a little time in which to relay it. But to set it out truly in all its parts, I must speak first of the realms of Faerie. Three kingdoms there are, of great import: Tir-Nan-Og, Erenn, and Annwyn. And three lesser exist as well: Norwald, Alban, and Prydain. A number of minor lands exist, too, and some there were which have vanished—of these Aelfheim is best known among your folk. Each touches your World at some point, ofttimes at many: Tir-Nan-Og here in America, Erenn in Ireland, Annwyn in Wales, and so on. But other, more obscure, realms there are, that join our World and no other. One of these, which brushes only Annwyn— so we thought—is known only as the Land of the Power-smiths, for they do not tell its true name. Lady Morwyn here is partly of that race, and also, of course, is her son Fionchadd." He paused to help himself to another sip of coffee.

"Now for centuries, the realms have been at peace except for the sort of intrigue one expects among restless princes, but lately there has been more trouble. Ailill has been the cause of much of it, but always there were the Laws of Dana maintaining balance. Such Laws were in force when David played the Riddle Game a year ago, and likewise they oversaw the Trial of Heroes he then assayed. But they govern many things, and not the least of them hospitality. Thus when Morwyn came to my land to seek her vengeance against the slayer of her son, as was her right, she was perfectly within the Law to take Ailill's life —or so she deemed, for at that time she believed Fionchadd dead beyond recall. That Ailill's sister, in trying to save him, brought about her own destruction was not Morwyn's doing—directly, though some may question it. But when Fionchadd returned to life again, the Laws suddenly became more complicated."

Lugh went on to explain how he had offered Morwyn hospitality, and she had accepted, all according to the Laws of Dana. He continued with the tale of Finvarra's wrath at the death of his kindred, though of his own admission he had not loved them. Next, he told of the messages exchanged: of surrender asked and denied, and of greater threats made and ignored. And at last he told of the blockade.

"*That*, at least, I may show you!" he said, whereupon he brought out the crystal disk and called the image of Finvarra's fleet into being in the space before the sofa.

David stared at it for a long, breathless moment, not only caught up by the wonder of the thousand ships of Erenn's navy stretched as far as he could see across the Faerie ocean, but also amazed at what Nuada—or someone—had made from what was obviously some mixture of holography and magic.

"Well, that's all real interestin'," Dale said, when a Word from Lugh had banished the image. "But what's all this got to do with me 'n Davy?"

"It is because we have a problem," Nuada replied. "We have a hard choice before us: war with Finvarra if we do not give up Morwyn, and war with Annwyn, and the Powersmiths if we do."

"An' let me guess," Dale said. "Them Powersmith folks is the stronger 'uns."

"Exactly!" Nuada nodded. "Fortunately, Oisin has remembered something which may save us."

All eyes turned expectantly toward the old seer. Oisin cleared his throat but had not even got out his first word when there was a commotion at the door and Froech shouldered noisily in.

A wet, wild-eyed, and totally limp Calvin McIntosh dangled in his arms. The boy was wrapped in Froech's black cloak but wore no other clothing. Froech dropped him to the floor with an unceremonious thump and there he remained with only his brown eyes moving. "A spy," he stated flatly.

Lugh inclined an eyebrow toward Nuada. "One of yours?"

Nuada scratched his jaw thoughtfully and dipped a brow in turn. "Not that I am aware of."

"I know him," David said heavily. "His name's Calvin —Calvin McIntosh."

"What shall I do with him?" Forech wondered.

"A very good question," Lugh replied. "Where did you find him?"

"I had just left the stable and saw him crouching on the porch. Apparently . . . apparently the Track washed him up."

"The *Track?*" Regan cried.

The Morrigu nodded. "He speaks truth, for I sense its music yet about the boy."

Lugh eyed Fionchadd narrowly. "Were you careless, lad?"

The young Faery would not meet his gaze. "I closed the Track in haste, I will admit; but I never thought any human could see, much less follow. Besides, you were there, *you* did not see him."

"But if anybody could follow us, I'll bet old Calvin could," David said slowly. "I'm pretty sure he's got some kind of Power," he added, and could have kicked himself, not the least because he had no real idea where the notion had come from.

Morwyn stared intently at the Indian. "Aye, Power there is, though not our kind, nor yet the common sort of Mortals."

"Tell us of yourself, boy," Lugh demanded, as with a subtle gesture of his thumb and forefinger he released whatever spell Froech had laid on their unexpected visitor.

"Not until you tell me what's goin' on!" Calvin cried, as soon as he found his voice. He glanced fearfully at David. "Help me, man, you've got to!"

David shook his head. "I *can't*."

"Silence!" Lugh snapped. He rose, strode around the room to glare at Calvin; locked gazes with him.

Nuada stroked his chin. "A spy you say, yet certainly an auspicious one, for it was of him we were about to speak."

"Of *me?*" Calvin sputtered. He leapt to his feet, coming

perilously close to colliding with the looming Lugh. "Who *are* you folks, anyway? Hey, Sullivan, what the hell's going *on?*"

"Sit down, Calvin," David said quietly. "Looks like you're gonna get your questions answered."

Calvin responded mutely, face pale.

"I think," Nuada said wryly, "that he is a very rare sort of human. As rare as young Master Sullivan—or rarer, if he is what I suspect: one of the old people of this land, one attuned to their Power."

"And the exact reason we are here," Oisin put in. "For it is because of this boy that I have summoned you."

"This *boy* has a name," Calvin gritted, "and he's not real keen on being talked about like he's not here! I'd *really* like to know what's goin' on."

Nuada looked at David. "Maybe you had better tell him, David, if"—he shifted his gaze to Lugh—"our King would be willing to lift the Ban?"

Lugh nodded his assent.

David sighed and rose, vaguely aware of a subtle difference somewhere between his brain and his tongue. "If you guys don't mind, I think this'd be easier if we just stepped into the bedroom for a minute. Nothing personal, or anything, but some things are just better one-on-one. Come on, Fargo, this is gonna take some explainin'."

Calvin nodded apprehensively, drew the cloak around him, and followed David out of the room.

"Okay, Calvin," David said wearily, after he had tossed his friend a pair of Uncle Dale's khaki britches and ensconced himself on the trunk at the foot of the old man's bed. "How much do you know?"

"How much you gonna tell me?"

"Look, guy, we don't have time for this!"

Calvin tugged on the borrowed garment and stared David squarely in the eye. "Okay, then: I know you've got a strange-lookin' swimmin' buddy who's hard to focus on, and then shows up again in your uncle's living room lookin' like something out of a movie. I know you've got a model ship that enlarges by what looks to me like some kinda magic. I know you came here some way I sure as hell don't understand, 'cept that it brought me too. And I know why these folks are here, 'cause I heard every word you folks said till that guy caught me." He folded his arms and flopped against the wall. "That enough?"

David eyed him narrowly. "But do you know who they are?"

"I've got an idea 'bout that too, but I'll let you tell me."

David took a deep breath and frowned. "Like I said, this is gonna take some explainin'."

"I kinda gathered that."

"Yeah, well, you know those books of mine? *Gods and Fighting Men, The Fairy-Faith,* and all? Well, almost all of 'em's true, or at least the stuff about Sidhe is. They're—"

"The old gods of Ireland," Calvin finished. "I know that much—and I think a bunch of 'em are sittin' in the living room right now, if I heard the introductions right."

David's eyes narrowed again. "You didn't know anything about this yesterday—or claimed not to."

Calvin met his glare. "I *didn't,* then; I do now."

"But how. . .?"

"You mean you haven't missed 'em?"

"Missed what?"

"Those books. I kinda borrowed 'em before I left last night. I really meant to ask, but—well, you'd kinda cashed in, and I didn't want to bother you. Your dad said you wouldn't mind, but I guess he forgot to tell you. You can ask him if you don't believe me."

"And *you* conveniently forgot to tell me this morning."

"Well, I was feelin' sorta guilty about it, so I thought I'd try to sneak 'em back in without you noticing. I guess that was a mistake."

"I guess it was."

"Sorry."

"But *why?*"

"Because I . . . I don't know, really. Call it instinct again. I just sensed there was something mysterious about you and that they were part of the mystery."

"There's that instinct again."

"Yeah, the same thing that told me to tell you my true name. At least we're even now: a secret for a secret."

"So you know about the trouble, too?"

"Not the background."

"Okay, well to start with . . ."

And as quickly as he could, David told him.

"Well, then, so maybe you can get on with your story, now," Dale said quietly when David and Calvin had returned and the Indian had settled himself into a place in the corner. The old man raised a prompting eyebrow at Oisin.

Oisin nodded. "We have a problem: We must somehow get Morwyn to the Land of the Powersmiths, or at least to Annwyn. Unfortunately, the only direct route there is blockaded, so that does not seem a likely possibility."

"But what good will that do?" David asked. "I mean, won't Finvarra just get pissed off and attack anyway?"

Lugh smiled grimly. "He might. But if we aid Annwyn and the Powersmiths by returning one of their own, they will be honor bound to aid us in return. Finvarra cannot stand against the combined might of the three of us—certainly not with the Powersmiths in the fray."

"But wait a minute," David said, frowning. "Isn't Annwyn more or less on top of Wales? And doesn't Faerie kinda overlap all over? If Tir-Nan-Og's here, and Annwyn's there, and this Powersmith place is next to—"

Nuada shook his head. "I see your thinking, David, but the Worlds do not fit together that way. You think we could simply bring Morwyn into this world, spirit her to Wales, then pass the World Walls again and so come to Arawn's kingdom. That is a reasonable thing to assume, but it could not be, because Annwyn overlaps this World at another time, as does Erenn. There are other reasons as well, having to do with how far one may stray from one's own World, but the simplest way to put it is that Annwyn has not reached this time yet. I know it is a complex notion, and one that is best understood by drawing pictures, but for that there is no time. Suffice to say it perplexes even the Sidhe."

"In other words," said Dale, "'t'ain't possible."

David blinked in confusion. "So that means . . . ?"

"—that some *other* way must be found to get Morwyn to the Land of the Powersmiths," Oisin finished. "And that is where you come in, you and Calvin McIntosh."

"Oh, no!" Calvin cried, shaking his head vigorously. "Not me, uh uh."

"You seek your heritage, do you not? Then perhaps you should listen further, for you may learn much about it."

Calvin scowled but kept his silence.

"I had been thinking on this problem, of course," Oisin continued, "and I was unable to see an answer—until I chanced to speak with young Fionchadd about his practice bout with David. Fionchadd mentioned a subsequent encounter with a strange boy, and said that he had sensed some sort of Power there. He let me read his memory, and suddenly I knew."

"Yes?"

"Galunlati." Oisin looked at Calvin. "Does that mean anything to you?"

Calvin's face brightened for the first time since his capture. "I've heard my grandfather speak of it. I think it's . . . it's kinda like the heaven of my people."

"As some Irish think Tir-Nan-Og is theirs," Oisin said, "which it is not. But you are right—and it truly does exist: It touches the Lands of Men on the other side from Faerie—"

"Uh-oh," Calvin interrupted. "You've lost me again."

Oisin looked at Nuada. "You had better explain this one, Silverhand."

Nuada did: how there were Worlds and Worlds: Worlds that touched but barely, that lay within each other or beside each other, all linked by the complex webwork of the Tracks. Galunlati was one of these. It joined the Lands of Men, but not Faerie. Tracks led there, presumably, as they did to all the Worlds, but the Sidhe did not know which ones. They did not even know how they would appear.

"But what does this here Galunlati place have to do with Miss Morwyn's situation?" Dale wanted to know.

"Just this," Oisin replied. "Two hundred years ago and more, as men measure time, I met a druid of Calvin's folk —an *adawehi*, they called him. He showed me the way to Galunlati, and I traveled there for a while. I met the men of that place—if men they may be called—and from one of them I heard of a land far to the east, beyond a golden strand and a sea of light. *Nundagunyi*, they named it: the Sun Land—a place of shifting smokes and strange landscape, where fires burn at the borders, and the people practice strange and terrible arts. This intrigued me, and I questioned him further and eventually was able to determine that this must be the Land of the Powersmiths, for no other folk work with flame in such a way. Finally he showed me a thing he had: a curious disk graven with the image of an eagle. The style was unmistakably Powersmith, and the material"—he paused for effect—"was Fire frozen in Time, which only the Powersmiths can master. Thus it seems that the Land of the Powersmiths must somewhere touch Galunlati."

Lugh nodded thoughtfully. "Have you anything to add to this, Lady Morwyn? Does this sound possible? I know little of your mother's folk, though rumor has always held it that only from Annwyn may their land be entered."

Morwyn nodded. "My mother's country touches Faerie only in Annwyn, but Tracks lead there from other lands as well, though they seldom use them because none of the places they reach are of any worth to them. I have heard of a sea far to the west, though, whose surface is afire with Tracks, and whose farther shore is sanded with gold and peopled by the red-skinned folk. The Powersmiths traded with them once, but they became too free with Iron and the trading stopped."

"Very good," the Morrigu said, reaching up to stroke the crow on her shoulder. "We will equip a host and escort Lady Morwyn there."

"That you will not," Oisin told her. "For those of pure Faerie blood may not travel in Galunlati. It is a World too far from their own, and the World Walls wreak a terrible change on those who would assay it. Only its own people,

those of one of the Worlds that adjoin it, or those who carry
the blood on one of those adjoining Worlds, may venture
there. Fionchadd could go, or Morwyn herself, but Nuada
could not, nor Lugh—nor the host you spoke of."

"*Nor* Finvarra," Lugh added triumphantly.

"Aye, I do not think so," Oisin said. "And that assumes
he would even search that way."

"So your suggestion is . . .?"

"I propose that David and Calvin, and perhaps other of
his mortal friends go to Galunlati and seek out this unwatched passage to the Land of the Powersmiths."

"You mean go *without* Morwyn?" David cried incredulously.

"Aye, to start with. I want her safe until I know otherwise. Is that acceptable to you, Lady?"

Morwyn nodded.

"But how do we get there?" David asked, "—assuming
I'm willing."

"By the ancient ritual," Oisin replied. "In that I will
instruct you: fasting, scourging, prayer, and vigil."

David grimaced. "That sounds painful."

"But we would owe you a mighty debt," Lugh noted.
"The King of the Sidhe does not take on such obligations
lightly."

"When would we go—if we did?" Liz wondered.

"As soon as possible, though it will take a day or two to
prepare."

She leaned against David's shoulder and sighed. "I can't
make it then. I've got to go back to school."

David looked beseechingly at Nuada. "Couldn't you
guys, like, fool with time or something, so she could go
and still get back okay?"

Nuada shook his head and glanced at Oisin. "I do not
think so . . ."

Oisin shook his head in turn. "No, David. The altering
of time is mostly a function of the Tracks, and since they
are not the same in Galunlati, and our Power does not work
reliably there, we could not guarantee your lady's return."

"This is the plan," Lugh said. "Fionchadd, being able to

travel in Galunlati by virtue of his mixed blood, and having kin-interest in this, will go as scout. He will attempt to cross this unknown sea and so reach the Land of the Powersmiths. He will use the ship *Waverider*, if David will permit it."

David nodded in resignation. "Sure."

"And Calvin and David will go with him as far as they may," Oisin added. "Calvin because his lineage may likewise be of some service there; and David because he is the link between: the one who knows most of men and Sidhe and the old folk."

"But assuming we're successful," David said, "how's Fionchadd going to get to Morwyn's country? I mean how is he goin' to know the right way?"

"In that I can aid," said Morwyn. "You know the way of the ship, do you not? Words may direct it, to some degree, even thought. But more certain than any of these is metal. This you have seen before, David Sullivan: a dagger, a sword—any worked metal when thrust into the deck will send the vessel to the place of that metal's forging."

"Oh, yeah—right," David said. "I see."

"*I* don't," Calvin muttered.

Morwyn reached to her waist and removed a small dagger in a sheath. "This I give to my son," she said. "It was forged in my mother's land. When he reaches the eastern shore of Galunlati, he will plunge the dagger into the ship's deck. The vessel will then take him to the place we seek."

"But why can't you just use the ship anyway?" David protested. "I mean it obviously doesn't have to follow Tracks. It can *fly*, for heaven's sake! Or why not go to Galunlati and take off from whatever place we land, or whatever?"

"As to the first," Morwyn said, "all the other ways east are being watched; thus this seems the only choice. As to the latter, to travel without the Tracks it must follow a source of great Power such as its master's blood. And since you are now its master, and you are here, that would be a futile effort."

"So I've gotta do this . . ."

"You do not *have* to," Nuada said. "But it would be very good if you did. It would aid your World as well as ours, for who can say what might transpire in the Lands of Men should war break out in Faerie? The Worlds are close here, David, very close. Anything of great force, be it of nature or of man's creation, that passes in one is reflected in the other. Thus the turmoil and torment of war would make men in this World sleep uneasily. There would be contention. Tempers would grow short."

"And with wind and weather as weapons . . ."

"A little you have seen already. There would be more and worse."

"Okay, then," David said heavily, "I reckon I don't have any real choice but to go. And I'll ask Alec, if you don't mind." He glanced at the Indian. "Calvin's his own man."

"Looks like I don't have a choice, either," the Indian answered slowly.

David held up his hand. "I have one condition, though."

"Yes?" Lugh asked curiously.

David took a deep breath. "Okay, well—I may be gone a while . . . and I'll have to explain that time. I can't just drop out of sight for who knows how long, and you guys evidently can't fool with time enough to cover me; and I'm sick of lying. So . . . I want to tell my pa. Ma already knows, so does Little Billy. It'd make it better for all of us."

"It is just," Nuada acknowledged, glancing at Lugh.

Lugh's brow furrowed for a long moment. "I will grant you this thing. But it will be hard for him to accept without proof."

"Proof's simple enough," David said. "Leave that to me."

"But what about you, Oisin?" Calvin interrupted. "Will you be our guide?"

"Alas, no," Oisin said sadly. "I am too old. I would age there, worse even than in this World. Such I learned by bitter experience during my brief visit."

"I'll go, then," Dale volunteered. "I've always been curious 'bout them Indian legends."

"But you would have the same trouble as I," said Oisin. "Your bones are not as strong as once they were."

"Well, you're right there," Dale admitted. "'Sides, who'd look after Davy's folks?"

"Oh, Christ," David groaned. "I can hear 'em now."

"Also," Oisin noted, "we will need a place to prepare the ritual, and there is a building here that would be ideal."

"So," said Lugh, standing. "It appears to be decided."

"I reckon so," David sighed. "Well, then, when do we start?"

"Two days hence, I should think," Oisin told him. "I must prepare certain formulae and refresh my memory of the ritual. Meanwhile, you should immediately begin your fast."

"Our *fast?*"

Oisin nodded. "Seven days is prescribed, though we may do with less if I alter certain other elements. But you should begin now: no food at all, and to drink—Calvin's folk drank a potion they called *black drink*. It was made of a type of holly, but it is rather similar to very strong coffee, so I think that would be a reasonable substitute."

"I reckon we can manage that," Dale said. "I make the strongest there is."

David sighed helplessly. It was happening again: He was off on another venture into the unknown, when all he wanted was to live a normal life—more normal now that he had his lady.

As if she read his mind, Liz's hand tightened around his own and she led him to the porch.

"David, I really do have to go," she said, glancing at her watch. "It's past midnight, and I have to get away early in the morning. But be careful—and remember one thing."

"And what's that?"

"That I love you."

"I love you too," David whispered, as they embraced and he buried his face in her hair. Her lips, when he found them, tasted of tears, and so, he knew, did his own.

Chapter XIII: Confessions

(Sullivan Cove, Georgia—
Sunday, August 18—morning)

"Pa," David said early the next morning, "I need to talk to you."

Big Billy regarded him curiously from around the side of Madam Bovary, the brown and white Guernsey cow. The splat of milk squirting into the galvanized bucket beneath her ceased abruptly. It was not quite dawn. Back in the house Uncle Dick and clan were still mercifully asleep, thralls to a night of revelry.

"I really *do*," David insisted, shifting his weight impatiently and trying not to think either about how sleepy he was or how hungry.

"Must be important," Big Billy observed, "to get you out here this early on Sunday mornin'." Sunday was not David's day to milk, and Calvin hadn't ventured down off the mountain yet. David wondered what was keeping him.

"Uh, yeah, actually it is. But look, could you come outside for a minute? There's something you need to see."

"Can't it wait? I gotta finish—"

David shook his head. "No . . . not really. This is as im-

140

portant as anything I've ever asked you. And it has to be now."

Big Billy nodded sullenly and stood. He slapped Madam Bovary on one bony hip and promised to return. "What is it, then?" he grumbled, when David had led him into the barnyard.

"I can't show you here. We need to go where we can see Bloody Bald."

"I've seen that blamed mountain plenty of times, boy. What's so special 'bout it now?"

"You'll find out," David replied, and ushered his father across the driveway and onto their upper pasture. A minute later they stood at the crest of a small hill, gazing west. Langford Lake was hidden in the same morning fog that shrouded most of the mountains. But they could see the pinnacle of Bloody Bald clearly from there, and that was all that mattered.

"Pa," David began hesitantly, "I . . . I know that you know there's been a lot of strange stuff going on around here lately—the last year especially."

Big Billy nodded uncertainly. "Well, *that's* a fact!"

"Okay, then," David went on. "Well . . . there's a reason for that, and that reason has to do mostly with me and something that happened to me one night."

Big Billy folded his arms and regarded his son imperiously. "Go on."

"Right. Well, do you remember last summer when I was so jumpy at breakfast and all? The day you found out I had that ring?"

"Yep, sure do."

David took a deep breath. "Well, what you *don't* know, what I never told you, is where I really got it. And the fact is that I got it from the Irish Faeries."

There, he had said it, and right up to the moment he had not been certain he would be able. But Lugh had been as good as his word: the Ban had been lifted, as least as far as his father was concerned.

Big Billy's face turned red as the eastern clouds. "Shit,"

he spat. "You brought me out here to tell me that! I ought to wear you out!"

"No!" David cried quickly. "Let me finish! There's a way I can prove it. It's gonna be strange, but you gotta trust me. Just do what I ask and . . . and I promise I'll never ask you another favor as long as I live. I'll do my chores and work in the sorghum and be the good little boy you want . . . just humor me this once."

Big Billy frowned but nodded. "What you want me to do?"

David glanced at his watch, then at the brightening sky. "It's gonna be sunrise in a minute or two. But right before that happens I want you to stand on my feet and look over my shoulder at Bloody Bald. Yeah, I know it sounds strange, but it's . . . well, it's magic, that's all. Just trust me this once, okay?"

Big Billy did not reply, but eased his Sears work boots awkwardly onto his far smaller son's Reeboks—not his full weight, David noticed, which was just as well.

Another glance at the watch. Twenty seconds, fifteen, ten, eight . . .

"Are you lookin' at the mountain, Pa?"

He could feel Big Billy nod clumsily. *Three, two, one* . . . As quickly as he could, David slapped his right hand atop his father's head and whispered very softly, "Everything between my hands and my feet is within my power, now see, Pa; oh, please *see!*"

The top edge of the sun cleared the horizon.

David did not move, for his father's breathing had gone very still. He was trembling slightly.

"Pa?" he cried. "Pa, are you okay?"

"Yeah," Big Billy gasped at last. "I don't have to see no more. I believe you."

"That's good," David sobbed in relief as he released his hold. "'Cause that's just the start of what I've gotta tell you. I—"

"*I've* got to finish the milkin'," Big Billy interrupted. "But I sure could use some company, 'specially if there's things that need explainin'."

David risked one final glance back toward the mountain —and saw the peak taller than it should be, saw a glitter of towers and pinnacles flash briefly from the summit—and heard twelve long notes of trumpet, one sounding from each tower to greet the sun.

"'The splendor falls on castle walls,'" he began.

"What's that?" Big Billy asked.

"Just a poem, Pa. Tennyson."

Big Billy's only answer was to lay an arm across his son's shoulders and draw him close for the first time in almost a year.

Because Lugh's proposal was not a matter he could discuss over the phone, David had to wait until church let out to get hold of Alec, and the waiting nearly drove him batty. What was he going to tell the guy, anyway? That the Sidhe wanted them to bop off on yet another quest into some other World? Did he have the right to ask such a thing, knowing that Alec had been grounded, never mind how he felt about Faery?

But did he dare *not* ask him? The Sidhe themselves had suggested he take other companions; that implied they felt very strongly that Alec *should* be a member of the expedition. And then David remembered something the fortune-teller had told him at last year's fair: *Three are mightier than on, but one is mightiest of the three.* Alec had been one, of the three then. Was he still?

David wondered. He'd been neglecting his buddy: paying a lot more attention to Liz, to Calvin, maybe even to the Sidhe. So to fail to ask him now would not only risk pissing Lugh and company, it would quite possibly further alienate his best friend. Besides, an adventure might be all well and good, but David was going off with a couple of guys he didn't really know, and while he liked both Fionchadd and Calvin, he was *comfortable* with Alec, and it might be real good to have somebody comfortable along.

So he sat in MacTyrie Methodist's newly paved parking lot, and waited, and every now and then glanced up at the four white Ionic columns, the red brick walls, and the tall metal steeple, and let the homey image soothe him. He hadn't planned this exactly, so the waiting gave him time to lay out his arguments, except he never could quite figure out where to get started. Eventually he turned on the radio. Atlanta's 96 Rock was playing Tom Petty's "Woman in Love," which was followed by Creedence's "Travelin' Band" and Fleetwood Mac's "Hypnotized." David found himself drowsing, but then the song ended and another began—right as the church door swung wide and a surge of people poured out. He strained his eyes in quest of his friend and found him, just as the Doors' ominous "Riders on the Storm" commenced. He flicked it off. Taking a deep breath, he climbed out of the Mustang, sprinted across the lot, and started across the grassy lawn. "Alec," he called. "Hey, guy, get over here!"

Alec pulled away from his mother's arm. David waved at tall, gray-haired Mrs. McLean and quickened his step. Alec was closer now; David could see his face brightening in the clear morning light. In his tan linen suit he looked very dapper—certainly more so than David, whose sole concessions to Sunday were white jeans instead of blue ones and a nondescript green dress shirt.

"So, oh Mad One, what brings you here?" Alec chuckled when they got within easy speaking range. "Surely they got that old time religion up on Sullivan Cove?"

"*Real* old time, as a matter of fact. But seriously, I've got to talk to you about . . ."

"If you're here, it must be about *that* stuff? Oh, jeeze, Davy; I don't know if I want to."

"Don't let me down before I've even started."

Alec's gaze shifted to the ground as they continued to walk toward the Mustang. "But it always gets me in trouble."

"Yeah, well, I'm afraid it will this time, too; but I have to tell you. Besides, you've got a right to know."

They reached the car and climbed inside. "Wanta come to lunch?" Alec asked suddenly, turning hopeful eyes toward his friend.

David thought about the fast he had begun that morning

and heard his stomach growl as if on cue. He shook his head sadly. "Can't."

"Oh, come on, it's lasagne!"

"I *can't*, Alec. That's part of the problem."

Alec scooted around to face him. "Maybe you'd better spill it, then."

David did.

"Whew," Alec said when he had finished. "That's a hell of a mess. And *naturally* the Sidhe need you to straighten it out."

"Well, not me specifically."

Suddenly Alec was giggling uncontrollably.

"What's so funny?"

"Oh, just that they're so bloody great, the immortal Sidhe. But give them one little problem, and what do they do? Come running to us—and not even to grown-ups, to kids! A bunch of stupid-ass kids!"

"I'm not a child, kiddo."

Alec raised a challenging eyebrow. "You're a man, then?"

David paused thoughtfully. So much had happened in the last twelve hours that one of the major events in his life had almost got lost in the shuffle. "In . . . one way at least," he said at last.

"And what's that supposed to mean?"

David flushed deep scarlet. "What do you *think?*"

Alec stared at him incredulously. "*You?* And . . . Liz? You mean you finally did it?"

David nodded sheepishly, certain his ears would self-combust from embarrassment. "I . . . well, I mean it's personal, and all. But . . . well, I I guess I'd feel worse if I didn't tell you. Besides, I remember what you told me once, that you'd know anyway 'cause she'd be grinnin' like a 'possum."

"I haven't seen her today," Alec noted dryly. "I'll have to be on the lookout for the mask of the great marsupial."

"Don't you trust me?"

Alec paused ever so briefly, but David caught it and frowned. "Uh, look, bro; I'll be glad to fill you in sometime, but what I *really* need to talk about's if you'll go to Galunlati with me. It's a week till school starts, and this shouldn't take that long—not long at all maybe, depending on how time runs in that other place. But I'd like to have you along."

Alec bit his lip in perplexity. "I don't know. I mean I'm grounded and all. It'd be hard to explain to my folks, especially about the fasting."

"What'd you *do,* anyway? I mean it's not like you to give them a lot of trouble or anything."

Alec's eyes went slightly out of focus, and he blinked several times in succession.

"You okay?"

"Huh? Oh yeah, sure. It's just that I had a flash of headache right then. Jeeze, I forgot what I was gonna say."

"Why you were grounded," David prompted.

"Oh, right. Well, it wasn't anything really, I was just . . . pissed and . . . and rode around about half the night. I was in Dad's new car, if you noticed, and that kinda did me in."

David laid a hand on his nearest shoulder. "Well, do what you can, 'cause I sure do want you with me!"

"Yeah," Alec said slowly, blinking again. "I will. Maybe if I make it clear that *you* asked . . ."

David heaved a sigh of relief. "I knew you wouldn't let me down."

"No," Alec replied hesitantly, "I . . . I won't."

David frowned again. "You *sure* you're okay?"

Alec shrugged. "Well I just got one humdinger of a headache all of a sudden. And there's something floating around the back of my mind I meant to tell you and can't recall, but I guess it's not important."

"Maybe you're catching something."

"Maybe I am."

"Maybe you should use that as an excuse to fast."

Alec chuckled wanly. "Maybe I will."

They talked on, planning, coordinating activities, plotting strategy to convince Dr. McLean, though the more they talked the more Alec seemed certain he would pose no problem. Thankfully the fair was ending that day, so there'd be no trouble as far as Alec's concession job was concerned. And when David dropped Alec off at his house and started home, one part of him, at least, was a tiny bit more comforted.

Alec, however, was anything but relieved. Why had he agreed to such a preposterous proposition anyway? He was supposed to meet Eva that evening, and had no idea when thereafter. But now, he would have to sandwich that in around packing for yet another trip to who-knew-where, all because he could not bear the idea of being left out—that somebody else might share something with David he could not.

Well, he had his own secrets now too: ones he had *not* shared, though he had intended to. That puzzled him a little, because he had been right on the edge of telling David about his own amorous escapade when something had made him substitute the same lie he had told his father. It wasn't the headache that had zapped him about that time, he realized, though that was what he had first thought; but simply the fact that to do so would be to sully his memory of Eva, and that was a notion he could not stand.

Eva! She would be leaving soon, though just when he wasn't certain. She looked about his age, so she probably had to get to school somewhere, which meant about a week, max. After all, she had said she was only visiting. But *then* where would she go? Alec found himself wondering, and wondering other things as well: like her last name. Like what her folks did. What had they talked about, anyway? He hardly recalled. Just him, and his hopes and desires, and his friends, and . . . and something else he could not clearly remember, that made his head hurt again when he tried to find it. Probably something about David. He was always talking about David.

Tonight, though, would be different. Tonight they would talk about her.

* * *

"Right on time," Eva whispered, as Alec made his way into the ruins late that evening. She rose from where she'd been sitting with her back against an ivy-covered wall. She had built a tiny fire, and Alec was grateful for it, for a sudden chill brushed him, even as his fingers caught hers. She was wearing a loose white dress, almost like a robe. Starlit against the dark leaves, the effect was truly breathtaking. He had swapped his suit for Bugle Boys and a Batman T-shirt. His parents had not heard him leave.

"I try to be punctual," he said. "I—"

"Still talk too much!" She laughed, silencing him with a smile.

They stood there for a moment, not speaking; Alec could feel his heart already racing, his body coming alive at that gentlest of touches. And then the caresses became more complex and longer, and very soon there was no fabric between them.

"Jesus," Alec gasped as he lay back at last, then realized he was naked and tugged on his pants while Eva looked on amused.

Alec caught her smile and returned it.

"And what's so funny, my Alec?"

"Oh, just that . . . I've never done it with someone like you."

"Nor anyone else, I suspect."

Alec colored to his spiky hairline.

"Well, no. But . . ."

She ran a hand along his ribs. "You were fine."

"Yeah, but I was thinking how funny it was for me of all people to just walk up to somebody and . . . well, you know. I mean, usually when I see somebody I like, I talk a lot, and . . ."

"We can talk now, if you want."

Alec leaned against her shoulder and stroked her bare thigh absently. "Sure. And as a matter of fact there's a bunch of stuff I've been meaning to ask you."

She caught his hand and brought it to her lips. Their

eyes met over the knuckles. "And I have a few things I need to ask you too."

"Me first."

"*No.*"

"What?" But Alec was gazing into her eyes and before he knew it was lost in them. The world tilted and swam, and suddenly he was at one remove from himself. It was like being drunk, watching his head swaying back and forth as Eva dropped his hands and regarded him with all traces of warmth gone from her exquisite features.

"Power walked this land last night, Alec McLean," she whispered. "Much of it I saw, but little read. Perhaps you could tell me more."

"Power?"

"You could start with David Sullivan. What has he told you lately? What that *mortal* men would not know?"

Alec opened his mouth to begin, but paused. He couldn't tell her, even if he wanted to. Yet . . . yet she *knew*, which meant . . . yet the Ban of Lugh . . . But . . . but something was wrong. Eva was suddenly not Eva but something far more sinister.

"What . . . how do you know of Power?"

A laugh, but not a pleasant one. "Because I was born to it, foolish boy. And I have your seed in me, and thereby have mastery of all that you are. You will tell me now— tell me all! What does Lugh intend?" She grasped his head, pulled it toward her, though he tried to wrench away. "Tell me, Alec McLean, by your Name I demand it!"

And Alec did: all he could recall, including everything David had said to him that morning word-for-word. Almost an hour passed before he sank back, exhausted.

"It is as I supposed," Eva said when he had finished. "And I know what I must do."

"What?" Alec asked sleepily. "Do for what?"

"Nothing that need concern you," she whispered, soothing damp hair off his brow. "You should rest here a time, while I procure a certain something that ought to prove very useful."

Alec started to rise, but she stopped him, and he sank down again. Their gazes locked briefly. "Sleep, my Alec," she said. "And dream exactly what I tell you."

Alec awoke somewhat later and sat up with a start. Where was he? He looked around, saw the comforting walls, the trickle of a fire. And Eva sitting beside him, calmly looking at him and smiling.

"I . . . Jesus, I'm sorry. I must have dropped off."

"It was the wine." Eva laughed softly, indicating a pair of silver goblets and an empty bottle that now rested between them, though Alec had no memory at all of how they had come there. "You apparently have little head for it."

"Evidently not," Alec said, rubbing his neck where it had stiffened. "I don't remember a thing about it."

"Not even why we drank it?"

Alec shook his head. "'Fraid not."

"I brought it to ease our parting. I fear it did its work too well."

"Our . . . parting?"

Eva nodded sadly. "Tonight is the last time we can be together. In fact, I must depart in a few moments. I had hoped you would remember."

Alec sat bolt upright. "Eva, no! There's so much I don't know!"

"And that you *should* not know," she whispered. "Sometimes remembered feelings are more pleasant than remembered facts."

"That's easy for you to say."

"Alec!"

He turned and stared at her, feeling tears start to burn in his eyes. "But you'll be gone! And I'll have . . . nobody."

"What of your friends?"

"It's not the same."

"I cannot help it."

His jaw tightened. "Can't you?"

"No."

"Stay."

"I cannot. I have work to do. One thing only I can give you to remember me by."

She reached into her purse—a fringed item made of soft leather that looked handmade—and removed a silver box, which she handed to him.

He took it and stared at her quizzically.

"Open it."

He did, and gasped as he saw what lay inside.

It was a dagger. Barely five inches long, that blade was; its hilt scarcely shorter. But it shimmered in the faint light. Simple was the design, yet perfectly proportioned and balanced. A leather sheath lay beside it. Alec drew it out and examined it.

"I made it," Eva said. "And now I give it to you."

"I can't accept this!"

"But you must, my Alec. You *must!*" She put a strange inflection on the final word, and Alec felt his thoughts slip out of focus. Suddenly he wanted nothing more than to look into those wonderful eyes. He did—and felt his head spin again as words slammed into his brain. *You must,* that voice repeated, *for that dagger has one particular use I would have you put it to. When the time comes you will know it, as you will know exactly what to tell your father so you can join your friend on his journey.*

She told him, then: both things; and Alec heard her words in his mind—but even as they were spoken, they seemed to sink out of sight, become drowned in his subconscious. When he came to himself, she was standing before him, smiling.

"Thank you again," she said, "for your most excellent company that has brought joy to a stranger in your land."

Alec gazed at the dagger in his hand. "And thank you for this most excellent present."

"Do not forget your promise."

Alec's mind blanked for a moment. "Promise . . . ?"

"That you will show my gift to no one else, nor tell anyone you have met me."

His face lit as he found the memory. "Of course. It'll be our secret."

"One of many," Eva said quietly, and rose.

"I'll come with you," Alec called, starting to join her.

"No," came her reply—already she was at the edge of the terrace. "I want to remember you exactly as you are." With a whisper of wind on fabric she entered the forest and was gone.

Alec slumped down by the fire and waited. Five minutes trickled by, then ten. He searched his memories, savored each one. And then tears started down his cheeks as he thought of Eva, how he would never see her again. They had done so much together, and there was so much left to do. But still, there were the memories. He did not know that not a single one of them was true.

PART II

GALUNLATI

Chapter XIV: Into the Asi

(Sullivan Cove, Georgia—
Monday, August 19—morning)

Monday dawned clear, though much cooler than was seasonable—as David discovered when he dashed down to the paper box barefoot and almost got frostbite along with the *Atlanta Constitution*. In spite of the sun, he shivered. An upward glance showed the familiar red disk peeking over the mountains to the east. *Last time I'll be seein'* you *for a while, old buddy,* he thought, and sighed.

Was he really about to embark on yet another foray into some other World? One where he would have nothing to guide him except what he'd learned from a few quick conversations with Uncle Dale and Calvin, neither of whom knew as much as he'd hoped; and a second, brief session with Oisin the previous evening. As for the sun, his companion of seventeen summers, he wondered what it would be like in Galunlati. Or would there even *be* one? He frowned thoughtfully, searching his memory. According to Oisin the Cherokee Overworld consisted basically of archetypical reflections of the natural world. Which meant

. . . Well, one thing it didn't mean was there'd be a sun. He shivered again and went inside.

Calvin looked up from the breakfast table as he entered. His new friend seemed calm, but a slight tic in his angular jaw showed that he was not. No plate sat before him, and the same prevailed at David's place. Only a half-empty mug of coffee gave any indication of sustenance. Little Billy by contrast looked smug, full, and well contented. Probably the little fiend had taken maximum advantage of the sudden lack of competition for the breakfast bacon and biscuits.

David tossed the paper in his father's general direction, dragged out a chair, and flopped down in it—and wished he hadn't, because it put him perfectly in range of a full whiff of breakfast. His stomach growled violently and twisted itself into a yet tighter knot—if that was possible. He rolled his eyes pitifully and tugged his already snug belt in a notch. It had been more than a day since he'd had anything to eat. Only the coffee kept him going.

"Sure you won't have something?" his mother asked. She actually seemed worried about him.

David shook his head. "Let's not start that again, Ma. You know what I'm doing, and why."

"It's all craziness, if you ask me," Big Billy opined, extracting the sports section. "Stickin' your nose in where it don't belong. Good thing I don't need you much this week or you'd be in trouble."

"It's only for a few days max, Pa," David protested, though he actually had no idea how long the quest would take, nor did it really matter, since Uncle Dale would be covering chores for him. It was too bad about his father, though; too bad that his earlier empathy had already faded. Things were back to normal—the same old contentious normal. Some folks simply had no sense of wonder.

"That's still too much time to be spendin' on foolishness," Big Billy snorted. "Fastin', and then settin' all day in a hot house tryin' to have a vision. You ain't gonna be smokin' dope, are you? Sounds 'spicious to me."

"Uncle Dale'll be checkin' on us," David replied. "Ask him. He'll see everything we do."

"Humph," Big Billy snorted again. "Don't trust *that* old buzzard not to try that stuff, now you mention it."

David rolled his eyes in resignation.

Calvin grinned wryly. "You 'bout ready?"

"Soon as Alec—"

Gravel crunched outside, and David looked through the open back door and across the porch, to see Alec's old burgundy Volvo putter into the yard. The car stumbled to a halt before Alec had truly stopped it.

"Fuel injectors," David said to Calvin's raised eyebrow. "G-Man must've got it running. I reckon miracles really do happen."

"That'll be two, then; considerin' what you said about him bein' grounded."

"Good point."

"His old man relent, or what?"

David shrugged. "That's what he told me when he called to say he was on his way. You never can tell about Dr. McLean."

By the time Alec disentangled himself from his seatbelt and climbed out of the car, David and Calvin had snagged their own gear and were waiting by the trunk to help him unload. David groaned when he saw the mass of equipment Alec had assembled.

"*All* this? I don't know if it's gonna be possible to take *anything*. I'm not even sure we'll be there in the flesh, exactly. Oisin wasn't clear on that point."

"Be prepared," Alec quoted, wiping his hands on his number-two pair of winter cammies before attacking the pile in the trunk. "Or have you forgotten your days in the Scouts?"

"I'm *almost* an Eagle," David reminded him haughtily. He pulled out the five-foot length of Alec's hiking stick-cum-runestaff—twin to the one he carried—and tossed it to him. Alec caught it deftly with his unencumbered hand. "Would have been if the troop hadn't folded."

"Water under the bridge, man. So, you ready?"

"After you, bro."

Alec started at that and looked thoughtful for the barest instant before slamming the deck lid. "Right."

"Into the breach, boys; into the breach."

An instant later they were marching down the Sullivan Cove road whistling "Darth Vader's Theme" from *Star Wars*, with Calvin accompanying on harmonica.

Uncle Dale was sitting on his front porch when they got there, calmly drinking hot cider—or what smelled like cider—with Oisin. But David knew his uncle well enough to know there was very likely more to it than what came out of store-bought jugs. "I don't suppose I could have some of that, could I?" he called when he came into hailing distance. "This fastin' business takes it out of a man."

"And you think this would put it back in?" Oisin laughed.

"Put *somethin'* in you's for sure," Dale rejoined.

David paused at the foot of the rickety steps and looked at them. Two old men, not that unlike, really: both with white hair that was longer than most men their age wore, though Oisin's held a hint of silver. Both lean and hard-looking, proof of a man's work done all their lives, except that Dale's had been in the Copper mines of Tennessee, and Oisin's—he'd been a warrior, David thought, before he was a philosopher or sage. Alike in truth, then, until you got to their clothes: Uncle Dale's inevitable khakis and hat; and Oisin's staff, rings, and the long velvet robe that was the color of moonlight. Even here in the clear light of day David could put no certain name to it, though it bore hints of silver and gray and white, even of gold and brown. Their eyes, too, were different: Dale's blue and penetrating behind their gold-framed lenses, Oisin's blind and filmed with shining silver.

"Are you ready to begin?" Oisin asked.

"Ready as we'll ever be, I guess," David told him. He patted his backpack. "I've got the two things I really need: the ship and the ring." He held up his hand where the twining dragons sparkled in the morning light.

"And you, Alec McLean?"

"Right as rain," Alec echoed.

"What about you, Mr. Calvin?" Dale inquired.

"Sure."

"But where's Finno?"

"Here," a voice called from inside, and the Faery pushed through the screen door, a tabby tomcat curled in the bare arms exposed by his sleeveless tunic. David started at that, first because Fionchadd had been inside at all, and second because the screen was steel mesh, which would manifest as fire to the Sidhe, as Fionchadd knew by bitter experience. Judging by his nonchalance around that metal, though, the Faery now wore the substance of David's World, as he must do for any lengthy sojourn there. He found himself wondering how that affected the prohibition against entering any dwelling unasked. Probably ought to ask sometime; find out if it was physical, psychological, or social.

"And what have *you* been about?" David asked him lightly.

"I was examining the—what is the word? Plumbing."

David and Alec exchanged amused glances. "Plumbing?"

"We do not have such things in Faerie," Fionchadd said deadpan.

"Jesus," David chortled. His gaze met Alec's, then Calvin's, and finally Uncle Dale's, and then he could control himself no longer. He doubled up with laughter. Tears started from his eyes, and every time he got close to regaining control, he would catch someone else's smirk and lose it all over—or worse, would catch Fionchadd's puzzled gape and really go over the edge. Eventually, though, his panting giggles subsided, leaving his sides sore. He felt distinctly lightheaded—probably a function of hyperventilation on an empty stomach.

Oisin laid a hand on his shoulder and dragged himself up. "An auspicious beginning," he said. "Let us hope the conclusion is as mirthful."

David tried to look sober, but kept catching glimpses of

his companions and sniggering again, as did they all, even Oisin.

"You will have to explain this to me sometime," the Faery said, obviously still mystified.

"I will, I promise," David told him.

"Let us proceed," Oisin prompted.

Wordlessly they followed him around the side of Uncle Dale's house that faced away from Big Billy's farm. A variety of outbuildings sprawled there amid a complexity of split rail fences, abandoned wagon wheels, miscellaneous farm equipment, and an even dozen indignant chickens. Oisin leveled his staff toward the shack in the middle. "That is your *asi*," he told them. "Dale Sullivan has made it to fit our need. The ritual will take place there."

"What's an *asi?*"

"A sweat lodge," Calvin volunteered. "It's a word from my language."

Alec puffed his cheeks doubtfully. "I don't think I'm gonna like this."

David thunked an arm across his shoulders. "Think of it as a sauna, Scotsguy: a very very *looong* sauna."

"What's a sauna?" Fionchadd wondered, but they shushed him.

David started toward the small building, but Oisin called him back. "No! You have not yet been purified! The sun will tell us when to begin, which is very soon. But before that happens, you must go to water. So if you will accompany me . . ."

David nudged Calvin in the ribs. "Going to water? Didn't I hear you say that one time?"

The Indian nodded mutely but did not elaborate as they followed Oisin to another ramshackle building, this one a former corncrib.

David stepped inside, the others following, with the old seer last of all. Though the outside air still had a bite to it, it was warm there, and dusty, and very dry, as if the ghosts of long defunct kernels and shucks sucked the moisture from the air. David licked his lips experimentally.

"Good folk," Oisin said formally, and their muffled comments and nervous snickers subsided instantly, for his voice had suddenly assumed an air of authority the like of which David had never heard in it before. No longer was he Oisin the friendly old man, but Oisin the arch-druid.

"Good folk, I say," he repeated, "you have come here to embark on a journey which may take you far from anything you know. I alone of any you have met have been there; even among our own folk, Fionchadd. But to approach Galunlati, you must travel by the Roads of that land. And in order to accomplish that you must undergo the fourfold preparation. The first part—the fasting—you have finished, though properly it should have lasted for seven days; yet I hope by certain things I have done at another stage, to have shortened that. But now come the other three portions, and these follow a form most ancient that I had from a druid of Calvin's people."

He paused for a moment to survey them.

"In a moment you will begin your quest. Yet you must not enter the asi as men from This World, as Calvin's people call it, bearing any outward sign of this land. Rather you must enter as man first came into This World: naked."

David sighed. He'd expected something like this, though it was really no big deal—it wasn't like any of them had anything to be ashamed of. He exchanged resigned glances with his companions, stuck the dragon ring in his pocket, and began to strip.

"What about this?" Fionchadd asked, fingering the elaborate gold-and-jeweled torque he wore around his neck. David hadn't noticed it before. "It takes great effort to remove, and it is important—as you know."

"You may retain that," Oisin said, "and likewise may Calvin retain the bag that lies upon his chest, if he wishes."

"How did you—" the Indian began.

"I heard it slide against your skin. Now hurry! There is not much time."

A moment later they all stood naked in the middle of the corncrib. Calvin had a tattoo, David noticed for the first time; a cross-in-circle on his right buttock.

"What does that signify?" Fionchadd asked, indicating the design on Calvin's butt.

"A sign of my people," Calvin said shortly; apparently he was taking the whole ritual very seriously. "It symbolizes the earth and the four cardinal directions."

"The Sidhe use a similar sign," Fionchadd said. "For the Four Elemental Powers and the Circle of Time that encloses all things."

"Four Elemental Powers," Calvin mused. "Like maybe the Four Councils Sent From Above in some of our legends."

"Maybe," Oisin said. "But this is a time for silence." He stared at them, then; and David could almost see them reflected in his silver eyes. "Four fine men, indeed," he murmured finally, nodding his approval. "And four finer men there never were to undertake such a quest. Now come!"

He ushered them through the door on the mountain-facing side. Cold air hit them, and they shivered. David wrapped his arms around himself. Calvin, ahead of him, was rubbing his ribs. At least the barn and the honeysuckle overgrowing a convenient fence shielded them from prying eyes.

"That way," Oisin called, pointing with his staff to the banks of a small stream that burbled along a few hundred yards behind Uncle Dale's house.

"The formula I will use is properly for reciting before ritual ball play," Oisin said, when they had halted by the banks. "But I think it will be fitting here, for you do not know what sort of enemies you may find, and whatever efforts we can make to thwart them would be well." He turned his face toward the rising sun and began to chant, his voice high and clear in the frosty air:

Sge! Ha-nagwa asti unega aksauntanu usinuli anetsa un-atsanuntselahi aktati adunniga.

The chant droned on for quite a while, but when it started around again Oisin turned south toward the boys, reached to the silver leather pouch that hung from his belt, and drew out a stick of some red material with which he marked each of them on cheek and nose, chin and brow. When he came to Calvin, the Indian boy stopped his hand, then stuck two fingers into his medicine bag and withdrew a sealed plastic bag from which he shook a similar stick, then placed it in Oisin's hand.

Oisin nodded and marked Calvin like the others before continuing with the third round, in which he faced west, and the fourth in which he spoke to the north.

He started over then, but this time, at a sign from him, the boys trooped into the water. It was not deep enough to truly cover them, but was sufficiently cold that it scarcely mattered. Still, they forced themselves to remain there through another complete fourfold repetition of the formula. By the time they emerged David's teeth were chattering. Alec was hopping from foot to foot.

"I have asked the aid of the Wardens of the Seven Heavens," Oisin told them. "You are now fit to enter the *asi*."

"'Bout bloody time," Alec muttered, as Oisin directed them back toward the small building.

Once they had returned to the farmyard, Oisin turned his empty gaze skyward. David saw the sun light his face with a ruddiness that was not usually present. And he saw the cracks, the seams and fissures of age beyond that given by rights to men—but saw too the hardness of the muscles, the strength of the bones beneath it.

"Oh, yes, I almost forgot," Oisin said. "There is one thing I would give you, David Sullivan." He reached into his robe and pulled out a pouch.

David weighed it in his hand. It felt heavy, as if it contained a rock. He curved his fingers around it and was pretty certain it held only one object. Quickly he loosened the drawstring, tipped the contents onto his hand—and gasped.

A tooth gleamed there—or at any rate it was shaped like one of the fossil shark teeth he had seen on display at the state capital, the kind they were always digging out of the sand pits in south Georgia—only this was larger than any he had seen. Three-cornered it was, with one point longer than the others and sharp along its sides. This point was milkily transparent with maybe a hint of red to it; whereas the other two were almost the color of rubies.

"Neat!" David cried. "What is it?"

Oisin shook his head. "It is a scale of the great *uktena* serpent that lives in Galunlati. My acquaintance there gave it to me upon parting. I do not know if it will serve you, or how; but he who gave it to me told me that it had much Power in that other World. Perhaps it does. Certainly it has none in the lands of the Sidhe, that I have found. As for Man's World, who can say? But bear it with you. At the very least, perhaps it will be a comfort."

David replaced the scale and knotted the long draw-strings around his neck.

"The moment comes," Oisin began. "Closer, closer, NOW! The asi awaits you!"

He wrenched the door open and stood aside as the boys stepped into the sweat lodge, then joined them and shut the door behind.

David gasped, already uncomfortably aware of stifling heat, though he supposed it was logical, considering why they were there. He looked around apprehensively. Once a smokehouse for tobacco when an ancestor had briefly toyed with that crop, and more lately used to cure the whole hogs that Uncle Dale had butchered every fall until Aunt Hattie died, the building had been abandoned in recent years. It was small, no more than three yards square and eight feet to the peak of its tin roof. No windows lit its gray board walls, and there was but a single door. The last time David had been inside, there had been shelves at two-foot intervals around the sides, and hams and shoulders and sides of bacon hanging by hooks from the rafters. That had been years ago, though; and things had obviously changed radically lately.

It was clean, for one thing: the red clay floor was spotless, and bare except for an ancient iron washpot toward the rear, and, in the exact center, a large pile of smooth stones. The shelves that had once filled the other three sides from floor to ceiling had now been removed except for the bottom range, which was just high enough to be used as a low bench around the perimeter. Their packs were there, along with their staffs and Fionchadd's bow; evidently Uncle Dale had been in charge of storing them. In spite of the hour, it was already uncomfortably hot, and a skyward glance showed him the source of the faint light that pervaded the building.

"It is the sun on the metal roof that does it," Oisin explained, apparently sensing his thoughts, "that, and another thing." He pointed upward, and David saw a basketball-size opening in the tin beside the ridgepole. Something sparked and glittered there, and David at last made out that it was a crystal.

"As the sun arcs the sky, the cystal will follow it and focus its heat onto the stones. When they grow red, you are to quench them in the tub of water you see yonder. Steam will rise, and with it heat. As soon as the steam begins to thin, remove the stones and return them to where I have placed them; the crystal will then reheat them."

"But what if we run out of steam before something happens?" David wondered.

"You will not."

"What about if *we* run out of steam," Alec muttered.

Oisin smiled sympathetically. "Unfortunately, you have eaten your last until the quest begins."

Alec's face fell.

"Ah, but I said nothing of *drink*." Oisin reached to his waist and withdrew a gray leather wineskin. David could hear its contents sloshing gently.

Alec's face brightened, but Oisin frowned. "No, boy, not yet, this too has a proper place in the ritual. First I must instruct you." He paused for effect before addressing them again.

"Hear my words, then: From now on you may not speak except to offer these prayers which I have written for you." He handed them sheets of vellum on which were words in a strange language. "Henceforth you follow the time and pattern of the ritual. As soon as the stones redden, you will place them in the cauldron. At this time David will read the first prayer. When the steam has settled, you will rise and flog each other with these." He reached into the corner by the door and brought out four bunches of willow withies bound together with rawhide. David groaned, remembering all too well the similar switches his mother had laid across his bare legs when he was younger. "Ten blows each, and each flogs another. There must be pain but not blood. The intention is partly to make you sweat even more, partly to free your spirit by forcing you to concentrate on your body, not your mind.

"Then must come the second prayer, which Fionchadd should read, and then you must sit silent and wait until the stones are red again, which will not be long, and then once more raise a steam. Once it too has passed and the stones have been set to reheat, Alec must read the third prayer, and you may each have one sip of this cordial." He handed Alec the skin, then paused and looked at Calvin. "It is the juice of a fruit that grows in Faerie, my young friend, not the wine you seem to dread."

At a nod from the Indian, Oisin continued. "When the stones glow red a fourth time, raise another steam and lay these upon them, while you, Calvin, read the final prayer." He passed Calvin a leather pouch. "It contains certain herbs; some to clear your vision, some to clear your way. Breathe deeply of their vapors, and when they have burned to ash, raise steam again, and repeat the ritual until a sign comes to you. Usually it will be an animal. You will know when that happens."

He turned and faced the fire pit. A single cone of sunlight shone there, focused on the mound of rocks in the center, which were already glowing red. Oisin took a wooden scoop from beside them and in quick succession dunked them in the washpot. They were immediately engulfed by steam.

"Begin the first prayer now," he cried, as he backed

through the door, and David did. It was the same formula, he realized, as before:

Sge! Ha-nagwa asti unega aksauntanu usinuli anetsa un-atsanuntselahi aktati adunniga.

Somewhere outside a low drumming started.
And so, inside, did the waiting.

Chapter XV: Tsistu

(the asi—no time)

Another hiss of hot stones into cold water, and the air in the asi grew even thicker.

David did not know how long he had been waiting, only that he was insanely tired of it. All he could be certain of now was that he was hot—hotter than he'd ever been. For the moment he simply slumped there, shoulders against the unplaned board wall and bare heels mired in red clay that was fast becoming mud as feet and steam worked their way on it. His body was sheened with sweat; he could feel it dripping out of his sodden hair and onto his forehead whence it slithered into his eyes, or sliding down his arms, or across his chest, or into the cleft of buttocks that were sore from sitting on splintery boards. All in all he was completely miserable.

The ritual must be working, though: because he was certainly becoming aware of a gradual altering of perception as reality shifted away from him. Every time he stood, he became dizzy; every breath was a battle with the hot, thick air. He was half dazed, and only a tiny part of him knew when it was time to ladle on more water, or drop more of the strange-smelling herbs on the hot stones, or read his particular prayer—except that he had long since stopped reading because he had it memorized.

Around him he could vaguely make out his companions. Alec on the bench beside him, leaning against the opposite corner post because they could not stand the notion of even accidental contact in a room that was already flooded with heat. Calvin to his left sitting stoically with his legs crossed and his hands folded in his lap, and Fionchadd simply sprawled as if at leisure opposite him. But even the Faery's face was now ruddy with heat and his hair hung in long, limp tendrils.

Alec sighed and began a mumbled repeat of his part of the invocation. David could have made out the words had he tried, but he shut them out because he had heard them a hundred times already, them and the incessant drumming that had begun to sound gently outside the moment Oisin had closed the door. He was not aware when the prayer ended.

Time passed; the building grew hotter.

Fionchadd rose and immersed the rocks again. He read his part, then they all stood and flicked each other with the willow switches for what seemed the thousandth time. There was no force behind their blows, though; and they stung but little.

The worst thing was the silence. Misery loved company, yet company was denied in that place. They could only stare at each other, groan, roll their eyes, and make simple signs of impatience or exasperation. Speech itself was forbidden.

Hotter and hotter, and the steam grew thicker yet.

David felt himself slipping away. He was getting sleepy, and golly but it was nice. It was great to have somewhere to retreat to, a place to go beyond the ever-increasing creep of heat across his body that was rapidly edging toward pain. He closed his eyes, dreamed.

There was a bear in that dream: a great white bear, ambling down a mountainside that looked familiar yet was not, as if the rocks and hills were the same as some he knew, but the trees were older and stronger and had never known the touch of an ax. *I come,* the white bear was muttering. *I come, I come, I come.*

Water hissed once more, and Calvin's chant followed.

David returned to the dream. The bear was still there, and likewise its chant: *I come, I come, I come.* Only there was another chant with it, lighter and mocking: *Too slow, Yanu Tsunega; too slow, Yanu Tsunega; too slow-o-o-o-o.*

A sudden draft of coolness coiled around his left ankle.

David jerked himself awake, thinking someone had opened the door. But no, from what he could see in the red-gray gloom it was still closed. His friends had evidently noticed it too, though, because they were every one sitting bolt upright. Fionchadd's eyes flashed green fire and Calvin rose to his feet. Alec started to follow, but David restrained him.

A noise, then, like something clawing the rough boards at the door. Something was trying to get in.

Another twitch of breeze found them, and with it the noise, ever more furiously, and then abruptly the scrabbling sounds stopped, though the draft grew stronger yet.

David strained his vision harder, gazing toward the light by the door—and saw, even as he heard Calvin's gasp, that they now shared the asi with a rabbit.

But it was no ordinary rabbit. It was larger than any David had even seen—easily eighteen inches at the shoulder. And its color . . . well, it was hard to tell in the uncertain light, but he thought it was brown. No, wait, it was white—no, gray. David rubbed its eyes. It was shifting colors, that's what it was doing. And its size wouldn't remain constant either.

When it hopped up to Calvin, it was the size of an average north Georgia cottontail; when it inspected Fionchadd, it seemed the size of a rat. But when it came up to where he sat beside Alec in the back, it was larger than it had been before—and perfectly black. Abruptly it rose up on its hind legs, set its forepaws on the board between him and Alec, and twisted its head sideways. Its eyes were red—and intelligent.

Yet David knew this was no animal of Faerie. He tried to will the Sight, tried with all his might—and failed.

"You will not see me that way," the rabbit said. "Nor ever see me in any form but this, though sometimes I like to change one thing or another. But rabbit I was born and rabbit I will ever be. I am *Tsistu*. I am to be your guide."

David stared at it keenly, more than a little unnerved. He had met talking animals before, but they had always been the Sidhe shapeshifted. This was not, yet it had spoken—or had it? Were those words he had heard, or thoughts?

The rabbit peered at him guilelessly, but David thought he saw a wicked flicker in its ruby eyes before they suddenly changed to brown.

David wondered if he dared reply, or if the ban on speech still held. They were supposed to await their guide, and this certainly seemed to be him. He exchanged glances with Calvin who shrugged helplessly.

"You may speak," Tsistu said, and there was a hint of mockery in his voice. "Though I would prefer you spoke very little, your kind can be so wearisome with it. Chatter-chatter-chatter, all day long."

"Would you rather we were so quiet we could hunt you?" Fionchadd asked unexpectedly.

"Would you rather *I* left you right now, and your quest undone?"

"No!" David cried. "But is it true? Did you really come in answer to our summons?"

"Of course not," Tsistu snorted. "I *always* come into the Lying World to be barked at by dogs, pecked by chickens, and stared at by idiot boys." He paused, looking contemptuously at David.

David, for his part, had seen that the movements of the rabbit's nose and mouth did not match either the sounds he thought he heard or the meanings that appeared in his head. He was gaping foolishly.

Tsistu snorted again, this time in what could only be

exasperation. "Of *course* I came to guide you! Your chants were echoing in Galunlati so loud I had no choice, if I would ever sleep again."

Calvin eyed him narrowly. "But I was dreaming of a bear."

"Me too," David confessed.

"So was I," Alec and Fionchadd acknowledged as one.

"Ah yes, a bear," said Tsistu, letting an ear droop ever so slightly. "Truly it *was* he you summoned, for it was he who woke me complaining of your noise, and sent me on ahead to see what you wanted. He is slow, you see; Yanu Tsunega is; and I much faster. I am to fetch you to him."

"You know our errand then?" Fionchadd asked.

"Of course I know: you would have me guide you to Galunlati."

"Well, I'm glad that's settled," Alec muttered.

The rabbit jerked its head toward him. "I heard that! I hear all. Mine are the finest ears in all of Galunlati, or the Lying World either. I can hear the clouds move or a shadow fall; I can hear the snap of the fires of your curious sun and the laughter of comets in the empty spaces."

"Can you hear our thoughts, I wonder," Fionchadd mused.

"I could if I chose," said Tsistu. "Though yours might be difficult, because your skull is so thick and your wits so dim. A shame in one with ears so nicely pointed."

Fionchadd glared at him.

Tsistu hopped toward the door. "Enough of chatter. Shall we be traveling?"

Calvin eyed David intently. Fionchadd saw that stare and appended one of his own. "I don't know, Lord Rabbit," the Faery said at last. "We have all dreamed of a bear, yet there is no bear, only a common hare. I have an ill feeling about this. I am not at all certain I trust you."

"You are a hunter," the rabbit replied calmly, though his eyes—blue now—had narrowed. "I smell the blood of many of my kin upon you, yet I came—and it is not a particularly pleasant journey. Would I have done so had I not been compelled?"

Fionchadd lifted an eyebrow. "I do not know. Would you?"

"Would you be happier if I swore that what I tell you is true?"

"And what would you swear on?" asked Fionchadd, and David knew his alert and devious mind was at work.

"On whatever pleases you."

"Would you swear on your life? Would you swear that what you say is fact; that you might drop dead should you be lying?"

"Gladly I will swear it."

"Finny, I—" Calvin began.

The Faery silenced him with a glare. "Oaths are a powerful thing among my people, red-one. Be sure I will listen clearly."

"Finny—"

"Silence! I will hear this one's oath." He gazed at the rabbit expectantly.

"Very well," Tsistu replied, sparing a wary glance at Calvin, who in turn eyed both him and the Faery with ill-concealed suspicion.

"The oath," Fionchadd prompted.

"Ah, yes. Well, since you insist." And with that the rabbit sat back on his haunches and drew himself up to his full height—presently three feet. "I, Tsistu, Lord of Rabbitkind in Galunlati and The World Beneath, and the Seven Levels of the Lying World, do swear that all I have said is true; that I have come in answer to a summons wrought by those here present and with the knowledge of Yanu Tsunega, the white bear who is their proper totem but too slow to meet them before the road to Galunlati passes. I likewise swear that should anything I say or have said prove false my life is forfeit, and may I fall down dead on the spot and be prey to worms and serpents."

Silence filled the asi.

"Was *that* sufficient?" asked Tsistu with more than a touch of sarcasm.

Fionchadd inclined his head. "No more may I demand. I will follow you."

David started toward the door, then hesitated and glanced down at his steam-slick nakedness. "Uh, what about our clothes?"

"Yeah," Alec said. "And our gear. Can we take our gear?"

"Take whatever you are willing to carry, though what *you* have is too much by far. Food and shelter will not concern you, though you might take what medicine things seem good to you. As for dress . . . my own skin does not shame me, and neither should yours, yet I understand you Pale-men are strange about such matters. But whatever you do, do it quickly!"

David breathed a sigh of relief and joined his friends in frantic dressing. A moment later he was ready, clad in jeans, Enotah County 'Possums T-shirt, and his worn hiking boots, with a denim jacket just in case. The medicine pouch he put in one of the pockets, then fished Morwyn's ring out of another and put it on. Finally he hoisted his khaki backpack onto his shoulders and grasped his runestaff, even as Alec took up its twin. Their eyes met. "Ready to travel, Fool of a Scotsman?"

"Ready as I'll ever be," Alec replied, slapping an arm around David's waist. "Come on, oh Mad One, let's boogie."

Calvin had also finished dressing: jeans, plain white T-shirt, hiking boots that were even more formidable than David's, his beaded sweatband—and a hunting knife David had not noticed before that now hung at his side in a beaded leather sheath.

For his part, Fionchadd wore loose gray trousers that were probably wool and a sleeveless, gray-and-green checked tunic cinched at his narrow waist by a belt of square gold links. He carried his bow, and on his back was a quiver full of pure white arrows. The dagger Morwyn had given him to direct *Waverider* was clipped inside the waistband of his trousers. His shoes were of pierced and gathered leather. The gold-and-jeweled torque encircled his neck.

Tsistu surveyed them critically, uttered a sort of half hiss of disgust, and hopped toward the door. It swung open at his approach, and David looked out into fog.

It was the densest he had ever seen, denser by far than the heavy steam in the asi—so dense that he could hardly breathe. He had not gone ten steps into its welcomed coolness before he knew he was not on the farm. Though he could not see his feet, he could feel that instead of the hard, dry earth of Uncle Dale's backyard, he now trod upon the sponginess of uncut grass. And the wind was strange, for it carried the rustle of leaves and the distant twitter of birds, not the rattle of roof tin and chicken squawks of his great-uncle's homestead.

He could see nothing beyond the swirling mist, except, when he glanced skyward, a vague yellowing that might be the sun; and at knee-level before him, a flash of white that was Tsistu's tail. Not daring to speak, he followed; felt the ground start to rise, and increased his pace as Tsistu increased his own, covering the unseen ground in great leaps and bounds.

"Hurry, hurry, Pale-men," Tsistu called back, though his pace never slackened. "Hurry, hurry, Slow-ones."

And David hurried as fast as he could—which was barely enough, because Tsistu's tail was vanishing, slipping so far ahead in the fog that he could only now and then glimpse it. Were it not for the muffled sound of the rabbit's tread, the constant taunts, he would surely have become lost.

"Slow-ones, Slow-ones, Slow-ones. Hurry, hurry, hurry. The sun soon melts the fog, and we will be stranded here in the Borderlands."

And David blundered on for what felt like hours, dimly aware of his friends panting along behind him. The world had narrowed to a flash of white tail before him, and to the pain that had quickly made its presence known in his side.

Other aches eventually joined it: in legs that were not used to constant running uphill, in lungs that were already tortured.

And still Tsistu led them onward.

"Faster, faster, faster. We will be lost, and all because of Slow-ones!"

David redoubled his efforts; ran as fast as he ever had, saving only that one terrible time he had blundered onto a Straight Track and been pursued by a then-far-more-threatening Fionchadd. And as if in answer the Faery's voice arrowed up from behind: "He sets a fearful pace indeed, my mortal friend; one that even I find hard pressed to maintain in the heavy substance of this World's body. I begin to appreciate the effort you made when first you eluded me."

"Yeah," David panted, "ain't it grand?"

"Faster, Pale-men; faster, Pale-men; faster. We are almost to the border."

David reached inside himself and found one last ounce of strength. He urged his body onward, trusting to his feet to find the path.

Tsistu's tail grew clearer. "Soon, now; soon, now; soon . . ."

Faster, for one more moment . . .

Abruptly David found himself enfolded by a cold that clamped around his heart and squeezed.

—and was gone. Before him Tsistu sat calmly, licking his front paws. Around him his friends sank down as one, even Fionchadd. David threw himself on the ground, and it was a moment before he could even open his eyes.

When he did, he saw that the fog still surrounded them —but there were shapes in it now: the pale outlines of bare trees that twined delicate limbs and empty branches among the drifting swirls. Light showed beyond them, unsourced but distinctly yellow. The only sound was the heavy pant of their breathing.

Tsistu hopped up to him and nudged him with a paw. "A pleasant morning's run, was it not? I do ten times as much and twice as fast each evening. Sometimes I race sounds for the joy of it."

David was too tired to even think.

"Rise now," said Tsistu after a moment, "for we are yet in the Borderlands. A fair way further we must travel."

David sighed and levered himself up with his staff. Tsistu hopped away to the right, and David saw a path there, a clearer place in the fog. He followed the rabbit—now gray-striped and the size of Darrell's worn-out sheltie, Scooter—onto it.

They had not traveled long—still at a steady jog—before the fog finally began to dissipate and the landscape to clarify. It was not much different from what David was accustomed to—except, he somehow knew, these tall, thick trees had never known the touch of man's metal, nor would. They had leaves now, though the small ones of early spring, but very soon those leaves became fuller and took on the darker shades of summer. A short while later they halted beside a river where water flashed among dark rocks jagged as tigers' teeth while steep banks loomed around it. Tsistu hopped calmly in and looked up at them from a point where the froth was just beginning.

"This is your path," the rabbit said. "You must follow me."

Calvin eyed the water skeptically, and Alec, if possible, even more so. "Just what I needed: cold feet to go with a blistered heinie."

David rolled his eyes in agreement. "Tell me about it! Fire and ice for certain."

Tsistu's right ear drooped quizzically. "Is something *wrong*?"

"We can't cross that!" David groaned.

Tsistu stared at him in obvious disgust. "You of all people should know not to trust your eyes. This is not water, it is the road to Galunlati."

David exchanged troubled glances with his friends. Fionchadd started forward nonchalantly, but David steeled himself as the Faery came abreast, so that they entered the river at the same time.

—and found themselves on a broad strip of soft grass that ran straight as an arrow in either direction.

"This has the feel of a Track," Fionchadd said, "yet it is unlike any I have encountered."

"Tell me about it," David replied, then motioned for his friends ashore to follow. "Come on, guys; it's an illusion."

Alec looked at Calvin, and Calvin at Alec, and together they joined David and Fionchadd.

Tsistu wrinkled his pink nose disdainfully and hopped onward.

They jogged on for a while, along the flat grassy trail. Forest flanked them on either side, but mist hung thick among the branches, and David could not make out what kind of trees they were, save that they were hardwoods.

Finally, just as David was beginning to think he could truly go no further, they stopped on the bank of a second river. A few yards to their left a tree-tall waterfall thundered into a pool of swirling black water before exploding over rocks taller than any of the boys and breaking into fast-moving channels.

Tsistu halted at its edge and hopped aside for them to enter.

"We can't go into that," Alec cried. "It'd carry us off in a second."

"Again, you rely on untrustworthy eyesight," Tsistu told them. "But it is to your souls you must harken, not my words."

"Doubtful, those," Fionchadd muttered.

"I heard that," Tsistu said. "Have I led you wrong so far?"

"Have we come to Galunlati?" Fionchadd retorted.

"We are very near. It lies beyond the falling water."

David looked at Alec and grimaced. "No choice, as best I can figure."

Calvin caught him by the arm and held him back. "I'll go first this time."

David stepped aside and let him. Calvin extended a foot tentatively, then squared his shoulders and put his full weight forward—and immediately slipped in over his head.

David stood horrified for a moment, then flung down his staff and leapt after, determined to do what he could.

But it was not water that met him. Instead he found himself standing in a field of thin, silky grasses that towered far above his head. A noise to his back was Fionchadd, and then a white-faced Alec joined them. He returned David's staff.

"Hurry, hurry, hurry, only one more ten-hops."

David sighed, and once more followed Tsistu through the grass. And then, abruptly, it parted, and he found himself gasping.

For the vista ahead quite literally took his breath. He had been to Faerie, of course, had seen its strange trees, impossibly tall; its peculiar beasts; something of its fair, distant people. That land held a hard, brittle brightness, a sort of glitter one could never truly rely on. But there was a subtle undercurrent of decay as well, of trees so extravagantly whorled they fell to pieces, of mosaics so finely made their designs produced not joy or wonder but confusion, of too *much* intricacy—in a word, of Power applied far and wide to warp the land to some secret master-image whose pattern was the interlacing spiral.

Here was none of that: here was nature itself: trees taller even than the giants of Faerie, some of them; and greener by far beneath a sky more blue. David glanced up, and saw the sun: white-yellow. There was absolute clarity here, absolute brightness, but without the hard edge of Faerie. Nature without the touch of mind at all. The air was also hotter.

Alec eventually commented on that.

"The sun is closer here," Tsistu told them over his shoulder. "And yet seven times it was moved before the men of this place could stand it."

None of them were inclined to respond, and they pressed on a way, through trees David could finally recognize: cedar and pine, spruce, holly, and laurel. But as he trotted by them, he felt a strange prickling on the back of his neck, as if someone was watching. Calvin saw his goose bumps, his furtive sideways glances. "I feel it too," he whispered. "But I reckon I oughta."

"How so?"

"Well," Calvin began, "according to my grandfather, when the plants and animals were first made they were supposed to stay awake for seven nights like we should have done; but to make a long story short, none of 'em made it except the owl and the panther and a couple more of the animals—the ones that can see in the dark, basically—and the evergreen plants. They were rewarded by being made strong medicine, and by not losing their leaves in the winter. They alone are still awake and watchful."

"Cute story," Alec said. "But not logical."

Calvin's face darkened. "Who's to say what logic is here?"

Alec's mouth popped open. "Yeah, right. I guess I should be more open-minded—I mean considering what I've already seen, and all."

Calvin only grunted.

They walked on a good while longer, only pausing when they passed from the forest at the edge of a large meadow. Broom sedge grew there, golden in the sun, and Tsistu paused at the first of it, gazing about warily, nose and ears a-twitch. David suddenly realized their guide had grown smaller, that his coat was now the same brown-ticked tan as the waving stems. He looked, in short, like an ordinary bunny.

"Something wrong?" David ventured, as Tsistu continued reconnoitering.

"Nothing is *ever* wrong with Tsistu," the rabbit replied haughtily, training a brown eye skyward. "I am bravest of the brave."

And with that he hopped into the field.

David started to follow, but had not taken two steps when a vast shadow darkened a wide swath of the meadow. David looked up, startled, even as he heard Alec shriek and saw from the corner of his eye Fionchadd bring his bow to bear.

"No!" Calvin hissed as he slammed into the Faery and flung him headlong to the ground, just as Alec likewise pushed David down. David rolled onto his side, but the shadow passed over again, and he raised himself cautiously to look.

It was an eagle, circling the meadow in a calm, lazy glide—and that eagle was black as polished coal. David's heart skipped a beat, for Ailill had once worn that shape, and had almost killed him while in it. Except—except now he looked at it, the eagle had a white head, like your regular red-blooded American bald . . . or . . . or wasn't there maybe a trace of gold among its feathers? He couldn't tell. The shadow touched him once more, then; and chills ran over him. David closed his eyes, expecting to feel talons in his back at any moment. Only the eagle seemed to be ignoring them, seemed to be searching for something closer to the meadow's heart. David shrugged Alec aside and rose to a cautious crouch, scanned the horizon, saw the shadow ripple across the grass, and a disturbance beneath it.

Abruptly the eagle folded its wings and dived, plummeting earthward more quickly than David's eyes could follow. It struck the sedge hard—David could hear the thunk, the rustle of displaced foliage. And then another, more troubling sound reached his ears: a long animal shriek full of terror and pain and anguish.

"Tsistu!" David screamed, leaping to his feet and rushing forward.

But it was already too late. The eagle rose in a series of awkward flaps, then caught an updraft and rode it into clearer air. From its claws a limp body hung. Higher it rose, and faster.

Fionchadd leapt up and once more drew his bow, only this time he got off an arrow.

Quickly it flew, and sure, and buried itself in the eagle's breast. With a single indignant squawk the bird folded upon itself and fell.

"You fool!" Calvin yelled at him. "You bloody, quickass, *idiot!*"

"What . . ." Fionchadd began, anger flashing in his eyes.

"The eagle is—"

"Help me!" a weak voice called: Tsistu.

Somehow they were there, standing in a shaky circle around the scene of carnage. The eagle was dead; of that, at least, there was no doubt, for Fionchadd's arrow had pierced its heart. Tsistu too lay still, but as Calvin knelt

beside him and laid a hand against his bloodstained fur, the
rabbit shuddered, then burst out in laughter that brought a
torrent of red from its mouth. "Awahili has slain me," he
said, chuckling, "and a thousand thousand times it has
done so; yet as long as my blood is spilled upon the land I
live again. You, however, have slain Awahili, and for that
your single lives are forfeit."

"What?" David cried. "Blast you! You've tricked us."

"But that is what I do!" Tsistu replied, still giggling.
"And a fine one it is, I must say!"

"I tried to tell you," Calvin spat, glaring at Fionchadd.
"It's taboo to kill an eagle."

"You should have said something earlier!"

The Indian grabbed the Faery's arm and jerked him
around to face him. "I *also* tried to tell you not to trust
him!"

Fionchadd knocked the hand roughly aside and turned
his gaze back on Tsistu. "You swore an *oath!*"

"On my life—and of lives I have very many, a thing
you, hunter-boy, should understand."

"Yet you swore."

"And I tricked."

"But what of the bear? That was no illusion."

"Oh, he is still coming somewhere, I have no doubt.
But I came sooner."

"I doubt it," Calvin snorted.

"You may doubt as you please, but the truth is—and
here I honestly tell it—that I was being pursued by Awahili
here: an ancient thing between us, a contest of wills and
wits that has no end. But then I heard your call and felt the
way between the lands slide open so that I could come to
you, and along the way I thought what an excellent trick it
would be to bring you back here and have you slay my
ancient rival, for—truth again—too often he has victory
over me. You were not the only ones fooled." Tsistu
laughed once more, and then his eyes glazed over. In death
he appeared no more than a common cottontail.

A rumble of thunder sounded in the distance, and a drift
of breeze slid over their skin.

David shuddered, then stood and eyed Fionchadd angrily. "Real cool, Finno. All we needed was for you to start shootin' up the wildlife."

"It is as the rabbit said," the Faery replied calmly. "I am a hunter, it is what I do. Besides, you yourself felt threatened. We all did. It could have been any of us dangling from that bird's talons."

"He's got a point there," Calvin noted. "But twenty-twenty hindsight's not real useful."

"What about foresight, then?" Alec said, as thunder rumbled again, nearer. "What do we do now that Finn's lost us our guide?"

"Yeah, and what was that about our lives being forfeit for killing an eagle? I mean, who's gonna enforce it?"

Calvin started to reply, but was drowned out by a third thunderclap, this one very close indeed, though the sky was still clear. Abruptly the Indian grabbed David's arm. "I think, my friend, we may be about to get a better answer than I could ever give you."

David twisted around, and saw two archers advancing from under the eaves of the forest. He stood stock still, knowing they had nowhere to go—not and outrun an arrow.

"People," Fionchadd hissed, and raised his own bow. Calvin reached for his hunting knife.

"Are you guys crazy?" David cried. "We've already got ourselves in deep shit from one piece of stupid violence. How 'bout we try to act civil for a change?"

"Tsistu was acting civil," Calvin began, but David shushed him.

The figures came nearer, two very tall women—as tall as the Sidhe, but more muscular. They were dressed in fringed white leather: knee-length skirts and ankle boots, all elaborately beaded in red. Nothing above the waist, though—save their own bare round breasts, which bobbed enticingly. Their ornaments were gold of a particularly ruddy shade, and their skin was white, almost as ice, though it seemed to hold an inner glow that was more like the hottest flames. Their knee-long hair was blacker than any David had ever seen, and seemed to crackle and pop in the suddenly dry air; their eyes were gray and glittering. They would have been beautiful, he thought, as not even the Sidhe were beautiful, had they not also sported tattoos in the shape of serpents that coiled their tails round those breasts, slithered up those smooth-skinned necks and bracketed those perfect mouths with their painted maws. Yet in spite of that, in spite of his own mistrust, David found his groin tightening; he had not, after all, seen that many bare-breasted women. He could not help himself, his eyes darted back and forth: from breasts to face and back, over and over. Not until it was too late did he find that he could not move a muscle.

"Oh, sh—!" David heard Calvin start, then fall silent.

Jesus, oh Jesus, oh Jesus was David's own litany of despair—but the women were upon him, binding his hands firmly before him with cords of the same soft leather as their clothing. Through the corner of his eye David could barely make out his companions in like circumstances. When the women had finished and Fionchadd had been relieved of his bow, he and Alec of their runestaves, and Calvin of his knife, the taller woman came and stood before them. A muttered word, a subtle hand motion, and David felt the paralysis slide from his head and arms, though his feet were still heavy as lead.

"Well done, sister," the tall woman said, flicking a glance briefly sideways. The movements of her mouth made the serpent tattoos look hungrily alive. "And well it was these strangers raised not their weapons, nor tried to flee, for then truly would our vengeance have been mighty!"

"Vengeance?" David croaked hopelessly, finding he could speak again, and wondering distantly if what he had just heard was really English. Whatever it was, it was different from Tsistu's speech.

"Vengeance!" the woman spat. "Know you not that it is taboo to kill Awahili? Even the foolish know as much, even the men of your land, once, and your kind best of all." This last she addressed to Calvin, who nodded grimly.

"But—" David began.

"Silence!" the woman whispered, though she might as well have screamed.

David was desperate now. He had to do something, had to. He focused on his legs, directed all his will on the paralysis there, felt it lessen minutely—and stumbled forward and fell.

The second woman kicked him hard, then jerked him roughly up by the bound wrists. "You will be first, little Pale-man. You will be first to—" She halted abruptly, staring at David's hand. David looked too, and realized they were gazing at the dragon ring. Abruptly the woman drew back, but her sister stepped forward and likewise examined his hand.

"Death may be their fate," she sighed, "but it is not for us to deliver."

David could only gape, not daring to hope.

"You bear the sign of the great uktena," the woman told him simply, the serpents bracing her lips gaping wide. "You must pass before our brother for judgment. Now come, for it is far and far we must travel."

Chapter XVI: Where-It-Made-a-Noise-as-of-Thunder

(Galunlati—day one—afternoon)

David never knew how long that forced march lasted, only that by the time it was over he would have welcomed anything short of a long painful death (a quick one was another matter) to bring it to an ending.

All morning they walked (he assumed it was morning by the slow ascent of the sun); and they were still trudging along far into the afternoon, always through mountainous woods. The scenery was magnificent; very like David's own north Georgia stomping grounds must have been after the last glaciation—before men came with slash-and-burn, the primal hardwoods gave way to fast-growing pines, and the gentle slopes had their innards exposed by developmental highways and their topknots crowned by Atlantans' condos.

Plant life was everywhere: trees and bushes and herbs with a thousand shapes and flowers of two thousand colors, all of it lush and healthy, and much of it of species none of them could immediately name. Most of it afforded them no problem, though every time the laurel or cedar grew thickly David felt that strange sensation of being watched.

Birds were omnipresent, too: jays and cardinals and mockingbirds and others David did not know, all crying out in tones that stopped just short of language. More than once David caught sight of Fionchadd cocking his head and looking thoughtful, and wondered if the Faery might hear more than mortal ears could discern.

Their captors, who had neither offered names nor demanded them, had loosened their bonds for a promise of good conduct, though David wondered why they had even bothered in the first place, since they obviously had the power of freezing men where they stood.

And powerful too was the white glare of sunlight that was both brighter and far, far hotter than the dry Georgia August they had abandoned. The women still had their staves, Calvin's knife, and Fionchadd's bow, but the boys had shed their shirts early on and now marched along with their packs slung across rapidly reddening shoulders. The greatest discomfort, though, came from the terrain itself: mile on mile of ever-steepening ascents followed by equally precipitous slopes that at times had them nigh onto sliding.

Eventually, though, the shadows began to lengthen and the landscape to grow even more rugged as the inclines grew sharper still and rocks began to thrust up among the trees. David became aware of an ever-increasing dull rumbling—half sound, half vibration—that buzzed in his ears and thrummed up through his feet to set his heart a-racing to some distant, subtle rhythm.

"Ahyuntikwalastihu," Calvin muttered behind him.

"Didn't know you spoke the lingo," David whispered back.

"I don't much, just a word here and there. I—"

"Silence," the taller woman hissed, and shoved him.

But still the sound grew louder.

It was almost exactly at sunset that their captors finally pushed through a high screen of laurel and brought them to a halt.

They stood on the edge of a vast canyon carved in the

hard rock of the mountains by the ribbon of river they saw far below. Mist rose from the left-hand side, where a cataract poured from some invisible crag into an unseen pool. The thunder of water was deafening—and was echoed, David realized suddenly, by a similar rumbling from above. He glanced up and saw the clear sky beyond the trees to their left suddenly obscured by fast-racing clouds rolling in from the north.

"Tallulah!" Calvin exclaimed. "I'll be damned if this isn't Tallulah Gorge!"

"It can't be!" David whispered. "Not the same one, anyway. Besides, that's miles and miles from where we started, and never mind that we're in another World. We can't have come that far."

"Miles in our World, maybe," was Calvin's cryptic reply.

Alec bent over to rub his thighs. "My legs certainly wouldn't argue."

"It is Hyuntikwalayi," their taller captor said.

The name buzzed in David's ears, definitely not English this time, perhaps because it was a name, yet slowly they rearranged themselves and he found he understood: *Hyuntikwalayi: Where-it-Made-a-Noise-as-of-Thunder*.

"It is not far now," the tall woman told them. "You will follow." She stepped toward the brink and turned abruptly left—apparently down the sheer cliff face. David saw her head bobbing along for a moment and then it was gone. His heart sank.

But when he got to the edge, prodded none too gently by the other woman, he saw a narrow trail gouged out of the sheer cliff face, nor more than two feet wide—but at least it wasn't a bridge. These kinds of heights he could handle—sort of.

The trail skirted along the cliffside for a way, growing ever closer to the waterfall. Soon David felt the first cool spray on his face, and in another instant found himself standing on wet rock not five feet away from the glittering froth. The lead woman motioned him forward and he followed her not under the falls, as he had expected, but around a sharp, almost invisible kink, and behind it. The ledge widened, and there they paused while the tall woman took a stick of dry wood from a stack nearby and, by some means David did not observe, lit it.

"Come," she mouthed above the din of the falls. "We are there."

David dragged himself up from where he'd been leaning against the damp wall and followed her up a short tunnel that grew wider and dryer as it gradually ascended.

A sudden turn of corner plunged them into blackness, save for the torch, but another brought them into the presence of light—an eerie flickering that seemed to come from the stone walls themselves.

They were in a cave, a vast chamber at least a hundred feet to the side and twenty high, studded here and there with clumps of dome-shaped boulders. Various dark openings appeared to lead off it—probably into other caverns. There were no direct signs of habitation, though the place was clean, if musty-smelling, and had a floor of white sand curiously marked with swirls and spirals.

"This is our house, come in," said the woman, and David realized he could hear again: the thunder of waters was reduced to a dull tremble in the rocks. He looked around as his companions crowded in behind, prodded by their shorter captor. His eyes were getting accustomed to the eerie lighting now, and could make out another light source as well: the true light of day streaming through a pair of openings high in the opposite wall. By the ruddiness of that light and the length of the fading shadows, David knew the sun had set.

The shorter woman had not followed them in. "I go to meet our brother," she told them.

"See that you tell him all," her sister replied.

The woman nodded silently and darted out.

David did not know what to expect next, so he simply waited, as poised for action as possible, exchanging nervous glances with his equally wary companions. It was hard though, he told himself wryly, to maintain one's guard when one's feet were reduced to blistered tatters.

Apparently the remaining woman did not fear their escape, because she completely ignored them and marched to the right-hand wall. There she set her hands to either side of her head just above the ears, and with the nonchalance with which an Atlanta matron might perform the same act in a wig shop, lifted off her long hair and hung it on a nearby peg. She turned then, and David started at the alienness of her hairless scalp. Bare breasts or no, bare scalp was an instant turnoff.

"Smooth as a damned pumpkin," Calvin muttered.

The woman's eyes flashed angrily. David could see, as she returned to them, that her head was not shaven but truly bald.

"You may sit for a while," she said brusquely. "Our brother will be home soon."

David could not help heaving a grateful sigh as he sought out a place on the nearest lumpy boulder. But just as his backside grazed the surface, it rose straight into the air and smacked into him.

"Christ!" he yelled as he tumbled forward. Then, "Shit!" as a glance over his shoulder showed him claws protruding from the bottom of that supposed boulder—claws and scaly legs above them, and a little further to the left a viciously beaked head big as his own where tiny red eyes stared balefully at him unwinking.

"Hell of a place to put a turtle!" David grumbled, struggling to his feet.

"You are not sitting," the woman noted with a touch of amusement.

"Not hardly," David snapped. "I . . . I'll stand, if you don't mind."

"You do not *like* our furnishings?"

"I'm . . . I'm used to stuff that's a little less lively's all."

"Please yourself."

"Can we sit on the floor, then?" Calvin ventured.

The woman shrugged and calmly arranged herself on the turtle David had vacated—which as calmly lowered itself and returned to somnolence.

Calvin apparently took the gesture as consent and sank

down on the white sand as far as possible from the nearest "stool." David slipped on his T-shirt and joined him against the cave wall. Alec did likewise; only Fionchadd remained standing.

David glared at him. "Even *you've* gotta be a little bit wasted!"

"Certainly I am. But there are more ways to rest than by sitting."

"Whatever," David grunted, and flopped his head back against the rock, already half asleep. And then he did sleep.

—Until something brushed his right hand, something cold and dry and scaly.

"Shit!" he cried, jerking upright. "What the *hell* was that?"

He glanced around and discovered that his friends were sleeping, even Fionchadd, who apparently dozed where he stood—and then realized, to his horror, that the floor was now crawling with snakes of every size and description and color—rattlers and copperheads prominent among them.

David did not dare move. He was not afraid of snakes, no way, not where he was from. But this many . . . and so many kinds . . . and a bunch of them definitely poisonous . . . and the rest—who could tell? He wondered what one did for snakebite here.

Scales brushed his bare side where his shirt had ridden up, and he held his breath as twin moccasins slid across his belly. A movement on his left showed him one lodging comfortably in the angle between his arm and body. He could not suppress a shudder.

Low laughter made him look up. The bald woman was still there, sitting calmly on her turtle as she played absently with a handsome diamondback as big around as her arms that she was allowing to twist and turn about her upper body until its spade-shaped head was opposite her tattoo-framed lips. The whole effect, David thought distantly, was rather kinky.

Thunder sounded then, and he started in spite of himself, and was only mildly relieved to find himself not full of fangs.

The woman slipped from her—mount or seat, David didn't know which to call them. "Our brother comes," she snapped. "Quick, Pale-man, I do not know how you are awake, but since you are, you must rise to meet him."

More thunder, and louder; and a blast of wind howled into the cavern from the gallery outside.

A man strode into the room—if man he might be called. Certainly he was the tallest man David had ever seen, and his thick chest and slender waist, his long legs and arms were perfectly proportioned—as was obvious from the near nakedness in which he presented himself. A knee-length loin cloth of white leather was his only clothing, though it bore beadwork designs that David supposed were meant to represent thunder and lightning. Twin golden bracelets coiled around each of his brawny arms, one above and one below the elbow, all of them gold and all of them in the form of serpents; and more ornaments of shell and metal and feathers glittered here and there upon him. His hair was as long as the woman's, though caught up in braids that hung to his hips; and his skin was as white as theirs, and held that same disconcerting glow. But what most caught David were his eyes: red, and glittering with fury. It was like glancing through clear air to far-off lightning.

As if feeling David's stare, the man locked gazes with him and returned it measure for measure before turning his face to the women, the shorter having joined her sister. "Who are these strangers that you have brought into my home?"

The tall woman inclined her head. "Strangers they are, in truth. They come from the Lying World. They killed Awahili."

"So I have heard," the man snorted. "Yet they live! Have I not taught you the Law? Begone from my sight! I will deal with them myself!" He reached for his waist, and suddenly a golden dagger glittered in his hand.

"Wait!" cried the woman, who had not moved an inch.

"The fairest one carries a mighty sign upon his finger!"

Her brother glared challenge at her, but reached out and grabbed David's hand, brought it roughly to chest level. He said nothing for a moment, but David could feel his eyes dancing over the ring, tracing the paths of the two intertwined dragons.

"He bears the image of the uktena," the woman ventured.

"That does no more than get him a hearing before I pronounce his doom," the man replied, then looked back at David. "Speak, Pale-man. Have you no tongue? Or"—he glanced at the women—"have my sisters stolen it from you? They are very fair, are they not? Neither of them have husbands."

David swallowed awkwardly and wished his friends would awaken, but they slept on. "No . . . sir," he managed. "I can talk."

"Then do so: why did you slay the eagle?"

"*I* didn't kill it," David protested, and immediately regretted it.

"Then who did?"

"The strange one," the woman inserted. "The one with hair like brass. He has a wondrous bow."

The man frowned at her, then inclined his head toward Fionchadd. "I would see this weapon."

The woman retrieved Fionchadd's bow and handed it to her brother, who studied it intently. "Yes, I have seen one almost this well made, once, in the house of my uncle, Asgaya Gigagei. A gift it was to him from an adawehi of the Nunnehi. Yet this surpasses even that one, for there are ten kinds of wood in it, each with its own medicine. He who made this was very wise in the ways of the spirit world. Truly he must have been an adawehiyu!"

Suddenly his gaze was back on David. "And *you* bear the sign of the uktena, which is very strange, and I feel an even stronger magic about you. Indeed, there must be, else you would not so easily have slipped my sisters' spells."

David's heart sank, but then he remembered the pouch

Oisin had given him. "Uh, could I, like, show you something?"

The man nodded.

David reached into his pocket, pulled out the pouch, and emptied the contents into his hand. The uktena scale glittered there in the half-light, strangely bright.

The man's eyes grew large. "Tell me your story," he said at last.

David took a deep breath and began. He tried to spend as little time as possible on cosmology (mostly because he only barely understood it himself), and devote as much time as possible to Oisin, whom he thought had left at least one favorable impression in this land, though evidently not with this man, who had only heard of him and identified him with the Nunnehi—which, David knew, was the Cherokee term for the Sidhe.

The man stared at him for a long time before he spoke again. "So the Nunnehi would have you seek passage through my land to Nundagunyi, and that is all?"

"If it's your land, then we'd certainly appreciate passage."

The man's brow wrinkled. "You flee war, yet you may bring war even to Galunlati—though I doubt such is your intent. I like not the sound of that."

David sighed. "Well, as best I understand it, the folks who may be going to war don't even know you're here, or at least very few do. And they can't get here without goin' through my World, which they wouldn't do 'cause they don't want to make waves there; or else goin' through the land of a powerful potential enemy, which they *really* don't wanta do."

The man stared at him for a while longer. "Did you win this scale yourself? Does the uktena yet creep through the woods of the Lying World?"

"No," David said. "It was a gift from the guy I told you about: the one who showed us how to get here."

"So it is no proof of *your* manhood?"

David hung his head. "I reckon not."

"Then it is no good."

"*Huh?*"

"Because *any* man may carry the scale of an uktena. All it requires is that he claim a warrior for a friend. It is quite another thing to bear one by right." The man's eyes narrowed, and David felt his heart flip-flop, for he knew the glint of craftiness when he saw it.

"Still," the man said, clearing his throat, "I may yet have a solution to your problem. I have myself been greatly vexed by an uktena of late, and yet I dare not slay him. Should you do what I cannot, and slay this uktena, I will grant you passage and aid you upon your return."

"But what *is* an uktena?" David asked. "Evidently it's some kind of snake, but what?"

The man laughed and pointed to the sand beneath their feet. "See you the grains there? Each is made of stone, and likewise is a mountain made. But as one of those grains is to a mountain, so the uktena is to a snake, in size, in cunning, in the danger it poses the unwary. Even I fear him."

David frowned suspiciously. "Uh, could you be a little more specific?"

"The uktena is the greatest of all serpents. As big around as the great trees of the west, he is; and longer than the tallest. Horns he has on his head, and red is his skin, usually, or white, or sometimes in between, for it changes. His scales are like crystal and glitter like sparks of fire. And on his head is a bright blazing crest like a diamond. *Ulunsuti,* that stone is called, and it has great virtue. That I claim as my portion if you slay him."

"Can it even *be* killed?"

"Proof of that you hold."

"So why don't *you* just kill it if it's givin' you trouble?"

The man's eyes flashed fire. "Because so dangerous is the uktena that even to see it is death!"

"Now wait a minute . . . How——?"

"Not the death of the *seer,* the death of his closest kin!"

David stood straight up, his face ablaze with rage. "His *kin!* I'm not gonna risk my—bloody hell, no!"

"That is why I asked you: you are not of this land. The

magic of the uktena does not extend beyond Galunlati. Thus you are the only ones who *can* slay him. It is either slay him or be slain, in any case. And if things transpire as you have said, your family may well die anyway."

David frowned; he was being manipulated again, and he didn't like it. And he was too tired to even think straight.

"This isn't one of those archetypal animals like Tsistu, or something?" he asked finally. "I won't get into trouble if I kill it, or anything?"

"Life *is* trouble," the man said. "But death is no escape, and since you mention Tsistu I will tell you what you doubtless already know, which is not to trust him. He is a trickster, and gamester worse than any in Galunlati. He has even dared to torment me with his tricks, and I am chief here."

"Chief?"

"Aye! I am Chief of Wahala, which is all the southern part of this land. Kanati has set me with enforcing His Laws here. You may call me Uki, which is a short form of that part of my true name which means Thunder."

David bowed automatically. "I'm—I'm sorry, sir. I didn't realize. Oh, crap, I should have introduced myself. My name's—"

"No!" Uki cautioned. "You are a stranger and a youth, and should not give your name so freely." He glanced at David's shirt for a moment, his eyes fixed on the insignia stenciled there. "Tell me, is that your totem?"

David glanced down in turn, saw the Enotah County High mascot: the winsomely grinning 'possum. "Uh, no, not really."

"It fits you, though, and you must have a name to go by here. I will call you *Sikwa Unega,* which means *White 'Possum,* for your grin and your cleverness and the paleness of your hair."

"Uh, thanks, sir," David said, blushing. "But, uh, what were you saying about how many uktenas there are?"

"There is only *one* uktena at any time; and he alone of the beasts here no longer has offspring in your land. And yes, he may be killed, and has been: though rarely. Yet his medicine is like that of all beasts here: whenever his blood is spilled he is reborn."

"So what's the point, then?"

"He returns no longer than your finger. Years it takes for him to grow large enough to cause trouble."

"So what've I gotta do to kill this thing? Can you give me any hints?"

Uki shook his head. "I will instruct you of the beast's habits and the proper means of his slaying tomorrow. For now, come; I am a bad host. Long you have walked, and weariness is in your eyes, if not your tongue. I will awaken your friends, and we will feast." He looked up, clapped his hands—which sounded unnaturally loud in the cavern— and David was certain he saw sparks leap from palm to palm. "Sisters, come: put on your fair seeming, and bring our guests to a place where they may rest for the night free of fear of your scaled companions. And bring food and drink."

"Food," David said heavily, "and rest."

Uki moved his hands a certain way, and the snakes began to slither away into the holes in the cavern walls. A second set the turtles lumbering to the corners. A third, and David's friends stirred and opened their eyes.

"Hey, Dave, what's happenin'?" Calvin yawned.

Fionchadd too awoke. He glanced from side to side, face dark with anger. "Power!" he whispered. "Power has been set on me against my will!"

"Against all our wills, Finno," David said as calmly as he could. "But oh, Jesus, guys; I think I've won us a re-prieve."

"What *kind* of reprieve?"

"Probably a fairly short one. I'll tell you about it over dinner."

"*After* dinner," Uki admonished. "It is impolite to speak of bargains while feasting. Now come, I must think of names for you others."

Dinner, which the men ate on the floor of a torch-lit adjoining, smaller cavern that was blessedly free of anything either tailed, scaled, or shelled, proved to be an excellent repast of corn cakes, tubers, berries, and cider, along with a generous portion of some fine-textured white meat that David could not identify and was not particularly eager to inquire about. Too late he wondered about the wisdom of eating here: Faery food was supposed to be perilous, was supposed to trap you forever in that World. Maybe the same applied to Galunlati.

But there was no sense worrying about it now, he decided, as he licked the last bit of grease off his fingers and burped contentedly. It was, after all, the first food he had eaten in two days.

"A fine meal," he told his host—and burped again.

Uki nodded, his face beaming. "My sisters are excellent cooks—and did I tell you? They are not married."

David yawned as the woman cleared away the feast.

"It is much better to be friendly, is it not?" Uki said after a moment. "—now that you have your names."

"Sure," said Alec, without conviction.

"That's easy for you to say, Tawiska," Calvin chided.

Alec blushed. The name Uki had given him upon awakening meant *smooth* or *slick*, in reference to his perpetually neat appearance.

"At least I can pronounce it, *Edahi*."

"At least *I* already had a proper name!"

"Yeah." David laughed. "And *you're* not named after a critter like me and Finno—'scuse me, *Dagantu,* here."

"It fits, though," Alec noted. "Dagantu's a kind of lizard—which is what Fionchadd used to be."

"It's 'cause of how he moves, though," Calvin noted, elbowing the Faery. "Ain't it, Finny?"

Uki cleared his throat and stood. "You seem to be entertaining each other, so I will leave you now. Sleep where you will in this chamber. My sisters will bring bedding. I will see you in the morning." He left, but the women soon returned carrying great piles of black fur which David thought must be bear.

He snuggled down into one, and regarded his friends, who had done the same.

"Okay, White 'Possum, spill it," Alec said, after a prodigious yawn. "What's this B.S. about a reprieve?"

David took a deep breath and told them.

"Kill an uktena?" Calvin cried. "You've *got* to be kiddin'! Those things are death even to look at!"

"Not for us, apparently," David replied. "Nor for our families, if you were worried about that." He explained what Uki had said about the World-walls being proof against that magic.

"Well, I don't like it at all," Calvin grumbled, though David thought he saw genuine fear hiding behind the Indian's recalcitrance.

"Know anything about how to kill one?" David asked him.

Calvin shook his head. "They're just not a thing you kill—not that it makes any difference, since there aren't any left in our World, according to my grandfather."

"Well, so much for that."

"Yeah," Alec snorted. "This is just great."

"It should be interesting," Fionchadd said. "I have never hunted an—what is the word? *Uktena?*"

"Welcome to the club, then," Alec sighed. "I haven't either."

"Just think of it as coming to terms with your heritage, Calvin," David said. "After all, you're the nature boy here."

"This is a little out of my league, though. Grandfather spoke of it only as a name, a child's threat. 'The uktena'll get you,' and that kinda thing."

"Redskin boogey-critters."

"Yeah, basically. Or boogey snake, in this case."

"And he never told you anything about how to kill one?"

Calvin shrugged helplessly. "Medicine's my thing, not warfare."

"Know anything to put us to sleep?" Alec asked.

"Only my fists carefully applied," Calvin said easily, then scowled as David glared at him. Alec's face, too, clouded; and David saw his jaw tighten and his lips go thin. But he had no time to worry about Alec now. All he was concerned with was finding his way to slumber.

The torches had burned to embers when Alec awoke, but there was still light to see by from the bluish lumine-scence that lit the cave. He had meant to examine it more closely, for it seemed to be comprised of sparks that slid through the stones themselves, but had not had an opportu-nity. Nor was this the time.

He had been dreaming of Eva, and in the dream she was gazing sadly into his eyes, slipping something in his hand. His eyes filled with tears when he thought of her, of how he would never see her again. Then that memory broke and shifted. He sat up and glanced around the room, saw the dim shapes of David lying close by him, of Calvin in the corner, of Fionchadd sprawling uncovered by the entrance.

Fionchadd! There was something about the Faery, something Alec was supposed to do. He frowned, straining his memory—and pain exploded in his head. Eva's face once more swam into his vision, only this time she looked terribly serious. *Maybe David is* not *your friend,* she was saying. *Would a true friend treat you so? And this Calvin is certainly not, for he builds barriers where none existed. As for the boy whom you name Fionchadd, I have met his kind before and they are not to be trusted. He is the heart of the problem, for he is the source of the strangeness, him and all his kind. If you would have David once more be your friend, you must remove Fionchadd's folk forever.*

Alec winced, shook his head, tried to think straight, to banish the soft, insistent tones, yet the voice droned on: *Only by one means may Fionchadd come to the place he seeks, and if he does not come there, he will no longer trouble you. You have already told me how that is to be accomplished, and for that end I have prepared a counter. When the time comes, you will know what to do.* She pointed to the small dagger Alec somehow had in his hand.

Alec blinked, shook his head again. Something was wrong, but he couldn't think what. There was something horribly different about Eva, she—she knew too much, he shouldn't have been able to tell her about Fionchadd, about the quest. . . . God, his head hurt; he had to get away from the pain, *had* to. He closed his eyes, and at once the agony left him. He dreamed once more.

And in the dream he crept out of his furs and slipped quietly across the sand to crouch beside Fionchadd. The Faery still slept, sprawled on his back, but Alec dared not trust his senses. He muttered a *Word* that came to him from somewhere, made a *Sign* he had no idea he knew, and paused, listening. The boy's breathing did not alter. Fionchadd had put aside his weapons and the belt that held them, but still wore breeches and tunic. The latter had ridden up somewhat during the night, and Alec eased his hand beneath the rough wool and across the Faery's belly until he found what he sought: the hard metal hilt of a dagger. Very slowly he removed it, all the while repeating the *Word*, then reached to his own waist, removed the dagger Eva had given him, and held the two side by side in the dim light. They were of similar size, and as he looked at them, his began to shimmer and twist, until an instant later it was a twin to Fionchadd's. Fionchadd's also changed, becoming a duplicate of Eva's gift. This he stuck back in his sheath and as carefully as possible, slid the other back into Fionchadd's keeping, and pulled his tunic back down.

Another *Word,* another *Sign,* and he returned to his bed.

Beside him David grunted and flopped onto his stomach. Alec smiled and rolled over as well. David's breathing had become a sort of chant: *sleep deep, sleep deep—and forget.* The voice, he thought, was Eva's. His hand curved around the hilt of his secret dagger, he too slept. And this time there was no dreaming.

Chapter XVII: The Great Uktena Hunt

(Galunlati—day two—morning)

"God, I must have died last night." Alec yawned from the entrance to the sleeping cavern. "Somebody point me to the john."

David glanced up from the breakfast they had found spread for them in the (still snakeless) outer cavern: honey and acorn bread, with blackberries and strips of smoked fish. Alec certainly looked the worse for wear—as worn as David had ever seen him. His frazzled hair, wrinkled clothing, and the dark bags under his eyes gave the lie to his new Cherokee name. Smooth, he was not.

Calvin gestured over his shoulder toward the entrance to the gallery that led outside. "We peed in the falls."

Alec grimaced wearily. "I don't have to—oh, crap, never mind."

"Exactly." David laughed, as his friend stumbled toward the opening.

"Washed up there too," Calvin called after.

"I do not understand the humor here," Fionchadd muttered.

David scratched his chin and grinned. "Well, crap's another word for—uh, you know..." He paused, looked at the Faery curiously. "Or do you?" he wondered aloud, then shrugged. "Well, all the parts are the same, anyway, so I'd guess that even you folk..."

"Yes?"

David rolled his eyes in exasperation. "Oh, never mind —how 'bout passin' me another bowl of berries?"

The next several minutes passed in relative silence as they availed themselves of Uki's bounty, but eventually David's impatience got the best of him. "Okay, Finno," he said. "Any idea how to kill this uktena-beastie?"

The Faery's brow wrinkled thoughtfully for a long moment. "I have been considering this," he said finally. "I have hunted monsters before, of course: manticores and krakens, even a dragon or two, yet nothing like this. I will need to spy out the creature's habits before I can choose a plan. It would be useful to speak to Uki, too. Do you know where our host might be?"

"If you're talking about Mr. Thunder," Alec said from the entrance, "he's standing up top making signs in the air. Looks like it's gonna rain down south, too."

David and Calvin exchanged meaningful glances. "I guess we're supposed to take his name literally."

"I guess."

Alec sauntered over, squatted beside David, and helped himself to a slice of bread and honey. His hair was dripping wet but had been combed carefully back. His shoulders and face were still damp. David chuckled to himself. Some things never changed, and one of them was Alec's compulsive neatness.

"What about the snake ladies, *Edahi?*"

A shrug. "Haven't seen 'em."

"Regular foxes, though—if you can get by the wigs and the warpaint."

"They're tattoos," Calvin corrected.

"Foxes?" Fionchadd wondered.

"A euphemism."

"A what?"

"Never mind."

"I cannot read the meaning in your mind in this country."

"Really?"

Fionchadd nodded. "That seems to be one of the qualities of this place. This far from my own source of Power I grow weaker, and the heavy flesh of your World does not help."

"The Lying World," Alec inserted. "That's what they call it here."

"Wonder why?"

"Think about it."

"Well, whatever they call it," David said, "couldn't you, like, change into the matter of Galunlati, or something?"

The Faery shook his head. "One may only wear the stuff of the Worlds that adjoin one's own."

"But Galunlati *does* join yours: your Powersmith part, anyway."

"Aye, but I am only of quarter blood. Besides, to do it here I would first have to put on the stuff of Faerie, which I cannot."

"Never mind, man; you just lost me."

"It is hard to explain. One may only wear the stuff of the Worlds that touch one's own—this much I have said. But one may *not* wear the stuff of Worlds that touch those that touch one's own—Worlds at two removes. The links become too tenuous."

"Gaaaa!" David cried, rising stiffly and stalking away. "It's too early for this, Finno; my poor, fried brain won't take it. I—"

"Ho," Calvin interrupted. "Thunder's here."

Uki was staring at them from the doorway. He looked calm and rested.

"I see you have found food," he said. "I trust your sleep was peaceful. But come, you must be about your hunting. I have seen the sign of the uktena closer than it has ever been. It would seem you have come just in time."

"Sure," Alec grunted, shrugging into his shirt, a hand

unconsciously seeking the dagger stuffed inside his waist-band.

David saw it and frowned, not having noticed it before, but before he could inquire further, Uki was speaking again. "Only one way may the uktena be slain," he said, "by an arrow through the seventh spot from the head. There is his heart and his life."

"But you said he was solid-colored," David noted.

"For the spots to show, he must be angry. They will appear as he changes color."

"And let me guess: we have to anger him."

"You are clever this morning, Sikwa Unega. You must have slept well indeed. It is a good thing I forbade my sisters to visit you!"

David only scowled.

"But there are certain things I must now warn you about," Uki went on, abruptly serious. "Whomever is seen by an uktena can become so dazed by the magic of the jewel in his head that he may forget himself and run toward it instead of away."

"I see," David said grimly, wondering for the millionth time what he had gotten himself into.

"The monster's blood is the final jeopardy," Uki continued. "It is poisonous to touch, even, almost, to smell. And of blood there is aplenty, let me warn you. The uktena lives mostly on it; it is the source of its red color and its major threat, for once pierced there will be blood in amounts you cannot imagine: whole rivers of it, it will seem."

"And we can't touch it?"

"Not if you value your lives."

"Well," said Fionchadd, springing to his feet and reaching for his bow. "I, for one, am ready to begin."

"Come then," Uki said, "array yourselves for war and I will show you the trail of the uktena."

Half an hour later David stood with his comrades atop the crag that hid Uki's home. To their right the river hurled itself out of sight into the gorge. A permanent cloud of spray showed there, but this morning the sun had caught it in such a way that a true half-circle of rainbow arced from cliff to cliff. David started to point, but Uki stopped him. "It will give you rheumatism," he said.

Alex nudged David with an elbow. "Wanta go looking for pots of gold?"

"That's another reality." David chuckled back.

"And false besides," Fionchadd added. "I know some leprechauns. All they hoard is beer and gossip."

"Wrong pot, Finno."

A sudden rustle of movement startled them, and David twisted around to see Calvin strip and dive into the river twenty or so yards upstream of the falls.

"Hey, what's *he* doing?" Alec wondered.

"Purifying himself, I guess," David said. "Must be his ancestry calling again."

Alec shuddered. "Some purification. Makes me shiver just to watch it."

"Then don't."

"It is a thing you all should have done," Uki said beside them. "And it surprised me that you did not. But perhaps you thought your own medicine sufficient, and in any case it is too late now, for we must hasten."

Alec hesitated. "But what about Calvin?"

"He will find us. Even if I hide my tracks, he will see yours, of that you may be certain."

"Some vote of confidence," David muttered.

"Hey, Calvin, get your ass in gear and come on," Alec hollered.

"Oh, for Chrissakes, McLean!"

Uki glared at him. "Come, noisy smooth one, we must go."

He led them single file into the dense tangle of laurel that flanked the river, and David was amazed at how uncannily quiet he was. He tried to move as silently, but instead became keenly aware of how every movement brought its own sound: the whispering press of boots upon dead leaves or fallen needles; the buzz of twigs along the denim of his jacket or their sharp cracks as they caught at pockets or sleeves. Suddenly he began to understand the minimalist school of dressing Uki employed. In a place where silence meant food, which meant survival, anything that made noise was to be avoided.

A moment later a gentle rustle in the bushes proved to be Calvin: shirtless and barefoot, though still wearing jeans and his pouch. Beneath his beaded sweatband, his hair was sopping. Stripes of black and red adorned his cheeks, chin, and forehead; a hunting knife glittered in his right hand.

They pressed onward for a fair while, tending always uphill, but over gentler slopes than they had encountered the previous day. When Uki brought them to it, the uktena sign was obvious even to David's eye. Straight ahead the earth had been rutted into a deep trough easily five feet wide, as though someone had dragged a vast tree through the woods, digging into the soil and bending bushes aside on either hand, where they were not crumpled underneath. Whatever had made that trail had been huge—unbelievably so.

"The beast will not be far off," Uki told them. "It sleeps by day, basking in the warmth of the high places, and it may be you will find it there. If you are not here at sunset I will go to seek your bodies."

"What if it takes longer?" Alec wondered.

"It will not. By day you have some chance. By night the uktena will find you."

"Well, I guess that's that," Calvin said grimly.

Alec twisted around, confused. "Uki's gone."

"He'll be back," Calvin said flatly. "Either way things go he solves one problem."

"Quiet," Fionchadd warned. "We must begin."

The trail was ridiculously easy to follow, but the Faery insisted on as much silence as was feasible, urging them along mostly by signs and the occasional irate whisper. It was like walking in a freshly plowed field, David thought. The earth was turned up in the same way, and even smelled the same: dim and musty—strong, even above the scent of pines. And it was soft underfoot: so soft he wanted to emulate Calvin and go barefoot, though he knew that his feet were no match for the Indian's—certainly not now, when his blisters had blisters. The *last* thing he needed in a moment of crisis was to worry about stepping on something sharp.

For perhaps an hour they traveled, always uphill. David became aware that the vegetation was changing: the oaks and maples were dwindling, becoming dwarf parodies of themselves before giving way entirely to shrubs and bushes. The air was cooler, too, and he shivered, grateful he had decided to bring along his jacket. Calvin ahead of him showed goose bumps across his smooth rusty skin.

"Burr," Alec said.

"Yeah," Calvin replied. "Must be true what they say about killing eagles."

David rolled his eyes. "Yeah, what now?"

"To kill an eagle in summer will bring a frost that'll kill the corn."

"Well, gee, Fargo, you're a regular mine of information this mornin'. You *sure* you don't know anything more about this uktena?"

"Scout's honor. Grandfather was real erratic."

"Will you humans please be silent!" Fionchadd hissed over his shoulder.

Smirking, they acceded.

A short while later the trail steepened perceptibly, and the last of the trees disappeared, leaving only stunted bushes. David realized they were approaching the top of a bald: one of those mountains whose summits barely passed the timberline. Georgia's highest peak, Brasstown Bald, over on the Towns-Union line was one such. He remembered the trip he'd made there with the 4-H Club when he was twelve. The visitor center on top had reminded him of a castle—only now he had seen a real mountaintop castle, and one much closer to home. Idly he wondered if the ground they currently trod had any analogs back in Georgia. Uki's place, he knew, had been so like Tallulah Gorge as to be identical, but the rest . . . some was familiar, some was not. Take here for instance: there were no other balds in Georgia save Brasstown (Bloody Bald was called that because it had bare rocks on its summit and slopes too steep to grow trees; its mortal summit came nowhere near the timberline), which meant this would have to be in North Carolina—only they hadn't gone anywhere like that far, not if they'd started from the Galunlati equivalent to Tallulah Falls.

Fionchadd's abrupt whispered "Halt!" jerked him from his reverie.

They had come much closer to it than they had intended. What David had taken to be an eruption of muddy-white quartz along the mountain's summit barely twenty yards above them had moved slightly: a barely discernible ripple across its ridged expanse. They were within easy striking distance of the uktena.

Fionchadd signed them to silence and slipped forward. His feet made no noise: none. David scarcely dared to breathe, and heard Alec's sudden awed gasp.

Fionchadd had frozen for a moment, still in a half crouch as he studied their quarry, and David found his eyes wandering toward the Faery as well—anywhere but toward the shape that lazed across the ridge line before them. Most of its mass, he realized, must be deposed down the opposite flank, for only a short section showed here: maybe five feet high and thirty long. By squinting he thought he could make out transparent scales with the merest hint of red to them, glistening in the sunlight.

Fionchadd crept closer, slipped sideways around the mountain.

"What's he doing?" Alec whispered.

"Trying to find out how big it is, I reckon," David told him.

"Damn big enough," was Calvin's only comment.

The Faery had disappeared over the left-hand crest by then, and for a long moment David held his breath, wondering if he should follow, or how long he should wait before acting. But then Fionchadd was back, coming around from the right, having evidently circled the summit. He motioned them downslope, and they were easily a hundred yards from the creature, though still in sight of it, before he dared to speak.

"Never have I seen anything like it," he said. "Vaster by far than any of the wyrms of Faerie, and thicker of skin, it appears, for I touched it."

"And we're supposed to *kill* it? Bloody hell!"

"Got any good ideas?" Alec asked pragmatically.

"Yes," Fionchadd said. "I have been thinking of how we solve such problems in Faerie, for beasts with poison blood are not unknown there. Three things we must do: first we must rouse it to anger."

"I was afraid of that," David groaned.

"The head lies on the opposite slope," the Faery continued. "And likewise the tail, both at least twenty arm spans either way, maybe forty-five overall. The head itself is roughly half the size of—what do you call your chariots, David?"

"You mean cars?"

"Right."

"Super," Alec snorted.

Fionchadd ignored him. "To attack the head directly would be folly. We must center our attention on this side, so that when it awakens, it will be at a disadvantage."

"Hold on a minute," Calvin broke in. "What makes you so sure about that?"

"The fact that the beast is, at heart, a serpent. It sleeps in the sun, its blood is cold. It will be slow to rouse, and lethargic. If we rouse it enough for the spots to show, then kill it before it fully wakens—"

"Lots of *ifs* there, Finno."

"Never mind," Alec interrupted. "What then?"

"Why, a simple thing: when the uktena angers—when its spots appear—I will shoot it."

Calvin bristled slightly. "Why you?"

"Because I am the best archer, and because my bow never misses."

"Are you *sure* about that? How do you know its magic still works here?"

"It does not matter. Magic or no, it is still an excellent bow, and I am an even more excellent archer." He pointed behind him. "If I could get above it would be best, but it already commands the highest ground, so that is impossible. Yet I will need to wait until I am sure of the seventh spot, and for that reason, I would prefer to be as far from the head as possible. Also," he added, "do not forget what Uki told us of the blinding glitter of the stone, to which even I may be not be immune."

"You didn't, by any chance, get a look at it, did you?"

"Only briefly from the corner of my eye, and even that caused me pain."

"But what about the blood?" Alec wondered

"That is the third thing. Down this side to our left is a deep cleft in the stone. If we can contrive it so the beast lodges there once it is wounded, that will control the blood as well as hold it fast. For safety, though, we should build a line of fire on the hollow's lower side as an additional shield between ourselves and both the blood and the creature itself. All beasts I know fear fire—save those that are born there, like salamanders. There is plenty of dry brush by the cleft, and these bushes should likewise burn well." He glanced at Alec. "You have fire sticks?"

"Matches?" Alec corrected. "Certainly." He patted his pocket.

"Very well: we will help you construct the barrier. When the time comes, you will light it. I can aid you there, for though I have little Power here, I think I have enough to fan a flame once started."

"That's a comfort," Alec said sullenly.

"It was meant to be."

"So," David said hesitantly, "if Alex's torchman, and you're the archer, I guess that leaves me and Calvin to wake up old Mr. Scaly here."

Fionchadd nodded. "If you are willing."

David winked at Calvin. "You up for it, Fargo?"

Calvin nodded and thumped a comradely arm on his shoulder. "I don't see we have any choice, White 'Possum; and as you say, it's one way to come to terms with my heritage."

"Or to meet your ancestors," Alec muttered.

"Enough of that," David snapped, then: "Sorry, but we're all kinda wired."

"'S'all right."

David fell silent for a moment, staring at Alec, then squared his shoulders and addressed Fionchadd. "So we've gotta piss this thing off, huh? Any notion how?"

"Simply waking it may be sufficient."

"Yeah, well, looks like it'd take a bloody cannon."

"I think I know a way," said Calvin. "It's a snake and snakes have scales. They also have skin underneath—sensitive skin, I hope."

"So you mean—?"

"Right: we simply walk up to it and poke it—hard."

David laughed in spite of himself. "Poke it with a sharp stick? I like that: poke a friggin' monster with a stick!"

"Or a knife, or your staff, or whatever."

"You have *got* to be kidding! I ain't gettin' close enough to stick that thing, uh uh, no way!"

"You got any other ideas?"

"I don't suppose your basic noise would help, would it?"

"Snakes are deaf. I don't think we'd better chance it."

"They must be," Calvin said. "Otherwise it'd already be on us."

"He is right," Fionchadd inserted, "though I did not know when I first urged you to silence that it has no ears. But Edahi speaks true: outright attack is the simplest way. Rouse the creature, and it will move—slowly, I hope, for that is usually the way of things so large."

"You hope."

"It is all I have."

"Well, then, boys; let's to it."

Half an hour later they were as ready as they could be. Fionchadd had shown them the chasm he had spoken of, and it did look promising: a deep gash, maybe eight feet across and a like amount to the bottom torn into the mountainside a little lower down to their left. It meandered along horizontally for a couple of hundred yards, tending gradually downhill, but the upper end was fairly narrow and fairly close by: an easy jump for a decent athlete, which they all were. They had cleared a space behind it to keep the flames from spreading that way, and piled brush along most of the length, aided, as it turned out, by the corpses of several derelict maples that lay there, apparently lightning struck in punishment for their ancient defiance of the treeline.

"Such trees are strong medicine," Calvin observed, kicking the one he had just helped heave into place.

"If you say so," David sighed, wiping his dripping forehead.

Alec picked up two bundles of reeds, lit one, and positioned himself midway along the line of brush. "This is it, guy," he whispered, gazing at David; and David thought he saw a gleam of tears. He reached out and clasped Alec roughly, and they remained that way for a moment, feeling for perhaps the final time their own aliveness reflected and given back. And then suddenly they were forced apart on one side, and other arms slapped across their backs, as Calvin came into the group. "Good luck, boys: break a leg."

An instant later Fionchadd completed the square. "Luck," he whispered. "Luck to all of us."

"Luck," Calvin echoed and broke away.

"Luck," David whispered in turn.

"Luck, you guys," from Alec.

"Yeee-aaaahhh-*hoooo!*" came David's drawn-out Rebel yell.

And then they could wait no longer.

Fionchadd skirted away to the left, toward the head; for they thought the seventh spot must surely lie that way, and there was also a gentle rise that would give him a better vantage point, though he would still be shooting uphill.

David and Calvin jogged off to the right and began to climb. David had his runestaff ready, with the sharpened point he had lately added to one end. Alec had offered Calvin his, but the Indian had shaken his head, saying his knife was sufficient.

All too soon they were there.

Close up David wondered how he could ever have mistaken the uktena for mere rock. It was like a wall of intricate glass mosaic: white, but shot with ruby and scarlet and crimson, the scales interlocking in a pattern of fabulous complexity that reminded him of some of the walls of Lugh's palace and made him wonder if perhaps there were not some greater scheme that ordered the aesthetics of all the Worlds.

Calvin gave him a brief thumbs up and darted forward, grabbed at one of the scales with a hand he had muffled in a protective wad of shirt, and thrust in his blade.

David took a deep breath and did the same, but from more distance, angling the staff up under the scales in a series of quick stabs that seemed to have no effect though he drove the point in over and over. Beside him he could hear Calvin swearing and grunting in apparent futility. David swore too, and stabbed harder—and somehow found a vulnerable spot, because the staff slid in deeper, and scarlet began oozing into the hollows between the scales. David jumped back reflexively, but only a thin trickle of blood welled out—though even that was enough to set the staff to smoking and wilt the foliage it fell on. The smell was horrible, too; for it was the stench of rotten blood.

"Jesus!" he whispered, as his gorge rose and he clamped a hand across his mouth.

Then, "Shit!" as the spot began to spread.

Abruptly the white wall twitched, scooted toward them.

One moment David was facing a section of uktena so long it resembled nothing animate, and the next it had slammed into him, and he was flying backward while a vast white cylinder arched into the blue sky above him—a cylinder that was quickly pinkening, and with a dazzling glare at one end that hurt to look at. Then he struck ground and rolled, and when he could see again, a second cylinder was also rising, only this one was smaller and had a point at its tip. Both head and tail, it appeared, had awakened.

The head was turning their way too, even as it rose, and

as it moved, the color changed: to pure, deep red, then to white, then to red again. Spots began to appear, blinking into existence along the whole vast length, exactly like the lights on a theater marquee. And each spot was as big as a man outspread, and red as blood.

"God*damn!*" Calvin yelled, and David glanced to his left to see the Indian charging downslope toward him, as a coil convulsed in his direction. Then, "Move it, Sullivan!" as Calvin reached down to yank him up. "Shit, man, we did it! But let's not hang around."

"Where's Finno?"

"Where he's supposed to be, I hope. Now let's go!"

Somehow David found both his feet and his staff. He could barely breathe, and his shoulder hurt abominably.

"*Now,* Sullivan! Oh Christ, *look out!*"

David looked up, could not help it. And for the first time he truly saw the uktena's head: huge and triangular, with twin red horns curving out behind like the arms of a lyre. Its eyes glowed yellow beneath the blaze of white light that sparked out from its forehead where the ulunsuti was. He shut his eyes quickly and jerked his head down to avoid the spell of that stone, whose afterimages were already dancing before him—but not before he had seen the mouth gape opened. The scarlet lining leered down at him from a hundred feet away, the whole horrible cavity bordered by teeth each as long as his arm. And then the uktena screamed its pain.

Abruptly the towering head plunged earthward, as if gravity had at last grown tired of being flaunted and yanked it down. David took advantage of the opportunity and rolled further downslope.

What was keeping Fionchadd?

Then he saw the Faery running toward the creature, saw him raise his bow and draw, tracking it along the beast's length. The spots glowed brighter, appeared and disappeared with even greater rapidity.

"Come on, Finny; shoot!" Calvin yelled.

But Fionchadd did not shoot. He stood as if dazed, as

the bulk of the creature looped across the top of the mountain.

"Now, Finno, *now!*"

An arrow flew, but struck home in a spot that was not the seventh. And David had a glimpse of Fionchadd staring dumbfounded at the bow while he nocked another arrow.

But the head was once more arcing toward them, ablaze with the light of the ulunsuti.

And David was running, Calvin beside him, down the slope and toward the barrier.

"Come on!" Calvin shouted. Then, "Look out!" as the tail snapped over the summit and kept coming, thumping and flopping as the beast flung almost its whole vast length into the sky, then folded upon itself and slid over the bracken toward them.

The barrier was ahead of them now: no more than fifty yards. David ran, fell, felt Calvin jerk him up, and ran again.

Forty yards. He could see Alec.

"Fire it," he heard Fionchadd cry. "Now, now!"

Thirty yards, and Alec was thrusting the reed torch into the tinder, as David and Calvin angled left toward the narrower part of the crevasse.

But suddenly that was cut off, because the tail whipped that way, and they had to dodge right while the monster slithered closer, moving faster than they ever could have suspected.

Twenty yards.

Ten.

This was the wide part, David realized suddenly, but by then he was jumping, clearing the pit as flames roared up before him and raced away on either side. Beside him was Calvin, before him was Alec's face. Heat slapped at him, but then arms grabbed him, and he stumbled, and then ran again, while flames raced along the edge of the gulley. Beyond them curled and twitched the uktena.

Abruptly they skidded to a halt: "Where's Finny?" Calvin gasped.

"He must be okay," David panted. "He helped spread the fire."

"But where *is* he?"

David scanned the upper slope, searching for the Faery amid the coils of the monster, but the rising pall of smoke made it impossible.

"Nowhere."

"Jesus, he's still there!"

"Then we better get him the hell out," Alec cried. He darted by them, leapt through the flames, and ran upslope, runestaff in hand.

"*No!*" David yelled, even as the flames licked higher into a wall that drove both him and Calvin back.

"I see him, guys. He's fallen!"

"Watch the head, Alec! The stone in the head!"

But Alec ran onward, toward coils that now undulated a bare twenty yards away. The head had stopped moving, though; had paused as if curious, poised above something that lay on the ground.

Behind the wall of fire, David could only stand beside Calvin and sob, as smoke stung his eyes, and flame poured its fury on his face, and he saw between the flickering tongues his best friend's figure still loping along, though the heat made his shape shimmer like a wraith. And above it all was the glare of the ulunsuti.

"Finn!" Alec shouted.

"I can't get a clear shot," the Faery answered, his voice shrill and shaky. "I— Oh, no!"

The head lowered, minutely, and at that moment a gust of wind tore the smoke and flame away and David saw Alec leap on the monster's back, saw him drive the sharp tip of his runestaff deep into the spot directly in front of the one from which Fionchadd's arrow still protruded.

Sound split the world then: a scream beyond all screams, a thunder beyond all thunders. David clamped his hands on his ears and shut his eyes reflexively.

When he opened them an instant later, the uktena was writhing and twisting along the ground exactly like a rattler he had seen that had had its head cut off by one of his crueler classmates. And each flop and jerk brought it closer to the gully.

But where was Alec?

David strained his eyes, but could find no sign of his friend amid the crumpled bushes. And then he had another concern, because suddenly the uktena was directly on the other side of the barrier.

It was stupid, David realized suddenly, for them ever to have assumed that anything so vast would be cowed by a simple wall of flame, especially when it was in its death throes.

Yet apparently the fire repelled it, because the creature thrust its head over once, then drew back; and, coil-by-coil, tumbled into the crevasse. A moment later it lay still, though dark blood continued to pump from the wounded spot, until the whole pit was awash with the foul-smelling fluid.

"Alec," David screamed, rushing as close to the wall of flame as he dared.

"Alec, can you hear me?"

No answer.

A quick glance at Calvin. "Come on!"

The two boys backed away downslope, then hurled themselves forward in twin leaps that brought them through the flame and across the uktena's back and into the smashed and wilted foliage on the upper side.

David was half hysterical. "Alec, goddamn it, answer me!"

A figure rose awkwardly, further to the left, and David's heart leapt, then sank again when he saw it was Fionchadd. The Faery looked dazed, was walking shakily and staring at the shattered remnants of his bow, but David had no time for him, beyond a brief sigh of relief.

Suddenly, from Calvin: "Dave, hurry, I've found him."

David darted to the right to where the Indian was kneeling by a crumpled figure. He had already started to reach out to him when Calvin stopped him. "He's alive—barely —but we don't dare move him until he regains consciousness. I can't tell how badly he's hurt, and we can't risk spinal damage."

David's blood turned to ice. "It's *that* serious?"

Calvin nodded grimly. "It might be," and then: "Oh, shit!"

David followed Calvin's gaze and saw to his horror that the skin of both of Alec's hands was hanging in tattered strips, as though he had held them in boiling water. They were red, too, though there was no sign of bleeding, just an ugly white-yellow pus oozing from the tortured flesh.

"It's the blood," David said. "The stuff must have squirted all over him when he stabbed it. Thank God he didn't get any on his face."

"No, but we've got to get it off him; it's still eating away, see?"

"Maybe this will help," a shaky voice said. Fionchadd's face was pale, his clothing tattered, and his hair filled with bits of brush. He held out the wineskin Oisin had given them in the asi and raised a slanted eyebrow. "It is the last of Oisin's cordial. I mixed it with water before we left the cave."

David scooted aside as Fionchadd poured the liquid on Alec's hands, then splashed more on any spot where the uktena blood made its presence known by holes or smoke or ulcers. Blessedly there were not many—evidently Alec had been flung off as soon as the runestaff found its mark. David looked around, saw it lying a few feet away—or what was left of it. The point end was eaten away entirely; and the remainder was reduced to a smoking nub no longer than his forearm.

A moan from Alec drew their attention then, though Calvin kept one eye peeled toward the uktena and the waning fire. Instantly David was by him, eyes fixed anxiously on his friend's face.

Alec's lids never opened, but his lips slowly found their way around words. "D . . . David?"

"I'm here, kid; you know it."

"Did we do it?"

"*You* did it, Mr. Smoothie, it was all you."

A faint smile. "I did?"

"You alone."

Alec's face contorted, and he coughed blood. "David?"

"What is it, bro?"

"I hurt."

"Where? You gotta tell us, so we can know how to make you better."

"Everywhere . . . but mostly hands—and eyes."

"*Eyes?* Oh, Jesus, no!"

Alec did not reply, but David saw his lids flicker, caught a glimpse of the familiar gray beneath. Then Alec screamed, "The light, the light! All I see is light."

"The stone," Fionchadd whispered. "I know it dazzled me; it must have completely blinded him."

"But not before he succeeded."

"Aye, where I did not."

"Never mind that." David looked back at his friend. "Just take it easy. We've done the hard part, the rest is all downhill."

"Literally," Alec whispered. He managed another weak smile. "But, David, there's something . . . something I've got to tell you."

"Sure, kid, anything."

"David . . . David, I've . . . I've done a real bad thing. I . . ."

And then consciousness left him and would not return.

Chapter XVIII: Regrouping

"I will go and find Uki," Fionchadd said. He sprang up from where he had been squatting at Calvin's side and darted off down the ridge.

"But what about Alec?" David cried frantically. "You know more about healing than any of us!"

"He is beyond my aid," the Faery called back. "But perhaps our host knows what I do not, for this is his land, not mine." He turned silently and was gone in a blur of fluid movement, the subtle grays and greens of his clothing merging with the landscape in some uncanny way long before he reached the treeline.

David and Calvin waited, though Calvin took the precaution of jogging down to check on the uktena, being careful to shield his eyes from the fading glare of the ulunsuti. David simply sat, holding Alec's head in his lap and wondering what to do; wondering how he would ever explain this to Alec's parents if the worst happened; wondering, more immediately, what he himself would do should he lose his oldest and truest friend.

A moment later Calvin was back.

"So how is it?" David asked dully, inclining his head toward the crevasse.

"Dead—I think," the Indian replied, squatting beside him. "At least it's not moving, and the flies seem to agree, to judge by the way they're already congregating." He glanced skyward and frowned. "Buzzards too," as a shadow slid across Alec's body.

David nodded grimly and wiped his eyes.

"How's the patient?"

A weary shrug. "Not moving—though I guess that's not necessarily bad, since we don't really know how bad he's hurt."

"He could feel pain, though. That's a good sign."

"I'm glad *something* is."

Calvin picked up the remnants of Fionchadd's shattered bow and began trying to rejoin the broken ends. "What do you suppose he meant there at the last? What was that bad thing he was talkin' about?"

David shook his head but did not turn his eyes from his friend's face. "I have no idea. I—" He broke off. "Why did he *do* it, Calvin? What was he trying to prove?"

The Indian shifted to a more comfortable position. "Uh, look, Dave, this is probably a bad time and all, and 'scuse me for butting in where it's none of my business, but since you asked . . . well, it seems to me like you guys have been —how shall I say?—having some trouble lately. Oh, you've probably not really noticed, what with being in love and all. But I've seen the way Alec looks at you, and me too, for that matter, and it's like . . . like . . ."

"Yeah?"

"Well, 'pears to me there's a lot of resentment there. I think that's what made him go crazy right there at the end."

David grimaced sourly and wiped his eyes again. "Yeah, well, maybe you're right. I guess I should have paid more attention to how he feels and all; but shoot, Fargo, a guy can't control who he falls in love with, or when, any more than he can control who his friends are."

"But he oughtn't to let it blind him."

"More red man's wisdom?"

Calvin shook his head and grinned wanly. "The North Carolina lady. She talked as much as she, ahem . . . acted."

David sighed heavily. "Maybe I *have* been blind—or at least selfish. But Jesus God, I'd sort of hoped that he'd understand that I had to take advantage of Liz's—availability while I had the chance. He'd have me all during school, after all. Besides, all I heard all summer was him egging me on about her."

Calvin gave up on the bow and laid it aside. "Well, as I said, it's none of my business."

David did not reply.

A rumble of thunder reached them, then; and Calvin looked up. "Well, that didn't take long," he said. "Here comes the Lizard. Looks like he found Thunderman."

David twisted around to see the Faery and the—what *was* Uki, anyway? Maybe an elemental?—trotting up the slope toward them.

Uki spared a brief glance toward the uktena, then joined them. He knelt by Alec's side, examined his hands, checked his eyes, and felt at his throat for a pulse. With each movement, his face grew grimmer. Finally he stood. "The boy lives," he said. "But he is fading, and will fade further."

"But can't you do something?" David almost sobbed. "You're the head honcho around here, aren't you?"

"Indeed I am not," Uki replied. "I am merely Chief of Wahala. Other Powers there are that rule me, Powers far, far greater."

David clenched his fists in despair. "Okay, so where are they? I'll ask *them*, by God!"

"Your flesh would not stand it," Uki told him softly, "For it is of the greater Thunders you speak: Kanati the hunter and Selu the corn; of the Sun and Moon, of the land above this one."

David's breath hissed out; he pounded his thighs ineffectually. "Worlds, Worlds, Worlds, always more goddamn Worlds. What do you do for wounds in *this* World?"

"We die. Usually blood is spilled and we are reborn. It

is a dangerous thing to die without blood being shed."

"But Alec's lost blood!" David wailed helplessly. "Lots of it!"

"But he is not of this World."

"So we've gotta get him back home, then."

Uki laid a hand on David's shoulder and squeezed gently. "Once again, that is impossible. He could never survive the journey. You have only to look at him to see that."

"And," Fionchadd reminded him, "we have still a quest to fulfill—or I have."

"Well *fulfill* it, then!" David snapped. "Just get the hell away if you're not gonna help me!"

The Faery danced back a step, startled. "I . . ."

David was on his feet in an instant. "You *what?* Do you think I care what you've got to do when my best friend's dying? Do you think I give one *fuck* about that? Your whole *friggin'* race can go to hell for all I care!"

Fionchadd started to reply, but David cut him off. "I'd be real careful what I said right now, Finno. *Real* careful. You might just find yourself in the same shape as Alec!"

The Faery tensed, and David tensed as well, balling his fists, and starting forward. But then strong arms wrapped him from behind. "Easy, Sullivan," Calvin murmured into his ear. "He's not your enemy, none of us are. We'll deal with that in due time. For now we've gotta get Alec outta here."

"Well spoken," said Uki. "We can take him to my house. There I can better care for him."

David relaxed a little and Calvin let him go, though fury still burned in his face as he fought to regain his composure. "But can you *heal* him?" he finally managed to sob.

"That is for time to tell."

Calvin pointed toward the crevasse and took a deep breath. "Well, we did one thing right, anyway: we killed your monster for you."

Uki followed his gaze. "That you did, and well, though perhaps too rashly." Abruptly he straightened and addressed them formally. "Know, oh travellers, that you have completed the task I have set you and by that have proven yourselves warriors. Thus it is that I hereby grant you passage through Wahala, to whatever honorable end awaits you.''

"But what about *Alec?*" David persisted, his control slipping again.

Calvin ruffled his hair. "Uki'll do what he can."

"So let's be at it, then."

"And so we will—in a moment. There is one thing still to do here. Come, Edahi, Dagantu—you also, Sikwa Unega, if you will—and I will show you the way to free the ulunsuti from the head of the uktena."

David hesitated. He didn't want to leave Alec, but knew there was no reason not to, and at least this way he could learn something. Wearily he rose and followed his companions toward the crevasse.

Uki stood on the gulley's edge, looking down; and David found himself forced to shield his nostrils with his shirttail at the stench—a reaction echoed, to his surprise, by Fionchadd. Calvin, who was shirtless, simply blanched and put his hand over his mouth.

"Gag, what a stink!"

"Foul, indeed."

"No fouler than that which breeds it," said Uki. "But it will not smell for long. Behold."

He raised his hands over his head and clapped them together four times in a certain rhythm. The sound was no louder than mortal men's hands performing the same gesture, but somehow the air seemed to thin, then thicken again, while the breeze brought the faint odor of ozone. David felt the hair prickle on his arms and neck, and gasped as sudden static charged everything around him, sending sparks crackling between his legs and the undergrowth if he so much as moved. And then sounds echoed in the sky: a booming of thunder, the intervals and cadence the same as Uki's clapping.

Silence hung heavy on the mountain for a time; then suddenly the air was alive with the chirps and hoots and twitters of thousands of birds that spun and arced in from all directions and arrowed straight toward them. Uki clapped another rhythm, and once more the swirling skies replied, and the birds began to circle, as more and more were added to their number. They were closer, too; and David could make out individual species: hawks and eagles, mostly—and buzzards with naked red heads. But there were crows among them, and ravens; and amid them all a smattering of smaller, brighter species: cardinals and blue jays and orioles. There were even some parrots, or something very like them: hook-billed green birds with brilliant orange heads.

"Carolina parakeet," Calvin gasped. "Extinct for a hundred years."

"And passenger pigeons, I bet," David added, becoming caught up in the excitement in spite of himself. He pointed to the northwest where a vast cloud of identical gray-brown shapes was joining the noisy array.

A third clapped rhythm, a third echo of thunder, and the birds descended upon the uktena's corpse. A cloud of flies rose, indignant over having their feast usurped, and became themselves feasts for the more fastidious. As for the rest—the ones with hooked beaks and rending talons—for them serpent's flesh was sufficient.

"In a few days only bones will remain," Uki said. "Then we will retrieve the ulunsuti."

Calvin grinned his appreciation. "Hey, neat trick, man."

Uki fixed him with a speculative stare. "I might be able to teach you; you have the power, I think."

David looked surprised. "I *knew* there was more to you than meets the eye."

Calvin would not meet his gaze. "I don't know what he's talking about. I only know what my grandfather taught me."

"Where few are strong it takes little strength to be greater," Uki observed.

Calvin's brow wrinkled in confusion. "I'll think about that later, if you don't mind. For now, we need to worry about our buddy."

Uki turned to Fionchadd. "You are fleet of foot and long

of wind, Dagantu. Go seek my sisters, they will help us
carry."

"And us?" David insisted. "What do we do?"

"We will prepare a litter."

Eventually they got Alec back to the cave. Impatient to
begin and unable to sit and wait while his friend might be
dying, David had demanded they start out as soon as the
litter was completed: two poles lashed together with deer-
hide Uki provided, and joined by Alec's shirt and David's
jacket and T-shirt. As it was, they met Uki's sisters less
than a third of the way down the trail, whereupon the
women took over the load and strode on ahead, making far
better time than David and Calvin ever could have, even
with Uki carrying half the weight at all times, and the three
boys taking turns.

David was still sitting by Alec's side in the sleeping
chamber when Calvin returned a few hours later, having
accompanied Fionchadd on a quest for some healing herb
Uki needed that he had suddenly found in short supply. He
supposed it was the Indian's way of cutting him some
slack, giving him some space while he got his head straight
and resigned himself to the—not the inevitable, he told
himself sternly—but to the distinctly probable.

Uki took the herbs, ground them into paste in a mortar,
and rubbed some on Alec's hands, then applied more to the
blisters that patterned his body where the uktena's blood
had burned through.

"Will that help any?" David asked, mostly to have
something to say.

"It will slow the poison," Uki replied, "but while any
remains in his body there is little hope. Now be silent, for I
must begin the prayers."

David nodded, and Uki closed his eyes and began to
chant, slowly and softly at first, then more loudly:

Dunuwa, dunuwa, dunuwa, dunuwa, dunuwa, dunuwa.
  Sge! Ha-Walasi-gwu tsunlun-taniga.

Dayuha, dayuha, dayuha, dayuha, dayuha.
    Sge! Ha-Usugi-gwu tsunlun-taniga.

Twice he repeated the formula, all the while pacing in counterclockwise circles around Alec, once for each line. He then made two more circuits, each time pursing his lips and blowing outward.

Finally he returned to his place at Alec's head. "It is a charm to cure snakebite," he said, "for I know none against the uktena's poison."

David had no choice but to accept his word, though he had only the vaguest idea what had transpired. But now he looked at the herbs, he recognized them.

"Tobacco!" he said. "That's tobacco."

Uki scratched his chin. "We know it as *tsalu*."

"And the blowing at the end?"

"Is it not obvious?"

" 'Fraid not."

"Serpents always coil to the right and the uktena is no exception. That part of the spell simply uncoiled his spirit from your friend's soul."

David did not reply, for he had suddenly found himself once more fighting back tears.

Uki stared at him for a long time, then spoke very quietly. "I have been thinking," he said, "and I have realized that one can sometimes become caught in just such a trap as snared the uktena: to assume that the answers one knows are the only ones."

"I don't understand."

"And I do not express myself well. But what I mean is this: I have been thinking of healing ways, and many I have tried as you have seen. Yet I have been considering ways to heal a man of *this* land—and your friend is not of this land."

David's heart skipped a beat. Was there hope then? He dared not think it, but already his thoughts were speeding ahead. "Whatever it is, I'll do," he said quickly.

"If it is a thing you *can* do," Uki answered softly. "But

what I have thought on is this: To the north of here, two days steady travel, lies Atagahi, the lake where the beasts go for healing."

David's eyes brightened. "And you think . . ."

"That if you were to go there and bring back some of that water it might heal your friend. The beasts who go there are more akin to those of your land than many here, ourselves included. Perhaps that will make the difference."

David leapt to his feet and started for the entrance. "You got it, man. I'm on my way."

Uki was beside him in an instant to restrain him. "No, not yet! There are things you must know, and I must give you very careful instructions, for this is not a journey to be undertaken lightly, nor is it certain you will succeed."

"Why not?"

"Because it is a place reserved for the beasts. My kind do not go there. Whether they will admit one like you, I know not."

"But we're both people, more or less!"

"Yet of neither the same blood nor much the same earth. It is my hope the beasts will see this and admit you."

"If not . . . ?"

"It will not be to your liking."

Fionchadd and Calvin had remained silent all this time, but Calvin finally spoke. "We've been talkin' too, David; me and Finny. We've still got the quest to go on, right? We can't change that, and too much depends on it to abandon it—and I'm not just talkin' 'bout Finny's mother."

David folded his arms across his chest. "Okay, go on."

"Right. So anyway, we've decided that you can stay here with Alec—or go searching for this lake, now, I guess. And we'll go on to look for the way to Powersmith-land, or whatever. We've been talking to Uki's sisters some, and they've told us they've seen a sea to the east where the sand glitters like gold and the farther shore burns like fire."

"That's it!" David cried. "It has to be!"

"Aye," Fionchadd said. "So we think. At least it

matches Oisin's description. But more to the point, they said there were paths there: paths of light across the waves."

David scowled. "But Nuada said there were no Tracks here."

"He said they had *found* no Tracks leading here from Faerie, and that they didn't know how they would appear. We've already seen that. I mean they're basically what brought us here, right?"

Uki frowned thoughtfully. "These things of which you speak, I know of them, but they are beyond my understanding, and to tell truth I fear them. They are things of the Greater Thunders."

"If we find one, though, that will speed our task tremendously," Fionchadd said.

David gazed up at Calvin. "Do *you* have to go, though? I'd . . . I'd like to have somebody with me when I go to this magic lake."

Calvin grimaced unhappily. "Yeah, well, we talked about that, too. But the bottom line comes down to logic, or common sense, or whatever, which is that if Fionchadd goes and finds what he's looking for and takes your boat and sails off, somebody's still gotta tell the folks waitin' back home that he's succeeded, so they can take whatever action they need to."

David grimaced in turn. "You're right, of course. But I was just hoping."

"You'll do fine," Calvin assured him. "I've seen enough of you these last few days to know that."

"Yeah, but sometimes I just get tired of trying."

"We all do, man. We all do."

"Well, maybe. But, hey, couldn't Uki's sisters go with Finno instead? I mean they know the lay of the land and all."

The Faery shook his head. "We have already asked them, and they say they have duties here." He smiled wickedly. "That is one thing I envy you, too: you will have more time with them."

"Thanks a bunch," David muttered, hoping the sarcasm would elude his hosts.

"There is one thing you must do, though," Fionchadd went on obliviously. "You must give me the boat and the ring."

"Sure," David said. "Boat's in the pack." He stuck out his hand and worked the ring from his finger, then dropped it into Fionchadd's palm. "Take care."

"I will bring it back to you someday, of that have no fear."

David gazed quizzically at Uki. "And this lake—can I go there and still be back before they return?"

Uki nodded slowly. "I think so, if what they seek is what I suspect it to be. In the meantime, you all should rest and leave at first light tomorrow."

"Well," Calvin said, slapping his hands on his thighs, 'I guess it's decided."

David stared down at Alec. "I guess so. For better or worse, let's do it."

Chapter XIX: Yanu

(Galunlati—day two—evening)

David slept very little that night, and not because of the distant rumble of thunder that began thrumming through the cavern as soon as Uki left them after dinner; *that,* as a matter of fact, was somewhat comforting. What was not comforting, though, was any thought of Alec, and he thought of him constantly: the things he'd never told him, though they'd been close as brothers; the minor slights of the last few weeks that his memory suddenly multiplied like the proverbial loaves and fishes, making every too-brief encounter a cause for remorse, every curtailed conversation a playground for guilt. And finally, the most difficult dilemma: *what would he tell Alec's parents if their son died?* That he could not imagine. He would have to talk to the Sidhe, he supposed, get them to intercede. No way he could manage by himself. And what about their M-Gang buddies? There'd be a shitload of explaining to do, and he wouldn't be able to do much of it with the Ban of Lugh in place, and . . . His eyes filled with tears, and he flopped over, saw Alec lying on his back on the fur beside him. Poor Alec, so alone. David scooted closer, nestled his friend's head in the crook of his arm—let the others think what they would.

With Alec's breath whispering in his ears, he dozed, and in the doze he seemed to her a chant:

> *Yu! Sge! Usinuli hatunganiga, Giyagiya Sakani, ewsatagi tsuldahisti. Usinuli hatlasiga. Tsiskwa-gwu ulsgeta uwutla-nilei. Usinuliyu atsahilugisiga. Utsinawa nutatanunta. Yu!*
>
> *Yu! Sge! Usinuli hatunganiga. Digatiski Watigei, galunlati iyunta ditsuldahisti. Ha-nagwa usinuli hatlasiga. Tsiskwa-gwu ditunilawitsuhi higesei. Usinuli ketatigulahiga. Utsinawa adunniga. Yu!*

David did not understand the words, but somehow they brought him comfort. It was women who sang, he realized distantly, probably Uki's weird sisters; but now their voices sighed like gentle rain on soft grasses. He stirred slightly, made himself more comfortable in his nest of fur. And then the song began again, only this time the sounds shifted in his head, and he found he could make out their meaning:

> Yu! Listen! Quickly you have drawn near to hearken, O Blue Sparrow Hawk; in the spreading tree tops you are at rest. Quickly you have come down. The intruder is only a bird which has overshadowed him. Swiftly you have swooped down upon it. Relief is accomplished. Yu!
>
> Yu! Listen! Quickly you have drawn near to hearken, O Brown Rabbit Hawk; you are at rest there above. Ha! Swiftly now you have come down. It is only the birds which have come together for council. Quickly you have come and scattered them. Relief is accomplished.

It started over, but by the time the second verse had begun, he was sleeping peacefully.

Morning found David unexpectedly refreshed. Indeed, he was awake and out of bed while both Calvin and Fionchadd were still snoring. After a quick check of Alec, who seemed to be at ease, he crept silently past his companions and into the outer cave. He paused there, warily searching the gloom for any sign of lurking reptiles, but saw only the rounded lumps of the huge tortoises that apparently had not moved from their corners since Uki had banished them there two days ago. Why did their host allow them there? he wondered, since he evidently did not like them. Or was he simply being hospitable? And who were those strange women, anyway? Were they really Uki's sisters? But if so, why were they so unlike their brother?

Well, there was no way to find out this time of day, that was for sure. He yawned, stretched, and padded down the corridor to the ledge behind the falls. In the ruddy light before dawn the cataract was a veil of pinkish silver, its rumble now somehow soothing. Hesitating only briefly, he stripped to his skivvies and thrust his head under, then his arms and face, and finally his feet and legs as far as he could, using cupped hands to slap more water on what the falls could not reach. The water was cold but invigorating. A quick concession to nature's call, and he returned to find his friends now stirring. Uki's sisters appeared from another way, bringing breakfast that was the same as the previous day's, then left again, just as Uki himself entered. He did not squat beside them, as David expected, but remained by the entrance, looking thoughtful. David found himself starting to fidget in anticipation and ate quickly, without really tasting the food.

Abruptly, Uki departed; but returned a moment later with his sisters once more in tow. Each bore a parcel wrapped in the same white deerskin they wore.

"Sikwa Unega, Dagantu, Edahi," he said solemnly. "Dawn fast approaches and with it you must depart, for all of you have long roads to walk before you find what you seek, and the sooner upon them the better, for even with my best aid, all of you will sleep in the forest tonight, and that is a thing not done lightly in Galunlati."

The companions did not reply, though Fionchadd slowly

rose to his feet. Calvin and David snagged final morsels and did likewise.

"Edahi, Dagantu, come forward," Uki said, nodding to Calvin and Fionchadd.

The Indian and the Faery exchanged glances, then shrugged and did as Uki bade them. Uki's sisters passed each of them a bundle.

"You may open them," Uki prompted, as they hesitated.

Calvin unwrapped his first. "Oh, neat!" he exclaimed. "This is brilliant!"

David wandered up to peer over his shoulder. It was a bow; not as intricate as Fionchadd's had been, but still showing many colors of wood layered within its elegant curves. A white leather quiver went with it, and white-fletched arrows.

"Thank you, *adawehiyu*," Calvin said, bowing; then prodded Fionchadd. "Well, go on, do yours too."

Fionchadd nodded, his face slightly clouded with what David suspected was envy. But it lit once more when he saw that his bundle held his old bow somehow made new again.

Uki smiled wanly. "It was a great medicine to fix that," he said. "And to accomplish it I had to ask the aid of all the trees in the forest and bury it in the ground and sing over it for half the night—perhaps you heard my singing. Its virtues are intact, I think, though I urge you to use great caution. Food you must have, of course, and you may freely slay any creatures you need. Only one thing I require: that you ask their permission before you shoot, and that you thank them upon their deaths and see that some of their blood returns to earth. By this they will know you an honorable man and honor you in turn with their lives to sustain you."

He turned to Calvin. "The bow I have given you is not so strong in medicine, I fear; but it should serve you equally well. You must bear the greater part of your journey, for you must both go and return, thus you too will need to hunt and eat. In your own land, also, you may find it useful, if the road you take be the one I begin to see for you. In return I ask only what I have asked of your friend: to ask, and to thank, and to be grateful."

Calvin smiled ruefully. "I think I can manage that, sir."

"I hope so," Uki said, then motioned David forward. David crossed the short distance and stood waiting expectantly while Uki picked up the bundle he himself had brought in. It was much larger and bulkier than the rest, and Uki unwrapped it before handing it over.

David could not suppress a gasp. It was a bearskin, longer by far than even Uki was tall, and far wider claw-to-claw than their host's outstretched arms, for the paws hung halfway to the ground from the places Uki held them. The long, coarse fur was black as coal.

"Alas," Uki said. "I cannot give you food, nor weapons for its finding, for you seek a medicine place, and for that you must follow the ritual and eat nothing that has not fallen upon the ground or grown from it—and even then you too should ask and thank. But never let it be said that Uki did not aid you as best he could, for though I cannot feed you, still I may provide you warmth and shelter." He held out the skin. "Galunlati is a hot land, yet the nights can be cold in the mountains. This will protect you in the bitterest of seasons."

"Thank you—what was that word you used, Fargo?"

"Adawehiyu. It means very great magician."

"Then thank you, *adawehiyu,"* David stammered. "I—"

Uki cut him off. "No magician I, only a humble Thunderer. But hurry now, the sun is risen and you must all be going. I will start you on your journeys."

A short time later they once more stood atop the waterfall. To the east, the sun poised over a double-knobbed mountain. To the north, clouds floated in a sky of palest lavender, their edges tinged with scarlet.

Uki pointed toward the sunrise. "That way lies your path," he told Fionchadd. "Walk ever with your shadow before or behind you and in two days you should find the golden sand."

He turned to David then, and nodded north. "And that way lies your road, Sikwa Unega. Follow the uktena trail first. When you come to its dying place, look to the north. There you will see another tall mountain, and beyond it another. Continue that way until dark. In the morning, do the same, sighting always by the tallest peaks." And with those words, he left them.

Calvin broke the ensuing silence. "Well, guys, it's been fun."

"Good luck, man," was all David could say at first, but then he added, "and thanks for the advice, Fargo. No hard feeings, I hope."

Calvin clapped a hand on his shoulder. "None."

"Luck," Fionchadd said, and suddenly enfolded David in a hearty hug, then kissed him on each cheek, leaving him blushing in confusion. "Luck, my friend—and fare-well, for we may not meet for long and long, though I *hope* it will be far sooner."

"Luck," David gave him back, and impulsively returned the kisses.

"Luck," called Uki, raising his hands skyward and clap-ping. Thunder sounded, and a veritable fusillade of light-ning crackled across the clear sky.

And then they were walking. David turned his face to the north, to where a cool wind was drifting down from among the trees. He did not look back, did not dare, not to see Calvin and Fionchadd start away to the east, not to see Uki and his sisters turn back toward the cliff that housed his best friend. He was doing what he had to do, he told himself. That would be enough. He would do this thing, *then* think about what came after.

Trees closed around him, and he was suddenly alone with the wild. Beauty surrounded him, and life, and with it came a ghost of healing, as sunlight swept the darkest of his thoughts aside. When he did look back, it was only to see the tops of a thousand maples, and beyond them a rainbow arching above the sound of thunder.

A little more than an hour later David passed the site of the struggle with the uktena, but he did not turn aside to survey the scavengers' progress, though they rose in indignant masses of flogging black wings at his coming. Rather, he moved on as quickly as he could, for with his return to that place came a return of his memories of Alec. Fight them though he would, he could still see the images: his slim, dark-haired friend astride the back of a vast red-and-white serpent, his runestaff plunging deep into the seventh spot. And then that friend lying bruised and broken on the ground with his hands in ruins and his face contorted with pain.

Unsummoned the inscription he had put on the staff came to him:

> Whoever holds to hinder here
> From road that's right, from quest that's clear;
> Think not to trick with tongue untrue,
> Nor veil the vision nor the view;
> Look not to lose nor lead astray
> Who wields this warden of the way.
>
> These runes were wrought, these spells were spun,
> By David Kevin Sullivan.

He patted the small backpack he wore beneath the bear-skin piled upon his shoulders. What remained of Alec's staff was still in there: his signature reworked and carved deeper from the earlier version: David, son of Sullivan. It was all he had of Alec now, all the proof that remained of the bond between them.

He passed the uktena place quickly, and headed down-hill, but the smell of decay and the cacophony of the birds stayed with him for more than a mile.

Slowly the day grew warmer, and at times he cursed the hot weight of the skin. In early afternoon he stopped by a lazy river and swam for a while. Afterward he found a patch of blackberries and ate so many he had to bathe again to remove the stains from this hands and face. A strip of sassafras bark served as a toothbrush as he walked on, climbing one mountain, then sighting another, descending the narrow valley between, and moving on again.

All day he tramped, at a steady pace, not so tired as he had been the first day he had come here; and he knew that even his own strong legs had strengthened under the constant stress of use. Uki had rubbed his blistered feet with a salve before he left, and they were also feeling much better. He was hungry, a little, but he found walnuts, which he cracked with stones, and hickory nuts, which he treated similarly, though the sweetmeats were so small and hard to get at he almost abandoned the effort in futility. And there were blackberries aplenty, as well as mushrooms. More than once he was grateful for the woodcraft David-the-elder had taught him, and his stint in the Scouts, for not everyone could tell which plants were edible, and certainly not among the fungi. For drink he had berry juices and water from the streams that seemed to trickle down from every mountaintop. But in spite of all this, his stomach soon began to knot and growl.

Eventually the sun nudged the horizon, and he began to search for a campsite. It would not require much: the sky did not look threatening. A place by the river would be ideal, one with high rocks to his back to guard against unwelcome intrusion would be even better.

He found such a site in a steep-sided gorge so overgrown with moss and conifers it was like twilight there long before the sun had truly set. It reminded him of an area near his mom's old stomping grounds in North Carolina; Nantahala, they called it: the Valley of the Noonday Sun. Well, this was Nantahala in spades.

There was even a stream, a wide shallow one tinkling melodiously across the golden rocks. And there were steep banks and mounds of granite, and over to the left by the blasted skeleton of a pine, three good-sized boulders together, all taller than he was and open toward the river. He stopped there, bathed again while the air was still warm, and built a small fire while he could still see to do it, collecting driftwood from up and down the bank. It was strange to see smoke there, he realized, as he stretched himself out in the last of the sunlight to dry.

At some point his thoughts turned to Liz. He wished she

was here now, Lordy Jesus did he wish it, and not just because he was naked and feeling a little bit horny. No, he needed her because he didn't want to be alone, and he was, and he was afraid he was going to screw up his mission. Liz wouldn't let that happen. She'd know what to do; would keep him from acting rash or stupid. Shoot, she'd have known how to stop Alec from that foolishness with the uktena.

"Liz," he whispered to the sky. "Girl, I want you with me."

Her name on his lips, he dozed—to jerk awake a short while later to a vision of the smoke drifting into the darkening heavens. Suddenly he felt guilty. Here he was, as conscientious an environmentalist as you could want, sullying the skies of a pristine World. Almost he put the fire out, trusting on the day's heat imprisoned in the rocks and the promised warmth of the fur to sustain him through what he had been warned would be a cold night.

But then rationality spoke, and he could almost hear Alec's voice in that supercilious tone he sometimes used, though it also carried a hint of wind among evergreen needles: *Yeah, sure, Sullivan. You can do without fire if you want to, but don't forget fire's good for keeping things off, and you don't know what's in the woods around here.*

And then Liz's voice answering, one with the tinkle of the river: *And just 'cause you haven't seen anything bigger than a rabbit doesn't mean they're not there. Remember the uktena.*

Bobcats—on the wind.

Wolves—from the riverside.

Mountain lions—from the standing pines.

"And bears," David said aloud, shaking himself from the half trance into which he had fallen: "Lions and tigers and bears, oh my!"

He dressed quickly and took a final long drink from the stream, then banked the coals and laid aside a pile of driftwood for predatory emergencies. One final careful survey of the site, and he set himself to digging a body-shaped hollow in the sand between the rocks. That accomplished, he wrapped himself in the bearskin and snuggled down to sleep.

For a time he dozed dreamlessly, but then came suddenly awake. Something was poking him. He started up, grabbing for his staff that lay close by, then realized what it had been and laughed. The moon had risen and poured its light into the gorge. The stream sparkled like molten silver, the woods hung dark as velvet against a deep blue sky. David could see by the light of that orb—uncannily huge and ruddy—that what had awakened him was nothing more than one of the bear paws that had come adrift when he had wiggled, and had slapped against his side. He batted it away playfully—to be rewarded with an unexpected wash of pain across his palm. He jerked it to his mouth, then brought it to eye level, squinting in the moonlight at the thin lines of blood welling out there. He shook it irritably, wiped it on the fur without thinking, then dabbed a bit of shirttail on it until it stopped. A quick check of the camp, an augmentation of the fire, and he returned to slumber.

This time his sleep was the heavy, dead falling of the truly tired—and yet he dreamed. Not of sights, though; but of sounds: a chant that began, one with the wind in the trees and the song of the river:

He-e! Hayuyahaniwa, hayuyahaniwa, hayuyaha-niwa, hayuyahaniwa,
   Tsistuyi nehanduyanu, Tsistuyi nehanduyanu— Yoho-o!
He-e! Hayuyahaniwa, hayuyahaniwa, huyuyaha-niwa, hayuyahaniwa,
   Kuwahi nehanduyanu, Kuwahi nehanduyanu— Yoho-o!
He-e! Hayuyahaniwa, hayuyahaniwa, hayuyaha-niwa, hayuyahaniwa,
   Uyahye nehanduyanu, Uyahye nehanduyanu— Yoho-o!
He-e! Hayuyahaniwa, hayuyahaniwa, hayuyaha-niwa, hayuyahaniwa,

Gategwa nehanduyanu, Gategwa nehanduyanu—
Yoho-o!
Ule-nu asehi tadeyastatakuhi gunnage astu tsiki.

Once more a part of him half understood the words, but
only when the last line had come around again for the
fourth time, could he truly make them focus:

*And now, surely we and the good black thing, the
best of all, shall see each other.*

David awoke with the sun shining on his face and something hot and heavy half suffocating him. He had slept
soundly: the sleep of the dead, his ma would have said.
And even now, as consciousness returned, he could not
shake the notion that something was not quite right, that
perhaps he was still dreaming. He rolled over, tugged at
the fur—and found that it did not follow. Rather, he heard
a heavy grunt, smelled a strong musky odor, and saw a
black-clawed paw slide onto his chest—and keep on moving, while muscles twitched there and the claws clicked
against each other as tendons flexed them.

David did not dare move, though he had to fight the
rush of adrenaline that suddenly tensed his every muscle
and erected his every hair. This was no longer merely skin,
the empty shell of a creature, but actual, living flesh,
which meant—

He twisted his head slowly to the left, to where the bulk
of fur should lie—too far, and something snorted.

Not wishing to disturb whatever it was, he tried to
relax, and suddenly became aware of a sort of low-pitched
gurgling growl that, now he thought of it, sounded exactly
like someone snoring. Risking a further glance to the left,
David discovered that his first wild notion had been correct. He was asleep in the arms of an immense black bear.

All at once the words to the song returned to him: *surely
we and the good black thing, the best of all, shall see each
other.*

The good black thing . . . surely not this.

Another grunt, and the bear moved; though it did not release David from its casual grasp. Well, he couldn't stay here like this all day, not when he had to get going, never mind the strange behavior of this critter. As cautiously as he could he eased back around and began to snake his left hand across the sand and toward his staff, thinking that any weapon when he truly tried to move was better than nothing. But as he did, his palm scraped something hard, and he winced, almost cried out, and then remembered that he had cut it last night on the bear's claws. He turned it over and stared at it in the pale light of morning, and saw the wound reduced to a line of red.

And then the bear moved in truth, and he felt hot breath on his neck.

"Ah, so that is what brought me back," a guttural voice whispered. Abruptly the weight across his body lessened, and David struggled up and around into a half crouch—as before him a vast shape unfolded itself from the sand, reared onto its hind legs, and raised a fanged and pig-eyed head ten feet above the ground.

"Jesus!"

The bear ignored him completely, sank to all fours, and ambled toward the river, leaving him gaping incredulously beside the remnants of the fire.

The bear slipped briefly into the water, then emerged and shook itself, showering David with spray.

"Thanks are in order, I suppose," it said. "For surely it was your blood that brought me back from the Ghost Country."

"My blood?" David stammered. "How?"

"But you must know, human, if you have come this far in Galunlati, that blood and life are one."

David suddenly felt very stupid, for now that he thought on it, remembering what Uki had said, it made a sort of sense.

"In fact," the bear continued, "I owe you a special debt, for I could not reclaim my body until blood brushed my hide—and stronger blood than now exists in this land— which is how I know you are a stranger here."

David relaxed a little, though it was hard to get used to talking beasts—harder, even than it had been when he first met the Sidhe and they began to speak to him in animal guise. At least then, once the shock had worn off, it was possible to accept that the minds that ruled the shapes were human. But beasts that had always been beasts—and still talked: that was much harder to swallow.

As if reading his mind the bear spoke again. "Ah, but I see confusion. You wonder how I speak so well, and the answer to that is simple: you and I are kin."

"Kin?" David gasped incredulously.

"Yes," said the bear. "Of all the Four-footed Tribes yours and mine are most alike, for many of my kind are descended of a clan of your folk who moved to the woods and grew hair upon their bodies. The *Ani-Tsaguhi,* we once were. I am a son of that clan."

"Then you're not a true bear?"

"By which you mean a bear which was never a man? No, I am not of that kind. There is still a chief bear, Yanu Tsunega, who dwells in *Kuwahi,* the Mulberry Place, to the north. I have never met him."

"Then you cannot help me?"

"That depends. I owe you a debt; if I can repay it, I will do so gladly."

"Well you see, *Ani . . . Ani—* What was your name again?"

"Names give power, so mine I will not speak until I know you better, but you may call me *Yanu,* which simply means *bear* in the tongue of this land."

"Right, okay then, Yanu; I guess I oughta tell you what they call me around here, though I'm not sure I want to."

"I am listening," Yanu said gravely.

"Sikwa Unega."

"White 'Possum, is it?" Yanu laughed (something between a growl and a snuffle). "Truly it suits you. But how came you by a name like that? You do not speak the tongue of Galunlati."

Ooops, David thought. That was a goof for certain.

Here he was spilling his guts to this blessed bruin when he didn't have the first idea he could trust him.

"If I wanted to kill you I would have already," Yanu said easily.

David started. "Jesus, man—can everybody around here read minds?"

"Only strong ones—those and the images behind your words."

David shook his head. "Yeah, well, I wondered about that, but every time I try to think about it—what I'm really saying, and all, I get a headache."

"I could tell you a good herb for that," Yanu volunteered.

David rolled his eyes. "So if you can read minds, I suppose you know why I'm here."

"I know the one you call Uki sent you. I know you are on a quest. I would be glad to hear the rest of the tale."

"Well, it's like this," David began, and told the whole story. By the time he had finished the sun was halfway up the morning sky. He was getting fidgety too, anxious to be on his way, anxious to bring healing to Alec. But the bear kept interrupting, kept asking questions.

"So you dreamed of a white bear while in the asi?" he asked once, when David had told of that part.

"Yeah, we all did. But all we got was that damned rabbit."

"That proves it, then!" Yanu exclaimed. "It was fated that I aid you, and aid I will."

David glossed over most of the rest, for Yanu was familiar of old with Uki and his sisters, though not particularly well disposed toward the latter.

"The younger sister took my skin, which was fine," he said. "She asked, and I gave permission, and then they killed me and apologized. But she did not cover my blood in the prescribed way, for when the time came for skinning, it was raining, which is her brother's province. Thus my blood washed away before it could return to the earth my mother, and so I was lost for ages until you restored me. She was scarcely more than a child then. How is she now?"

"Grown, I guess," David said, and continued.

"And now you seek Atagahi?" Yanu mused when the narrative was finally over. "Well, that is easy enough to find. Come, follow, and I will show you."

"I . . ."

"Hurry, for only at sunset may your kind see it."

David made haste in gathering his pack, staff, and canteen. And though he was careful not to mention it, he was grateful to be relieved of the weight of bearskin that had burdened him the previous day.

The rest of the forenoon they filled with the easy chatter of two friends getting to know one another. David told as much as he dared of his World and discovered that Yanu knew something of it as well; and then, inevitably, the discussion turned to the riddle of the overlapping Worlds.

"This only I know," Yanu said. "Galunlati is far younger than the Lying World, and the two once lay much closer. But then your kind came, and the wise among the Ani-Yunwiya grew afraid and restless, for your folk would keep no treaties and honor no words. And so eventually a secret council was held, and the great wizards and witches were summoned, and together they fasted for seven nights and prayed for seven sevens of days, asking aid of Galunlati. But the chiefs of this land were also afraid, and turned a deaf ear on them, and used certain magics they have that not even the wise of your land know, nor these ones you call the Sidhe either, if what you say of these things called Tracks is true, and together they moved the whole land. Now it floats, touching your land but in fogs and the dreams of madmen and children."

"And there's still a World beyond this?"

"There is one where the Great Thunders live: Kanati and Selu and their like. They made this place; to them it was that the chiefs of this land appealed when we drew apart."

"I see," David said slowly. "Circles within circles."

"And gods within gods," Yanu added. "For even Kanati is not his own master."

"Is Uki a god?"

"That is hard to say," Yanu replied. "His father was one of Kanati's sons, but his mother was a woman from the Lying World."

David frowned. "His sisters too?"

Yanu sighed. "Perhaps I should tell you the whole story."

"Please."

"Very well. Years and years ago, in *hilahiya*, in the Ancient Times, before the lands were split, a woman of the Ani-Yunwiya chanced to find her way to Galunlati. She met a man there and spent many nights with him, but one morning she rose earlier than usual and found that he was not a man at all, but a serpent, one of the monsters from the Underworld who had put on man's shape to trick her. She cried out at this, but nothing could be done, and she was not strong enough herself to kill the snake man, who then escaped her. For the whole next winter she wandered Galunlati demanding justice, but no one heard her, and in the spring she gave birth to one daughter and in the fall to another, both of whom proved wild and unruly."

"Makes sense so far," David noted. "But what about Uki?"

Yanu cleared his throat and continued. "Now one of the Thunder Boys, who are Kanati's sons, saw this, and feared both for the woman and for Galunlati; for he did not know what sort of mischief the snake girls might cause when they were older. So one day he came upon the baby girls where they slept and tattooed their faces so that men might know them for what they were, and set some of his spittle in their mouths so that they might become more like him —and then himself visited the woman in the shape of a handsome man and begat another child on her, who was born the next year. That child is the one you call Uki, and he is set to rule Wahala, but more importantly, to watch over his sisters, the snake women, and see that they not grow too powerful or too wicked. Mostly, I am told, he has succeeded."

"Yeah, well, it all kinda falls together now," David said.

"Though I still don't quite know what's up with him and the weather."

"This only I know," said Yanu. "As I said, this land is young compared with yours and parts of it are yet unfinished. Perhaps Uki's magic is needed to make the rain until Galunlati can bring forth its own."

"Maybe," David said, and threw a stone into the water. The ripples, he thought, were like Worlds—and so, too, were the leaves on the surface, and the pebbles beneath.

Lunch was persimmons washed down with stream water, and in mid-afternoon Yanu found a honey tree, and David helped himself, sucking the sweet stuff off his fingers, then chewing the waxy comb like it was gum. He had, truth to tell, almost forgotten the gravity of his mission.

Toward late afternoon, though, he began to become apprehensive. The sky was darkening, veiled by high, thin clouds, and the wind was growing more chill. The woods were growing denser, too: with black-trunked pines crowding out everything else, the odor of their blue-green needles masking even the high thick musk of Yanu's coarse fur.

Abruptly, Yanu stopped. David halted beside him, and sank down gratefully on a large boulder. Beyond them was a vast, open mud flat overgrown here and there with reeds and short grasses. Far on the opposite side more mountains showed dark beneath a westering sun. It was hot there; heat devils shimmered in the heavy air above the exposed earth. David squinted into the glare—and then his eyes began to burn exactly as they did in the presence of Faery magic. He winced, rubbed them furiously. Was it possible? He strained his vision, tried to summon the Sight—and caught a shift in the air, as of a veil of half-visible breeze swept aside.

The sun touched the roof of the mountains and suddenly it was there:

He stood not at the edge of a plain at all, but on the shores of a vast lake that glowed ruddy in the waning light.

Where grass had sprouted, now ranged cattails and rushes; and where silence had reigned, now was a veritable symphony of bird calls: ducks, mostly, but the honks of geese and the chirps and warbles of countless others as well. He dashed forward, and saw a whole regiment of mallards wing skyward, then glanced sideways, and saw waddling toward him what could only be the awkward shape of the extinct great auk.

"Behold Atagahi!" Yanu said. "It shows itself to you without my intervention, a wondrous thing that. Surely you must be an *adawehiyu*.

"No," David whispered. "I'm only a boy with a very sick buddy." And with that he unscrewed his canteen and filled it to overflowing.

Chapter XX: Shifting Scales

"You have what you came for," a voice growled behind him. "But that does not mean you will take it away."

David leapt to his feet and spun around, still clutching the precious canteen. Six feet away was a bear—but not the familiar roly-poly Yanu, who was now cowering beneath the eaves of the wood. No, *this* bear was white and at least half-again as tall as his recent companion. *A polar bear,* he thought in panic.

Except . . . except . . . Weren't polar bear heads more pointed than this one's, which was rather round? And of course there was the question of what a polar bear might be doing so far south . . .

The bear stayed where it was, but sat back heavily on its massive haunches, still staring at him with its little pig-eyes, while it clicked its fine black claws together across its bulging stomach. David thought of making a break, but knew that the beast could be on its feet quicker than he could imagine, and that even if he could reach the nearest trees, which were several yards away, they would do him no good because bears could climb.

"I agree," the bear drawled. "Running would not help. But it would help *me* a great deal if you would explain why you have come here. This is a place for my wounded kin, and you are no kin of mine."

A quick sideways glance showed David that Yanu had crept back a little closer and was shaping sounds with his mouth without giving them voice. David cocked his head and frowned uncertainly. But suddenly an image came to him: a white bear shambling through the woods; and the words *I come, I come, I come*.

And this *was* a white bear. Maybe . . .

He took a deep breath. "Then why did you answer our summons, oh Great White One?"

The white bear flopped forward, which brought its muzzle within bare inches of David's face. Its breath smelled of fish and watercress. *"You!"* it roared, showing David a mouthful of curving white fangs. "You it was who called but did not wait! Truly I should eat you now, for not only have you stolen from my lake, but you have stolen from my time as well, and made me an object of laughter!"

David swallowed hopelessly. "It was Tsistu. He . . . he tricked us. He said you were coming too slowly and had sent him ahead to meet us."

"You are a double fool, then: to come here, and to listen to fools. Did you not know Tsistu was a famous trickster?"

A helpless shrug. "Not at the time."

"You do now!"

"I'm . . . I'm sorry, sir."

"Sorry is not enough!" the bear growled, rising to its feet. "You owe me twice! Once for your theft, and once for your impatience that cost me great trouble."

"No, oh Grandfather," Yanu interrupted suddenly. "He owes you but one time. For I am one of your people and he has restored me to life."

The white bear swung its head toward his smaller counterpart. "And who are *you*," it asked, "who wear the fur of the West?"

"I am—" and here Yanu gave a name that truly sounded like the grumblings of a bear.

The white bear stared at him for a moment, then nodded. "Very well, since you have given me your name, I will accept your word." He turned back toward David. "You owe me your life but once, now. Is there a way you would prefer to die?" He cocked his head inquiringly and sat back again, waiting.

David had no idea what to do. Was this *it?* Was he going to snuff it here by the shores of a magic lake of healing? He gazed once more toward Atagahi, felt his eyes burn— and suddenly an idea occurred to him.

"Wait," he said slowly. "Isn't it true that most of us human folks can't see this place?" He gestured toward the expanse of shimmering water.

"That is so," the white bear acknowledged, "and truly I wondered that you found it. Yet that will not save you."

"But it means that there's more to me than . . . uh, meets the eye."

"That is possible," the white bear conceded. "To eat a wizard will greatly enhance my power."

"But—" David began.

"He is right," Yanu interrupted. "I was called back for a reason, I knew it when I came. The lake showed itself to him without your will. And I have sensed strong medicine about him, as would you, should you choose to look for it."

The white bear bared its teeth at him and narrowed its eyes. "You are saying . . ."

"You must see for yourself."

The white bear did, surveyed David from muddy boots to uncombed crown. "He does have strong medicine; that much I will acknowledge. Very well, what is it you wish?"

"That you engage him in combat, and if he wins, you let him go free."

"He will not win," the white bear said amiably. "But that sounds very fair to me."

"Well it doesn't to *me!*" David cried, unable to stand

any more. "What the hell are you trying to do, anyway, Yanu? I can't fight this thing!"

"Yes you can," Yanu said calmly. "And I will tell you how."

David's eyes narrowed suspiciously. "I'm listening."

Yanu cast a warning glare toward the white bear, then turned back to David. "You have with you a scale of the great uktena; and more than that, you have helped to slay one."

"You did not tell me *that*," the white bear noted.

"You were too busy being angry to ask," Yanu replied, " . . . or to look."

The white bear bared its fangs again. Its breath, David thought, was considerably hotter than before.

"Nevertheless it is true," Yanu told him. "The scale has great magic, but you yourself are not lacking or you could not have come here. You can use the pain to take on the shape of a bear, and thus fight my Chief here, on equal terms."

David stared at his would-be adversary. "But . . . " He swallowed. "But couldn't he just as well become human and fight me?"

The white bear laughed. "Me? Become human? I who never was?"

"I've never been a *bear,* either," David reminded him archly.

"No, but you have tasted our flesh and drunk our blood, and that is enough to work the change!"

"I have not!" David cried, before he remembered that in fact he had—once, when Uncle Dale had shot a nosy black fellow that had hung around his farm too long. The meat had been pungent and greasy. "Besides, you just said yourself that you eat people, so that makes us even."

"Alas, desire and fact are not always the same," the white bear observed wistfully.

"Well," David said, folding his arms on his chest, "I reckon I've got to do it."

"I reckon," the white bear said, "you do."

* * *

"And just *how* am I gonna pull this off?" David raged at Yanu a short while later. They had retreated to the edge of the forest to confer; the white bear had drawn away to a patch of short green grass and was patiently grooming its fur with claws as long as David's hands. And watching.

Yanu grinned at him. "A simple thing: the mingling of blood and magic. You cut yourself with the uktena scale; your blood awakens it; its magic awakens you. Then you must think on the thing you would become."

David regarded him skeptically. "How deep a cut?"

"Deep, if you would live. Nothing is ever free, and there can be no magic without pain."

David grimaced sourly and fished the pouch out of his backpack. An instant later the uktena scale glittered in his palm. He raised a brow at Yanu. "What about my clothes?"

"They will not change with you."

David rolled his eyes and stripped. The setting sun was warm across his shoulders. A mallard waddled up to watch.

"Does it matter which I cut?"

"That with which you fight."

Biting his lip, David took the scale in his left hand and slashed it across his other palm—too lightly, for only a trickle of blood showed.

"You must do it with more force than that," Yanu told him. "You spilt far more blood to bring me back and endured far more pain."

David frowned and set his jaw. This time he folded the scale in his right hand and squeezed as hard as he could, feeling the glassy edges gouge against fingers and palm. Harder . . . harder. He closed his eyes, and with his other hand grasped the protruding two arms of the scale (the root-ends, he supposed)—and yanked suddenly upward.

Blood flowed out and dripped between his fingers to stain a stand of daisies. Yanu licked it up greedily, and before David could stop him, had likewise slapped his tongue along his hand. "Blood on the earth is dangerous," he said. "Yours is much safer inside me."

David stared at the hand incredulously. It was no longer bleeding.

"Now close your eyes," Yanu said, licking his lips, "and think how it would be to be a bear."

David did, or tried. At first nothing came to him. It was nerves, he supposed, one more delay—and, he admitted, more than a little plain, raw fear. He would be marching off to fight in a minute, after all: and fight a friggin' *bear* in the bargain. It was a little frightening how matter-of-fact that suddenly was. But a part of him—the part that wanted very badly to be back on his front porch in north Georgia drinking Dr Pepper and talking to Liz—was scared well beyond shitless.

That kind of thinking wasn't going to get the work done, though. He had to do this, had to do it *right*, and had to get it over with. Which meant he had to concentrate on nothing except the problem at hand.

But how did it feel to be a bear?

It would feel . . . heavy, first of all; clumsy, hot, *big*. The muscles would be thick and strong and methodical, not slim and supple like his own. He took a deep breath, felt his chest expand, released it—and found that it did not sink back as far as he had expected. His shoulders felt funny, too; as if they wanted to slump forward. His hip joints hurt. The sun across his back made it itch abominably. But that was distracting. *Bear*, he had to think; *bear, bear, bear*.

He would have a big black nose, and long claws, and little pig eyes. And fur—lots of that, black and wiry. He would have ears that twitched, and jaw muscles like iron that would pull back over long white teeth of which he would be very proud.

That was it: heart and blood and muscle, bones and fur and skin. And brain: a beast brain, but one that loved its children, that enjoyed playing in the meadows, that liked to eat wild honey, and—

Pain exploded through him, and he gasped, then threw himself to the ground and rolled in a vain attempt to escape

the agony that was suddenly threatening to turn his inside
out.

Abruptly the pain was gone. He staggered onto his
hands and knees—*no*, his feet! And was a bear.

By the banks of Atagahi twenty yards away the white
bear was still grooming itself and swatting bees.

They came together without fanfare on the reedy shores
of the magic lake, but David could never quite recall how
it began. One moment he was simply approaching his foe
at a cautious amble; an instant later they were regarding
each other across an ever-decreasing distance—decreas-
ing, he realized dimly, because he was covering it at full
gallop. And then the white bear was rearing up on its hind
legs, and then *he* was—rising higher and higher to match
that impossibly tall form. And then they had crashed together and were grappling on the ground.

Claws slashed him, bringing quick blood across his fore-
legs, and with it pain like raw fire. He lashed out with his
own, defending his face, protecting his belly, landing a few
blows here and there, suddenly blind and reckless with
very human fear. Then agony flared through his legs, and
he realized he'd been clawed there too.

Growls filled the lakeside, echoing off the looming
pines: his, and the white bear's—and Yanu's.

"Let the bear fight," Yanu shouted in his own tongue.
"It knows how. Your body is young and will give it
strength. That is all you need!"

David recalled dimly how it had been when Fionchadd
had fought through him before—how much he had resisted. He gasped, and prayed it was the right thing, and let
go.

His bear shape *did* know how to fight, all right; how to
use teeth and claws—all four sets of those. Somehow he
climbed atop his adversary and gave him a good raking,
but then the white bear flipped him over again, and they
tumbled together toward the lake. Water lapped them, cold
and clear, and with it fled part of the pain. But hot blood

flowed over them more quickly; and David realized he was seeing through thickening veils of red.

Back on dry land now, and more blows thrown and taken. His left arm was so savaged it was useless, he could not even curve the claws there. And jaws were coming toward his neck. No, were *on* his neck and gnawing toward his life. Already the world was darkening. He was going to die. Why had Yanu done this to him? It was all a trick, a horrible, bloody trick.

"You can stop now," Yanu called.

Nothing happened.

"I said *stop*," he called again. And this time the pressure vanished from David's neck. He dared open his eyes, saw his foe sit back abruptly.

"What do you want?" the white bear snarled. "Another few nips and he would have been dead."

"And you would have slain Uki's chosen," Yanu replied promptly. "But there is another reason."

"Very well," the white bear snapped, "I would like to hear it."

Yanu scratched his side absently. His small eyes glittered. "Why are you fighting?" he asked.

"You were here, you know the answer."

"Suppose you tell me, though."

"Because he took water from Atagahi unasked."

"Do all who come here crave your permission?"

The white bear shook his head slowly. "They do not."

"And why do they not?"

"Because it is a place of healing for all the Four-footed Tribes. In particular for my wounded kin."

An ear twitched. "And just who *are* your kin?"

"Are you *stupid?* Your kind, my kind: the Bear-tribe."

"And what is that?" Yanu cried triumphantly, waving a paw toward David.

The white bear's mouth dropped open (rather foolishly, David thought distantly).

"I would say," Yanu went on before the other could reply, "that that is a wounded bear!"

"You have tricked me," the white bear spat, leaping to its feet and lumbering toward him.

"Maybe I have spent too much time with Tsistu," Yanu replied dryly, not moving. "His soul came so often to the Ghost Country during my long years there that he and I have become close friends."

"And it would seem," the white bear snarled, halting in mid-step, "that you have now made another." He said nothing for a minute, simply stood staring at the placid-seeming Yanu, but gradually the fire faded from his eyes. "Very well," he said at last, "you have defeated me." He turned and retraced his steps toward David.

David saw him coming, but hardly cared. He hurt all over. His body was a mass of gouges; but worse, tendons had been severed in his left foreleg so that he could not move it. He tried to speak, to cry out his pain, but could only manage something between a growl and a whimper.

The white bear shuffled up to him and poked him in the side with his muzzle. "I am weary of this, human; and truly you have shown yourself a worthy opponent. I suppose I could argue that you are not truly a bear, but the Ani-Tsaguhi themselves are not all of that seeming, and I do not stop them. You are injured, and I have injured you. Go into Atagahi, drink the water. It will heal your body and restore your form. And take away what you will; for any man for whom you would risk so much surely deserves to live."

David managed a grunted thanks, dragged himself to his feet, and limped toward the lake.

An instant later, he was both whole and human.

And the white bear was nowhere in sight.

Chapter XXI: Healing

(Galunlati—day four—evening)

The journey back from Atagahi was not remarkable—except for the haste with which it was begun. David had the healing water now, the precious fluid that would—he hoped—save his best friend. It only remained to get it to him and pray it arrived in time. So it was, then, that he jogged as fast as he could through the darkening woods, with only a panting Yanu for company, all the while cursing himself for the casual pace he had maintained the day before. It was pretty damned irresponsible, he told himself, to have taken it easy when Alec's life hung in the balance. And as for diversions like bathing, eating—sleeping, even. Why, he could certainly have gone without them for a day or two.

"You beat yourself too much," Yanu told him when they paused by a stream to slake their thirsts. It was an hour past sunset and night was fast enfolding them. David's stomach was an agony of emptiness.

"I have to," David gasped between swallows. "I've got a sick friend, remember?"

"But you will do him no good if you kill yourself before you come to him. And as for that other thing that is hurting you: you did the right thing by taking your time. Why, think, boy; had you come to Atagahi as you are now: tired, without sleep or food; do you think you could have fared as you did against Yanu Tsunega? There had to be a battle, I knew that as soon as I saw him there. And you had to be wounded for my plan to succeed. But it took careful timing, for I had to be certain he would admit that you were wounded, yet could not wait too long for fear you *would* die. Had you arrived fatigued, and I then overestimated your strength, he might have killed you before I could stop him, and then where would you be?"

"Dead," David panted, and threw himself on his back by the stream, gazing past the tall pines to the ragged doily of purpling sky beyond. "One thing still puzzles me, though."

"What might that be?" Yanu wondered absently, as he waded into the stream to fish.

David propped himself up on his elbows. "Well . . . gee, this is hard to put. But, well, I'm confused about how I was able to shapeshift. From what I've heard, magic—or medicine, or whatever—is supposed to always be strongest in one's own World—or at least that's what the Sidhe —the *Nunnehi*—say, and it seems to be true, as far as I can tell. But I can't shapeshift back home, so according to them, I shouldn't have been able to here, either."

"Have you ever tried?"

"Once," David replied sheepishly. "It didn't work."

"It was mostly the scale, then," Yanu told him, snapping a paw into the water to casually flip a shining rainbow trout onto the gravelly shore. Another followed immediately. They lay beside David's feet, bodies arcing up and down in blind panic, gills fanning helplessly for air.

"I know *that* much!"

"Very well, I will tell you. You have magic, Sikwa Unega; that much is obvious—and evidently in both lands. In that you are like the uktena, for it is a unique creature, being part of many things at once, thus it was only reasonable that you would respond to a part of it. You needed only to be awakened."

David frowned uncertainly. "Sorry, but you've lost me."

"The uktena is neither serpent nor beast nor vermin. It has the form of a rattlesnake, but the horns of a goat; it lives mostly on blood like a leech or a tick, but has the soul of a man."

"Wha . . . ?"

"The uktena was formerly one like yourself, did you not know that? Once, when your folk came often to Galunlati, one of them insulted the Sun, and She sent heat to burn this land. But the people asked Kanati to help them, and he turned two men into serpents and sent them to kill the Sun, knowing She would not die, but would well learn a lesson. So it was that he made the rattlesnake and the uktena. The former succeeded, but the uktena was afraid when it saw the Sun and crawled away into the Lying World, where it stayed and terrorized the Ani-Yunwiya for many years. Always, though, it held a grudge against the folk of Galunlati who had made light of its cowardice, and so, when it heard that the Ani-Yunwiya had asked deliverance from your kind, it saw a chance for revenge and crept back into this land. And when Galunlati was removed from the Lying World, here it remained to torment its former tormentors."

"So," David said finally. "Its power really comes from my World?"

Yanu shook his heavy head. "Its *substance* comes from your land, its power both from Galunlati and the World Above; it is some of all, and all of neither. But because part of it *is* of your land, its power responds to you—and yours to it."

"I see," David sighed, though he didn't. He could go to sleep so easily . . . so easily.

"Eat those fish," Yanu said. "And I will let you."

For the first time in two days David slept with a full stomach that evening.

* * *

Toward sunset on the second day David found himself
once more cresting the ridge where Alec had slain the uktena. The charnel reek was fading now, the scavenger birds
gone except for a few sated buzzards staggering among the
withered bracken. David allowed himself a side jaunt to
survey the remains. From a little distance, the gully appeared empty, the burn scars on the far side already putting
forth new growth. But as he stepped nearer and peered in,
he saw what he expected: a vast skeleton, intact in places,
disrupted in others, its half-moons of ribs describing a century of seasons across the land. Scales lay about in profu-
sion, proving dangerous underfoot—as he learned to his
regret when he kicked at one and found the edge piercing
not only his boot, but his big toe besides. Ignoring the pain
as much as he could, he limped downward where the head
had been. Like an alligator's skull it was, or more like that
than anything else—except that the upper jaw was about
the size of the hood of his car, and the eyeholes big as
schoolroom trash cans. Of the ulunsuti there was no sign
save a small cavity in the middle of the forehead between
the two ivory horns.

"A mighty victory that must have been," Yanu said.
"The uktena has grown since last I saw him. And truly I
hope it is a year for every rib, and that times the sunrises in
those years, before I see him again—though everything
has its season and I know someday we will come against
each other once more."

"The price of immortality," David murmured.

"All things have their price," Yanu answered: "Joy and
sorrow besides."

"Yeah, and speaking of sorrow, I'd better boogie on and
see to Alec."

Yanu followed him to the first line of trees below the
summit. "I must leave you here, Sikwa Unega. It has been
long since I wore my hide, and I would not leave it again
as soon as I might were I to venture further. Uki's sisters
have sharp eyes, as I have learned to my pain. I think I will
journey in the north for a while—or maybe westward," he

added, "for I am not certain I want to see my chief again so soon."

David nodded mutely, and a sort of snuffle from Yanu seemed to express a like sentiment. Impulsively, David grasped the bear around the neck and hugged him tight. "Thanks a bunch, man. I don't know what I'd have done without you."

"Died, most likely: frozen or eaten. I did not tell you that Spearfinger came near last night."

"Spearfinger?"

"An old woman with an immense finger like an awl which she keeps hidden until she is close to a victim—whereupon she stabs him. She likes to eat livers."

David could only gape.

"She has followed us since our first night together," Yanu continued, "but she fears me. Beware, though, for she is likewise a shapeshifter."

David scanned the surrounding woods nervously. "We're clear now, though, right?"

Yanu raised his head and scented the breezes. "I do not smell her, and I would, for she reeks of blood."

"I *bet*!"

"Truly I must be going," Yanu said, turning.

"Carry on, then," David called, as the bear started back up the trail.

"Farewell to you too, Sikwa Unega," Yanu growled over his shoulder. "And be kind to my kin in your land."

"I sure will," David replied, and continued on down the mountain.

Little more than an hour later he trotted out of the woods above Uki's cave. Coolness struck his skin, and he realized the close-grown forest had been almost stiflingly warm. But he was in clear air now, and the strong evening breeze brought with it a tickle of spray and the tingle of ionized air. He halted for a long, breathless moment, and simply stood there, enjoying the breeze, letting the falls' steady pounding slowly drum the fatigue from his bones.

He had just started on again when another sound insinuated its way into the water's rhythm: the high, sweet buzz of a harmonica playing Beethoven's "Ode to Joy."

"Calvin!" David shouted, gazing left to where the trees blazed red with sunset fires above a ruby river. Before he knew it, he was running.

The music stopped in mid-note, and another voice rang out, "*Siyu*, White-Possum-Man!"

Calvin himself came into view an instant later; prancing along the opposite bank with his shirt tied round his waist and his boots thumping against either hip. The new bow was slung across his back, and he had acquired different war paint, if the lightning bolts of blue and yellow slashing across his chest, shoulders, and cheekbones were any indication. An explosion of pheasant feathers was knotted in his hair, and instead of his headband he was wearing Fionchadd's torque.

David waited on the nearer side, while Calvin made his way along the stepping stones as if he had been crossing them all his life. A yard from shore, the Indian suddenly paused, threw back his chest—and frowned sullenly, his arms folded across his gaudy pecs.

David froze in the act of extending a hand, but then Calvin's jaw muscles twitched, his eyes sparkled, and he broke into a grin.

David grinned too, and then the two of them were standing in knee-deep water, arms wrapped around each other, giggling like utter fools.

"I did it!" David gasped.

"So did Finny and me."

"You're kiddin'!"

"No way."

"I . . ."

Calvin's face turned suddenly serious. "I wasn't sure we'd ever make it, either, Dave. It was just . . . too remote, I guess. I've just been kinda drifting along like all this was an extended dream, or something—kinda goin' with the flow and all. But when I saw Fionchadd put that ship in the water and sail off, suddenly I knew it was real. That . . ."

"Let's finish inside, okay?" David interrupted. "My feet are killing me—and I've *got* to see to Alec."

"Sorry, man; it's just that I haven't said a word for two days."

David flopped an arm across Calvin's shoulders and steered him toward the cliffside trail. "I figured you'd be used to your own company by now, what with a year on the road, and all."

"Well, you can only live in your own head so long 'fore you start to go crazy."

"With only a crazy man to talk to? I don't doubt it! Or maybe you already have; ever think about that? This may really *be* a dream. You may still be up on Lookout Rock!"

"Or with Our Lady of the Smokies."

"Nah, you wouldn't have any clothes on then."

"Good point." Calvin laughed, and followed David toward the gorge.

Alec was no better when David arrived, but neither was he any worse, though his sleeping face was gaunt and pale and he had obviously lost more weight than a few days without food could account for. His hands had healed a little—maybe; but David wondered if he'd ever be able to use them properly again, because a closer inspection revealed a drawing of tendons and muscles he did not like, as if they were drying out like the body of some dead animal left in a parching sun.

"He sleeps mostly, now," Uki told him, as David crouched by the pile of furs. "We wake him for what food he will take, but I doubt it is sufficient. And the charms are no longer working."

David shrugged helplessly. "Well, you tried, that's all you can do. But I guess he's just not designed for it—the medicine can't get a hold on him, or something."

"I fear not," Uki said. "But perhaps you will be more successful."

"No time like the present," Calvin said, squatting beside them and pointing to the canteen. "How do we do this?"

"Good question," David echoed. "Does he drink it, or do we bathe him in it, or what?"

"All," said Uki. "But to drink he must awaken."

"Alec!" David whispered, reaching out to gently shake his friend's shoulder. "Alec, it's me, Davy."

The only reply was a faint moan.

"Alec? Come on, man, wake up! Speak to me!"

Uki drew him back. "I think part of him hears you and would answer, but there is another trouble: he has waited so long that he has lost the way. Anticipation has kept him alive; now the relief that replaces it may kill him."

"Can't you do anything?"

"One thing more I will try. You bathe his limbs. I will do what I can."

David nodded and drew back the furs that covered his friend, and now he saw how completely the uktena's poison had wasted Alec's body. Ribs showed like fences where before had been smooth flesh; muscles hung slack; hip bones arched high above a shrunken belly. He looked, David, thought, like one of those AIDS victims he was constantly seeing on television. Calvin's only reaction was a half-suppressed whistle of dismay.

"What now?"

"Rub the water over his arms and legs," Uki said. "But save some for him to drink. My charm requires access to his chest."

David did as instructed, pouring a thin trickle of the water across Alec's shins and spreading it out with his palms; feeling, as he worked his fingers around, how flabby the calf muscles had already become.

For his part, Uki reached into a pouch at his side and took out a small brown stone pierced with a tiny hole through which ran a string. Grasping one end of the string between his thumb and forefinger, he let the rock drop first to Alec's lips, then to the center of his chest, and finally to his manhood. "The centers of life," Uki murmured. Centering the stone above Alec's solar plexus, he gave it a gentle shake and slowly began to twirl it, then let his hand go still. The stone continued circling for a time, but gradually the figure it inscribed became an ellipse, which in turn became a simple arc along the length of Alec's body.

Eventually it stopped, but David could see that it did not

lie vertically beneath Uki's hand, but tended slightly toward Alec's right side as if drawn there by some invisible magnet.

"It is as I thought," Uki told them. "His soul lies in the west; it is there I must face to call it."

"Just tell me what to do," David said.

"Continue bathing," Uki replied, standing and striding around so that he faced away from David, with his feet to either side of Alec's head. "Do the arms next, then work upward along the torso. The face must follow; when you reach the mouth, call me."

"Got it."

Uki did not reply, but secreted the stone, raised his arms, and began to chant:

> *Sge! Ha-nagwa hatunganiga Nunya Watigei, ga-husti tsuts-kadi nigesunna. Ha-nagwa dungihyali. Agiyahusa aginalii, ha-ga tsun-nu iyunta datsiwak-tuhi. Tla-ke aya akwatseliga. Hyuntikwala Usunhi digwadaita.*

This time David understood the words—perhaps, he decided later, because he did not truly listen.

> Hear! Ha! Now you have drawn near to hearken, O Brown Rock; you never lie about anything. Ha! Now I am about to seek for it. I have lost a friend and now tell me about where I shall find him. For is he not mine? My name is Uki."

As David worked his way higher, Uki started over. The third time he joined in, not consciously, simply letting his tongue follow the flow of rhythm and accent. By the fourth round he had reached Alec's forehead. By the fifth his mouth.

"I'm there," he said clearly, whereupon Uki repeated the verse more loudly and clapped his hands three times, sending thunder echoing through the cave.

"Now!" he cried. "Now!"

For with the first clap Alec's mouth had sagged open. David wasted no time and sloshed a little of the water from the canteen across his lips. They moved involuntarily. Alec's eyelids fluttered. More water, and Alec's tongue twitched. An instant later he swallowed, choked softly, then gulped more, and finally—to David's vast relief— reached up, took the canteen, and drank greedily.

"*No!*" Uki warned, when Alec would have drained it. "You must save some for your eyes!" David pried the canteen gently from Alec's fingers and poured a little on each of his friend's rheumy lids.

He blinked, shut them again, blinked twice more, and squinted. "Jeeze, it's bright in here," he mumbled.

"You're back!" David sobbed, lifting Alec's torso off the furs to hug him. "Oh, Jesus, man, you're back! You're back! I—" He paused then, suddenly terrified. "Oh crap, I haven't hurt you or anything, have I? Can you . . . can you see, and all?" He thrust himself away and regarded his friend at arm's length.

"Davy?" Alec said slowly. "Things're a little . . . fuzzy right now, but I . . . think they're getting clearer." He twisted free, tried to stand, but sank back down. "Oops, maybe not quite yet."

"Not hardly," David chided. "But Jesus God, I'm glad you're okay." He peered up at Uki. "He is, isn't he?"

"He will be fine. As the waters of Atagahi spread through him he will grow stronger. By tomorrow he will be well enough to travel."

"That's good," David said, nudging Calvin, "'cause we need to be gettin' home. We've still got a message to deliver."

"I will show you a short way," Uki said, "one that will keep you clear of Tsistu."

"You mean he's already back again?" Calvin asked. "Reincarnated, and all . . . ?"

Uki shrugged. "It would not be at all unlikely. But enough of him, *you* must eat—both of you. You have fasted long enough."

"I could eat a horse," Alec volunteered.

"Alas," Uki replied sadly, "none of those beasts live here. What you need is the flesh of a strong animal to give you its strength in turn. Bear would be perfect. I will send my sisters to hunt one."

David's heart flip-flopped. "Uh, please *not* bear!"

Uki's eyes narrowed, but David thought he saw a spark of mischief there. "What do you suggest instead?"

"Buffalo," Calvin said with conviction. "I saw a herd not an hour's walk from here."

"And fish," said one of the sisters from the entrance. "To aid in speed and quickness. Perhaps *you* could procure some, brother?"

Uki rose wordlessly and left.

David looked puzzled, but Alec was laughing. "More magic," he giggled. "Always more magic. The whole blessed world's made of magic."

"Fool-of-a-Scotsman, get real," David giggled back, risking a friendly jab to his buddy's shoulder.

"I'd *rather* get dressed," Alec replied archly. "Has anybody got a comb?"

"Now I *know* you're cured." David laughed, as Alec staggered to his feet and let his friends steer him to the ledge behind the falls.

By the time Alec had made himself presentable, the snake women were back with a huge haunch of meat; and by the time it was prepared the three boys were famished. The fish Uki had caught, they ate raw, but the herbs sprinkled over them tasted wonderful, and their flesh was firm and sweet.

Finally David flopped onto his side and looked at Calvin. "Well, I guess it's time you told us *your* story."

"Yeah," Alec chimed in. "What were *you* up to while I was watching horror movies on my eyelids?"

"Boy, *that's* a long one," Calvin sighed. "I don't think I wanta go into it now." He leaned back and folded his arms contentedly across his chest.

"The *hell* you don't!" David cried indignantly. He leapt forward and prisoned the Indian's body beneath his own.

Calvin's mouth popped open in surprise. "What're you *doin'*, Sullivan?"

"It's called coercion," David hissed, grinning fiendishly as he secured his hold on Calvin's wrists. "Now would you like to reconsider your decision?"

A bored yawn followed. "I don't really think so, at least not now." His lids drifted down, and David felt Calvin's body relax.

"*Fargo!*"

One twinkling eye slitted open. "Oh, well gee, guys; if you're *that* interested . . ."

"We are," David said, releasing him.

"Okay then, but only a short version, 'cause I really *am* beat." He sat up and crossed his legs, rested his hands in his lap, and began.

He made short work of the trip to the golden sand. The journey itself had been uneventful, except for one harrowing moment when Calvin had misjudged a bow shot and nearly been gored by a charging buffalo before Fionchadd saved him; and the fact that they had been attacked by a monstrous leech at another place, when they had been forced to ford a river.

"That would be Tlanusi," Uki said. "I should have warned you, though usually he is sleeping this time of year. Perhaps the death of the uktena has disturbed him, for they are kindred, and the beast would know of his passing."

Calvin shrugged. "Whatever you say."

"What *I* want to say"—David chuckled pointedly—"is for *you* to say how the quest ended."

Calvin smiled cryptically. "Maybe it'd be easier if I *showed* you."

"Showed us? How . . . ?"

The smile widened as Calvin reached into his pocket and pulled out a thin crystal disk exactly like the one Lugh had used earlier to show them Finvarra's navy.

"Hey, where'd you get *that?*" David exclaimed.

"Finny gave it to me," Calvin replied smugly, setting the disk on edge in the sand between them. "But old Silverhand invented 'em. There're these jewels in this torque, see, that are kinda like movie cameras, 'cept they're magic; and whatever Finny saw they imprinted on these disks that he had stashed in that fancy gold belt."

"Oh, Christ," David groaned, rolling his eyes. "High-tech comes to Faerie and the little fiend never even told me!"

"Magi-tech," Calvin corrected. "Pure mumbo-jumbo. Frankly, I'm not real sure this thing'll work here," he added, "but Finny thinks it will, since it is partly magic from our World that runs it." He muttered a word and sat back expectantly.

The disk immediately began to expand, until all they could see was a five-foot circle of light in which shapes were quickly taking form.

"It's got the whole record of our trip in there," Calvin told them as the shapes became rapidly clearer. "But he's got it set on the last part."

The first thing David could make out was a sandy shore, and he thought briefly that Calvin had somehow come into possession of the disk he had seen before—except, he realized quickly, that the sand this one showed was gold, and the waves beyond were empty of ships but alive with webs of glitter that could only be Straight Tracks.

"You must have been very near Nundagunyi," Uki observed. "For only there do the Great Waters look so."

David studied the image more intently and saw beyond the waves and webs of light a curtain of reddish fog that his vision could not penetrate. The image spun for a moment, then; first showing Calvin's face, and then, after more chaos, Fionchadd's.

"You must record my departure," the Faery was saying. "I have given you my torque to accomplish that, and also to remember me by."

"But what are you gonna use? I mean, don't you need to record this too?"

Fionchadd patted his gold-linked belt. "I have a dupli-cate disk here, and another on which to place further happenings. There are two seeing-stones as well, and one of those I will take with me."

The Faery's hand filled the disk for an instant, then pulled back to show him holding one of the torque's jeweled end-knobs. "This will record my voyage," he said. "And now I must be upon it."

The rest of the departure looked familiar: the toy ship was placed in the water; Fionchadd rubbed the ring; the flames sprang forth; the ship expanded. The Faery's face loomed large again as good-byes were said and he and Calvin hugged each other. Calvin gave Fionchadd his beaded headband, and then the Faery splashed through the waves and leapt onto the deck, waving, and brandishing his bow. "I go to my grandmother's country," he cried. "Tell my mother I will return for her with an army!"

"Just bring *yourself* back, Lizardman," Calvin shouted, as the disk showed Fionchadd reaching to his waist, drawing out a dagger, and striding to the angle behind the dragonhead. For a moment he hesitated, weighing the weapon in his hand as if something were not quite right, then squared his shoulders and drove it home.

A strangled gasp from Alec startled them all, and when David turned that way, he was crying.

"Hey, what is it, man?" he asked, more than half afraid his friend had suffered some sort of relapse. "He's okay, we're all gonna miss him."

"Yeah," Alec sobbed. "But . . . but something's *wrong*. I don't know what it is, but it's my fault, I know it is!"

"*Your* fault," David snorted. "How could that possibly be?"

Alec shook his head. "I don't know, but I've done a bad thing, I *know* I have."

David took a deep breath and let it out very slowly. "What *kind* of bad thing?"

"I told you, I don't know! All I know is that . . ." His face contorted with pain. "Oh, God, I get a headache when I even try to think about it!"

David exchanged troubled scowls with Calvin and Uki.

"He is weak," Uki said, "and dreams no doubt torment

him, for he was nearly Tsusginai, in the Ghost Country in Usunhiyi—and that is a fearful place indeed!"

"I don't know," Calvin said, frowning. "He was talking about that bad thing before he started fading."

"Alec, can you tell us—" David began urgently.

But Alec was asleep.

Chapter XXII: Home

(Galunlati—day seven—morning)

Alec's memory was no better when Uki roused them the next morning. He was immeasurably stronger though, if by no means fully recovered, and David decided not to quiz him about the nameless "bad thing" until later.

"It's funny," Calvin said, as he sorted the small museum of herbs and mineral specimens he had accumulated the last few days, "how we could be here doing all this stuff, and almost forget why we really came."

"Running around in other Worlds'll do it to you," David replied sagely, applying himself to his own gear. "Trust me. I've met my myths, and now you've met yours. You'll never be the same after—and I tell you what, it's a mixed blessing. I'm *still* figurin' things out."

Alec snugged the last buckle on his pack. "Yeah, and I don't even believe in this stuff!"

"Do you not?" Uki said behind him. "Well, do you believe in thunder or in rain? In the green earth? In living things?"

"Of course!"

"Then surely it is not that much harder to believe in me."

"Well," Alec hedged, "I've *seen* you."

"And I you, but a hundred years from now when I tell my sisters' sons—should they ever be so fortunate as to marry," he added wryly, "that I entertained the likes of you, do you suppose they will believe me? They will not have known a time when our lands lay close together and it was as easy for our folk to visit you as it is for your folk to come here. You, at least, have songs and prayers; we have none for such a purpose, and in your land, who would listen?"

"We would," Calvin affirmed instantly.

"No doubt," Uki sighed. "But come, you have a pressing errand and should be about it."

"Right," said David, getting up. "Just let me get my staff."

"Speaking of which," Calvin said, "I guess I should return my bow."

"No," Uki told him. "It is yours. Perhaps it will lose some medicine in your world, but much of its strength is in the thing itself, and that will not change wherever you take it. And," he added with a twinkle in his eye, "while we talk of gifts, I have others for you."

"But we don't have anything to give you in return," David protested, "and you've helped us out so much!"

"You have given me tales for a long evening's telling, and food for thoughts that will span longer still."

"Well, if that's enough . . ."

"And more than enough. But come."

Uki led them into the outer cavern (the snakes were beginning to re-emerge, David noticed, stepping over one). There he opened a chest made of the shells of two tortoises hinged together with rawhide thongs. From it he took a small earthenware jar and a pouch of the ubiquitous white deerskin. The latter he passed to Calvin, which proved, upon being emptied, to be an uktena scale.

"I have given it a special power," Uki said. "Too long I have ignored happenings in your land, and from what you have told me, perhaps that has been an error. It would be good for me to learn more; and you, Edahi, would be an excellent teacher. Should you ever desire to return to Galunlati, burn this scale and step into the smoke that ensues, call my true name, and you will be here."

"But what *is* your name?" Calvin asked suddenly. "I mean, you've never told us."

Uki lifted an eyebrow. "I have not, have I? Here we hide our names, for fear they be used to witch by; yet I have just asked you to conjure by mine! But since you are leaving, I think I can trust you with it." He paused, took a deep breath. "Know, then, all of you, that I am called *Hyuntikwala Usunhi,* which in your tongue means Darkthunder."

"Darkthunder," David whispered. "Nice!"

"The thunder in the heavy clouds at the end of a hot summer day," Uki said. "I trust it to you; use it wisely."

"But wait a minute," David blurted out. "If all we had to do to get here was to burn a scale, why'd we have to spend all that time sitting around in an asi?"

"For several good reasons," Uki told them. "The first is that the scale requires special preparation which few here know how to do. The second is that your friend had only one scale, which would not have sufficed for the four of you. Thirdly the scale can only take you to places where you yourself have been, and none of you had been to Galunlati. And finally, it requires that you know the true name of someone of power in this place, and my uncle with whom your friend visited gives his true name to none."

"Makes sense, I guess," was all David could manage in reply. Uki smiled at him. "Ah, you are ever the clever one, Sikwa Unega; I believe you would find out every secret in all the lands, given time—but for now I would have you discover a closer one: your gift." He paused, and motioned his sisters forward. "Since you already possess an uktena scale, I have for you a twin bow to Edahi's. To this I would add what you have already won: the waters of the lake Atagahi. Little remains in your strange metal flask, but it may still do you some service. I have mixed it with water from my own river, and said certain Words over it. I cannot be certain that its magic will go with you into your land, but my hope is it will retain some of its healing virtue even there. One thing more I should tell you, though: Not only can it heal the body, but also the spirit. Use it sparingly."

David took the gifts, bowed solemnly, and backed away.

Finally Uki faced Alec. "I have already spoken of the power of names, my young friend; and well have you worn that which I gave you: Tawiska: the Smooth One. But you have passed a mighty trial since I called you so, and have thereby earned another. I hereby declare Tawiska dead and your new name to be Tsulehisanunhi: the Resurrected One!"

"Uh . . . thank you, sir," Alec stammered.

Uki did not reply, but took the jar, uncapped it, and shook out a second leather pouch, which he gave to Alec. David could tell by the way Alec's hand sagged beneath it that whatever it contained was disproportionately heavy for its size. Alec hesitated a moment before emptying the contents into his palm.

A glitter of jewel-broken colors told David what it was before Uki identified it.

"It is what you have earned at great cost," their host said: "It is the ulunsuti, the stone from the head of the uktena. The beaks of the birds have freed it."

It glittered in Alec's hand, like an immense rough diamond: crystal-clear except for one vein of red through its center. That vein seemed to pulse in a gentle, subtle rhythm.

"It has many powers," Uki continued, "but I know not how they may work in your land, or if; except to say that its primary virtue is to prophesy. You must keep it in both jar and pouch at all times, and once a week it must have blood—a single drop will suffice. Twice a year it must have the blood of some large animal or it will grow restless and seek sustenance on its own. Blood also it must have for any major working. It is a dangerous thing to deliver into the hands of the inexperienced, but I give it to you with a wish for luck, and a warning: Study it, but use it not capriciously or in vain, for it marks you a strong adawehi. See that it not make you a foolish one."

"But I don't deserve this," Alec protested, as Uki passed him the jar.

"You rid me of a threat I could not have done myself," Uki replied. "You risked your life for your friends. That marks you a man of great honor and power."

Alec flushed and stared at his feet. "I . . . I'm not at all sure that's why I did it, actually. I . . ."

Uki cut him off. "But you did it, which is what is important. The stone is, in truth, far too little reward." He paused and grinned—disarming in one so tall and stately. "Perhaps you would like one of my sisters as well? Or perhaps the set. Or perhaps one of your companions would like one."

"Uh, thanks," David said quickly, "but—well, they'd be hard to explain, and we . . ."

"We—" Alec began, but then broke off, blinking rapidly. "We— *Damn,* what a headache!"

"We already *have* girlfriends," Calvin finished obliviously.

"Ah, but what of wives? Of those how many?"

"None."

"None! But surely you are of an age . . . Why had I known I would have performed the ceremonies myself!"

David exchanged horrified groans with Calvin, then risked a surreptitious glance back at Uki and saw that his eyes were twinkling. "It was a thing to be hoped," their host said, "not expected."

"Sorry," David managed.

"I guess we'd best be going," Calvin prompted. "Hey, you okay, McLean?"

Alec shook his head. "Just a twinge of migraine, I reckon."

"A result of too much excitement so soon after his illness, no doubt," Uki said, as he led them to the ledge behind the falls. "Here lies the fastest way back to your world. Though it is not without peril, it is best that Tsulehisanunhi return to his own country as soon as possible. A day's journey overland would do him no good service."

"Anything," David said. "I'm bloody sick of walking."

"Right," Alec agreed, having evidently recovered.

"Good-bye," David said, extending his hand.

Uki hesitated for a moment as if confused, then took it, and followed David's lead in a handshake.

Alec and Calvin did the same.

"I meant what I said about returning," Uki told them. "I grow tired of my own company—and all these women and their pets."

Alec cleared his throat self-consciously. "Come on, guys," he said. "Let's boogie."

"Very well," Uki replied. He reached into his pouch and produced three more uktena scales, which he distributed among the boys. "When I tell you, hold the scales aloft and close your eyes. The rest will be as happens."

A moment only they stood there, lids shut, arms extended over their heads. David could feel the prickle of spray against his skin, the energy of the ionized air. Behind them, Uki begin to chant: louder and louder, until his voice screamed above the thunder of falling water. Then, as abruptly as he had begun, there was silence—followed by three hand claps, which were answered immediately by three flashes of lightning that crackled down from heaven and smashed through the falls to enfold the scales.

"Farewell!" David heard Uki call as fire exploded through him. Then he was falling into blue-white flames.

His eyes popped open—saw only mist. But around him the heat grew greater as phantom hells consumed him, crisped his skin black, then sent it flaking away into ashes. Hotter and hotter, and pain beyond pain. And a distant thunder, like drums.

—which grew steadily louder until an agony of sound banished that all-consuming heat with an even more appalling agony: one that shook his very being into fragments of fire and rained them into the mist.

One final clap of white noise, and abruptly there was solidity beneath his feet.

White still filled his eyes, though; and the heat had scarce diminished. But an instant later a brush of clean air broke in upon them, ripping the veils from their eyes, as the thunder rumbled away.

They were standing in the wreckage of Uncle Dale's smokehouse. Apparently it had been struck by lightning.

"You are back," Oisin said, rising from the porch of the nearby corncrib, a puzzled frown creasing his forehead. "Yet surely you did not have to arrive with so much...exuberance. Could some other way not have been found...?"

"We did it!" David gasped, leaping across the blasted threshold. "We did it, Oisin! Finno's on his way."

"Yeah," said Calvin, shouldering past David while he dug in his pocket for the precious disk. "And here's a record of everything that happened." He froze, and David saw his face darken as he realized what he had just done to a blind man. "Sorry," he mumbled quickly. "I forgot."

"So do I, sometimes," Oisin said quietly, taking the disk. "But I must leave now to deliver the tidings to Lugh. I am certain he will be pleased."

"I hope so," Calvin sighed.

"Me too," David added.

"Farewell, young heroes," Oisin called, turning. "And congratulations." With that he started up the hill toward the forest.

"He's sure in a hurry," Calvin noted.

"You're not kiddin'."

"You know what *I* want to do?" Alec asked suddenly.

David grinned at him. "I'll let you tell me."

"Take a hot bath and go to bed."

"That," David said, laughing, "sounds like a remarkably good idea!"

"Now why would you want to do somethin' like that?" Uncle Dale chuckled, sauntering into the backyard. "Seems to me you'd be more interested in explainin' how you came to blow up my pore ole smokehouse. Boy howdy! Bolt of lightnin' falls out of a clear sky in the middle of the mornin'! I've seen it all now, I reckon."

"Sorry," David said sheepishly.

Dale shot a bemused glance at the departing Oisin. "Well, *he's* makin' tracks, ain't he?—though I 'spect he don't have much say in the matter." He winked at David. "Reckon I oughta send them folks a bill for a little construction one of these days?"

Alec had managed a glimpse at the old man's watch. "And speaking of days, guys, whatever one it is, it's nine-thirty in the morning."

"It's Friday," Dale said, laying an arm across David's shoulders and drawing him toward the house. "You boys was gone four days."

"More than that passed in Galunlati, though."

The old man ruffled his nephew's hair. "You can tell me about it over breakfast—that is, if you fellers're up for any."

David shook his head and patted his tummy. "We ate before we left."

Dale stared at him fondly. "Well, you better get on home, then. Or"—he shifted his gaze to the ruined asi—"I *might* just decide to put your young fanny to work! Seems to me like you owe me 'bout a week's worth."

David rolled his eyes. "I'll never get out from under at this rate. Unless . . ." He eyed Calvin speculatively.

"Uh-uh, not me, man. I gotta be movin' on."

"But *Calvin*," David teased, grabbing him by the arm. "That nice hot bath's waitin'. Alec, you coming, or you gonna boogie?"

Alec shrugged indecisively. "Best be travelin', I reckon. I imagine the folks'll be wanting to see me."

Five minutes later they trudged up the Sullivan's driveway. The Mustang was where he had left it; the Volvo had been moved at least once.

"Well, take care of your own bad self," David said, as

Alec opened his trunk. "And hey, thanks a bunch, man—and I'm sorry." He hugged his friend impulsively.

Alec's response lacked conviction. "My bad self," he whispered absently, staring at his hands. "Yeah, for certain."

PART III

THE CENTER HOLDS

Chapter XXIII: Bad Things

(MacTyrie, Georgia—
Friday, August 24—afternoon)

My bad self, Alec was still repeating silently as he sprawled across the bed in his attic sanctum late that afternoon. He had showered, shaved—all but the shred of moustache—and was wearing clean clothes for the first time in ages. But in spite of those concessions to normalcy, one thing alone was on his mind: that disturbing uneasiness which twisted through his thoughts every time that phrase boomeranged back to him—as it had been doing ever since David had tossed it off so casually that morning. *My bad self,* came the litany again; *I have done a bad thing.*

But what?

Much of his disquiet was doubtlessly simple letdown, his trusty left brain insisted: the sudden release of the tension that had filled his last few subjective days. And a big chunk of it was certainly disappointment over Eva's departure, now that he was back in his own right world where things like girlfriends were important—as he had suddenly recalled all too well when he'd searched in vain for someone to whom he could relate his amazing tale.

It was strange, though, now he considered it, how seldom he had actually *thought* of Eva while in Galunlati. In fact she'd almost slipped his mind entirely. Still, there'd been so much else to occupy his time that he supposed such lapses were understandable. And in any event he had no such diversions now; he *would* think of her; *would* take time to logic everything through and hopefully recover from his lost first love. That done, he would turn his attention to his late adventures and try to assimilate yet another mass of data that expanded his world on the one hand, but threatened the rationality that was his core and center on the other. It didn't do, he thought; to feel the things he felt—or know the things he knew.

And the one thing he did *not* know.

"I have done a bad thing." There, he had named it aloud. But another scouring of his memory still rendered up no answers.

Idly he reached into his nightstand, snagged the jar that contained the ulunsuti, and removed the jewel, placing it on the fake-Persian throw rug beside his bed, while he lay athwart the covers, bare feet dangling off the opposite side. A blowup of R.E.M.'s latest album cover peered down at him from the ceiling; Metallica's newest buzzed tinnily on a boom box turned too low to do the song justice. His folks were out: some faculty dinner or other.

Prophecy, huh? He wished it could show him the *past*.

Maybe it could. Or maybe . . .

He stared at the crystal and tried to concentrate on the bad thing, but that only made his head hurt. Perhaps if he tried to get at it sideways. . . . Let's see, when had he first become aware of the wretched notion?

Well, he'd noticed a sort of vague apprehensiveness ever since he had shown up at David's to begin their quest, but it had more or less been overshadowed, first by the minutiae of the ritual, then by the hypnotic languor of the asi. After that he'd been too distracted. But when . . . ?

He had it! It was when he'd rushed in to stab the uktena and it had rolled over him. For that horrible instant, when

ne had truly believed he was dead, he had *known,* had held
that terrible knowledge just long enough to proclaim it to
the world and preserve it in David's mind, whence it had
come shrieking back to haunt him.

But what was it? He'd been jealous, he admitted, jealous of David and Liz and Fionchadd and Calvin. So jealous that he suspected he had snapped just a little there at
the battle and hurled himself into the fray, recklessly desperate—he now acknowledged—to prove himself once
and for all as heroic as David's flashier friends. But it had
rebounded on him, leaving him . . . *dying,* he supposed.
The jealousy was bad, but he didn't think it was the bad
thing itself.

He had let his eyes slip out of focus as he continued to
stare at the ulunsuti. He was getting sleepy, too; beginning
to drift, yet he could not tear his gaze from the pulse of the
red line that bisected the jewel. But he had to close his
eyes, *had* to. He blinked, let his lids slide down—and the
line was still before him and growing brighter. It started to
spiral to the left, then shifted abruptly and began coiling
toward him, boring into his brain, twisting a hole in his
memory and laying its secrets bare.

Bad thing, bad thing, bad thing, he heard himself
chanting—though whether aloud or not, he did not know.

And then he did not care, because his head was awash
with pain—exactly like an old house must feel if three
centuries of hoarded cobwebs suddenly took flame in the
attic.

Fire! That was it! There had been a fire . . . and an enclosed place—a place of bricks. *His* place: the ruins! And
there had been Eva, and she'd given him a dagger, and—
no! It wasn't possible. Yet it was, for Alec finally knew, as
the power of the ulunsuti crisped the last shreds of glamour
from his mind, what that bad thing was, who had done it,
and why.

He stumbled to his desk, snatched up his phone, and
called David.

* * *

David jerked his foot away an instant before the brick dislodged and went crashing noisily into the honeysuckle below.

"Careful," Alec warned, "these old steps can be a little tippy."

"Tell me about it," David grumbled. "How come you never showed me this before?"

An hour had passed since Alec's cryptic phone call; thirty minutes since the Volvo had scrunched into his yard (Alec had had no choice but to drive; the Mustang's battery was dead as a doornail), and there was still no answer to the mystery. *Something to show you; something to tell you,* that was all he'd said.

Alec, trudging up the steps ahead of David, hunched his shoulders and navigated three more of the half-hidden treads before responding. "I was *afraid* you'd ask that," he panted. "And truly I don't know. I guess"—he halted at the top and turned around, face flushed beneath the remnants of Galunlati sunburn—"I guess I just wanted to keep one place for me alone—my own Place of Power, like. You've got Lookout Rock, and all. But when you first showed it to me back when we were little, I . . . I wanted one for myself. So I prowled all over MacTyrie and finally found this. I can't believe nobody else has discovered it after all these years."

"I can't believe you've kept your mouth shut about it all these years," David gasped, joining his friend on the terrace and flopping onto his back in the suppertime sun with his faithful knapsack for a pillow. "For that matter, I can't believe I didn't find it on my own—or that G-man or Darrell didn't. I mean, the kids from the college must've been all over this part of the county. It's not *that* far from town."

"Just luck, I guess," Alec said. "But swear to God I've never found a sign of a soul. Not so much as a cigarette butt."

David raised an eyebrow. "So those are all *yours?*" He stared appreciatively at the neatly triangulated stack of beer cans that lined most of one inner wall.

Alec nodded sheepishly. "Four years' accumulation. Hey, wanta go inside? Feel up to it, *old man?*"

"Don't press it, McLean! I've only got six months on ou, and I've regained my weight advantage, thanks to our little indiscretion, so don't think I won't beat your ass f you give me grief!" He laughed then, to prove he wasn't erious, and regarded his buddy curiously.

Things were better with Alec than they'd been in a vhile—partly because their stay in Galunlati had given hem time to rediscover the joys of each other's company. 3ut there was a new bond between them, too, because, for he first time in his almost-adult life, David had realized hat friendships were *not* immortal, and that friends veren't either, no more than family. In the past such things 1ad been remote, even when confronting the Sidhe; for in 1is riskier encounters with them he had been most con-cerned with the preservation of his own life, endangered though others might be. But Alec lying wasted in another World was not an image that rested easily with him, nor had he rested easily the few nights of his friend's illness. In fact, it had caused him to do a lot of thinking, both about Alec and, more pleasantly, Liz, and the whole dynamics of their triune friendship.

Liz! She'd be back tonight; had promised, via a noon-time phone call, to drop by around eight. There'd been vague rumblings about catching the new Bond flick, which still gave him a couple of hours to find out what was up with his buddy.

"David?" Alec's voice jogged him from his reverie.

"Sure thing, man. Lead the way." He followed Alec across the terrace and into the shell of building, noting the sudden coolness inside the thick walls. Goose bumps prickled across the bare arms below his U-2 T-shirt. "Burr," he muttered, "least you don't have to worry 'bout air-conditioning."

"Yeah, great, isn't it? You can lie on the terrace and toast, then come in here and cool off."

"With a little help from the brew?" David giggled, indi-cating the stacked cans.

"Like I said, four years of cloak-and-dagger."

David cocked his head toward the fireplace. "Tha
work?"

Alec nodded. "Sure does—cleaned the chimney ou
myself, and if you think I didn't have fun explaining that
Came home black as a coal miner's heinie. Have to watcl
it, though; can't use it by day, and generally only or
cloudy nights—'cause of the smoke, and all."

David scanned the horizon. "Folks can't see the
flames?"

"Not as far as I can tell. I'm careful, anyway."

"No doubt," David replied, knowing it was true. Alec
was nothing if not circumspect—and evidently much
sneakier than he'd ever suspected.

Alec slipped off his backpack and helped himself to a
seat on the hearth. He unzipped a compartment and
dragged out a paper bag that proved to be full of sand-
wiches and chips—and two cans of Miller, one of which
he tossed to David.

"Mr. Sullivan," he said, "would you do me the honor of
being the first outsider to contribute to yon stack of dead
soldiers?"

"My honor, indeed!" David chuckled, popping the top.
"But just one, and same for you: you're drivin', remember?"

"Two's all I could make off with anyway, without 'em
being missed."

"I *thought* they kept pretty close tabs."

Alec sniggered and took an appreciative swig. "Mom
thinks it's Dad, and Dad thinks it's Mom."

David took a long swig and set the can down beside
him. "So why now, Resurrection Man? Why, after all these
years?"

Alec's face grew serious. "It's like I said, Davy: I truly
don't know." He paused, swallowed distractedly, then
looked at David again. "No, maybe I *do* know: maybe . . . I
guess it was almost dying. Week before last was real shitty
and all, and to be honest, once or twice I wanted to trash
myself—until I met Eva."

David's eyes narrowed. "Who's Eva?"

Alec froze, unable to meet David's stare. "Well, that's a real interesting question—but I don't want to get into it quite yet. Or actually, I *do*, but I need to get some other things out first."

"Your move, man."

Another swig, longer this time. "Right. Well, anyway, I guess when you—when you went to so much trouble to save me, I realized that I'd been a real asshole, being jealous of you and Liz and all. But worse, I knew I'd been keeping some things from you, and I didn't want to do that anymore. This is one of them."

"Oh, gee—thanks. I appreciate it."

"Yeah, well, you've trusted me with so much, and it was the least I could do. I don't want any more barriers."

"Hey, don't worry, things are fine. We're off to school in a couple of days; Calvin's 'bout ready to hit the trail again; Liz'll only be here on weekends. That only leaves my weapons sessions with the Sidhe—if Silverhand still wants to do 'em, now that Finno's gone. You wanta come along?"

"Thanks, but no," Alec said quickly. "I prefer pixels to pixies."

"I'm sure the Lizard would resent that bitterly."

"Let him!"

"I wouldn't fool with that kind of stuff either, if I had any choice, but I don't—you know that. But truly, if I could do it all over and not have it happen, I would. I was happier when the Sidhe were only myths."

"I don't doubt it—"

"Did I hear the ghost of a *but?*"

"Not a *but*, exactly...well, maybe. I guess I was gonna say 'but it's not that simple.'" Alec took a deep breath. "There're a couple of things I have to tell you."

"You mean besides about this Eva person?"

Alec nodded. *"And* about her."

"So shoot!"

"This is gonna be a big one."

"I'm ready."

"Okay, then. Davy, I . . . I know what the bad thing is."

A chill raced down David's spine. "Oh jeeze, man, I'₋
'bout forgot about that."

"I wish *I* could," Alec snorted. "But it came back to me
That's the reason I called you, why I brought you here."

"Okay..."

"It's Eva, David. The girl I told you about—that ₋
couldn't tell you about before today. I met her at the fai₋
and kinda fell for her. Just an infatuation to start with—₋
thought—but then it just sorta grew. I guess I needed
somebody and she was available. Anyway, she's the reason
I got grounded: I was out with her. Well, actually I came
up here, and she just kinda found me—and we...uh,
well, we kinda did it."

David's mouth popped open, and it was a moment before he could speak. "All right!" he began, then broke off.
"But...but if that's the bad thing, I don't see why you
couldn't remember it. I—"

"She's one of the Sidhe, Davy—probably one of Ailill's flunkies."

"Oh God, *no!*"

Alec nodded grimly. "'Fraid so. I should have known. I
should have seen it in her face, or heard it in her voice, or
something. Worse, I should have known when I found out I
could tell her things—except."

"Except?"

"Except I don't think I could."

David rose abruptly and paced to the empty doorway to
gaze out at the lengthening shadows. Jesus, he would have
to be going soon, to clean up for his date with Liz. And
now to have something like this dropped on him.... He
whirled around in place, trying not to betray the confusion,
the anger that was welling up in him. This was important
to Alec; he would let him have his say.

"She played with my *mind!*" Alec sobbed wretchedly. "I
didn't know at the time, but I...I think the magic water
helped some, and then I looked at the stone, and suddenly
it all came clear. None of the memories I had were real,
they were only what she wanted me to believe. But Eva

umped me for everything I was worth, and then left lies in
my head."

David cleared his throat awkwardly. "So you *didn't* do it
then?"

"Oh, no, *that* really happened, believe me."

"Well, that's some comfort I guess."

"Comfort *hell!* That's the biggest thing a guy our age
can do, and I had it stolen. Do you think I was anything to
her but a grunt and a thrust?"

"Well, she wouldn't have done it unless she wanted to,"
David replied lamely, trying frantically to consider the implications—none of which were encouraging.

"Bullshit. You know enough of Faery morality to know
that's a lie. All I was was a warm body to her—that, and I
think she had to do it to get power over me. Deep power, I
mean: the kind that let her play with my mind. I've been
thinking about that a lot, and it's all starting to make sense.
Blood, semen, whatever; they're the stuff of life. One sus-
tains it, one makes it. Think about all the Faery magic
you've seen. Half of it depends on blood. Our blood to
reanimate Finn, that sorta thing."

David resumed his pacing. He would have to be away
soon, but—Jesus, he couldn't resolve all this that quick.

"There's still one more thing: the *really* bad thing."

"So spill it, bro. You know you can tell me anything."

Tears trembled in Alec's eyes. "There's a real good
chance I've betrayed the Sidhe. I . . . Eva gave me a dagger
as a so-called going-away present, and apparently made
some kind of posthypnotic suggestion, so that when we got
to Galunlati I switched it with Finn's."

"Oh, Christ, Alec—*Jesus!* Finno needed that dagger to
get to the Powersmiths! Any other would take him . . .
Shit!" David froze in mid-step, at a loss as to how to continue. "If you're right, if you *have* betrayed them, God
knows what they'll do!"

Alec sighed. "I keep telling myself maybe it wasn't be-
trayal. Honestly, I don't know what the dagger would do,
but . . ."

"I do," David spat. "I'll bet you dollars to donuts it' take Finno straight to Finvarra."

Alec fell silent, staring helplessly at David. "I just don know what to do!"

"Well, one thing's clear, we've gotta tell the Sidh pronto. At least that way they can't accuse us of holdin out on 'em."

Alec's lips thinned as if he fought back some remark but finally he nodded. "I was afraid you'd say that, bu you're right, of course." He stood, drained the beer, and started toward the door. "Come on, White 'Possum, reckon it's time I found out what the old 240'll do."

David's only response was a resigned roll of his eyes as he snagged his pack and followed Alec back down the se-cret stair. Why did it have to come to this? Why now of all times, when an hour before all he'd wanted to do was find out what his buddy's minor mysteries were, then go home and see his lady? Liz—Lord how he'd missed her. He'd spent half the day rehashing their adventures so he could tell them to her just perfect. And now he was gonna have to tell her something much more sinister.

They had reached the field by then, and sprinted toward the waiting Volvo. Alec started it up, gunned the engine furiously, then shifted into drive and tore up the turf for yards before his surge of panic slackened.

Halfway between Enotah and Sullivan Cove, David made a disturbing discovery.

Alec had made the right turn off Courthouse Square and headed toward the less-populous southern end of the county. No problem so far—except that his friend's unex-pectedly heavy right foot was threatening to attract consta-bulatory attention they neither desired nor could afford. But a mile or so past the city limits, the national forest closed in around them, and it was then that David caught the first faint warning tingle from his eyes as the Sight began to kick in. It didn't usually bother him now; or else he had got so used to it from frequent contact with Faery that he no longer noticed its minor manifestations. Maybe

: was the fact that the Sidhe usually showed themselves to im willingly these days.

But this time, he somehow knew, was different—and uddenly, as they swung around a particularly tight curve,)avid caught sight of something that proved to him just ow different it was.

It was a rider—no, a *pack* of riders, all on horseback, ill galloping through the woods to the right where the mountains had been scooped out to make the road. Those orsemen were following them, too, of that he had no loubt, pacing the Volvo along the edges of cuts that fre- quently rose far above their heads in an arch of red clay ind black stone, or just as often dived beneath the level of he road where the highway department had filled a hollow. n and out, up and down, but never losing sight of them, ind oh so very slowly growing closer.

And his eyes were burning abominably, which meant hat they were Sidhe (as if he had any doubt, once he could see their dress: black mail and ornate black helms and flowing cloaks black as their horses), and that they were ising Power in profligate amounts to sustain their glamour here at this time of day and off the Tracks.

"Faster, Alec," he shouted. "Christ, won't this thing go any faster?"

"I'm going as fast as I dare!"

"Bullshit. It ain't to the floorboards yet!"

"Davy—"

"The Sidhe are after us, McLean! We gotta run for it, get to the house as fast as we can and get behind doors."

"Won't the car protect us? It's steel, after all."

"Sure, but what good's it gonna do if we're stuck in the car? There's no telling what the Sidhe are up to, but those are Lugh's *guardsmen*, guy! And—oh shit!"

For the hump of mountain had swept suddenly lower as they entered a long straight roughly a mile from David's house. And as the crest of the cut dipped along with the road, the lead rider veered sharply toward them. Closer he came, then was pounding along the pavement, while the westering sun slashed his shadow long before them.

David's breath hissed as that man turned his face their way, then reached to his scabbard and slid out a sword. He could see the Faery's mouth move in words he could not understand; could feel a buzz in his head that was his telepathy muted to incomprehensibility by the presence of so much steel; could see the stallion's eyes growing wide with pain and horror as its rider drove it nearer to what was for it, in all likelihood, a lump of red-hot flame.

Closer the rider urged his steed, and nearer—even with David's door, now; with the others charging up behind and splitting off to either side to surround them.

"Goddamn it, McLean, *move* it!"

Alec floored the accelerator, straining his body forward, as if that effort would give them more momentum. David saw the riders fall back a little—evidently their mounts, no matter how fast in Faery, were somewhat limited here.

They crested a hill—too fast, and Alec had to fight to retain control in the hairpin curve that followed. But they got a little grace from that, as the shrinking right-of-way forced their pursuers behind again.

But then they were on another straight, and ahead was the hump of mountain that hid the approach to the Sullivan Cove road. Less than a mile to go.

David twisted around once more, saw the riders spur their mounts and surge forward.

"Hurry, man! You've gotta get to the turn before they recover their ground, that's our most vulnerable place— Oh, God, here they come!"

Alec's brow furrowed, but he kept his foot on the floor, while David watched the rear. The Volvo's engine began to buck and hiccup.

The leader was gaining—gaining too fast. A stab of spur and suddenly he was even with David's window, the stallion's eyes wide and wary, its nostrils flecked with foam. Teeth showed in tortured jaws as the rider fought the reins, his own teeth flashing a terrible whiteness as he grimaced—swore.

The turn was upon them.

Alec jammed on the brakes, jerked the car into a half

slide, and swung around into the narrower dirt road. Something thumped hard against David's door, and he heard a muffled scream that might be either animal or human. A glance sideways showed him the horse's legs pounding beside him, the rider's knees practically in his face. And then that rider was slashing out with his sword—not toward the car, but further back and down. Light flared there and metal screeched.

"The tires! Oh Jesus, man; give it all she's got!"

Alec flicked the wheel toward the rider. The Volvo shuddered and the rear end threatened to come around. A hail of gravel exploded behind them.

"Shit—he got it!"

"Tell me about it," Alec muttered, fighting the wheel.

They were nearly at David's driveway now, thundering along between the river bottoms. "Where to? Your house or . . ."

"Yes!" David shouted. *"No!* I don't want those things there. Go to—to Uncle Dale's, I guess. We've got to get inside! Got to find time to think."

Alec scowled. "I don't think the car'll make it that far."

"It's *got* to!"

"Davy—"

"Would you rather fuck up the rim or get slashed by one of those guys? They mean *business*. And I don't think it's me they're after."

It was all Alec could do to keep the car on the road. The riders had dropped back a little, which David thought was curious—until he realized, with sick dread, that they'd probably done exactly what the Sidhe wanted. They were being herded, there was no doubt about it.

"Should have stayed in civilization," he groaned dully. "No way they'd have come after us in the middle of Mac-Tyrie."

"Wanta bet?" Alec spat. "Given enough time those guys'd do anything—oh *shit!*"

The car slewed wildly, and David heard the pounding of rubber against metal as the tire rubbed itself to ribbons and tore away.

"Here! Turn here!"

Alec swung the wheel hard left, hurling the Volvo across the culvert and into Uncle Dale's drive. It bounced twice and something metal broke with a resounding clank as he forced it mercilessly up the steep slope.

"By the porch! Park by the porch!"

Alec tried, lost control—and slammed with a sickening crunch into the solid wood.

A check down the hill showed the riders close behind.

Alec flung his door open and leapt out. David followed the same way, his own door blocked by splintered timber.

As they pounded up the rough gray steps, Uncle Dale dashed out from the gloom inside. "What in blue-blazes is a-goin' on?" he hollered. He was as angry as David had ever seen him.

"It's the Sidhe," David panted. "Quick, inside!" He shoved Alec through the door, dragged his uncle in afterwards.

"'Bout *time* you got here, David Sullivan!" a female voice drawled from the sofa.

"Liz! What're you—?" David began, his heart beating double from conflicting emotions that flip-flopped once more as a familiar black-haired figure dashed in from the kitchen with a paring knife in his hand.

"And *Calvin!* I—"

Hooves sounded in the yard. Metal rustled. Someone coughed, a horse snuffled, and then there was silence but for the sudden whistle of wind.

Alec tugged the curtains aside and gazed out—and froze. "It's too late, folks," he managed, and buried his face in his hands.

David eased him aside and took his place. And felt the hair rise up along his arms and legs.

For the whole yard was fenced by a line of mounted Faery warriors in jet-black mail. Tall they were, and black-helmed so that David could not see their faces. But the livery—golden suns-in-splendor emblazoned on the black velvet surcotes revealed by their billowing cloaks— marked them as Lugh's personal guard. Their ranks continued out of sight to either side, probably encircling the house. As one they reached to their hips, and as one laid naked black swords crossways across the pommels of their saddles.

"What do we do now?" Alec whispered.

"We wait," David replied, as Liz came up behind him and made her own recognizance. "That's all we *can* do."

But he could not help another glance; and so he saw a man detach himself from the ranks and urge his black stallion two paces nearer. He did not look familiar, though it was hard to tell for the ornate nasal and cheek guards that hid most of his face, but he alone wore a sun disk centered on the front of his conical helm. Evidently he was the captain.

"Alexander McLean," the man called clearly in burred and accented English. "In the name of Lugh Samildinach, High King of the Daoine Sidhe in Tir-Nan-Og, I demand that you surrender!"

Chapter XXIV: Words on the Winds

(Sullivan Cove, Georgia—
Friday, August 24—late afternoon)

"So what do we do?" Alec said at last. "We can't wait here forever."

David dropped the curtain and swung around to face him. "No," he said grimly, "but *they* can."

"Why don't they do something, then? There's a zillion of them and only five of us!"

David shrugged and surveyed the worried group ranged around his uncle's living room: Alec by the fireplace, fidgeting with the poker; Dale himself on the sofa; Calvin now peering out the front door—apparently he'd come by for supper and pitched in to help; and Liz beside him, having arrived early and walked over with a batch of fudge, leaving her car at his folks' place. What shitty luck that was, too; here she'd come home expecting to carry him off to a movie and found herself up to her neck in disaster instead.

As if reading his mind, she took his hand. Her eyes were fearful, but the set of her jaw was firm. "Looks like I've walked into a frying pan that's just been turned on high," she said philosophically. "I guess my timing's not real good, is it?"

"No," David said dully. "I'm sorry." Her grip tightened, and he kissed her forehead.

"You wanta tell us what's goin' on?" Calvin inquired with a touch of sarcasm, having finished his surveilance.

"I better do it," Alec sighed, "since it's my fault we're in this." As quickly as he could he briefed them. Fortunately David had told his uncle the gist of their story that afternoon, and Calvin had apparently just told Liz a fair bit as well, so there was no need to back up that far.

"Whew," Calvin said when Alec had finished, "but you've got a point. What *are* they waiting for? I mean we're obviously not goin' anywhere."

"Your guess, man," David replied. "No, wait!" he added suddenly, his voice rising with excitement. "I've got it! The Sidhe can't enter a dwelling without permission; there's some kind of taboo against it. As long as there're walls and a roof, we're safe." He tried to make his words sound more hopeful than he felt.

"But that's *stupid!*" Alec cried. "Half the windows are open anyway."

"So's the chimney," David replied quickly. "So was the one at my house when the Sidhe were after Little Billy last year, though I never thought about it. I thought it was the steel in the screens, but that small amount wouldn't bother 'em if they were really out to get you."

Liz's brow wrinkled uncertainly. "So you think that's all that's holding them off? A simple no-no?"

"What else could it be?"

"Taboos can be pretty strong stuff," Calvin noted.

"Maybe you're right," Alec said slowly. "When you remove the impossible, whatever's left, no matter how unlikely, is true."

"Or something to that effect."

"Which leads me back to my first question: *what're we gonna do?*"

"Well," David said, gazing thoughtfully at his friend, "I

reckon the first thing is to talk to 'em. Find out exactly what it is they think you've done."

"I *know* what I've done."

"But do the Sidhe know—precisely?"

Alec shook his head helplessly and slumped down on the hearth.

"No, David!" Liz cried, as David eased out of her grasp and started toward the door. "Don't go out there!"

Calvin stepped forward to intercept him, but David fixed him with a glare and he froze.

"Wait," Dale said, rising abruptly to block the opening with a wiry arm while Calvin looked on, scowling. "You *sure* 'bout this, boy? Maybe I oughta be the one to do the talkin'."

"The hell you are!" David flared, reaching past him for the knob. "It's gotta be me. I've got more experience in bargaining with the Sidhe than anybody here."

Anger sparked briefly in the old man's eyes, but then his face softened. "Well that's a fact," he said at last, still unmoving. "Ain't too smart to try to bargain mad, though."

David regarded the insubstantial barrier of his uncle's flesh. "But what else can I do?"

"Whatever you think's best, I reckon—but keep a close watch on your tongue—and be careful."

"You got it."

The old man grunted and lowered his arm.

David gave him a quick hug, squared his shoulders, turned the knob, and eased onto the porch.

Wind bit at him, unexpectedly cold and cruel. What he first thought was thunder was the crack and rip of the riders' satin cloaks billowing unrestrained before the hissing gusts; lightning was frightened rays of sunlight glancing off gold-toned gems on helms and reins and weapons. Behind the horsemen, the ancient cedars that bordered the yard twisted like corkscrews in fey whirlwinds that seemed determined to suck away the very air. The sky above the mountains was a tumble of clouds dark as the riders' clothing and as ominously shiny. It was, he thought, exactly like the first tentative forays of a monstrous storm, and he had seen what the Sidhe could do with the weather. In spite of himself, he shivered as he strode to the top of the steps.

The captain raised his head a fraction and urged his horse forward a step. His eyes blazed beneath his visor. "You are not the one we requested," he said coldly.

"No," David replied, his eyes flashing warning as the man brought his mount another pace closer. They were no more than ten feet apart, now; and nearly at eye level. "Alec McLean is his own man," David continued, trying to choose his words with utmost care. "He can come and go as he pleases—and we won't give him up unless we know what crime he's committed."

"That crime you know yourself," the captain told him. "Had you *not* known, you would not have feared; had you not feared, you would not have fled. Guilt is an easy thing to read in a Mortal's face—or actions."

David swallowed thickly. "I . . . I'd still like to know the charge."

The Faery glared at him contemptuously, and David suddenly realized that a cold dread was creeping into him, the return of a long-banished nightmare. Barely a year ago it had been, when he had stood in the woods no more than a mile from here and bargained with Ailill for possession of Little Billy. He'd stumbled into their World then; the Sidhe were in his now, and he had learned a great deal in that year. But suddenly he was once more a teenage boy finding himself completely outgunned. Well, he'd begun it; now he had to brazen it out.

"The charge," David repeated as clearly as he could. He clenched his jaw to keep it from shaking, and not alone from the cold.

"Very well," the captain said. "The charge is treason against Tir-Nan-Og." As if to reinforce his accusation, the wind picked up another notch. Somewhere something wooden slammed into metal. A brick dislodged from the chimney and smashed onto the tin below.

"What *kind* of treason?" David found himself shouting

over a particularly strong gust that made the whole porch rattle.

"He has delivered Fionchadd mac Ailill to the enemy."

"*Alec* did?" David laughed, much to his surprise. "And how, may I ask, did he do that? He's certainly no sorcerer. Shoot, he doesn't even *like* you folks—or magic. Science is his thing, for God's sake; he'd forget all about you guys if he could. You don't fit his worldview."

"Would that we could forget him as well," the captain replied. "But he it was betrayed Fionchadd; the seeing-disk showed the act. Would you behold our proof?"

Without waiting for an answer the Faery reached into his surcote and produced a familiar-looking gold-and-crystal object, mouthed a Word, and held it out in his palm. The wind did not disturb the image as it expanded and showed David what he had hoped not to see.

It was their sleeping chamber in Uki's cave. The walls and ceiling showed vaguely; the dimness of the strange, furtive lighting marking it as night. Familiar shapes lay about, snuggled in piles of furs. David recognized himself, and Alec next to him—an Alex who was suddenly rising, who had a strange glint in his eyes as he crept forward, reached under Fionchadd's tunic, removed the daggers and exchanged their shapes by the use of Power he should not have had, then crept away once more.

"Oh my God!" David whispered hopelessly, aware by a gasp of dismay that Alec was now standing in the half-open doorway behind him. "The bad thing."

"A bad thing indeed," the captain acknowledged as he banished the image and secreted the disk. "And a worse thing if you do not surrender him. He alone can name the traitor amongst us."

"You still haven't told us what happened to Fionchadd," David noted, though he had a pretty good idea.

"Is it not obvious?" the captain hissed. "That dagger took him not to the land of the Powersmiths but back to the seas of Faerie by a route we did not suspect. Finvarra caught him there. He holds him hostage in exchange for the lady Morwyn whom he has already claimed. He threatens the Death of Iron for Fionchadd if she does not accede. No one returns from that twice."

David could feel the hair start to crawl on the back of his neck. He swallowed again and cleared his throat. "So what you really need," he managed, "is to know who betrayed Alec. Well, that's easy enough: it was—"

"Davy, *no!*" Alec screamed, hurling himself across the porch to clamp a hand across David's mouth. The Sidhe raised their swords warily, but Alec had already dragged David inside. Never had he felt so much strength in Alec's grip or heard so much raw fury in his voice.

"What the hell are you *doing?*" David yelled furiously as the wind sucked the door closed behind them and they tumbled together onto the rug. Dale and Calvin were on Alec in an instant, dragging him back, prying at the hands that still clamped unnaturally tight around David. Liz hauled at David himself, and with her aid he managed to wrench away from his friend, whose suddenly murderous grip had only barely lessened in spite of two men's efforts. Alec's eyes, when David saw them, were blazing with anger—and, he feared, something worse.

"God*damn*, McLean," he shouted. "There's no sense in this! They don't want *you,* they want *Eva!* That's all, just you to tell them who used you!"

"But I can't let you tell them," Alec gasped. "I *can't!* She's got back in control somehow. Oh, God, my head hurts!" He slumped against the sofa and buried his face in his hands. Liz bit her lip and scooted over beside him, laid an arm around his heaving shoulders. Calvin simply stood where he was and frowned.

"But *how?*" David choked, his voice shaking as he tried to regain control and fight back his own sudden tears. "She didn't have any trouble with you telling me—or the whole mess of us just a minute ago! For that matter, what difference does it make if she prevents you? I'm my own man. What I say is on my conscience."

"No," Alec sobbed. "You don't understand; she'll kill me if you do. She'll blow up my head, I can feel it." He clutched his temples.

"But wouldn't that mean she's around here some-where?" Liz wondered.

"Maybe," David said. "Or maybe she'd left some kind of really weird safeguards that just kicked in again—who knows. Shoot, maybe the ulunsuti wore off, or something. But this is a real mess. I mean, I . . . I can't tell them *any-thing* now, not with Alec's life at stake. Besides, I doubt the name she gave him's even the right one."

"Prob'ly not," Dale agreed. "But they might be able to figger out something from it."

"They oughta've been able to read our minds out there on the porch too, but evidently didn't."

"They can't read through strong emotions," Calvin said unexpectedly. "Least that's what Finny told me on our little jaunt. And they have to be close to you, or touching you, unless they're really strong themselves. Either that, or have some other hold on you, like Alec told us Eva's got on him."

"So what do we do?"

"I've heard that question before," David sighed. "I reckon I'd better talk to 'em some more."

A moment later he was back on the porch.

Though he had braced himself for it this time, the wind still startled him with its ever-rising fury, and there was now a hint of hard, stinging moisture in the frigid gusts.

"Have you come to deliver the traitor?" the captain asked casually, black-gloved hands draped across his pommel.

David grimaced and shook his head. "I . . . I can't. And if I tell you what you want to know, it might kill him. Apparently . . . whoever it was left a pile of safeguards on his memory. If he talks, or if . . . if *I* talk, he'll die. And if that happens, you'll never find out."

"We will find out," the man said flatly, "if we have to search every mind in Faery."

David glared at him. "So why bother Alec, then?"

"It was the simple way, so the Ard Rhi thought."

"Well, I guess he was wrong then."

The man glanced around suspiciously. "Perhaps he was."

"Then why don't you leave him alone, since you have other options? Why don't y'all just go away?"

"Because we have no choice! Our king was in a rage when he dispatched us; he placed us under *geas* not to return without McLean, and we dare not defy that prohibition. He can find what he wants among the boy's memories."

"And maybe kill him or drive him mad?" David shouted back. "But I reckon I shouldn't be surprised. It'd be just like you folks: take what you need and leave the rest, no matter how you leave it, huh?"

"It is not our intention to harm him."

"But you don't care if you do!"

"This accomplishes nothing, Mortal."

"It keeps Alec alive longer!"

The captain snorted and turned away, scanning the horizon. "This is not your house," he said. "Your family lives nearby."

David's blood froze. "You wouldn't dare!"

"We would dare anything, except defy the laws of Dana. Do you think mere walls of wood dissuade us?"

"But you can't risk hurting my folks," David protested. "There's been too much strange stuff around here already. More would bring the very thing you hate: people with questions and machines."

The captain smiled fiendishly. "We do not have to *enter* dwellings, Mortal; for we have eternity to wait, which you do not. Eventually they will fall down; but long before that, someone will step outside. It is an easy thing, do not forget, to make changelings or drive men mad."

A hand clamped down on David's shoulder then; a hand old and rough and gnarled. "Enough, boy," Dale said softly. "Maybe you oughta let me talk to 'em. I've argued me a case or two in my life. 'Sides," he added, grinning smugly as he reached into his pocket, "I've got me a little something here from Mr. Lugh ought to change things right quick."

David swung around and stared at him in wonder, then noticed what his uncle had in his hand. It was the birthday scroll, and in the other he held a cigarette lighter. His thumb was tapping nervously against the striker.

"'Pears to me I can finish this right now, just by wishin'," the old man called, louder, fixing his eyes on the captain. "This here gives me one boon, and I'm thinkin' I just may use it."

"You may try," the captain sneered. "You will not succeed."

A grizzled eyebrow lifted. "Suppose," Dale said. "just *suppose*—and mind you I ain't wished yet, nor lit no fire —but just suppose I wished for you all to go away and leave us alone."

"You could wish that," the Faery acknowledged. "But more of us would return, and you would have no more wish, and would thus still be where you are. Also," he added, "we might choose to interpret *us* in a way that you did not find pleasing."

"What if I said for all the Sidhe to leave all mortals alone for . . . for ten thousand years, maybe?"

"We have allies."

"So maybe . . ."

"Enough, mortal," the captain snapped. "We could stand here a month with you proposing *ifs* and myself countering with *thens*. Do you not remember the conditions of the gift? Lugh promises you a boon, aye; but he promised not *any* boon. Remember the words, *see* them, mortal, with your own poor eyes! Do they not say, *'if it be within my power and a just thing'*? Some things you might ask for would not be within the Ard Rhi's power—to lift the spell on young McLean, for instance, for he did not set it. To abandon this effort would not be a just thing, for it would put at risk his kingdom. Do you not see? Someone has betrayed him, he wants the betrayer back— The same betrayer who has also betrayed your young friend."

"Then I reckon we ought to both be lookin' for a common enemy."

"Perhaps we should. But until we hear otherwise, we wait."

"Seems to me," Dale noted, "that you're askin' us to do the same thing that started this mess in the first place. Didn't somebody ask Mr. Lugh to give up somebody who took shelter with him? And didn't that boy in there just spend 'bout a week and nearly die tryin' to get her to safety? And now you want me to hand him over 'cause you think he's a traitor? Shoot! He may be, to you. But he's innocent to us. And we've got him!"

"Fool of a mortal, we can wait forever."

"I can wait till hell freezes over too," Dale shot back. "Even if we starve to death and you find the bodies, you still won't have no answer. But I'll tell you *this:* sooner or later somebody'll come by. Oh, you might hide yourself, but they'll find out something's up, and they'll be here with iron. Or Bill will, or JoAnne. You may think you can wait forever, but you may just find out that's over a fair bit sooner than you thought it was." And with that he took David by the arm, dragged him inside, and slammed the door.

"Jeeze," David gasped, when he had recovered from the shock of their precipitous departure and had ensconced himself in a rocker by another window. "That was . . . was damned eloquent. You should've been a lawyer."

The old man favored him with a ironic smirk. "Thought about it once. Wanted David-the-elder to be one. No point in worryin' 'bout it now, though, with all these other things goin' on."

"What're they doing?" Alec asked from the couch.

David squinted through a grimy pane that rattled until he touched it. The circle around the house appeared to have tightened, and more riders had evidently joined the ranks. He rose and checked the other windows, saw the same thing. On his circuit he also discovered something else that disturbed him. Four riders had dismounted: three men and a woman. They had cast aside their cloaks and stood revealed in pure white robes. For a moment they consulted together, then separated, skirting around the house until

one faced each quadrant of the compass. David could no
hear them, but could tell by the movements of thei
mouths, the rhythm of the half-heard words buzzing in hi
head that they had begun to chant.

And in answer to that invocation the sky grew darke,
still, and thunder slammed the heavens in earnest. The
wind picked up too, its gusts louder and longer and wilder
Rain began to fall, the drops heavy as liquid steel, and
lightning prodded the mountains with fearful glee, then
danced quickly closer. A bolt struck one of the cedars and
split it to the roots, and it blazed up, burning. None of this
fazed the Riders of the Sidhe, though; still as statues, they
sat their horses, frozen except for the wild billowing of
their cloaks, and the glint of arrogant disdain in their inhu-
man eyes.

It looked like night out there, David thought, what with
the clouds piled in huge masses over the ridges and the sun
hidden behind them. Night—or a vision from Doré's Hell,
as larger drops smashed into the earth and beat the clay
until the yard looked like raw meat. The metallic clatter on
the roof changed pitch, as hail mixed into the rain and
smashed the summer foliage.

"I don't think they can attack us directly," David said.
"But they can use the things of this World and augment
'em with their magic."

Dale eyed the ceiling, where a steady drip had made its
presence known. "Yeah, and I was just wonderin' how it is
'zactly they define a dwellin'?"

David stared at the others. And shivered.

Chapter XXV: Thunders of the Mind

The telephone rang.

David, leaning against the wall by the porch window, jumped at least a foot and headed for it, but Calvin was there before him and wordlessly handed it to Uncle Dale.

"Hello?" the old man said tentatively, and David could hear the pops and crackles halfway across the room. The voice too: female and agitated.

Dale frowned. "Maybe I better let you talk to him." He motioned David over and passed him the receiver.

"Hello?" David began, and jerked his head away from a second barrage of static. *"Hello?"*

"David? David, is that *you?*" It was his mother. She sounded scared.

"Yeah, Ma," David sighed. "I guess you know we've got a problem."

"I reckon *so!* What the hell's goin' on? It's rainin' like Revelations over here, and the power's done flickered twice."

"It's . . . it's worse than that here," David said, wonder-

ing if his mother had figured out the true gravity of thei
predicament. "It's . . . one of *those* situations."

The phone fell silent for a moment. Then, distinctly
"Shit."

"Uh, yeah," David muttered, glancing around the room
"Hey, look, Ma, don't do anything. Don't do anything a
all. They're after Alec, not me, but we're not gonna le
'em have him. Do me one favor, though—don't go out
side. Don't—" Another burst of static made him hold the
receiver away. "Ma? Are you there?"

"Barely. Lightnin' just blew off the whole front of the
hayloft." She sounded breathless and even more frightened.

"The hayloft?" That was where the whole thing had
begun, with him reading *Gods and Fighting Men* and fan-
tasizing about Faerie. And now it was gone, and those
same gods were fighting men with lightning in his uncle's
front yard.

Abruptly the lights flickered. David saw Calvin scurry-
ing to light the oil lamps that flanked the rough stone mantel. "Look, Ma," he shouted, trying to make himself heard
over a rising storm of white noise. "This can't last forever.
We've got to wait it out, but whatever you do, don't go
outside, and don't let anybody else over there go out either.
Just sit tight. We're gonna—"

The world turned white, then; and the air seemed to
vanish for an instant, then came crashing back with almost
visible force as lightning struck the porch. David heard tin
shriek and the slow rip of overstressed wood splintering,
but even before it had truly registered, he had flung the
phone away. Something lifted him and hurled him into the
wall and he saw whole constellations of stars. When his
vision cleared, he was lying on the floor gazing up at the
hole his shoulder had made in the cheap paneling four feet
above him. The receiver was a mass of melted plastic,
twisting on a cord, its gyres highlighted by the flames of
the oil lamps.

"Jesus," Liz cried, rushing over to help him to his feet,
while Calvin gingerly re-hung the useless appliance.

"Or somebody," David sighed. He started to rejoin Dale and the white-faced Alec in front of the fireplace, but could not resist another glimpse outside.

The Sidhe were still there, still waiting; but the sky was aflame with lightning that leapt and cavorted among masses of clouds that were roiling so fast their ephemeral streamers made patterns—patterns which the bolts limned or erased or ripped asunder. It was hard to believe it was the real world out there, for the elements had gone crazy; water was acting like a solid thing, and so was the wind; and solid matter had become soft metal for their forging. Even colors had ceased to matter, for the darkness was not uniform, and the clouds were at one moment red, then gray, and then a sick greenish-silver; and the half-seen forms of the cedars and the Faery warriors (apparently quite dry) outlined now in blue, now in gold, now in crimson. And through it all was the distant buzz of chanting, the roar of the wind, and the incessant thunder that was like the booming of not-so-distant cannon.

It was hopeless, he thought, as he slumped down beside Alec, with Liz on his other side. Calvin stood stoic in the corner, brow furrowed. Uncle Dale was simply staring.

For the first time in his life David was utterly without resource, without idea. His brain felt as though someone had drained it of all intelligence, as though thunder and lightning and fear and waiting had pounded his senses numb.

Idly he fished in his pocket and curled his fingers around the pouch that held the uktena scale. Unbidden he found his thoughts returning to the serpent. That had been no worse than this, really; though they'd known they were going into battle, and had therefore had time to plan. But the odds had been just as bad—worse, actually. He could still remember the image: that one heart-stopping moment when the uktena had loomed over him in all its terrible, wonderful glory, with light flashing from between its eyes that was whiter than the Faery druids' lightning, and the power of red blood flooding through its whole massive body. He knew what it was like, now; how it was to have one's innocent sleep disturbed by outside forces bent on one's destruction. *God*, how nice that would be: to turn himself into a giant snake with a jewel of fire in his skull and lash out at those who tormented him; to feel his body swell with rage as hot blood surged through him, filling him with fire and strength and power.

"David! What's happening to you!" It was Liz's voice, but she sounded strangely distant. "David! Oh *no!* David—"

Suddenly there was no more sound. As suddenly, Liz and Alec were leaping away from him. David's eyes started to burn, he blinked—once, twice; looked down—and saw his knees as from a distance. But there was a rip in his jeans that hadn't been there, and they felt suddenly tighter. A sharp pain prodded him, and he yanked his hand from his pocket (such a strange movement, such a long way) and stared at it. Blood was oozing out of his fist, but there was something still in his hand. He willed his fingers open (though he could not seem to get them to separate), and saw the white leather pouch that housed the scale, saw how its glassy edges glittered there, having sliced through the leather and into his palm. He had just time to realize what had happened before the uktena brain took over. In that one moment he hurled himself through the living room window and into the yard. When he touched ground he had no arms and his clothes were in tatters.

Before him the Riders of the Sidhe drew back a fraction, their faces awash with sudden wonder.

Fury took David: blind hate, and with it a joying in power he had never known before.

A glance skyward, veiled in red, but with light stabbing the sky like a searchlight as he jerked his head upright—and found himself rising higher and higher, above the cabin's roof. And then he was staring down on the riders —open-mouthed horsemen in helmets and swirling cloaks, who were drawing swords and nocking bows but too caught up in wonder to use them.

Riders!

The ones who would kill his friend. His friend above all

riends, who had almost died for him. And these folks wanted to kill him. He opened his mouth and screamed, but the scream came out a roar. He tried to run forward, but could not—and found he was coiling instead.

And then David Sullivan, who was rapidly drowning in the half-mad brain of the uktena, looped himself around the house and waited, his yellow eyes ever in motion.

"Jesus God," Alec gasped, staring at the wreckage of the window through which both wind and rain were now whipping. "He always wanted to be a skin-changer, but I never thought he'd get to be one!"

"But *why?*" Liz cried. "That's just not the kind of thing he'd do, not now when we need him!"

"Unfortunately," Calvin said. "I'm afraid there's a good chance he couldn't help himself. We talked a little about this while Alec was sick, and he told me how it works. But the real danger is that once it's happened, you've gotta constantly keep in mind that you're human, or you'll lose yourself in the beast mind real fast. He had to let go before he could really fight properly when he was a bear—and bears are pretty smart. But as an uktena . . . who knows? One thing, though: he better change back pronto or we're *all* goners."

"But how *did* he change back?" Liz demanded, her face pale with horror.

"*Then* he had water from Atagahi. He's supposed to have brought some of it back, but I don't know where it is."

"I bet I do," Alec said shakily. "David likes to have all his magic whatsis around him, 'specially if it's not obvious that's what they are."

"Like the ring," Liz whispered, staring at the band of interlaced silver on her finger.

"Like the scale itself," Calvin echoed. "I've got a twin, you know . . . I wonder if I could—"

"Don't you dare!" Liz snapped, grabbing his arm before it could reach the white pouch that hung at his belt.

"No," Alec agreed. "But as I was about to say, it's prob ably in his backpack, which is in my car."

"So near, yet so far," Liz groaned.

"And if we got it, what would we do with it?" Calvin asked. "I mean it's one thing to force-feed a sick guy, and something else entirely to feed a hundred-foot half-crazy monster."

Alec glared at him. "Well, if you're supposed to be so damned smart, why don't you crank up that blessed Cherokee juju you're always talking about and do something? Maybe—"

A bestial scream from the yard interrupted them. Liz glanced out the window just in time to see the uktena's head jerk skyward with something writhing in its jaws— something that fell to earth an instant later: the severed hindquarters of a horse. She wondered dully where the rider was, but a sheet of rain obscured her vision. Whatever blood there had been was already on its way to the sea. That was a strange thing to think of: Faery blood at one with Sullivan Branch, which was tributary to the mighty Chattahoochee, which was an Indian name. Suddenly the walls between the lurking Worlds collapsed in her brain and rushed together. This World, the Lands of Men —and Galunlati—and Faerie and all its satellites were one. David—Fionchadd—Calvin, all different, all alike, all boys with flashing eyes and good bods and laughing faces and brilliant minds. Uncle Dale, Nuada, this Uki fellow—Darkthunder, or whatever he was: they were alike as well. This Faery woman who had loved—had *claimed* to love Alec—was even she a shadow? But of whom? It was all too much. With the world gone wild, her senses pounded to numbness, and her emotions tied into knots in the bargain, she just didn't know.

It was more than she could stand. She retreated to the sofa and sank down there; closed her eyes. *Hold on, girl,* she told herself. *You gotta get yourself together.*

A particularly violent thunder clap jolted her from her reverie and made her cry out in alarm. She looked around, saw Uncle Dale and Alec staring out the door—and then ne saw something far more alarming. She had only time to asp, but by then it was too late.

For while Uncle Dale and Alec had been despairing ver David, Calvin had very quietly crept to the fireplace nd removed one of the oil lamps from the mantel. Before he knew what he was about, certainly before she could top him, he had hurled it into the fireplace, where it exploded in a poppy of pungent flame. He flung something else there too: something that glittered white and red and silver as fire took eager hold of it.

Flame filled the room, then; and heat beyond fire, and in that final flash, she had only time to see Calvin fold his arms around himself and hear him cry out in a language she did not know, and he was gone. The word remained behind him, though, echoing through the suddenly silent room. *Hyuntikwala Usunhi*.

She wondered what it meant.

Outside the rain had not abated; and the click and slide of glassy scales and the screams of men and horses told of a monster that had not stopped hunting.

Chapter XXVI: Masks

"What was *that?*" Alec shouted, jerking around and gazing over his shoulder.

"It was Calvin," Liz managed. "He . . . he threw something in the fire and . . . and just *vanished!*"

"The scale," Alec stated with conviction, nodding and biting his upper lip. "I'll bet he's—"

He had no time to finish, for he was flung to the floor as the uktena slammed into the far side of the house. With it came the creak of tortured timbers, the tinkle of shattering glass, and the resounding crash of something large toppling in the adjoining bedroom. The drip in the ceiling worsened to a steady stream that rapidly grew into a puddle on the now-slanted floor. The mounted deer's head above the mantel listed precariously.

Alec staggered to his feet, leaning heavily against the sofa while Liz tried to sit up and Uncle Dale steadied the remaining oil lamp, then set it on the floor and wedged it with a stack of Sears catalogs. Every shadow in the room

...ifted as faces became lit from below, giving them the
...ok of masks in some pagan mystery.

Another thump, not so hard, but more glass broke. A
...hair toppled over in the kitchen.

"I'm goin' out there," Dale announced. "If I don't, that
...ing'll wreck the whole bloomin' place."

"No!" Liz cried, rising. "It's too dangerous. It'll . . . it'll
...ill you, maybe."

Bony shoulders shrugged. "Better to die fightin' then
...aitin'. 'Sides, that's still Davy, whatever else it is. I'm
...ettin' he won't hurt me."

Alec grabbed his arm. "No, you don't understand! That
...nay be David, but it's an uktena, too: the jewel in the head
...lone'll drive you crazy if you look at it straight. Besides,
...lo you think David would act like that if he was in control?
...He may be pissed, but he's no killer! You saw what he did
...to that horse. That's the uktena! If David's in there, he
...can't get out!"

"He won't hurt me, though," the old man repeated,
shaking off Alec's grip. "I'm countin' on that. And I'm a
right fair poker player."

"Uncle Dale . . ."

"I'm sorry, boy, but I gotta try. You stay here; take care
of Miss Lizzy. See that the house don't catch fire."

"Uncle Dale—" Liz protested.

"No!"

And with that Dale Yearwood Sullivan pushed through
the doorway and stepped onto the wreckage of his porch.

Tornado.

That's what it was like out there, Dale thought, as he let
the screen door handle slip through his gnarled fingers and
slam closed. It reminded him of the one that had gone
through Gainesville back in '36 and leveled the whole
blamed town. The wind howled just as strong, the air felt
just as strange: heavy and light at once. And that awful
sensation of the whole world out of control and threatening
to fly apart. Even the light was the same: that sickly green-
ish sky awash with lightning and latent power. Before,

though, it had been electric lines that spat and arced and
hissed, not the skies themselves. And there had been no
galloping horses, no shrieking Faery warriors.

And no uktena.

He had never seen anything so huge that yet lived, not
even the whales that had followed the ship which had taken
him to fight the Reich. Part of it was squirming right below
him, too: a section of back as high as the porch and nearly
as wide, that slid and twisted by him like a red brick wall
dimly marked with man-sized spots. He wondered where
the head was, then saw a flash of whiter light over to the
left where the vegetable garden once had been.

Poor little 'taters, he thought absently, and headed for
the steps. "David!" he shouted, his voice thin and frail
above the roar of the weather. "David, boy, it's me: your
Uncle Dale!"

But the uktena could not hear him. It thrashed on in its
deafness, hunting, scouting out Riders with its piercing
eyes, then fixing them with the jewel in its skull and tear-
ing the life from their bodies. Three it had caught already,
and their blood tasted good. (No it didn't, a part protested,
a part that was sick at heart, that wanted to gag, that
wished at once to break free and to hide itself utterly and
never come out again while the greater, wilder self went on
with revenge and killing.) Others came nearer to slash at it
with swords and stab ineffectually with Faery knives, but
those he scarcely noticed, for his scales were hard as the
diamonds they resembled and though many a weapon
broke on them, not a single blow found his flesh. He was
the uktena! He was unstoppable! Those attacks served only
to fuel his fury, which in turn redoubled his power—power
he could use in his hunting.

"Davy boy, stop!"

With that shout, Dale fell silent. *Reckon it ain't gonna
listen,* he told himself when the thing showed no signs of
heeding. *All right, then; the danged thing's still got eyes!*

He stepped off the bottom tread into the yard. An hour

arlier it had been green grass, bright and healthy, if maybe
in need of a mow. Now it was all but gone, beaten into the
hick soup of mud that was being churned even deeper and
hicker by the rain and the monster's writhings.

Head must be over there, he supposed, glancing left to
where the white light was brightest. He started that way,
but a movement to his other side stopped him. A Rider had
ventured closer: the captain, he thought it was. Must be
risking a close inspection while the head was occupied
elsewhere. But then he saw to his horror that the man had a
bow, was raising it and nocking an arrow.

Dale knew in an instant what he was about, but it was
already too late. For a bare second his weary eyes met the
Faery captain's hard, bright ones across the vast cylinder of
the serpent. "The seventh spot," the Faery said, and took
aim.

"No!" Dale hollered. "You goddamn son of a bitch!"

The bowstring twanged, the sound delicately clear amid
the harsh cacophony.

Dale froze as he saw the arrow fly. He prayed that the
wind would take it, whip it away to fall uselessly on the
roof, but he knew from bitter experience of the prowess of
Lugh's archers, and thus knew that such hopes were in
vain. He did not even blink when the shaft struck home in
the scaled back of the monster that had once been his favorite nephew.

The ensuing scream was louder than the thunder.

Abruptly the vast body heaved toward him, touched
gently, almost casually . . . and sent the ground rushing up
to knock the air from his lungs. For the first time that
terrible evening he was grateful for the mud. He scrambled
up, made for the steps, had barely reached them when a
second heave jerked a massive coil his way once more. It
missed, and he almost made the porch before a third blow
caught him and smashed the steps to kindling. Trapped
between the creature's rock-hard scales and the equally
solid wood of the porch sill, he heard his shinbone crack.
The sound reached his ears before he felt the pain.

* * *

It was a miracle either Alec or Liz could act, so stunne
were they by what they had witnessed. It was just ther
now, Alec realized. Bare moments before they had bee
five, then four, three. Him and Liz now: two fingers wher
once had been a hand. And two fingers weren't enough fc
holding.

"Alec!" Liz's shout wrenched him from the awful rev
erie. "Come on, we've gotta get him in." Already she wa
pushing through the door.

"Right," Alec grunted dully, and plodded after.

"Now!" Green fire lit Liz's eyes, visible through th
tears.

Somehow he was on the porch. Lashing rain soaked hir
in an instant. Dale had made it halfway across the shatterec
porch, but his face was near as white as his beard. Liz wa:
beside him, wind whipping her hair into her face. Alec
grabbed a shoulder, heaved, as Liz took the other. He
heard the old man cry out, saw his face blanch whiter still
as he gritted his teeth and closed his eyes against the
agony.

Four feet to the door; three . . . two . . .

—inside, and dragging Dale through the puddle by the
door to the relatively greater safety of the sofa. They could
not raise him onto it, but Liz snagged one of the throw
cushions and stuffed it under his head.

Alec stood and faced the door.

And decided.

The pain was still there: the fire that flooded his mind
every time he thought of betraying Eva. But it had lessened
slightly, though he did not know why. Perhaps the recent
stress had driven it deeper into his mind. Perhaps there was
another reason he could not know. Probably she had some
idea what was going on, so maybe she was distracted.

But for whatever reason, he had to do something—now,
while he could. It was him and Liz; everyone else had
fallen. And it was all his fault. There was only one slim
chance, and it depended on more *ifs* than he could imagine.

But did he really have any choice?

"Stay here," he told Liz flatly. "There's one possible thing I can do. If not . . . I just don't know."

"What—?"

He reached out and laid a strangely calm hand on her shoulder. "Just trust me, girl. And if it doesn't work, I'm sorry."

She started to rise, but he was already gone.

Out the door, onto the ruined porch once more. A glimpse at the uktena, lit now by a veritable wall of light-ning flashes. It was writhing more wildly than ever, but the glow from the head was getting closer. Alec strained his eyes, seeking the arrow that had impaled his friend. Where was it? There? No, that was a splinter of siding caught between two scales. But, *there* it was. His heart skipped a beat: it was in one of the spots. He counted, and his heart skipped again. The captain's aim had been true: it had found the seventh spot. Still, maybe there was hope, for the arrow had struck right at the edge. Maybe that would make a difference; maybe David would not die.

The Volvo was where he had left it, wedged between the house and a scaly coil that had slid into it and warped the whole front end out of shape. Its roof was on a level with the porch floor. He had to get in, though; had to. A piece of banister had torn loose and was flopping danger-ously against the wall, bristling with rusty nails. He grabbed it, wrenched it free—and slammed it into the car's windshield. The first blow bounced off; the second starred the safety glass; with the third it shattered. Alec leapt down onto the hood, promptly slipped on the wet metal, and had to grab the wipers to right himself. Metal cut his hand. He swore, but dragged himself up, using the scrap of wood to clear a larger hole in the windshield. He crawled inside, dodging shifter and steering wheel. Only one chance now, if he was right, and he had to be. Not in the front seat though, maybe the back. He slid into the passenger bucket, twisted around, scoured the rear footwell—and found David's backpack and his own. He grabbed them, dragged them out, hauled them behind him onto the hood, and flung them on the porch.

Light flooded over him, and he realized the uktena ha
brought its head around. He was vaguely aware of th
Riders still there, but circling much further out. The chan
ing had stopped some time ago, but the rain had n
abated.

Leaning against the front wall of the house, he franti
cally unzipped David's pack and rifled through it. Bless
edly the canteen was still there. He shook it to be sure i
was not empty and heard a gratifying slosh.

His own pack, next, and thank God he had yielded t
caprice and stashed the ulunsuti there. He shook out th
jar, emptied it, and stuffed the bag in his pocket.

"Wish me luck, Liz," he called to the open window, an
leapt onto the uktena. A quick roll through mud, and h
was past it and standing, though the rain almost knocke
him flat again and he had to dodge a segment of scale
body that twitched toward him.

Where was the head? Light answered him: a whiteness
flickering across the trees. Behind him the Sidhe drew
nearer. He didn't care.

A moment only it took him to unscrew the canteen,
another to free the jewel. The instant it touched his flesh it
took fire, blazing so brightly he had to close his eyes,
though that made little difference. Power was awake there
—Power he had not expected. But he had cut himself when
he'd climbed into the car, and the blood must be feeding
the jewel. What had Uki said? Blood to work the great
magics. But what to do with them? he wondered.

Gritting his teeth, he raised the stone above his head and
opened his eyes. The glow was dazzling, brighter than full
day.

—and was evidently doing what he needed it to, because the head was coming toward him. Recklessly he
splashed water from the canteen along the glistening
scales, saw the serpent's flesh shimmer and contract, continuing along the length, but not fast enough, not nearly
fast enough to save him.

For the head was leering down at him, closer,
closer. . . . He had a horrible moment of déjà vu, as he saw

e light of the living ulunsuti merge with the light of his
wn. Teeth and jaws and flaming eyes filled the world as
e uktena stretched its maw to the limit—and paused.

For an instant the monstrous eyes calmed, looked, in
pite of the glare, in spite of the rain, in spite of the veil of
ngers Alec had raised to protect his sanity, like David's.
hen madness roared into them once more, and the head
rched down.

I'm going to die.

But the teeth did not sink into him, though the heat of
he serpent's breath fell on him and made him gag.

"Alec," a woman's voice shouted to his left. "The
mouth! Throw it in the mouth!"

"What?" Alec had time to call, and then black-gloved
hands had jerked the canteen from his fingers and hurled it
into the gaping jaws. He glanced around, just as lightning
imned a figure standing beside him—a familiar one.
Guardsman, unmistakably, by the cloak and helm. But . . .

Then there was no more time, because the mouth had
closed on the canteen and was rising high as the surviving
cedars. It remained there for a moment, bright against the
clouds, then convulsed and slammed heavily to earth—directly atop the guard.

The change began suddenly and took only seconds to
effect. The uktena shuddered, then shrank and paled. It
was impossible to describe, almost impossible to see
through the driving rain, and perhaps that was fortunate.
One moment there were uncontrollable masses of coiling
monster; the next a human boy lying face down, naked,
and unconscious across the legs of a slender Faery warrior.
Between them was a lump of pierced and twisted metal that
might once have been a canteen.

Alec realized dimly that the pain in his head was gone.

Lightning flashed once more, and he became aware of
Faery warriors regrouping and nudging their mounts cautiously forward. He reached out toward David, but a voice
stopped him.

"Alec . . ." The woman's voice again, faint but clear—
and somehow familiar.

He paused, his hand already on David's shoulder, a
looked around at the injured Faery.

"Alec?"

Could it be? A mad scramble that way, as prioriti
warred within him.

"Alec?"

The full lips inside the black helm moved. Scarcely da
ing to breathe, Alec eased it up and set it aside. An
looked on the face of Eva.

"Aife," the captain said behind him. "She was the new
est among us."

"Eva . . . why?" Alec sobbed, his eyes burning wit
tears.

Her eyes slitted open, sick with pain. "At first because
loved Ailill and hated those who brought his doom," sh
whispered. "But now because, in spite of myself, I find
love you more, and that love is a far finer thing than hate."

"Eva . . ."

A finger to his lips. "At first you were a weapon, my
Alec, to be used, then set aside. And when I saw you agair
in the chariot you were still no more than a thing. Even on
the porch you were little more than an obstacle and a
threat. But here, face-to-face, risking all for the life of your
friend, I suddenly knew you were the one I love. You
would have done for your brother what I could not do for
Ailill, though in trying I have betrayed you and also my
land and king. My soul and my body must sunder."

"And will pay the price when they reunite," the captain
said, as Aife's eyes glazed over. "We will be waiting for
your return." He passed a hand over her lids, then frowned
and removed a coil of gold from behind her ear.

"I have heard of these things," he said. "Some at Finvarra's court use them. They make clear the words of
others, but likewise hide one's own thoughts. No wonder
we could not unmask the traitor."

A whimper made Alec turn. Liz had come into the yard,
so quietly he could not hear her. Wordlessly she sank down
in the mud beside David's filthy form. The rain slackened

she tried to lift his head, but her own green eyes were
reaming.

"I am sorry," the Faery captain told her. "But I have
one enough harm for one day, perhaps I can aid his heal-
ng." He knelt and reached toward David's back where a
plinter of arrow still protruded from beneath the left
houlder blade, then grasped it, set his teeth, and yanked.

David shuddered and moaned softly, but the wound was
lready closing. Alec and Liz turned him over, stared at his
ace. The Faery flung a cloak over his shivering body.

"David," Alec said woodenly. "Not you too."

The rain had stopped.

David's face was still.

"Alec, do something," Liz groaned.

"I can't, girl, I *can't.*" His voice was thick with misery.

"His body lives," said the Faery. "But his *self* seems to
be far away."

Liz buried her face against Alec's shoulder.

Alec put his arm around her and bowed his head. It was
too much. He couldn't stand it anymore. He had tried and
failed. And so close to success.

"You've been gone as far," a male voice drawled
quietly. "You made it back; so can he."

Alec glanced around and saw Calvin.

Chapter XXVII: Turned Stones

The Indian had been standing on the edge of the porch when he spoke, but already he had leapt down the ruined steps and was sprinting across the yard.

Alec rose and faced him, frowning. "What do you *mean?* And for that matter, what the hell were you trying to do, zapping off like that in the middle of a crisis?"

"I didn't think I had a choice," Calvin replied. "And I didn't have time to argue. Things were gettin' out of control real fast, and I knew there wasn't a thing to do on this end. So I did the only thing I could: I went to see Uki. I wanted to bring him here, but he wouldn't come—or couldn't." He crossed and knelt beside David. "He's got one of those crystals like he gave you, though: and he's been watching what's goin' on through it—not that he didn't already have an idea something was up, since the whole sky over there was goin' crazy when I arrived—apparently this mess was reflected even in Galunlati. Anyway, when he saw David change back, he sent me off to—"

"Never mind," Alec broke in sharply. "Come on, let's get him inside."

Calvin grunted his assent, and with help from the Faery captain—whom he gave permission to enter—managed to carry the unconscious boy into the house.

Uncle Dale was no worse, though his face was far too pale—and grew paler when he saw his nephew. "Put him here," he said, patting the sofa next to which he lay. "I'll be all right in my rocker; just watch out for my old leg bone."

Alec nodded and he and Calvin helped him to a seat there. He did not cry out, but Alec heard the bones grinding together, and saw his face knot in pain.

"I'll be okay," Dale repeated stiffly, as the captain knelt to examine his leg. "Get me a shot of 'shine and tend to the boy."

Calvin trotted off to the kitchen, and Alec joined him there, oblivious to the shattered crockery that littered the floor. He clamped a hand on the Indian's shoulder. "Sorry I cut you off earlier, man. Now what was it you were saying about me having been gone as far?"

Calvin found the 'shine in Dale's pantry and poured a shot into one of the few surviving glasses, then stared at it for a moment and, to Alec's surprise, took a healthy hit before offering him one as well. "Isn't it obvious? The same thing's happened to David as happened to you. And apparently Uki thinks we have what it takes to fix it."

"Well that's just great," Alec spat bitterly, as they returned to the living room.

"Ycah," Calvin said, handing the glass to Dale, who took it gratefully. The captain had set his leg during their brief absence, and already some of the pain had vanished from the old man's face.

"So what do we do?" Alec asked, once more at David's side.

"Well," the Indian replied, "in your case Uki found where your soul had gone and chanted it back, then we fed you the healing water."

"But David's *already* healed!"

"Which means we've just gotta get his soul back, I guess."

"That is what I said," the Faery captain noted testily, as he joined them.

Alec scowled at him. "Any idea how?"

"Not with your kind."

"I have an idea, though," Calvin volunteered. "If we could remember the chant."

"You're the one who heard it, not me."

"But you're the one who answered."

Liz stood suddenly and stared at them. "Could you two stop arguing and start thinking? What *kind* of chant are you talking about?"

"One in Cherokee," Alec began. "I—"

Calvin interrupted. "You use a stone to find out which direction the soul's in, then call it back."

"But we don't have a stone."

"Oh yes, we do," Alec said, brightening. "We've got a stone of great Power." He brought out the ulunsuti and held it in his hand. It still glittered, but not with the arcane brightness it had earlier held.

"Hmm," Calvin mused thoughtfully, "could you maybe use that to heal him?"

"I don't know how," Alec groaned. "I'm afraid—something would go wrong."

"Maybe you could use it as a focus," Liz suggested. "Or I could. I've done things like that before. Remember when Nuada used me to find David when Morwyn captured him?"

"A fine notion," the captain acknowledged, "for love is a great aid in such things."

"But we still don't have the words to the chant."

"No," Calvin said slowly. "But . . . I sort of remember 'em; I mean I heard 'em a bunch of times, and I think I've heard my grandfather use 'em. If I could only get started . . ."

Alec's face brightened. "Wait a minute! When I figured out what was going on with all this, I was just kinda gazing into the stone and wondering, and I got an answer. Maybe if we looked into it now, and wondered, we'd get one to this too."

"And with four of us healthy, we could each cover a direction. That is, if this guy here'll help." Calvin eyed the Faery captain.

"Forgoll, I am called," the Faery said. "And yes, I will aid you."

"I'll help too," said Dale, trying to stand.

"No, you'd best stay were you are," Alec told him. "Soon as we get David squared away we'll call a doctor for you."

"I'd like to help, though."

Liz crossed to him. "I know you would, but—well, you're hurt too, and—"

"And we don't know what kind of effort this will take," Alec finished.

The old man nodded and leaned back reluctantly.

Calvin popped his knuckles. "Okay, folks, let's get at it."

"Right."

They laid the jewel in the center of David's chest, directly above the heart, and gathered round the sofa facing inward, all holding hands, and each taking a cardinal point, with Liz to the south, by his head. She took three deep breaths and slowly let her eyes go out of focus. "I'll concentrate on David," she whispered. "You folks stare at the line in the stone, and try to remember that formula. If anything starts to happen, I'll try to bring us together."

Alec nodded and followed her lead, letting his eyes shift to the ulunsuti. At first all he saw was simply a rough, shiny dome, more or less like a lump of melted glass. But the focus of his vision quickly narrowed to the thin line of red that pulsed there. Brighter and brighter it grew, until all he could see was a veil of red.

Davy? Davy— can you hear me?

No answer.

David?

He changed tactics, tried to remember the cave, himself lying unconscious, then words calling him back. No response first, but then, very faintly, he heard them.

Abruptly another presence was there, another mind; finding those words too, and drawing them closer. Liz, he knew, and once more was glad for the granny who had taught her to scry. He reached out to her, touched, and joined his thought with hers, then felt a surge of strength as Forgoll slid in with them and made their linkage firm. Last of all came Calvin, for he alone had never done such things. But with the Indian's memory, and Alec's as well laid bare, the words were suddenly clear:

> *Sge! Ha-nagwa hatunganiga Nunya ulunsuti, ga-husti tsuts-kadi nigesunna. Ha-nagwa dungihyali. Agiyahusa aginalii, ha-ga tsun-nu iyunta datsiwak-tuhi. Tla-ke aya akwatseliga. Tsulehisanunhi/Liz/ Edahi/Forgoll digwadaita.*

Listen! Ha! Now you have drawn near to hearken, O ulunsuti; you never lie about anything. Ha! Now I am about to seek for it. I have lost a friend and now tell me about where I shall find him. For is he not mine? My name is Alec/Liz/Calvin/Forgoll.

Four times they repeated that litany, and on the fifth, Uncle Dale chimed in from his place by the chair.

And then David's eyelids flickered open.

"He was not without at all," Forgoll said, "but within."

"What happened?" David mumbled. "Last thing I remember's gettin' really pissed, and then I was an uktena, and—" He buried his face in his hands. "Oh Jesus, what I did! I—"

Liz's arms folded around him, as she helped him sit up and offered him a taste of 'shine. "Alec saved you with that magic water of yours—that and the ulunsuti."

"Alec!" David cried, trying to rise. "Oh no. But . . . but the water was in my pack and— He didn't . . . did he?"

"I'm fine," Alec said, joining David on the other side. "Eva's dead, David. She was one of the guards."

"Oh Jesus, man . . ."

"And a sad thing that was," said a voice from the door.

Alec looked up. Standing in the remains of the doorway—but with his feet obviously planted on the porch—was the tall figure of Lugh Samildinach himself. A beautiful red-clad woman behind him was the Fireshaper Morwyn.

"May we come in?" the High King inquired.

"Don't know as you can," Dale said feistily. "Seems to me you've been actin' might hasty lately and causin' a heap of trouble. Sure have messed up my house somethin' fierce. I don't believe I want you in here."

Lugh regarded him mildly but gave no sign of protest. "The house can be repaired with no trouble," he said. "As for the rest, I do not know that I blame you. But when Finvarra sent word that Fionchadd was captured and demanded that I render up Morwyn, I was beside myself. I do not like my plans to go awry. My only thought was to find the traitor."

Dale's eyes narrowed thoughtfully. "You 'uz just takin' care of your kingdom? Is that it?"

"Something to that effect, yes."

"So what're you gonna do now?" David asked.

"Truly I do not know," Lugh replied. "I suppose it will be war. Before I had a choice of yea or nay; now I have only the choice of whom."

"It will be Erenn," Morwyn said. "I have already decided. Finvarra threatens my son with the Death of Iron if I do not give myself up. I therefore will do so. My people will then attack Erenn, if Arawn will let them through; otherwise, there will be war with Annwyn as well. If you join them, they may forgive you for what has happened here. If you do not, who can say?"

"Aye," Lugh sighed heavily. "And I have further cause for war, now that I have found another of Ailill's spies in my very household."

"That's all real good," David said, "but where does that leave us?"

Lugh eyed him curiously. "Where indeed?"

"I know where I *wish* it left us," Dale said. "I wish left us alone!"

"*Is* that a wish?" Lugh asked quickly.

"What do you mean?"

"I mean, was that a wish? A real wish? A desire of you heart? You still have a boon from me, you know."

Dale eyed Forgoll distrustfully. "Your man here told m that wouldn't work."

"I know," Lugh said, "and as you would have used i then, he was correct. But things have . . . changed."

"You mean . . ." David began.

"It is certainly within my power to forbid my people t come here," Lugh said. "And I begin to think it is an hon orable thing. Too often the ills of Faerie have broker through of late. This one almost embraced a whole othe World as well, and we need no more enemies than we have now. Perhaps Ailill was right, perhaps we should not trou ble with men. Perhaps if we ignore them, they will forget us." He peered at David speculatively. "Would you like that, David Sullivan? Would you forget the Sidhe? That choice is yours."

David blanched at that. It *was* a choice: a mighty one, and he did not know what to say. Once before Nuada had tempted him so, and he had turned him down. But that had been under duress, with other trouble pending. Now, with things at peace in his world . . . maybe he ought to recon sider. Hadn't he himself said a few days ago that he wanted to be a normal kid? Well, if he accepted Lugh's offer, he would be that very thing: just another north Georgia teen ager. But still . . .

"What about my friends?" he asked. "What about my folks?"

"They as well, if you would have it."

David frowned. A normal life: him and Liz and Alec and his buddies—Calvin too, if he decided to hang around. But he was being asked to make the same decision for himself *and* his friends—and he knew he could not do that. He could choose for himself, but if his friends still knew, there'd be barriers. If he chose for them and kept his wn knowledge, once more there'd be walls. If he decided or them all he'd be playing God, and he had no right to do lat either.

"I can't," he said finally. "Lord knows I'd like to forget ll this, but I can't. It's part of me, part of what I am, part f what's made me a stronger person. I can't undo it."

Dale cleared his throat and looked up at Lugh. "Seems ike the best thing, then, is for you to just do what you aid: go away and leave us alone."

"If that is your wish," Lugh said, "you have only to tate it aloud and burn the scroll."

"But why bother with that?" Liz wondered. "If you're gonna do that anyway."

"Because the paper contains my blood and thus controls a bit of my Power," Lugh replied. "Were I to declare the borders closed, you might someday use it against me. I want nothing of Power where I cannot control it."

Liz gazed at the ring David had given her. Once it had belonged to Oisin. *"Nothing?"* she whispered.

"That you may keep," Lugh told her. "Its virtue has vanished, and in any event we did not make it." He paused. "All other gifts you may keep as well, for they are not many, and cut off from my land whatever Power they may have will fade."

"But what about *Katie's* wish?" David wondered.

"She has already used it: she asked for new wagons for her people to replace those young Froech destroyed."

"Sounds like her," Dale mused.

"She distrusts magic; she said it should only be used to correct what magic has damaged."

"Yeah, that's her all right."

"It's decided then?" From Calvin.

"So it would seem," Lugh said heavily. "Dale Sullivan, have you so chosen?"

The old man nodded. "I have, sir. I . . . I want the borders closed twixt here and Faerie, I want you and your folk to leave us alone."

"Two wishes but one thought," Lugh said. "But it is within my power and a just thing, and so I will have it be."

"There is one thing I would first ask," Morwyn said.

Lugh turned toward her. "And what is that?"

"It is a favor I would ask of young McLean..."

Alec frowned at her. "I'm listening."

The Fireshaper took a deep breath. "The jewel has th gift of prophecy, does it not? I would ask that you allow m to use it so."

Alec eyed her uncertainly but crossed to the doorwa and held out the ulunsuti.

She did not touch it, but gazed at it for a long time, he green eyes narrowed to slits. Then she blinked and returned to herself.

"And what did you see, Lady?" Lugh asked her curiously.

Morwyn's face lit in a smile of peace. "I... I saw myself and Fionchadd alive and happy together. He was older, but not so very much. That will give me comfort."

"Very well," Lugh said. "Now let us depart. We have a grim business ahead of us." He turned at the edge of the porch and spoke through the gaping doorway. "Truly Mortals—friends I would still say, whether you would or no—I grieve for all that has happened. Perhaps one day we will meet again, though it will certainly be of your asking. I go now to prepare for war. Think of me. Remember when the skies grow dark and rain falls heavy and you dream of death and murder that they are perhaps reflections of darker things in Faerie. I say that not as a threat, but as a warning. I may declare the borders closed, but when has war kept borders?"

"Good-bye," David called from the sofa. "Give my regards to Nuada and Oisin." He paused, swallowed, eyes suddenly misting. "And... and if you can, tell Finno I'm sorry."

"I will do all those things," Lugh said sadly. "When you are ready to empower your wish, burn the scroll."

And he was gone.

Epilogue: Ashes

(Sullivan Cove, Georgia—
Friday, August 24—night)

David stared at the pile of crisp ashes in the fireplace. If he squinted very hard he could still make out the lettering there: the delicate black uncials, the wonder of interlace, all now gone to nothing. A drop of Lugh's blood had vanished with it, too; they had known when that happened, for the vellum had flared briefly as bright as the sun. Uncle Dale had cried out then—and had leapt to his feet, newly healed, though he had not put that in his wish.

Now was only ashes and fading fire, but the oil lamp's glow was steady as the world slowly slid back to normal. Somewhere in the kitchen Dale and Liz were putting together supper. Calvin had gone to David's house to brief his folks on the situation. Alec sat on the sofa beside him, munching fudge and also staring.

"It's over, bro," Alec whispered, laying a hand on David's knee squeezing.

David nodded glumly. "Yeah, but how *much* is over? Did we go too far? Should I have let Uncle Dale make that wish?"

337

"Could you have stopped him? It was his to use, after all."

"Yeah," David sighed and fell silent.

His wish.

But it wasn't over, not for him anyway. There was still Power in the world: the Power of Galunlati. It was in that jewel Alec had, and in the scale *he* had, and in another one Calvin had brought back with him, and in the chants and magic Calvin had already sworn he would learn at Uki's side.

And there were other things that weren't over, either. A friend was hostage somewhere, perhaps under threat of a death that even for his immortal kind might well be final. Oh, he knew Morwyn had seen Fionchadd free and happy in the ulunsuti, but did that necessarily mean it would happen? It was *a* future, but was it the only one? And even if Fionchadd was somehow released, did that mean they would still be friends? Once more their relationship hung on forgiveness.

Then there was the last, and most troubling thing: he had killed. Oh, they had been Sidhe; and he knew he had done that before, when Lugh's guards had attacked him in Tir-Nan-Og. Rationally he knew there was nothing to worry about—the Sidhe were immortal, would be reborn. Those deaths were not forever. But would those he had slain hold a grudge? He didn't know. The worst thing, though, was the way he had done it: with the mouth and fangs of a monster. He shuddered at that, at how easily the uktena had taken control. Did that mean it was still in there somewhere? Was there a beast forever locked inside him waiting to get free? He shuddered again and leaned back, eyes closed.

And felt something warm brush the top of his head. He looked up and saw Liz smiling.

"You're worrying about the passing of magic, aren't you?"

He shrugged.

"You're all the magic *I'll* ever need," she whispered.

He took her hand. "You're all I'll ever need too—or ever want."

Headlights slashed into the yard, then; and he heard the distinctive bellow of Big Billy's old Ford truck.

Voices danced into the clear, silent night: his pa's grumbles and his ma's protests and Calvin's calm weaving between them. And Little Billy bursting through the door, shouting, "Is it true, Davy? Are the Shiny Folks really gone?"

"It's true, kid," David said. "But there's still a heap of magic in the world."

Author's Note

In this and the two previous adventures of David Sullivan, I have derived much of the background information on Celtic mythology and folklore from David's favorite book, Lady Augusta Gregory's *Gods and Fighting Men;* though Reverend Robert Kirk's *The Secret Commonwealth*, Katharine Briggs's *An Encyclopedia of Fairies*, and W. Y. Evans-Wentz's *The Fairy-Faith in Celtic Countries* have also proved invaluable, as have many other works too numerous to mention. But since with *Darkthunder's Way* I have expanded my amoebic cosmology to embrace an additional mythos to which I have only tangentially referred before, that of the Cherokee Indians, I have inevitably found myself mining a new set of sources. The most important of these were James Mooney's *Myths of the Cherokee* and *Sacred Formulas of the Cherokee*, both originally complied in the late 1800s; but I have also drawn a fair bit of cultural information from Charles Hudson's much more recent *The Southeastern Indians*. In utilizing the Cherokee myths, I have attempted to do what I did with the Celtic myths before: preserve the essential character, attributes,

...d institutions, while at the same time filling in some of
...e blanks and ambiguities in—hopefully—a rational
...anner. This has not always been easy, and in some cases
...y previously established cosmology has required devia-
...ons from strictest conformity.

My depiction of Galunlati, for instant, is a sort of syn-
...esis between the traditional one, which was the home of
...e gods and archetypal animals and lay beyond the Sky
...ault, and This World, with which those same beings fre-
...uently had commerce until it became too corrupt (hence
...y term: Lying World) and they departed.

The notion of the removal of Galunlati from This World
...s also essentially my own, though consistent with Chero-
...ee cosmology, which not only gave This World several
...evels (of which what *I* call Galunlati is the topmost
...kimmed off and attached to the Upper World), but also
...poke of two types of time: recent, when things were as
...hey are now; and *hilahiya*, or Ancient Time, when the
...nimals (but never *all* the animals) could speak and the
...gods walked freely among men.

Finally, a different kind of deviation occurs in *Sikwa
Unega*, the Cherokee name I have given David, which is
...not a strictly correct translation of "White 'Possum." The
word *sikwa* did, indeed, originally mean 'possum, but with
the introduction of hogs, it became attached to those creatures, with the term for 'possum becoming *sikwa-utsetsti*
("grinning hog"). I found this latter too cumbersome when
compounded with *unega* ("white"); so, since the change
was apparently made fairly recently, I decided to revert to
the original term, on the theory that Galunlati split off from
This World before that usage became common.

In all other cases, however, the Cherokee words,
phrases, and chants are as accurate as I could make them;
most of the words being derived directly from the glossary
or text of *Myths of the Cherokee*, and the chants from
Sacred Formulas of the Cherokee—though once or twice I
have had to depart slightly from the standard usage of a
formula. The spell that comforts David, for instance, is
rightly sung to soothe the night fears of small children, not

boys on the edge of manhood, but the circumstances, think, allow this slight variation. Once or twice, too, have had to reconstruct a Cherokee word from guesswor that is, lift it from another formula, insert it in one of tho: here, and hope I got it right. Finally, for the sake of sin plicity, I have eliminated all diacritical marks. Any error linguistic or otherwise, are strictly of my own making.

TFD
Athens, Georgi
30 May 1989

TOM DEITZ grew up in Young Harris, Georgia, a sma
town not far from the fictitious Enotah County of *Dar
thunder's Way*, and has Bachelor of Arts and Master of Ar
degrees from the University of Georgia. His major in med
eval English literature led Mr. Deitz to the Society for Cr
ative Anachronism, which in turn generated a particula
interest in heraldry, castle architecture, British folk musi
and all things Celtic.

Darkthunder's Way is the third adventure of David Su
livan and his friends, whose story began in *Windmaster*
Bane and *Fireshaper's Doom*. Tom Deitz is also the autho
of *The Gryphon King*, an unrelated contemporary fantas
set in Athens, Georgia. All of Mr. Deitz's novels are avai
able from Avon Books.